OC 1 7

The Christmas Room

The
Christmas
Room

CATHERINE ANDERSON

BERKLEY
NEW YORK

BERKLEY
An imprint of Penguin Random House LLC
375 Hudson Street, New York, New York 10014

Copyright © 2017 by Adeline Catherine Anderson

Library of Congress Cataloging-in-Publication Data

Names: Anderson, Catherine (Adeline Catherine), author.
Title: The Christmas room/Catherine Anderson.
Description: First edition. | New York : Berkley, 2017.
Identifiers: LCCN 2017011151 (print) | LCCN 2017016327 (ebook) |
ISBN 9780399586330 (ebook) | ISBN 9780399586316 (hardcover)
Subjects: LCSH: Parent and adult child—Fiction. | Domestic fiction. |
BISAC: FICTION / Romance / Contemporary. | FICTION / Family Life. |
GSAFD: Love stories.
Classification: LCC PS3551.N34557 (ebook) | LCC PS3551.N34557 C48 2017 (print) |
DDC 813/.54—dc23
LC record available at https://lccn.loc.gov/2017011151

First Edition: September 2017

Printed in the United States of America
1 3 5 7 9 10 8 6 4 2

Jacket art by Tom Hallman
Jacket design by Colleen Reinhart
Book design by Kristin del Rosario

This book is dedicated to my son John, who brought me to the state of Montana, and to the wonderful Montanans in the Bitterroot Valley who welcomed me with unconditional friendliness and warmth. In particular I want to mention Renee, Ryan, Todd, Doris, Kim, Pam, Sarah, Anita, Cindy, Nikki, Alex, Danny, Jason, Joy, Amber, Anna, Kaz, Harry, Tina, David, Connie, Mike, Jim, Trevor the vet, Tom the teacher, and Keith the joke teller. I also want to acknowledge a fabulous lady named Dallas who knocked on my door one day to say that she wasn't there to sell me anything or to give me anything. She is just a *real* Montanan, and she noticed she had new neighbors, so she stopped by to introduce herself. Well, she did sell me something. She sold me on the state of Montana. And she did give me something, the gift of friendship, and later when we sat with her at a fund-raiser for a local woman stricken with cancer, she gave me a dozen farm-fresh eggs. I also want to thank Clearwater Builders for its excellent work ethic and for all the talented and amicable people employed by the company.

God bless Montana.

The Christmas Room

Chapter One

WARM AUGUST SUNLIGHT SLANTED ACROSS THE DUSTY WIND-shield of Cameron McLendon's blue Ford pickup as he drove south on Highway 93. It was such a beautiful day in Montana's gorgeous Bitterroot Valley that he rolled down the front windows to enjoy the afternoon breeze, redolent with the scent of pine. He released a deep breath and tried to toss aside his worries.

West of the four-lane thoroughfare, the Bitterroot Mountains rose with splendid majesty to the clear blue sky, their glacier-chiseled canyons inviting the eye to delve deeper into the Selway-Bitterroot Wilderness. Cam, with a professional background in both fish and game biology, knew a totally different world existed in that remote area, a place so rugged and wild that some people couldn't comprehend it. He kept a close eye on the traffic as he took in the magnificent scenery with quick glances. Someday soon he hoped to have the time to take his son on a hike into those canyons.

His tight grip on the steering wheel relaxed. The tension eased from his neck and shoulders. Then he noticed that a light dusting of snow capped the mountain peaks. *Only a little,* he reassured himself. *Only a freak dusting.* But it was still a warning that those locals who were predicting an early winter might be right. *Damn. Isn't it just my luck? If winter strikes sooner than anticipated, my mother will have difficulty navigating our camp.*

Upset, tired, and hungry, Cam bypassed the turn that led to his new hometown, Rustlers' Gulch, and drove farther south to a place called the Cowboy Tree. A bar-and-eatery combo with rustic decor, it offered only limited menu choices, but the food was tasty and easy on the wallet. After parking in the long rectangular lot, Cam checked his reflection in the rearview mirror to finger-comb his hair. Tiny lines had appeared at the corners of his blue eyes. He was only thirty-five, but it had been a stressful summer, and all the worry had taken its toll.

As he pushed through the double doors of the establishment, he felt the casual, welcoming atmosphere surround him. The walls had been papered here and there with dollar bills autographed by customers. Bistro-height tables, handmade from knotty pine and rectangular in shape, flanked the front windows, while regular tables out of the same wood peppered the inner section of the dining room. A bank of poker machines cozied up to a jukebox at one side. Lighted beer signs offset the darkness of aged wood paneling. Three televisions, kept at a low volume, entertained those interested in sports or a news channel.

Though the establishment was busier than usual at this time of day, Cam found an empty place near a window and swung up onto a stool, allowing the hum of conversation behind him to become white noise. A little girl with golden curls wandered over and said hi. He guessed her to be about three, and she was adorable. Cam returned the greeting and watched her toddle back to her parents' table.

At first it had surprised Cam to see minors in places that served hard liquor. Now he took it in stride. Kids weren't allowed to sit at the bar, but they were welcome to come in with adults to eat. The state of Montana apparently believed it was up to parents to decide if a place of business provided an appropriate environment for their children.

Long ago, the Cowboy Tree had been constructed around a ponderosa pine that had developed an impressive circumference over the years, necessitating periodic enlargements of the hole in the roof that accommodated the conifer's massive trunk. Back in his home state of California, Cam had seen trees inside structures, but for some reason they had never seemed so impressive. This pine and the old building appeared to have sprung up from the earth together. The framed hole in the ceiling allowed precipitation to seep in and collect in the massive rock planter at the base. Staff and patrons added water regularly to keep the roots well hydrated, and Cam believed that water had also been plumbed in under the building.

"Hi, Cam!" Trish, an attractive bartender with curly, shoulder-length red hair, flashed a bright smile. "You snuck in on me. Long day?"

Cam laughed and then groaned. "I showed a ranch north of here. Had breakfast at five and not so much as a sip of water since. The potential buyer wanted to walk the land. It's a twelve-hundred-acre parcel. When I make my first sale, buying a side-by-side will be at the top of my list I can tell you that."

"What's a side-by-side?"

"A powerful ATV that seats five. They're built sort of like a golf cart and are awesome for showing property. Not much will slow them down."

"Ah. I've only ever heard them called mules." Trish chuckled. "So thirst and hunger drove you here. I can't imagine trying to walk every inch of that much land. Sounds to me like you should carry a cooler filled with sandwiches and drinks." She circled the bar to serve him a tall glass of water. "The chicken wings are on special, fifty cents apiece, minimum order of five."

Cam thanked her for the drink. "I'll take ten with the apple-cherry glaze. That should hold me until I get supper on the table tonight."

"Your mom still on deadline?" Trish asked.

"Oh, yeah." Cam's mother, Madeline McLendon, was a murder mystery writer of some acclaim. "She'll be too busy killing someone this evening to help me cook. She's always there for cleanup, though."

Trish took a seat across from him. Her green eyes sparkled with amusement. "I finally found time to read one of her books— her most recent, I think, *Death by Potato Sprouts*. Do you ever worry when she makes you a fruit smoothie that you might not live to drink all of it?"

Cam burst out laughing.

Trish left to place his order, then reappeared behind the bar and held up an empty tumbler. "One for the road?"

"Only one. Make it my usual, please." Cam stood and took his glass of water to the bar, where he could chat with Trish while he ate. Normally a serving of wings arrived quickly, but the cook seemed to be taking his time today. Trish soon grew busy busing tables. One of her helpers, a thin blonde everyone called Cowgirl, refilled Cam's water glass. "How's your day going?" he asked.

"Good," she said without enthusiasm. Cam could tell she hated being there and wondered why she stayed on. Maybe she couldn't find other work. "Not much news to report. Same-old, same-old."

Trish returned, and Cam was glad to see her. At least she knew how to carry on a casual conversation. "I think the cook must have driven to Missoula for more wings," she teased. She made Cam's drink, a dash of Apple Crown over ice, and slid it across the counter to him. Then she held up a leather dice cup. "Want to try your luck while you're waiting?"

The Cowboy Tree ran daily dice games, the details scrawled on a white dry-erase board. The jackpots were often handsome, sometimes as much as a thousand dollars. Cam had won eight hundred one night when his mom had visited Montana to see their land before they purchased it. He'd never thrown a good roll since.

"Nah. I think Mom's my lucky charm. I'll bring her back in for dinner some night and try a few rolls then."

Trish shook the dice, and her cheek dimpled with a saucy grin. "I have a feeling it's your day to win. Roll a full house, and you'll have eight big ones in your pocket."

Cam shrugged, slapped a five-dollar bill on the counter, and stood up. It was only a few bucks, and he rarely gambled. Why not? He took the cup, gave it a shake, and slapped the mouth down on the counter so the dice wouldn't go every which way.

"Oh, my God!" Trish cried in a hushed voice. Then she yelled, "He won. First roll, five of a kind! A thousand bucks, people!"

Cam had four more tries to go. He sensed a crowd gathering behind him. Then, from the corner of his eye, he glimpsed a woman next to him. When he glanced down at her, he felt as if every brain cell he possessed went AWOL. She was beautiful, not the dolled-up kind of beautiful, but naturally lovely. Her straight black hair fell over her slender shoulders like shimmering silk. As far as he could detect, she wore no cosmetics, but that didn't detract from her features, which were delicately molded and enhanced her large dark blue eyes, outlined in long sooty lashes untouched by mascara.

She arched an eyebrow. "Aren't you going to roll again?"

Cam realized that he held the cup frozen at shoulder height.

"Sure," he found the presence of mind to say. "You just took the wind out of my sails."

"That's a line that's seen its day," she said with a laugh. "Roll hot, cowboy. I like winners."

Cam shook the dice, and one die shot off the counter. He winced as Trish picked it up, wondering what the hell had gotten into him. He wasn't a hormone-driven teenager.

"Free roll," Trish said.

Cam took another turn. Trish shrieked. When Cam focused, he saw that he'd rolled another five of a kind. He tossed the dice three more times and got zip. After Trish counted his winnings onto the bar, he plucked one bill from the pile and handed it to her.

"You don't have to do *that*, Cam. A hundred bucks? No way."

"Hey, you're the one who convinced me it might be my lucky day."

As Cam collected his money, the other woman shifted closer and asked, "Would you like to join me at my table?"

Cam swept his gaze downward from her remarkable face to take in the rest of her. She wore a fitted plaid Western shirt that had endured some wear, faded Wrangler jeans, and scuffed riding boots, the toe of one sporting a piece of hay. He also caught the familiar scent of horses mingling faintly with her perfume. He grabbed his drink. *Just my kind of gal,* he thought. *Maybe it really is my lucky day.*

AS KIRSTIN CONACHER LED THE WAY TO HER TABLE, SHE WAS acutely aware of the man behind her. He'd caught her attention the moment he entered the building—muscular, six feet of handsome, with tousled hair that gleamed like the well-varnished knotty pine bar. His eyes were a radiant sky blue, and he had a burnished tone to his skin that pegged him as an outdoor enthusiast. She could tell with only a look that he was no stranger to physical labor, and she'd been impressed by the easy, warm way he conversed with Trish. No fake charm, no canned lines. She found the sense of authenticity that he gave off very refreshing. There was also something vaguely familiar about him, but she couldn't recall ever having met him.

Oh, Kirstin, she mentally scolded herself, *what on earth were you thinking to hit on him like that?* Her cheeks burned with embarrassment. So what if she'd been searching for the right guy for six years and could hear her biological clock ticking? That was no excuse for her to be so forward. Normally she waited for a man to hit on *her*, not the other way around.

She resumed her seat, where a martini, extra dirty and straight up, still awaited her. In Kirstin's opinion, Trish made the best one in the valley. Only she hadn't come here for an afternoon drink. The martini was merely one of her stage props. She'd learned over time that men in bars tended to steer clear of a lone woman having a soda. A recognizable mixed drink seemed to spur on conversation.

Cam took a stool across from her. "Have you already ordered?"

She met his gaze, and a tingling sensation moved up her spine. That surprised her. She'd met dozens of handsome men, but she'd never felt like this. "Yes. The cook seems to be dragging his feet today."

"Come here often?"

"Not that often." *Liar, liar, boots on fire.* She came to the Cowboy Tree as often as she was able to escape from her dad's ranch for a couple of hours. The male patrons tended to be landowners who put in an honest day's work. She knew most of them, and unfortunately, they also knew her. Local men didn't mess with Sam Conacher's daughter. She kept hoping for a stranger to drop in, someone wonderful who wouldn't know about her dad. "Are you new to the valley?"

"Oh, yeah." He flashed a dazzling grin that creased his lean cheeks and displayed straight white teeth. "Anyone whose family hasn't been in the valley for three generations is a newcomer, or so I'm told. It'll be years before I earn the privilege of being recognized as a Bitterrooter."

She bent her head and toyed with her olive pick. Her cheeks went warm again. When she looked up, she said, "I hope I didn't give you the wrong impression. I don't habitually hit on guys."

A twinkle danced in his eyes. "Did you hit on me? It went over my head. I guess I need to get out more."

"My name's Kirstin."

"Cam."

"I know. I heard Trish talking with you after you came in. Short for Cameron?"

"Yep. Cameron McLendon."

Her fingers tightened on the olive pick. "Scottish?"

"Only half. My mom's Irish."

Kirstin's father was a Scot, and he was the most stubborn, irascible man she'd ever known. He hadn't always been that way, though. The death of her mother six years earlier had changed him. "Well, half Scottish or not, you seem nice."

He chuckled. "I take it you have a low opinion of Scots."

"Not really. Just a difficult experience with one in particular." She took a sip of her drink. "So, Cameron McLendon, tell me about yourself."

He smiled. "Boring story."

"So is mine, I'm afraid, but to get acquainted, we have to start somewhere, and I asked first."

He chuckled. "Want me to get two toothpicks so you can prop

your eyelids open?" He followed the question with a sigh. "Okay, here goes. I got a job opportunity with Long Barrel Ranches, and I've wanted to live here or in northern Idaho most of my adult life. It was finally my chance to chase my dreams, so I took the position."

"I'm not bored yet. Keep talking."

He shrugged. "For a long time, my dreams took second seat to my responsibilities, and I got stuck in Northern California. It's not that I dislike California, but after a couple of trips to this area, I fell in love. I kept hoping I might settle here, but life kept throwing me curveballs."

"Still interesting. What kind of curveballs?"

"It's kind of personal to share with a stranger."

Kirstin huffed. "Oh, boy. You haven't been in the valley long enough. No one can keep a secret here. You may as well spill your guts."

"I guess it's not *that* personal." He shrugged. "I got my girlfriend pregnant in high school."

"Uh-oh. I'm not sure that qualifies as a curveball. More like a demolition ball."

He paused to search her gaze, his expression conveying a mixture of surprise and appreciation. "Most people just say 'tough luck' and then move on to more interesting subjects."

Kirstin had met individuals who skimmed only the surface with her in conversations. When she told people about a life-altering event and they barely acknowledged her comment, she felt unimportant if not invisible. It also hinted that the other person had little emotional depth. "It *was* tough luck, I suppose, but the ramifications go well beyond that and probably lasted for years."

His cheek creased again in a suppressed smile. "Voice of experience?"

She shook her head. "No. I lived a very sheltered life in high school." She wanted to add that she still lived a sheltered experience, but that would shift the conversation to her, and her own life bored her to tears. "I did have a friend who got pregnant, though. She kept the baby, and her future was totally steered off course." She popped a green olive in her mouth. "So what happened? After you learned of the pregnancy, I mean."

He took a sip of his drink. "Well, it didn't demolish my life, but it did drastically alter it. My dad insisted that I marry her."

"At seventeen?" If Kirstin ever had kids, which seemed more unlikely with each passing year, she'd never force her son or daughter to get married that young. "That must have been a recipe for disaster."

"Pretty much. Our feelings for each other—or at least hers—weren't strong enough to withstand the trials of a teen pregnancy, and she filed for divorce before the baby was born. I think it was the shortest marriage on record." He shrugged. "Not all her fault, not entirely mine, either. She wanted to put our child up for adoption, but my parents helped me get custody. Right after she had the baby, she faded from the picture completely. No phone calls, no visitations. But even so, she refused to give up her parental rights. That ended up being a mess when I tried to get authorization from her to move my son out of state. She wouldn't cooperate. I think that, for whatever reason, she still holds a grudge against me. I'm not sure for what. Both of us were just kids."

Kirstin nodded. "At that point she should have turned loose of it. But apparently she didn't, and without her authorization to relocate, you were screwed."

"Pretty much stuck in California, for sure. And then, about five years ago, my dad was diagnosed with stage-four colon cancer."

She glimpsed a shimmer of moisture in his eyes and felt a

burn in her own. She knew how devastating it was to lose a beloved parent to cancer. Kirstin would never forget the day her mother had been diagnosed. "That must have been rough."

"Three years of rough. He was stubborn and didn't give up easily. My mother, God bless her, stood by him and cared for him until the end. All during his illness, I lived and worked an hour and a half away. They had a gorgeous home in snow country, and when a storm came during the winter, my first call of the day was to my folks to see how deep the white stuff was. Anything over three inches had me hauling ass north so I could clear their driveway, a necessity in case Mom had to call for an ambulance." He shook his head. "As Dad's illness worsened, her burdens increased, and my father needed moral support. What kind of son would have left them?"

Kirstin's heart squeezed. Though his story differed from hers, she *completely* understood how he must have felt back then. "No siblings to help you out?"

"I've got an awesome older sister." His eyes warmed with fondness. "She loves our parents as much as I do. But she'd gotten married before Dad got sick, has a family, lives on the East Coast, and has a challenging career. It was really hard on her when things got bad. She couldn't come home for every rough spot in the road. Airline fares alone made that impossible. Our folks helped with her travel costs, but mostly she tried to come when she could spend quality time with them."

"When her visits really counted." Kirstin remembered how her own life had become centered on her parents during her mom's illness. When she wasn't needed to care for her mother, she'd been trying to comfort her father. "That must have been so awful for her, wanting to be there all the time and unable to be."

"Exactly. She couldn't just abandon her family and career to be around constantly. She did what she could. And at the end, even though she couldn't catch a flight to get there before he died, she was there when it mattered most, to support me and Mom afterward." He took a sip of his drink. "It was difficult for me. I won't say it wasn't, or that I didn't feel resentful sometimes. I know she felt awful about it. But, hey, I'd chosen my path, mistake driven though it was, and that left me being the only kid on the ground to take care of our folks."

Trish delivered their meals. Kirstin smiled when she saw that they'd both ordered wings. "Great minds think alike." She eyed her basket of food and cringed. Eating chicken wings was messy and required no fewer than ten napkins to keep the sauce off her hands and face. For reasons she had no time to analyze right now, she wanted to be at her best as she got to know this guy. "This isn't what I would have ordered if I'd known I'd be eating with you."

He seemed to welcome the distraction, and Kirstin understood that. When she recalled her mother's painful death, she felt as if her heart was being pushed through a meat grinder.

"Chow down," he said. "If you smear sauce all over your face, I won't hold it against you. Just do me the same favor."

Kirstin grabbed a pile of table napkins and set it between them. "We have a deal. But don't let good table manners take precedence over telling me the rest of your story."

Around a bite of food, he said, "Only if you play fair and tell me yours."

"I can do that."

He frowned as if trying to remember what he'd been saying. "Anyway, my dad passed away almost two years ago. I think Mom was in shock the first year. Me too, I suppose. And my son took it really hard. Dad was our patriarch, the hub of our lives." He took two of the napkins. "Last spring, when I got a chance to work for Long Barrel Ranches, selling exclusive agricultural or recreational properties, I really wanted to grab the opportunity. Only I couldn't leave my mother behind in Northern California. What family she has there is spread out over the state and up into Oregon. She had some friends, of course, but that isn't the same as people who love you."

"So she agreed to move here with you?" Kirstin guessed, dabbing the corners of her mouth.

"She said she was ready for a change so she wouldn't constantly be reminded of Dad—their favorite restaurants, the trails they loved to walk, things like that. So I took my son before a judge. He was nearly sixteen. Caleb told the judge that he had never heard from his mom, that she had never even sent him a birthday card, and he didn't think it was fair that he couldn't move to Montana with me. The judge deemed Caleb to be old enough and mature enough to make that choice for himself. In a little over a week, I had permission to relocate my son. I put my farm on the market and came to the Bitterroot Valley to find a piece of land. Now we're here on our property, essentially camping out while our residences are being built."

Kirstin nearly choked as she swallowed. "Is your property on the river?"

He wiped his mouth. "Oh, yeah. We got so lucky. A large chunk of property with a lot of river frontage. Gorgeous piece of land. As rough as our living conditions are right now, even my mother loves it. Incredible three-hundred-and-sixty-degree views of the mountains. Fairly private. Good soil for alfalfa. The only problem is that Murphy's Law reigned supreme this summer, slowing things down as far as construction went. We had to get septic system approval, and the county is especially careful about granting that on river property. The builder hasn't even broken ground yet. He will soon, though."

Kirstin collected her composure. "I think we're neighbors. You're the people with the—um—huge camp."

Cam looked startled for a moment and then smiled. "Everyone who drives along Fox Hollow Road probably sees it. I think it's become a conversation piece, with people speculating about what crazy thing I might do next. When you're trying to create comfort for your family out in an alfalfa field, you have to be inventive. I've nicknamed it the Hillbilly Village."

"I'm glad you have a sense of humor about it. My father says we've been invaded by the Clampetts."

He threw back his tawny head and barked with laughter. She loved his broad smile. "Fair enough. I got everything in our camp functional, but I couldn't make it pretty. We tried to rent a house, but no landlord would accept us. We have three dogs and six cats, not to mention horses."

"We drive by your place going to and from town." She fiddled with a crumpled napkin. "When I first saw you walk in, something about you seemed familiar. Now I know why. At a distance, I see you all the time. My father owns the ranch behind your property."

Cam stared at her. "You're Kirstin *Conacher*? Sam Conacher's daughter?" He thumped himself on the forehead with the heel of his hand, leaving a smear of red sauce above his left eyebrow. "Oh, shit!"

Kirstin realized that he was already aware of her father's reputation. "My dad isn't as bad as rumor makes him out to be." The moment she spoke, she knew she needed to make a retraction. "Well, he actually *is* pretty bad, but I've learned ways around him."

• • •

CAM COULDN'T BELIEVE HIS BAD LUCK. HE'D ACTUALLY BEEN thinking about asking Kirstie out on a date. *Not happening.* Rumor had it that Sam Conacher went way over the top when it came to protecting his daughter. Some people even said he could be violent, but Cam doubted that was true. Mostly the man just destroyed the reputation of any guy who was dumb enough to mess with her. Supposedly she didn't date. He'd heard that she was beautiful, of course, but he had envisioned a spoiled, snotty rich girl with salon-conditioned hair and pampered skin. Kirstin Conacher didn't fit that mold. Her nails were clipped short. Her hands, though small, looked strong and hardened from physical work. Her clothing was ordinary.

"Is it true that you're still a virgin?" Cam wanted to kick himself the moment he asked the question.

She laughed. "Is that what people still say? No, definitely not, but only because I've been creative a few times, sneaking out behind my dad's back." She passed him a napkin. "Forehead. Right above your left eyebrow." As Cam scrubbed his skin, she added, "I know sneaking out sounds absurd. I'm a grown woman and should just get a place of my own. But it's more complicated than that."

Cam saw sadness in her eyes, and her mouth drew into a pinched line. "Hey, if it's something that's hard for you to talk about, there's no need to get into it. We didn't sign a full-disclosure agreement, after all."

"That wouldn't be fair. Me sharing my details was part of the bargain. Besides, in some ways, our stories are alike. Six years ago we lost my mom to ovarian cancer, and I'm an only child. I had to carry the load, making sure she got her medicine on time and playing roulette with opiates when she couldn't bear the pain. Convincing my father to put her in hospice was difficult. To him it was like giving up and signing her death warrant. I was nearly eighteen when we found out. She died when I was twenty. It was a terrible two years."

Cam's stomach knotted. He'd lived through times like that and knew how horrible they were. "I'm sure you made all the right choices."

"I don't know about that." Her eyes glistened with unshed tears. She looked out the window instead of holding his gaze. Cam studied her profile. He thought it was perfect, featuring a short delicately bridged nose, lush lips, and a small chin that suggested she might have a stubborn streak. "I was so young. Death had always been something distant to me—an awful thing that would happen way off in the future. Only suddenly, there it was, taking my mom from us." She took a bracing breath and looked back at Cam with a self-derisive smile. "Sorry. It's been six years. One would think I'd be over it."

"Do we ever really get over it?" Cam asked. "Two years, six years. That's not long enough. Twenty maybe. And then it'll still make us sad if we let ourselves think about it."

She nodded. "Losing Mom nearly destroyed my dad. Right after her funeral, he took his first drink, and I didn't see him sober for two years."

"Oh, man." Cam felt grateful that his mother was such a strong woman. After losing her husband, she had never turned to alcohol or tranquilizers to survive. "That must have made things harder."

"It was horrible. Drunk as a lord, he ran heavy equipment, rode horses, and herded cows. He took stupid risks countless times a day, and I lived on the edge of panic, afraid that he'd kill himself. Finally I told him one morning that I couldn't take it anymore and was moving out." She took a sip of her martini and sighed. "Until that moment, I'd never seen my father cry except for when Mama died. But he sank onto the stairs, stared at me with tears rolling down his cheeks, and begged me not to leave. I was all he had left, he said, and if I abandoned him he'd have nothing to live for."

"Oh, Kirstie."

She set her glass down with a loud *click*. "He sobered up to appease me." She lifted her hands. "When you talked about feeling stuck— Well, that's how I felt that morning and how I still feel now. He kept his side of the bargain, and I've never seen him drunk again. He'll have a couple of beers or a little wine. I don't mind that." Her gaze clung to Cam's. "I didn't leave that morning. I realized that he needed me, and I couldn't abandon him."

"Of course you couldn't. He's your father, and you love him."

"You'd be amazed by how many people tell me to run for my life and let the ornery old bastard dive back into a whiskey jug."

"People call him that to your face?"

"That and worse. And it's not entirely undeserved. My dad is old, he's ornery, and he can be extremely difficult. He hasn't always been that way. Before Mama died, he was a great guy—a good neighbor, a wonderful boss, and a fabulous father." She grimaced. "Now it's a different story. He treats me as if I'm sixteen. He grew so impossible to work with that all but one of his hired hands quit. He has me and a man named Miguel who shares the responsibilities of ranch manager with me. His wife cleans and cooks for Dad, so she makes a good income as well." Kirstin pushed the last olive around in her glass. "They're family-oriented people. I think Miguel understands my dad in ways that others don't."

Cam heard the pain that laced her words. Kirstin's feelings ran deep, and he totally understood how her emotions worked against her. She deserved to live her own life, to feel free to date and maybe fall in love. Yet she'd become trapped by a sense of obligation—just as he had. No longer hungry, he pushed his plate aside and noticed that she had done the same.

"I'm sorry, Kirstin. When our folks get older, it can be hard. I loved my dad. I love my mom. What I wanted to do with my own life got lost in the shuffle. But I wouldn't go back in time to change a thing. I did no more for them than either of them would have done for me. That's what family is all about. I know that it's a small consolation, but someday when you look back, you'll have no regrets."

Her gaze clung to his. "I hope for that. But what about my life now? We only get one shot."

Cam couldn't dismiss her concerns. He'd felt them himself. "I'm not going to say you're not missing out on things. I used to worry that I'd bypassed my window of opportunity to meet the right person, and sometimes I still do. All I can do is trust that I'll meet her soon and get my shot at happiness. Not that I'm unhappy. I love my work. Our new land is beautiful. And my son is a precious gift in my life. But when this chapter ends, will another one open up for me?"

She nodded. "Right. I hear you. Ever since my mom's death, I've felt like a figurine trapped in a snow globe. When I finally couldn't take it anymore, I started sneaking out." She gestured at the window. "As often as I can, I visit the restaurants and bars on Highway 93, for better company."

Cam knew firsthand that most of the bars were similar to the Cowboy Tree, low-key, friendly, and suitable for family dining. "How has that worked out?"

"Well, the overall picture is pretty dismal, but at least I'm no longer a virgin."

Cam arched his eyebrows. "And how did that happen?" He winced. "I mean the circumstances, not the nuts and bolts."

"I met a nice guy, arranged to meet him in Missoula, where I can get lost in a crowd, and went to bed with him." She shrugged. "Nothing spectacular. But after he left my motel room, I went to the lounge and had a drink to celebrate my coming-of-age. I know it sounds sleazy. I didn't care if I ever saw him again. He was my means to an end."

Cam thought she was far too lovely and special to waste herself on some guy who meant nothing to her. On the other hand, he'd been intimate with people who didn't really matter to him, so maybe his opinion was sexist.

She scrunched up her nose. "I've dated only a few guys since then. Nobody memorable. Maybe an HEA isn't in the stars for me." She laid a crumpled napkin on her plate. "My opportunities to spend a night away from home are at a minimum." Another sigh conveyed to him her sense of frustration. "I never pictured my life like this. Dad let me attend college in Missoula, but he refused to let me live on campus. He said he wasn't about to let some 'liberal pip-squeak' seduce me. In fair weather, I drove back and forth. If I wasn't home by six, he was wearing a path on his slate floor, worried sick. In bad weather, he drove me to campus and picked me up when I finished my last class. I felt like an overlarge kindergartner."

Cam appreciated her honesty. He hadn't been held back by an overprotective parent, but he had been hemmed in by familial obligations. He wondered if she regretted not leaving the ranch over her father's drinking. Conacher had been in the wrong, and she'd missed her opportunity to escape by giving him a second chance. Cam knew he couldn't learn the answer to that question over one order of wings, and there would never be a next time. She was pretty. She was interesting. But with her father as part of the equation, she was also dangerous.

"I'm thirty-five," he told her. "A little too old for you."

She gave him a smile that didn't reach her eyes. "I'm an extremely mature twenty-six, going on twenty-seven. The age difference doesn't seem that important to me. This will sound bold—it seems to be my day for it. But, please, I'd like to get to know you better."

He glanced at his watch. "Damn, it's already four thirty. I've got livestock to care for, and then I have to fix dinner."

"Well, I can see I've scared you off. Is it my age, or do you just feel that the situation is too complicated because of my father?"

Cam hated being put on the spot, but she was a nice young woman and deserved an honest answer. "I'm taking a huge risk just by sitting here with you."

"Yes, you probably are," she conceded.

"If someone in here told your father that we were seen together, I could become his next target. I've heard the stories. He goes after any man who messes with you. Gets them fired from their jobs, ruins their reputations."

She sighed. "I won't deny it, Cam. By seeing me, you'd be putting yourself in his line of fire."

"Right, and I have my family to think of. I came with savings to back us up, but buying the land was expensive, so I need to start selling ranches before my money runs out. I don't want my mom shouldering the load, which she will if I don't hit my stride in the valley."

She nodded as if she understood, but she didn't look happy about it. "Just in case you change your mind, would you like to have my cell number?"

Cam saw no harm in that. "Sure." He exchanged devices with her and punched in his name and number on her phone while she did the same on his.

She returned his cell. He slipped hers back across the table. An edgy feeling moved up his spine. He couldn't shake the thought that he was making a huge mistake.

She searched his expression and smiled. "Hey, don't feel bad about this. You're playing it smart. My father can be bad news."

Cam didn't want to sound as if he were throwing her a crumb to make her feel better, but at the same time, he couldn't just walk away, either. "You're a very attractive lady, Kirstin. I have a feeling I'm going to regret not seeing you again."

"If so, you've got my number." She collected a hand-tooled leather purse from where it sat on a stool beside her. Cam knew with one look that it had probably cost a small fortune. If he'd seen it earlier, he would have known she had money and lots of it. "My fair share," she said, placing a twenty on the table.

"You don't have to do that. My treat."

"Nonsense. Two ships passing in the night should go Dutch." She stood and extended her hand to him before he could gain his feet. He grasped her fingers. She responded with a strong grip that told him more than she could know, particularly how hard she worked on her father's ranch. "It's been a pleasure to meet you, Cam. I've enjoyed it."

He nodded, still feeling off-center. Looking up at her, he couldn't recall ever having met someone who appealed to him quite as much or on so many levels. In a short span of time, he'd learned so much about her, namely that she was a devoted daughter, that life had challenged her at nearly every turn, and that she had the capacity to be loyal, even when the circumstances were completely unfair to her. "Likewise. Take care of yourself, Kirstin.

When you drive by the Hillbilly Village, toot your horn to say hello. I doubt that your father will go off the deep end over a little neighborly horn honking."

"You might be surprised what my father could read into a friendly honk."

Pulling the purse strap over her shoulder, she walked away. With every click of her boots, Cam silently called himself an idiot.

Chapter Two

AS KIRSTIN TURNED OFF ONTO FOX HOLLOW ROAD, SHE DE-cided she shouldn't go home just yet. If her father looked the wrong way at her, she might bite his head off. Just before the bridge that spanned the river to touch the west corner of the McLendon property, there was a pullout where people parked to launch their boats from state land or to take their dogs for runs off leash. She decided to take a short walk. A cooling-off period.

She turned left and pulled in beside an old Camaro with a dented back fender. Then she cut the engine of her truck. *Correction,* she reminded herself. *It's not my truck. Like everything else in my life, it belongs to the Conacher Ranch.* She couldn't help but resent that even though she knew that someday the entire operation would become hers. That wasn't the same as working to buy something for herself. Not the same as having a sense of accomplishment and pride. Even her savings account didn't feel as if it were truly hers. Every dollar had come from her father's pocket.

So many people thought she was lucky. Kirstin Conacher, the girl who'd been born with a silver spoon in her mouth, a girl who played at being a rancher and had never had to work hard for anything. They were so mistaken. She busted her ass every single day, and anyone who'd ever held a genuine silver spoon in their mouth knew that it soon started to taste like cheap metal, bitter on the tongue.

She swung out of the truck, beeped the remote to lock the cab, and pushed the keys into her jeans pocket. A walk would take the edge off. She set her stride along the well-traveled trail, trying to appreciate the natural beauty that surrounded her. Groves of aspen and cottonwood lent touches of apple green to the thick stands of evergreen. Rocky beaches curved in and out along the river's edge. Craggy mountain peaks rose like divine sculptures against the azure Montana sky. The air cooled her cheeks and tasted of the flora that thrived in the riparian area. To her, it was home, and nowhere else in the world could ever equal it.

She just wished she could feel happy and content here. But meeting Cam and then being rejected by him had felt like the final blow in a sense, dashing her hopes of ever having a normal life. Her father, as much as she loved him, was to single men what bear spray was to grizzlies. What guy in his right mind would ever put his livelihood at risk to start a relationship with her? Not even Cam, who seemed to have depth and be a caring person, had wanted to tangle with her dad. And she couldn't blame him. He had a mother and a son for whom he was responsible.

She walked over the rocks to reach the water's edge and stared across the river at Cam McLendon's camp. She supposed he'd been right to nickname it the Hillbilly Village. A small vintage travel trailer sat facing her. It must have been renovated, because the exterior paint, crisp white divided by a blue stripe, looked brand-new. It was an adorable RV, reminiscent of days gone by, and she would have loved to see the interior. Behind it were two dusty-looking tents, and to the left of them sat a small reddish brown cabin. A gray late-model SUV was parked near the trailer. An old Ford truck sat behind it, sporting so many dents and scrapes that it looked as if it might have been entered in a demolition derby.

Not much to look at, she thought. But to her, that camp represented all the things she wanted in her own life. The people there were chasing a dream, and they were enduring hardship as a family to grab hold of it. The present, and all its daily trials, wasn't their focus. In their minds, they saw what the land could one day be, and they were determined to make it happen. Cam had created a home from very little. And, yes, he'd been inventive to make his mother and son comfortable. But even from where she stood, she could sense the intense love that emanated from the hodgepodge. If only some of it would rub off on her.

Tears filled her eyes and ran in scalding streams down her cheeks. Cam might not even know how very blessed he was. In the end, he and his family would achieve their dreams, and together they would enjoy the fruits of their determination and sacrifice. The way things were going, she doubted she might ever experience the love of a good man or get to have a child of her own. And, if her dad had his way, nothing she ever possessed would truly belong to her.

Daddy would just give her everything.

She turned and moved back up the slight grade to the forest. Pieces of driftwood had been cast upon the rocks, left by a swift winter current to lie there, harden, and lose all semblance of life. They were beautiful—twisted and weathered pieces of what had once been gorgeous trees. Someday when she grew old, she might resemble that wood, a withered outline of what she might have been.

Good luck, Cam, she thought. *I hope a new chapter opens up for you and that it's wonderful beyond all your expectations.*

MADDIE McLENDON HAD BEEN WORRIED FOR HOURS. HER SON, Cam, had left at six that morning, and he still wasn't back at camp. Her biggest fear was that something horrible might happen to him. Every time her grandson, Caleb, was late, she fretted about him, too. She didn't know how she could survive losing another loved one. Since her husband Graham's death, her boys had become her everything. She'd read that her fears about losing someone else were a normal part of the grieving process, but Maddie disliked being *normal*. And she sure as heck didn't want to be a weight around her son's neck.

Relief flooded through her when she heard the rumbling sound of Cam's diesel truck. She shut down her computer and got up from her office chair, groaning under her breath because her legs were stiff from sitting for so long. Her right knee sometimes gave her fits, and that was the case today. She felt pretty good, though, and that was a bonus. She'd gotten a treatment last week and had suffered through most of what she thought of as her chemo hangover days. Though Cam was gone a lot working, even he had started to notice that she felt under the weather every couple of weeks, and he kept asking if she was okay.

Last spring, she'd made a judicious decision not to tell him that she'd been diagnosed with colon cancer. The same disease had killed his father less than a year and a half before, and when she learned she had it herself, she couldn't manage to hit Cam with the news. He was a strong-willed and resilient man, but he loved people to a fault, investing too much of his heart and often too much of his time into caring for others and trying to make them happy. He'd spent most of his adult life focused on rearing his son and supporting his parents. She wanted Cam to chase after his dreams and to have his own piece of the pie.

Maddie had achieved all her dreams. She'd been blessed with a wonderful husband, the love of her life who'd fulfilled all her girlhood yearnings for a hero and romance. For years, they'd stood side by side, working to create their own little dynasty and raising their children. Maddie never looked back and felt that she'd been cheated out of anything. She'd had it all.

Now it was Cam's turn, and she wouldn't derail him by telling him that she was battling for her life. Heck, no. If she lost the war, she'd have plenty of time to warn him, but until then, she was a tough old broad, she was responding well to treatments, and she could get through this without her son holding her hand.

As was her evening habit, Maddie quickly tidied her work space and then the tiny kitchen. She'd already made her bed that morning. The vintage trailer had been redone, inside and out, and it amazed her how perfectly the designers had utilized the square footage. Compared to her former home, this place was a postage stamp, but it was cozy and warm, and she tried to keep it looking nice.

She stepped into the miniature full bath to brush her hair, originally a short cut that had grown out a bit, much to her relief. Cropping her mane had seemed like a practical choice for camping, but instead she'd awakened each day to a nightmare of reddish brown spikes that refused to lie flat until she wet them down and blew them dry. With the extra length she had now, the style was more controllable. Not that tamer hair helped much with her looks. Light though her treatments were, the new chemo drug that was regularly infused into her bloodstream had taken its toll. Her skin was dry and crinkly. She'd been what she liked to think of as pleasingly plump before her surgery. Now her fat deposits felt like balloons that had lost all their air.

Oh, well, she thought. *I'm not losing my hair. That's a miracle. And I'll gain all the weight back when I get through this and be a plump grandma again. Caleb won't worry aloud about me getting too thin anymore after he hugs me.*

As she stepped out of the trailer, she skimmed an appreciative glance over the sturdy wooden steps with a handrailing that Cam and Caleb had built for her. *So sweet.* They had done everything they could to make her comfortable here. It had been a difficult transition at first. She'd missed her spacious high-end home. But now she loved being here. The relaxing sound of the river, the breathtaking views of the Bitterroot Mountains from her windows, and the forest across the stream seemed to embrace and soothe her.

Once on the rocky gravel that Caleb had spread over her front yard to cut down on mud being tracked inside, she made a mental note to call her sister in Missouri soon. Maddie had flown back there to have her tumor removed, and she'd stayed with Naomi for the first few rounds of her chemo. Now they chatted as often as possible. Naomi and her husband, Chuck, were the only members of Maddie's family who knew about her cancer, and during those first three months, they'd been so supportive. Naomi loved getting phone calls from Maddie that began with "I'm still cancer-free!"

She pushed open the gate and left her spacious front yard, wondering where Caleb had gotten off to. He'd come to her trailer after he'd gotten home from school and eaten a snack to hold him over until dinner. But she hadn't seen him since, and until now she hadn't missed him. That was one drawback of being a writer. She slipped away into another world and forgot all about the real one.

She went directly to the wall tent that Cam had transformed into a multifunctional living area. He called it the cook shack. She found her son already standing over the propane stove, preparing a cast-iron skillet for cooking. He'd put on a bibbed apron because he still wore his work clothes: a crisp dress shirt, Western jeans, and well-conditioned riding boots. In Maddie's opinion, he was an extremely handsome man. Whenever she told him so, he laughed and said she saw him through the eyes of love.

"You sure had a long day," she said. "Did the guy make an offer?"

Maddie hoped that Cam had gotten a nibble. He needed to make a ranch sale. She wasn't overly worried about money, but for Cam's peace of mind, he needed to carve his own niche in this market.

"Nope. He just walked the land and found fault with everything. It's a gorgeous property. I don't know what his problem is." He stepped over to give her a quick hug. "No worries. Someone else will go wild over it."

Maddie flashed a smile. "Only a matter of time." She glanced at the skillet. "What are we making tonight? I'm done working for the day and ready to help."

"I'm going for simple tonight with ground beef goulash."

Maddie knew that no meal Cam cooked was ever simple. He loved to create different dishes from scratch and had an uncanny sense of what flavors complemented others. She stepped over to the utility sink, a stand-alone fiberglass tub with running water, to wash her hands. Then she set herself to the task of rinsing and chopping the vegetables he'd taken from the fridge.

"Mom," Cam said. "You don't need to do that. Standing in one spot makes your back hurt."

Maddie had fibbed about her bimonthly chemo treatments, telling her boys that she was going into Missoula for physical therapy. She'd had minor back surgery several years ago, so they had accepted that explanation without question. "My back feels awesome tonight. Where's Caleb?"

"He offered to take care of the horses for me." Cam winked over his shoulder at her. "It's my turn, but I think hunger drove him to be generous."

Maddie laughed. "When he got home from school, he ate an entire row of Oreos, an orange, a bunch of carrot sticks, and then half a bag of chips. I think he volunteered out of the goodness of his heart, not because he's starving."

DINNER WAS OVER AND THE KITCHEN WAS CLEAN IN WHAT SEEMED to Maddie a blink.

Caleb dried the last skillet and then turned to them. "Let's take the dogs for a walk," he said. "It's, like, still way light out. We've got time."

"I walked a huge ranch today, son. Can we save it for tomorrow night?"

Caleb groaned, which made Cam sigh.

"All right," Cam said. "I'm in, but no farther than the slough tonight. Deal?"

Cam quickly laid a fire in the woodstove so that the wall tent would be toasty warm when they returned. Along the river, it grew cold as the sun went down, and of an evening, they liked to sit in here to catch up on each other's day. Cam had found upholstered swivel rockers and created a comfortable conversation area. Sometimes Caleb did his homework while they chatted. Other nights he went to the prefab cabin that he and his father shared as sleeping quarters to watch TV on Cam's sixty-inch flat-screen. High-speed Internet had been installed shortly after Maddie had arrived in mid-August.

As they set off for their walk, Maddie and Cam set a slower pace while Caleb raced ahead with the dogs, Boomer, Bingo, and Bear, all three black-tri Australian shepherds. Maddie's six cats joined the parade at varying distances. Cam had ordered an eight-by-eight shed to house the felines, and Maddie went out each day to care for them. Coyotes were numerous around their land, so she put her cats inside at night to keep them safe.

"Oh, how I love it here," Maddie said.

"I'm glad you like it, Mom. When I brought you here, I worried that it wouldn't be your cup of tea. It's a big change."

"It's gorgeous, and I have no regrets," Maddie assured him.

And it truly was gorgeous. The cottonwood and aspen leaves added lighter dollops of green to the verdant slough terrain. To her left, Cam and Caleb had fenced nearly twenty acres for the horses, and the equines were enjoying their newfound freedom. All four of them came running to the barrier to greet them. Maddie and her son stopped to pet them before resuming their pace. She was glad Cam was tired and walking slowly. That allowed her to watch her step and protect her knee. She had no idea what was wrong with it, only that it didn't trouble her all the time.

Her arm bumped Cam's as they ambled along. "Caleb's right, Mom. You're getting thin. I just felt your shoulder bone."

Maddie forced a laugh. "Bless your heart. But the truth is, I still can't feel my ribs."

He sighed. "I know you want to be a good sport about our move, but you'll tell me if you aren't feeling well. Right?"

Maddie evaded giving a direct answer. "I'm feeling as fit as a fiddle!"

"Well, I'm glad. And it'll be much nicer for you once our residences are built."

He bent his head, watching his feet as he walked. Normally he threw sticks for the dogs or played around with Caleb, but that evening he seemed to be in a thoughtful mood.

"What is it, Cam? Did something go wrong during the land showing?"

His hair lifted in the breeze and shone like shellacked hickory in the fading sunlight. "Not during the showing, but afterward."

She studied his profile. He had his father's chiseled features and generous mouth. "Want to talk about it?"

A hint of a smile curved his lips. "I was starving on the way home and stopped at the Cowboy Tree for a bite to eat. I met a beautiful young woman while I was there. She asked me to sit at her table, and I really enjoyed chatting with her." He watched Caleb romping with the dogs. The teen had grown muscular over the summer, filling out his jeans and Western shirt in places he previously hadn't. "Have you ever met a perfect stranger and started talking as if you'd been friends for years?"

Maddie nodded. "How do you think I ended up with your dad? So this lady is pretty special, I take it."

"I think so. I shared things with her that I'd never blurt out to other people, and she reciprocated. But as intriguing as I found her to be, I can't see her again."

"Why?" Mystified, Maddie sent him a questioning look. "You finally meet someone appealing and put the kibosh on the possibilities without going on a date?"

"Her name is Kirstin Conacher."

Maddie stopped dead in her tracks. Cam slowed to a halt and turned to face her. "You see? That put chocks in front of your wheels, just like it did mine. I know what you're thinking: that seeing her only once could mean big trouble for me. But I didn't know who she was until after I sat down with her."

"Yes, it could mean trouble," Maddie agreed. "With a few negative comments about you to key people, Conacher could ruin your reputation across this valley before you get your first sale."

"So you've heard about what he does to guys who mess with his daughter." Cam didn't phrase it as a question.

"Everyone in this valley has heard about it. I may stay busy with my work, but I do get out sometimes. I go to book club meetings at the Rustlers' Gulch Library now. I play bingo. I visit the little bookstore and chat with people. Everyone knows we bought the land that borders his, and I've been told more than once not to get on his bad side."

Cam nodded. "That's why I told her I couldn't see her again. She didn't seem angry, but I could tell she was disappointed."

"And?" Maddie prodded.

"The minute I told her, I wondered if it was a mistake."

Maddie huffed out a breath and gazed off through the trees. She wanted so badly for her son to stop putting everyone else first and follow his heart for once. But Sam Conacher could destroy him. "I've seen her in town, driving a pickup with the name of her father's ranch painted on the door. Though I suspect she's a spoiled brat, she appeared to be friendly with everyone she encountered, so maybe I'm wrong about her. And I have to admit she is lovely."

"I thought she'd be spoiled, too. But she's not. It's too bad she's Conacher's daughter. If she weren't, I'd be like a bear after honey."

A wave of regret washed over Maddie. Was she really going to let Cam put his own life on the back burner again? She was a firm believer that some people were fated to be together. What if Cam passed on the opportunity to get better acquainted with Kirstin and never met another young lady who intrigued him as much?

Maddie's income could cover their expenses. Besides, even if Conacher did his worst, Cam could always practice his profession in Idaho, where he also had a license. It would be rough on him to travel back and forth, but he could roll with the punches and eventually recover.

"You rarely meet a woman and feel this interested."

He shrugged. "It's no big deal. There are other fish in the sea."

"Yes, but when are you going to find one that makes you happy?"

"What are you saying, that I should risk ruining my future in this valley? She seems nice, but dating often comes with promising starts and dismal endings. Not to mention that Conacher would squash me like a bug as the finale. I've heard stories that curl my hair. Some young car salesman ended up losing his job for riding with Kirstin when she took a Corvette off the lot for a spin. When Conacher heard about it, he got him fired."

"And you're going to take a pass just because her father's a jerk."

Cam gave Maddie a bewildered look that made her laugh.

"Think about it, Cam. My income will cover us during a slump, and you can always travel south to sell property. What would your father say if he were here?"

Cam shoved his hands into his back pockets. "That I've got a fabulous chance to be successful here and not to blow it."

"Graham McLendon never backed down from anyone," Maddie reminded him. "Men like Sam Conacher are bullies, and he hated bullies. If he were here right now, he'd tell you to see the lady again, and to hell with her father."

Cam finally smiled. "He would, wouldn't he? I can almost hear him." After a moment, he added, "I got her phone number. Maybe we can arrange to meet again somewhere. If so, I'll be extra careful."

"Careful as in careful not to be seen with her?" Maddie hated the thought of that, but she also understood Cam's sense of obligation to her and his son. "It's beautiful weather. A long walk and a picnic would be fun. You could walk over the bridge and meet her across the river. That way, your vehicles wouldn't be seen together."

"That's a great idea."

Maddie heard the dogs moving toward them. Both she and her son turned to watch Caleb circle the bounding balls of multicolored fur as he ran. She could only pray that Cam could satisfy his curiosity about Kirstin without crossing swords with her father. People who lived in Rustlers' Gulch referred to Sam Conacher as an ornery old son of a bitch.

CAM HAD NO REAL ESTATE APPOINTMENTS THE FOLLOWING DAY, so he texted Kirstin.

> *I knew I'd regret not seeing you again. Is there any way you can meet me tomorrow for a walk along the river and a picnic afterward? I'll bring the food and drink.*

She didn't text back right away, and Cam sat staring at his phone like an idiot. When it finally hummed a notification tone, he jerked as if he'd been stuck with a pin.

> *I can only get away around noon, our lunch hour. I can tell Dad that I'm taking two hours and work late tomorrow night. Where should we meet?*

Cam smiled. As crazy as it was, he felt better now. He sensed that they had a lot in common, and he hated when he liked the first part of a story and never got to find out how it ended.

JUST BEFORE NOON THE NEXT MORNING THE FARRIER CAME. Kirstin's father said that he didn't want a bunch of stuff going on around the horses while they were being reshod. A few of them were still green and got nervous. He gave both Kirstin and Miguel a large chunk of the afternoon off. Kirstin feigned reluctance to be gone for so long, saying she'd planned to do this or that. He waved her away and told her to get her hair cut or something.

Kirstin couldn't believe her good luck. She could spend more time with Cam than she'd hoped. She arrived before he did and left her truck where she had parked it the prior afternoon. Then she moved into the cover of the trees to wait for him. Leaning against the rough bark of a ponderosa, she watched the roadside pullout for his vehicle to appear. Instead he arrived on foot, carrying a medium-size cooler in one hand. The blue lid matched the deep color of his eyes.

Her heart leaped, and excitement coursed through her. Today he wore old jeans, faded with wear, and a denim shirt, sleeves rolled back over his thick forearms, tails tucked in at the waist to reveal his Western belt and shiny buckle. When he reached the forest and caught sight of her, he waved. Sunlight slanted through the tree boughs, dappling his hair and making it gleam one moment, then casting him in shadow the next.

"Hey!" he called out.

"Hey, yourself." She walked to meet him. When they drew close, he flashed her a grin that sent shivers down her spine. What was it about him that made her feel like this? "This was a fabulous suggestion, Cam. It's a great day for a walk and a picnic."

"I'd like to leave this where we're going to eat." He lifted the cooler slightly. "You have any ideas?"

Kirstin knew this side of the riverbank by heart. "Farther downstream, there's a grassy knoll that would be perfect. It's a little too close to our ranch proper for comfort, but Dad's supervising the farrier. I'm pretty sure he won't go riding and possibly see us."

"Sounds perfect."

They struck off, walking side by side. The occasional brushes of his sleeve against hers made her acutely aware of him. He moved with an easy grace, as sure-footed on the rocks as she was. Faint hints of warmth emanated from his solid body. She caught the scent of his woodsy cologne and suspected that he'd shaved recently.

"You've got a better view of our camp from here," he told her. "What do you think?"

She stopped to study the Hillbilly Village even though she'd done so only yesterday. He described how he had buried a three-hundred-gallon tank at the other side of his mother's trailer to serve as a makeshift septic tank and regularly filled another tank the same size to supply them with water.

He pointed out where their first building would go up. "It'll be a huge workshop. Some might call it a barn, I guess. We'll have residences at the front—one upstairs, which will be mine and my son's, and one downstairs for Mom. It'll be nice, with wood siding and shingled rooflines. I think we'll be happy there. Later we plan to build a nice home."

"What'll happen with the shop residences afterward?"

"We have a conservation easement in our riparian area, so the rules are strict to protect the property. But I talked with a conservation agent, and it'll be okay if we rent them out."

"Awesome. It's always good if a property produces income. Will you farm the land?"

"Oh, yeah, although I may not do it myself. I'm better off selling real estate. But I've been approached by a couple of guys who might grow alfalfa each year for a large percentage of the cuts. That works for me. It won't cost me a fortune to feed my horses and cows over the winter, and I won't be neglecting my career."

"You have cows?"

"I sold them before coming here, but I plan to buy more."

They reached the grassy knoll and left the cooler while they continued to walk. She hadn't misjudged him in the bar yesterday. He could walk at a fast clip over rugged terrain without getting winded. Their conversation bounced like a Ping-Pong ball from one topic to another, an easy flow of exchanges that relaxed her. Then he slowed the pace a bit. "You have only two hours. We should probably go back now to eat."

Kirstin told him how she'd gotten an unexpected leave of absence for the afternoon. "Dad thinks I'm getting a haircut."

"Won't he notice if you don't?"

"I only get the ends trimmed when I go in. He won't notice." He shot her an irresistible grin.

When they struck off walking again, it was her turn to point out and identify different parts of the Conacher Ranch, which now lay across the river from them. When he saw the post-and-beam houses and the outbuildings in the distance, he whistled.

"Wow. That stable is incredible. Not that the homes aren't. Only I can't help but think your horses have better digs than we will when our place is finished."

She laughed. "You'll have a great home, all that you need, anyway. I get lost in the ranch manager's house. It's too big for one person. I'd rather have a small bungalow."

LATER THEY SAT SIDE BY SIDE ON THE GRASSY KNOLL WITH THE cooler in front of them. Cam was glad that he'd decided to see her again. She was absolutely beautiful, and he still had the feeling that she was one of a kind. He knew for certain now that he should make it a point to get better acquainted with her. He liked her down-to-earth view of life. She'd proven herself to be a good walking partner, fit enough to give him a run for his money, yet still feminine. There was so much about her that appealed to him, especially her low-key laugh, which rang with sincere humor and wasn't loud or obnoxious. He'd dated a gal once who sounded like a horse neighing. Her laughter had seemed forced and had driven him crazy.

Kirstin complimented him on the picnic offerings, simple fare but homemade. Thick turkey sandwiches with all the trimmings; potato salad made from scratch, a portion of which he would serve to his family that night; a light cucumber salsa; and a cream cheese dip, accompanied by corn tortilla chips. He'd brought chilled white wine and canned soda as well. She chose to have wine, which he poured into red plastic cups.

"This is fabulous, Cam."

She ate as if she were starving, and he liked that about her, too. Women who picked at food and pretended to have no appetite bothered him. He enjoyed cooking, and food, it seemed to him, should be appreciated, not necessarily in large amounts, but with enthusiasm.

When she tasted his cucumber salsa, she closed her eyes with a blissful expression on her face. "Oh, my God, that's good. Recipe, please. Sometimes, just for the heck of it, I cook for myself at my place, and I'd love to make that. It would be great as a veggie dip."

"I'll text it to you," he promised. "Why don't you cook more often?"

"My father has a housekeeper who prepares all his meals, so I mostly eat at his place. But I don't want to end up being a person who can't put a meal together, so at least once a week I make a nice dinner, cutting down the recipe as much as I can. I do leftovers only twice." She held up two fingers. "No matter how good something is, I can't stomach anything for more than three days."

"I'm the same way." Cam studied her profile as she dabbed the corners of her mouth with a section from a paper towel roll. "What kind of stuff do you cook?"

"I'm clear across the board." She talked about surfing the Internet for dishes that sounded good. He chuckled when she shared stories about her abysmal failures, his favorite being a homemade bread recipe to which she'd added three times more yeast than needed, resulting in dough overflowing the bowl inside her oven. "What a mess! Now I make sure that I've read the amounts correctly."

She sobered, fell quiet, and stared at the river. Cam hoped he hadn't said or done something to offend her. Finally she said, "I feel kind of bad about yesterday, the things I said about my dad. I thought it was important to be honest with you, but now I wonder if I was entirely fair to him." A flush rode her cheeks. "I shouldn't talk negatively about my father. He's a good person at heart, and there are underlying reasons for his behavior that I didn't mention yesterday."

Cam could think of no good reason for a man to hold his daughter hostage at home. "Well, nothing you said about him differed much from things I'd already heard."

She sighed. "My poor dad. His behavior has become legend in this valley. People wag their tongues constantly about him, never stopping to wonder what changed him."

"What did?"

She shook her head. "If we see each other again, maybe I'll tell you. I promised myself that I wouldn't be glum today."

"Aw, come on. Now you have piqued my curiosity."

She wrinkled her nose. "It's just a very sad situation, Cam. That's not how I want you to think of me, some gal who always talks about herself."

"I don't think that, so let loose."

She hesitated. "Okay. You asked for it. I believe my dad holds himself to blame for my mother's death."

Cam winced. "Why? She died from cancer. That's a natural cause."

She glanced over at him. "I need to have your word that you'll never repeat this. I've never told anyone, and my father would be extremely upset if this became more fodder for the gossip mills."

Cam never gave his word lightly. "I can't think of anyone I'd want to tell or need to tell. So you have my word that I won't."

She took a deep breath and released it. "After I was born, my mother started having female trouble. Eventually her gynecologist wanted her to have a complete hysterectomy. She kept getting cysts on her ovaries." She lifted her cup to take a sip of wine and then sent him a questioning look. "Are you uncomfortable discussing female stuff?"

Cam shook his head. "No, of course not."

She licked her lips and swallowed, her dainty larynx bobbing in her slender throat. "Her periods were extremely heavy, so much so that she grew anemic. I can actually remember that, so it must have spanned several years. It got so bad that she had to get iron shots fairly often, and the injection site always burned and ached afterward, sometimes for days. It was as if she had a reaction or something." She gazed across the river. "Both my parents wanted more children, my father especially. He hoped to have a son who'd someday run the ranch." She forced a smile. "Not that he feels a woman can't do that. It's just easier on a man physically. One night—I can't remember how old I was, maybe eight—I heard them arguing upstairs in their bedroom. They rarely fought, so it frightened me, and I huddled at the bottom of the steps, listening. Mama was crying. She told Daddy that she wanted another child as much as he did, but she couldn't go on like she was. Daddy asked her if she could hang tough for another six months. If they couldn't make a baby in that amount of time, she would have the surgery."

Cam's stomach knotted. "Oh, God."

Kirstin nodded. "Yes, oh, God, and I say it prayerfully." She shrugged her shoulders. "I was just a kid. I didn't understand any of it then. I only knew my mama was sick, and my daddy didn't want her to let a doctor make her feel better. After that, it seemed to me that she just got well. I know now that she stopped getting any cysts. She never got one again so far as I know. She remained healthy, had regular exams, and went through what seemed to be a normal menopause.

"When I was sixteen—maybe just turned seventeen—she started getting what she called 'whinges' in her side. Sharp pains. They'd come and go. They'd last for only a little bit, making her press a hand over the spot and gasp, but she felt fine otherwise. I remember her saying that she thought it was her appendix flaring up. When she went for a checkup, the gyn found nothing that alarmed him. He said the appendix can become inflamed. He'd known patients who had warning flare-ups but had never gone into full-blown appendicitis. He told her what to expect if she did and to go directly to the hospital."

"Was your dad concerned?"

Kirstin sent him a scolding look. "Of course he was concerned. He loved her with all his heart. But she'd been thoroughly examined and there was nothing to indicate something serious was wrong. And he was no longer bent on having another kid. I was born in his early forties. He was in his late fifties by then."

Cam had heard his mom say that ovarian cancer was a stealthy killer that often went undiscovered until it was too late. "So the gyn missed the cancer."

She nodded. "It was probably a tiny tumor at the time. He had no reason to suspect cancer, so he palpated her ovaries like a doctor does in any routine exam."

"Dear God. He missed it, and she ended up dying."

Kirstin nodded. Her face had gone pale. "I helped Dad care for her. If I hadn't, the ranch might have gone under. He was with her as much as he could be. At the end, he bought her things she liked to eat, things she craved. If he thought she might like something we didn't have on hand, he'd drive to town late at night even though he was exhausted from busting his ass all day. Raspberry sherbet. Later, when dairy upset her stomach, he got different flavors of sorbet. He spooned broth into her mouth. He adored her, and watching her die nearly killed him."

Cam didn't need her to connect all the dots. "So your dad blames himself because he asked her to postpone getting a complete hysterectomy years earlier."

She nodded. "If he hadn't asked her to wait another six months, she would have had no ovaries later, thus no ovarian cancer to kill her. I can see his reasoning, flawed though it may be."

Cam digested that. He tried to imagine how he might feel in a similar situation, and he had to admit he would wish he'd never asked his wife to wait before she had a surgery that would have eventually saved her life. Of course, Sam Conacher hadn't known back then that she would never have the surgery at all. "Damn, that's rough."

"One night right after she died, he got roaring drunk—even drunker than usual. I was awakened by a loud crash, and I found him on his knees in the living room. He was sobbing, rocking back and forth, and saying, 'Annie, forgive me. Annie, forgive me.'" She shivered. "He was so plastered he never even knew I was there. He said, 'If it would bring you back, I'd put a bullet in my brain. I swear to God I would. But nothing will bring you back, and with me gone, our baby girl would have this ranch dumped on her shoulders. I can't do that to her.'"

Cam understood Sam Conacher now in ways he almost wished he didn't. It was a lot easier to just dislike the guy.

"I don't know why I'm telling you this."

"I believe I asked you to," he replied. "Besides, yesterday I told you stuff I rarely talk about. I'm not proud of that period in my life, the mistakes I made, not only getting Becky pregnant but also putting her through a disastrous marriage that never should have happened. I haven't seen her since Caleb's birth, but I don't think her life has gone well. Multiple marriages with kids from different fathers. Sometimes I wonder if her inability to stick with one man is my fault."

"That's crazy. I'm sure having a baby and then giving it up left her with some emotional scars, but you were no more responsible for that than she was."

"Do you know how weird this feels?" he asked, giving her a long look. "We're friends. I don't know how that happened so fast."

"Me, either. Something just clicked between us. I felt the connection yesterday and still do today."

"It's a good thing, making friends," Cam told her. "None of us ever has enough of them."

"I have fewer than most," she confessed. "Lots of acquaintances, and I think most of them like me, but not many people I can call whenever I just need to talk. Those kind of relationships require an investment of time, and I don't have much to spare."

Cam heard what she didn't say, that it was easier to stay home than to go out with acquaintances and upset her father. She was such a pretty woman and sweet as well. She was wasting the best years of her life. But who was he to talk? Back in California, others had thought the same thing about him, but Cam would never feel that he had misspent a single day. He'd raised a fine son, and he'd been there for his parents when they needed him.

She grew quiet again. Then she said, "If my dad knew I told you all that, he'd want to wring my neck."

Cam hooked an arm around her shoulders and gave her a quick hug. He could tell by a quick inhalation of the scent of her hair and shirt that she'd worked on the ranch until she'd left to meet him. The varied scents told a story of haying horses and cows and feeding grain. To him it was familiar and yet alluring when combined with her feminine essence.

"Your father will never hear it from me," he assured her. "And it's probably been good for you to get it off your chest."

She looked him directly in the eye. "So, tell me, Cam. Do you plan to see me again?"

"That depends on you."

"I'd love to," she replied. "Just say the word."

"Tomorrow?"

She smiled. "Is this our version of jumping in with both feet?"

"I'm not one to jump into anything, but I don't hesitate to move cautiously forward when something feels right."

"Lunchtime works great for me. There's a place farther downstream where rocky fingers divide the river into thirds, creating narrows I can jump across. I can walk here from the ranch, and my father won't think twice about it. I often go walking during my break, and this has always been one of my favorite places to do that."

Cam yearned to kiss her. Her lips, a pale rose-pink color, shimmered in the sunlight. A strand of jet hair lifted in the breeze and slid over her cheek. He decided to resist the urge, though. They were, as she'd pointed out, close to her father's ranch, and they were in plain sight.

"Can you be gone long enough for a walk and lunch?" he asked her.

"Yes, around two hours, and tomorrow I'll bring the food. I'll make our picnic tonight and hide my cooler out in the woods so Dad will never know I'm meeting you."

"Normally when my schedule is clear, I do a lot of driving around, looking at expired listings and watching for property for sale by owners, but I can head home for lunch."

"We're on," she said with a grin.

Chapter Three

THERE HAD BEEN A HALF DAY AT CALEB'S NEW HIGH SCHOOL. HE hated going to classes in August, so he'd been glad to get out early and have a chance to do something fun. Only, Gram was writing, and he wasn't supposed to disturb her unless he was bleeding to death. He'd checked on the horses. The dogs were huddled and sound asleep at the base of Gram's yard table, so he couldn't take them for a walk. And he didn't feel like watching flicks on TV that he'd already seen.

Last night he'd watched his dad make a picnic lunch for himself and Kirstin Conacher, so he knew they were on the opposite bank somewhere. He decided to walk downriver until he spotted them. Then he'd drop to his belly in the tall grass along their side to spy, since he had nothing better to do and no one would ever know, and maybe he'd learn something about the opposite sex.

Caleb didn't have to walk that far before he saw them. As planned, he dived to the ground and parted the grass. Before five minutes passed, he realized that this was going to be *way* more boring than anything else he could have done. From a distance, Caleb decided that the guys at school were so right. Kirstin Conacher was hot, and his father was totally blowing it with her. He wasn't even holding her hand. It looked to Caleb as if all they'd done so far was talk. That was so lame. In the locker room, he heard other boys discussing how they didn't waste any time with girls, not even on a first date. Maybe his dad needed to read a how-to book, or something.

Finally he saw his father give her a loose hug. All he did was curl his arm around her shoulders, though. What was he thinking? Was he bashful? As he watched his dad put what remained of the picnic back into the cooler, Caleb decided he should stay hidden until they walked upriver toward the pullout, where he'd seen her truck parked. It would take his dad a while to walk back to camp. He'd have to lug that cooler across the bridge and along the paved road to the automatic gate. Then it was a long way down the gravel lane to their driveway. Even if he cut across the alfalfa field, it would take time. Caleb could race back to the cabin and turn on the TV, and nobody would ever know he'd been gone.

Only when he got home, Gram was outside, letting the dogs out of her yard for a short run. He slowed his pace as he drew near his grandmother. Sunlight beamed down on her, making her look like an angel with a halo. Maybe it was only that he'd gotten taller over the summer, but she suddenly looked so small and skinny to him. He couldn't make the heavy feeling that something wasn't quite right with Gram go away. Losing Gramps had been horrible, and now Caleb felt a clawing fear that he might lose her, too. She was more a mother to him than a grandmother, and he didn't know how he and his dad would live without her.

"Why are you home so early?" she called out.

"We got out before lunch," he yelled back.

"You should have knocked. I have a coffee cake cooling on the counter for your afternoon snack. I would have made you a sandwich, and you could have had some cake for dessert while it was still hot from the oven."

Caleb drew up in front of her. "I didn't want to disturb you, and I got bored, so I walked downriver."

Her blue eyes sharpened on his face. "Caleb McLendon, have you been spying on your father?"

Caleb tried never to fib. It was the one thing that really pissed Gram off, and his dad, too, for that matter. "I couldn't rent a movie without permission. I had hardly any homework and got it done in five minutes. I checked all the animals, and I'm not supposed to bother you while you're working. What was I supposed to do, play games on my phone? I get in trouble for doing that too much, too."

Gram's eyes transformed from looking like high-tech sensors to warm and twinkly. "Well. Don't keep me in suspense. How did their walk and picnic go?"

That was one of the things he loved about Gram. She hardly ever got upset about stupid stuff that she could let slide. "My dad crashed and burned."

"What?"

"You need to talk to him, Gram. He never even kissed her. I don't think he knows much about girls."

His gram burst out laughing. "I don't think your father needs dating instructions from me. He barely knows Kirstin yet. Sometimes when you're older, you're not as impulsive. Personally, I'd be offended if a man tried to kiss me too soon."

Yeah, well, Caleb thought, *you're so old that you're almost an antique.* But he didn't say it aloud. "I'm starving. Can I have some coffee cake?"

She hugged his waist and led him toward her trailer. He draped an arm over her shoulders, and under the layers of her clothing and light jacket, he felt the bony ridges of her shoulders poking against him. It made him want to feed her vanilla ice cream with extra caramel topping, her favorite. Maybe he could do that later if she'd watch a movie with him. "I hope Dad gets his act together. It'd be awesome if his girlfriend lived next door. Less gas to go see her."

Gram laid her head on his shoulder. "Oh, Caleb, you're good for me. You lighten my mood. I don't think your father is thinking about fuel consumption right now."

"Maybe not. The guys at school talk about Kirstin Conacher a lot. They all think she's hot, and now that I've seen her, I think so, too."

Gram chuckled. "Oh, dear, the terrible sixteens have arrived."

WHEN CAM AND KIRSTIN REACHED HER TRUCK, HE FOUND HIMSELF wishing that he didn't have to end their time together so quickly. But he sensed she felt the same way, and he'd see her again tomorrow. Meeting here was a great idea. Except for occasional pedestrians or a raft of fishermen drifting downstream, they would have privacy. And even if someone saw them, they probably wouldn't recognize Kirstin from a distance.

Cam no longer felt so concerned about her father's reaction if he learned they were seeing each other. As his mother had reminded him, his own dad would have told the old fart to do his worst and seen Kirstin, anyway. Cam did worry about the repercussions for Kirstin, though. The longer they could meet in secret, the more time she would have to decide if seeing him was important enough to her that she was willing to pay the price.

He let the cooler slip from his grip and *plunk* on the gravel. At the door of her truck, emblazoned with CONACHER RANCH in bold green, she turned to smile up at him. "I still feel bad about boo-hooing to you about my father. Tomorrow I promise to be lighthearted."

"You didn't boo-hoo, and I enjoyed listening," Cam assured her, and he meant it. "Small talk is boring, so I'm glad you shared more of your family history. It sheds a whole new light on your father for me. Helps me understand where he's at in his life. Maybe he could benefit from some counseling."

Her cheek dimpled in a smile. He longed to touch his fingertip to the indentation before it disappeared. "Dad will *never* go to a shrink. 'Any man who seeks advice from an academic who learned about life by reading textbooks is a damned fool and a pansy-ass.'"

Cam threw back his head and laughed. "That sounds like *my* old man. Stubbornness must be a trait of that generation."

"Or of Scotsmen."

She tipped her head to give him a questioning look. Cam stepped in close, curled an index finger under her chin, and bent to touch his lips to hers. He meant it to be a sweet, getting-acquainted kiss, but the instant their mouths touched, heat ignited between them. She tasted of wine, heady and intoxicating. Desire punched into him like a clenched fist. She melted against him and curled one slender leg over the backs of his knees. He felt his arms lock around her as if of their own volition. At the edges of his mind, he knew this was crazy. They were standing near a fricking road where anyone could see them. Her truck could be easily identified by those who drove by.

He forced himself to end the kiss, hauling in a steadying breath as he backed away from her. She wobbled on her feet, making him grab her arm to lend her balance. Her gunmetal blue eyes were unfocused, her expression dazed. He wondered if he looked just as stunned.

"Wow," she said softly. "Did I imagine that, or did it really happen?"

"I'm not sure. But we're not going to try it again to find out."

He gestured at the ribbon of pavement just behind her. "Not here, anyway. Down in the trees, maybe, where we won't be seen. I don't want your dad to find out about this and get all bent out of shape before we can get to know each other better."

She nodded and pushed her hair back from her face. "Right." Her lips curved in a shaky grin. Her dimple flashed at him again. "That's never happened to me. It felt like spontaneous combustion."

"That's as good a description as any, I guess. It's never happened to me, either."

She glanced at her watch, which rode a simple leather band. He noticed that her hand shook slightly. "No hiding in the trees for us today. My time off is over."

"What time should we meet tomorrow?" he said. "At noon?"

"Fifteen after. It'll take me a few minutes to walk over."

"I'll head downriver to meet you and help carry the cooler. Why waste the time alone when we can be together?"

OVER THE NEXT TWO WEEKS, AS AUGUST GAVE WAY TO SEPTEMBER and September crept toward October, Cam and Kirstin met along the river nearly every day. Cam discovered that she didn't always get days off, which he felt was over-the-top. Kirstin explained that her father didn't force her to work so much.

"It's a matter of necessity. Dad and Miguel are dividing their time right now between haying on the ranch and rounding up cattle from our grazing lands." She smiled up at him. "When I say *our* grazing lands, I mean Dad owns them. Back in the late sixties, he saw the writing on the wall and knew there would be more and more restrictions placed on public lands, so he scrimped and saved to buy parcels of land. He didn't care if some or nearly all of the property was mountainous. All he needed was a good road in, plenty of grass, and a bountiful water source. When I say he's land poor, I mean he's *really* land poor. But he has plenty of property to summer his cows on while he farms the fields here. At the end of haying season, he takes the excess cattle to auction and keeps his base herd here."

They circled a fallen log. "Wow. Instead of counting on public land, he bought his own? That must have cost him a bundle."

"Yes, but he did it over a thirty-year period of time. Even longer than that, actually. My mother called him a visionary, and I think she had it right. Dad bought his first parcel back in seventy-one, and he picked up the last piece in two thousand fifteen. I think he stretched his financial limits on that one, but it's a gorgeous acreage on the east side of the valley. The last of the cattle he needs to round up are grazing there." She walked around a large chunk of driftwood and met him on the other side. "My mom shared his vision, thank goodness, and didn't mind when he saved his profit each year to buy more land. It meant she didn't get diamonds on her birthday, or that her kitchen didn't get remodeled, and she waited a lot of years for her beautiful house to be built. But she supported him as he built an inheritance for me.

"When a ranch came on the market and it matched his criteria, he grabbed it. He didn't care if there was a nice house. He picked up large parcels that were other people's mistakes. They couldn't farm the land to feed their animals over the winter, so they went bust, and Dad got the properties for a great price. He picked areas where he knew the land might sell for a song, purchased one piece, and then waited for others to come up for sale, allowing him, in some areas, to collect contiguous acreages. He's a favorite with agencies that are trying to preserve the open land of Montana, because in areas where he can, he legally adjoins the parcels and places a conservation easement on them so they can never be sold separately or subdivided."

"That may make them hard to sell."

She nodded. "Yes, but he may never want to sell them. When the ranch passes down to me, I probably won't, either. Owning them protects us. Weather providing, we can run cattle for as long as we want to, and if public grazing land is decreased or snatched away, it shouldn't affect us. I will feel bad for ranchers who are impacted by grazing-land cutbacks, though. Their way of life is being attacked." She kicked a rock and winked at him. "Just like that. I can't say whether grazing allotments are actually destroying our public lands. All I know is that the activists might be wise to consider becoming vegans, and even then, they'd better stop depriving farmers of irrigation water across the country, because they'll have nothing much to eat."

Cam laughed. An eagle soared up from a tree and then dived toward the ground. "Somebody just caught his lunch. As for the effect of grazing on public lands, I can't cast a vote without doing an extensive study. That's no longer my field, though. Don't laugh. I have a degree in game biology, and now I sell real estate."

She smiled. "Sounds familiar. I got a degree in business management and don't use it."

He slanted her an inquiring look. "You're totally into raising cattle, aren't you?"

"It's in my blood. As a little girl, I'd sit on Dad's knee while he ran the numbers on a piece of land he was considering. When I was six, I already knew how to calculate cows per acre. I'd go with him to walk a parcel. I'd get really excited over grass and sources of water, or if there was a nice house my father could lease out." Her cheeks went rosy. "Sorry. Most women get excited about jewelry. I'm turned on by grazing land. Now my father has his operation covered with land of his own. A lot of it. He leases some of it out, but mostly he uses it himself and rents out the houses. People who enjoy having horses and a few cows, but can't afford a large ranch, are delighted to have him for a landlord, and in exchange for low rent, they're happy to do fence repairs if he pays for the materials. It's all land that Mother Nature waters and his cows keep mowed in the summer."

Cam whistled. "Holy hell. How many acres does he have?"

"I'm not sure. I'd have to do a spreadsheet." She tapped her temple. "Dad has it all up here."

"And with all that wealth, his daughter rarely gets a day off."

"You've got it. What's said about my dad in town is true. He's ornery and impossible. The one flaw in his youthful dream was failing to anticipate that he'd grow so mean after Mom died that men wouldn't want to work for him. So now he has four hundred pair on mountainous and rough terrain with no hired hands to help gather them. Last spring he sold his double-deck stock trailer. He didn't tell me why. I think he ran short on money. His remaining stock trailer carries twenty head, maximum. He's already collected cattle off the properties that are farther away. But losing those four hundred pair, around eight hundred head in total, and the bulls left there to propagate that herd, will possibly put him in the red." She lifted her hands. "So I work seven days a week. That's ranching for you. It's not for sissies. Someday I hope to have a full crew on the payroll again. I think I can keep workers happier than Dad presently can."

"But, for right now, you're flat out because your inheritance is at risk."

"It's not quite as dire as that." She shrugged. "That's where the grazing land will probably save us. Dad can use it as collateral to get a loan to keep us afloat, and hopefully next year will be better.

But it's never good when a ranch goes in the hole. If next year isn't better, and you just never know, we'll go deeper into debt if we borrow against the assets again."

"He needs to hire some temps."

She laughed, her eyes twinkling up at him as they walked. "Cowboys, you mean? Trust me, he's tried. But there are a lot of jobs in this valley for good hands, and they'd rather work for less money than put up with my dad's foul temper. The seasoned guys don't apply, and the bad ones aren't worth hiring."

Cam's entire picture of ranching had changed from the pastoral images of peace and tranquillity that floated through most people's minds to the trials of reality.

ANOTHER AFTERNOON THEY PLAYED QUESTION AND ANSWER. What is your favorite band? What's your favorite color? Your absolute favorite food? What's your favorite love song of all time? The questions they came up with were many, and they spent a lot of time laughing over each other's answers.

"Really?" Cam asked. "Your favorite song is 'The Way We Were'?"

"Well, yours is 'Those Were the Days.' How is that any better?"

"It's just that 'The Way We Were' was a hit way back in seventy-four, following the release of the Streisand-Redford film. You weren't even born yet."

She narrowed her eyes. "Unless you're older than you say you are, you weren't either."

"No, I wasn't. But I grew up listening to my parents' all-time favorites playing on the stereo, which familiarized me with the music of their generation. Somehow I can't picture Samuel Conacher listening to old love songs."

"Oh, but he enjoyed romantic music before Mom died, and I was twenty by then, so I remember all the songs they played."

"Do you like old hits more than you do the contemporary ones?"

"Some of the old ones just speak to me. 'The Way We Were' has beautiful lyrics with wistful undertones. And I can picture different scenarios involving two people who once loved each other and broke up. How much they might regret their mistakes. How much they might wish they could go back in time and do it differently. You know?"

He guided her around a fallen log, his much larger hand locked around hers. "That's why I like 'Those Were the Days,'" he told her. "I picture a group of young friends who have no idea what awaits them in the future. They feel invincible. The reason the song speaks to me is because it feels timeless and the same scenario is probably still playing out at university nightspots all over the country."

"It's kind of sad, though, isn't it?" She leaned her head against his arm. "When they were young, everything seemed possible, and later they faced the hard knocks of life."

Kirstin straightened and studied the expressions that flitted over his chiseled features. She was already falling in love with him. Maybe it was impulsive and far too soon, but she couldn't seem to stop herself. It wasn't only that he was handsome and fun to be with, but also that he felt things as deeply as she did and wasn't embarrassed to reveal it.

"In the end, Kirstin, all of us end up facing hard knocks. For me, the most important thing is finding someone I can make the journey with who'll always stand beside me, no matter what."

She nodded. "I want to find someone who will also remind me to laugh. My mom's gift to our family was her ability to look at a complete disaster and find something to laugh about. She used to say, 'Sam, if we don't laugh, we're going to cry.' And she was right. So most of the time she'd get Dad to laugh with her. And pretty soon they felt better."

"Laughter is good medicine," he agreed. "They say people who pray together stay together, but I think laughing together is almost as important."

He looped his arms around her and drew her close against his chest. She had come to cherish these moments when the heat and strength of him surrounded her. She yearned for him to make love to her soon. Only that could never happen out here in a public-use area.

His thumbs trailed lightly over her cheeks, igniting the nerve endings just under her skin. Kirstin went up on her tiptoes to wrap her arms around his neck. "Kiss me, Cam."

He angled his mouth over hers and delved deeply with his tongue. She savored the taste of him and wished they could find a grassy spot in the forest to spend the entire day together. When he ended the kiss, she whispered, "I'm falling in love with you, Cameron McLendon."

"Don't go into overdrive, honey. We've only just begun."

She drew back and stared up at him. "Oh, my God, the Carpenters? Don't deny it, Cam. You're a romantic-song junkie."

"I guess maybe I am. And if you know that song, so are you."

ANOTHER AFTERNOON KIRSTIN NOTICED THAT CAM SEEMED pensive as they walked along the path that led through the trees. The rush of the river came from their right. Sunlight beamed down through the evergreen boughs from directly overhead. The air felt cooler than it had yesterday, making her wonder how long it might be before the first snow. She hoped the white stuff would be a long while in coming. It would be hard on Cam and his family to endure the winter cold, and if her father couldn't get all the cattle home, the ranch would take a huge financial hit. But she knew from experience that Mother Nature seldom changed her schedule for anyone or anything.

"Is something troubling you, Cam?"

He smiled. "Yes, sort of. My mom hasn't been herself the last couple of days. It's been happening a couple of times a month—nothing I can put my finger on, but she sleeps more and her color isn't good. She doesn't eat much, either. I can't tell if she's sick or just having bad days, like she says."

"Oh, I'm sorry." Kirstin hadn't met the woman yet, but judging by things Cam had told her, his mother was a wonderful lady. "Can you get her in to see a doctor?"

"She says she just saw one and got a clean bill of health."

"Would she lie about that?"

He frowned. "My mom doesn't normally lie, but I have seen her be evasive." He flexed his shoulders. "Enough of that. I'm shaking it off." He grabbed her hand. "It's a beautiful day, so let's enjoy it."

Before they returned to their picnic cooler to have lunch, they saw the nest of a bald eagle at the top of a dead snag. Kirstin had never been with someone who was as reverent about wildlife as she was. Now she had Cam to marvel with her over the beauty of nature.

"I'd love to climb up and have a look," he told her, "but sometimes they reuse their nests."

Kirstin squeezed his fingers. "I've noticed that. We wouldn't want to ruin it." Her neck started to ache from leaning her head so far back. "Do you realize that I've never known anybody who's as much fun as you are on a walk? We've visited here how many times now? And every single time, I've enjoyed myself."

"Me, too. You're a cheap date."

She laughed and elbowed him in the ribs. As they cut through the trees toward their lunch spot, he said, "We've met here a lot. Not counting the day we met, how many hours have we been together so far?"

"You're wanting to calculate the hours?"

"Sorry. I need to measure time against my emotions. Always before, I've been able to depend on my common sense to guide me, but with you, I'm not sure I've got any."

"What a sweet compliment." She leaned forward to peer up at him. "Really, Cam? Your good sense flies out the window when you're with me?"

He narrowed his eyes at her. "It's not a good thing, Kirstin. I made one serious mistake in the past, and maybe that's made me way too careful. But I think we'll both be better off if we keep our heads firmly attached to our shoulders."

Kirstin wanted no part of that. For once in her life she wanted to be silly and reckless. She jerked her hand away from his, spun off a rock into a run, and cried over her shoulder, "Race you!"

She thought she had a lead on him, but he was upon her in seconds and grabbed her around the waist. Even as she shrieked and laughed, he turned her in his arms and started to kiss her. Then he stiffened before their lips met.

"We're right out in the open."

"Dad is riding the grazing land today with Miguel."

"You think. Things happen. He may have come back for some reason."

Cam had left their lunch in a more private place at the edge of the trees. Grasping her hand, he led her there. After digging all their food from the cooler, they settled down to eat. He had consumed half his sandwich when he said, "I know you've dated several guys. Has none of them had the courage to approach your father and ask his permission to see you?"

Kirstin's pulse skittered. "Don't even *think* about it, Cam. My father won't see it as you doing the honorable thing. He'll go straight into attack mode. Please wait until you're certain I'm worth the risk."

She hoped he might say he was already certain, but of course, he didn't. Cam was a careful, thoughtful man who wanted to be sure they were right for each other. With someone else, Kirstin might have resented that, but with Cam, she understood. As much as he loved his son, that didn't negate the fact that he'd paid dearly for years for that one mistake in his late teens. She also felt flattered. His cautious forward momentum told her that he took their relationship seriously.

Kirstin caught a flash of movement off in the woods, and she fixed her gaze on something large and such a dark brown that it was nearly black. She stared as it moved toward them and its outline took on a distinct shape. Her heart started to pound. "Cam," she said softly.

"You do understand that I'm uncomfortable with all this sneaking around," he said.

"*Cam,*" she said with more urgency while not raising her voice. "There's a bull moose coming in our direction."

He followed her gaze with his own. "Wow. I've seen them along the roads while driving, but never up close like this."

"Keep your voice down!" she said in a stage whisper. "Seeing it up close is *not* good. Look around you for the biggest tree, and run for it. I'll go the opposite direction. Moose are stupid. We might gain a few precious seconds if we confuse it."

Cam finally seemed to register that she was frightened. "You're going to climb a tree? Is it really that dangerous? I've never studied moose."

"I haven't either, but I grew up with them." Kirstin shifted her hips to get her feet under her. "You don't need to climb the tree. Just do an earthbound version of pole dancing. If he lunges at you, keep the tree in front of you as a barrier."

From the corner of her eye, she saw Cam work his way into a crouch.

"One, two, *three*!" She sprang forward, moving to her left. Cam lurched into a run, going the opposite direction. "Zigzag!" she yelled. "Big zigzags! Don't run in a straight line!"

As Kirstin ran, she saw the animal start after Cam, but then it changed its mind and lunged after her. *Good,* she thought. *By running in two different directions, we got a slight edge.* She reached her chosen tree, a medium-size ponderosa, and planted the flats of her hands against its red bark. The moose was right behind her. She circled to put the massive trunk between her and Bullwinkle. The moose, broad head lowered, rammed into the conifer with its antlers, which her dad called paddles because of their shape. To her horror, she felt the tree shudder under the impact.

"Kirstin?" Cam cried. Then she heard him yell, "Oh, shit!"

She was too focused on the bull to even glance toward Cam. She heard the animal grunting. If she made one wrong move, circling right when she needed to go left, or vice versa, she could end up dead. The next instant, she felt hard bands clamp around her hips. Then her weight was lifted upward with such speed that she thought the moose's paddles had caught her and thrown her upward.

"Grab the limb!" Cam yelled. "Fast! Hold on and swing a leg over it."

Kirstin had no time to consider the wisdom of these directives. Cam was on the ground and presently holding her up. He'd be injured or killed if she didn't move quickly. She threw her arms around a limb and hooked a knee over it. As she sat up to scoot closer to the conifer's trunk, she saw Cam leap up to grab another limb across from hers. He swung forward, then back, and then forward again as he lifted his weight. The bull rammed his lower legs with its paddles, and she thought Cam might be jerked to the ground. But with a show of incredible strength, he muscled himself up to safety with only one arm.

He inched toward her to hug the trunk just as she was. Just then she felt the pine shudder again. Cam, heaving for breath, tipped his head to one side and met her gaze. "We need a bigger tree."

CAM HAD HEARD MONTANANS SAY THAT MOOSE WERE MORE dangerous than grizzlies. But he had taken that warning with a grain of salt. People loved to tell newcomers scary tales, and he'd figured the moose-attack stories were just more of the same. Apparently he should have listened. But he'd been told that moose rarely visited this stretch of river bottom, so he hadn't been worried about encounters. Now he sat in a tree and under him a bull moose was punching the trunk with such force the pine's roots were in danger of being jerked loose.

"Now what?" he asked Kirstin.

She tightened her hold on the trunk as the bull battered the tree again. Her eyes were as round as quarters, and her face had gone pale. "Pray," she said. "We pray. It's all we can do." She leaned sideways to study his legs. "Your feet hang down too low. You need to move up a rung."

Cam craned his neck to examine the protrusion of wood

growth above him. "I don't know, Kirstin. It may not bear my weight."

Just then the moose caught the side of his boot with an antler and nearly jerked him off his perch. He scrambled upward to sit on the higher limb. As he'd feared, it sank under his body, but it didn't break. "How did this happen? We've never seen a moose around here."

"We have them on the ranch." She peered down. "Where'd he go?"

"He's under me," Cam told her. "He appears to be wondering if he could uproot this tree and kill me that way."

"It's mating season. He thinks we're a threat to his procreation plan."

Cam, who felt at least halfway safe now, said, "I'd be a threat if I had a gun."

Kirstin rested her forehead against the bark, blocking his view of her face. "A bull destroyed a tree on the ranch last year. It was about this size."

"He *destroyed* it?"

"Completely, but it did take him a while. It became his daily hobby."

Just then the moose rammed the pine again. Cam felt the shudder clear to his bones. He gave the surrounding area a thoughtful study. He saw only more trees. "How long do you think we'll be his entertainment of the day?"

"Maybe only a few minutes, possibly until dark. He's mad because we invaded his trysting spot. Shit. I am so screwed. Dad will notice that I didn't get half the chores done."

Cam groaned. Kirstin added, "We need to sit still and be quiet. The sound of our voices is agitating him."

Silence settled between them. Cam's pulse was still racing.

Every time he looked down, he saw the moose circling below. Occasionally the animal would circle out, turn to face the tree, and then charge. It was as scary as hell.

Cam guessed that about an hour passed. The moose gave the ponderosa one final butt with its massive antlers and then wandered a few feet away to vent his anger on Cam's cooler, which flew into the river. Then he grazed on grass near the water's edge. Cam and Kirstin watched the animal's slow retreat until it disappeared.

"Do you think it's safe to get down?" he asked.

Kirstin shook her head. "Let's give it a few more minutes."

"I can't believe this happened," Cam said. "Damn! That creature was freaking massive. Almost as big as an elephant."

Kirstin started to laugh. Cam wasn't sure how this was funny, but he soon joined her. They both hugged the tree trunk. Tears of mirth ran down their cheeks. When they both felt drained and exhausted, they swung from their perches and dropped to the ground. Kirstin landed with catlike grace, exhibiting to Cam a strength that he doubted most women had.

"I'm walking you home."

"Not all the way," she protested.

"Most of the way. We don't know where that bastard went."

When they had almost reached the grassy knoll where they'd lunched that first afternoon, Cam deemed it safe for Kirstin to go the rest of the way by herself. Still shaken by their close call, he drew her into his arms, which quivered like plucked bowstrings as he tightened his hold on her. It hit him then how much he'd come to care for her.

"Ah, Kirstin."

She lifted her face to his. "I know. It all happened so fast that it's a blur in my mind, but I was terrified. The moose could have nailed you as you lifted me up."

"He tried."

"How did you evade him?"

"I pole-danced. I should visit some nightspots and apply for a job."

Cam was so glad to have her there, safe, uninjured, and so lovely, he forgot about the damned moose. He forgot nearly everything but this slender woman who had turned his world upside down. He bent his head to kiss her. She melted against him. He felt as if he'd waded into electrified water and gotten in over his head. Zings of sensation skipped over his nerve endings. He couldn't hold her closely enough. When he finally drew back for air, they were both breathing heavily.

"Be careful walking home. Don't linger anywhere. Okay? And keep your eyes peeled for moose."

She nodded. Then she retreated a step and swung away to start moving over the rocky beach. "Text me!" she yelled, and then she broke into a run.

CALEB HAD SKIPPED LUNCH HOUR AND WOODSHOP FOR A chance to spy on his dad. Now he wanted to punch his fist into the air and do a victory dance. His father had finally laid one on Kirstin, a big, long kiss with lots of tongue. *Yes. Way to go, Dad!* Caleb suspected they'd done it before, because they seemed pretty practiced at it. But it was the first time he had seen them kiss. Maybe there was hope for his father, after all.

He didn't dare get up from his hiding place, though. He didn't want to get a long lecture tonight about respecting the privacy of others. He wasn't hurting anybody, and by cutting woodshop class, he had avoided what he now thought of as *the big chill*. Not even the two girls who were taking the course got the cold shoulder from all the guys the same way Caleb did. In his other classes, Caleb didn't mind being the odd one out. Nobody could talk but the teacher. At least he could pretend during those periods that someone liked him.

Head still hidden below the grass, Caleb glimpsed movement off to his right. His nerves jangled. He'd walked quite a distance downstream and might be on Conacher land. What if he got caught trespassing? He shifted to peer through the tall weeds. He saw an old man on a sorrel horse. The guy wore a light tan Stetson, a wrinkled faded blue shirt, and jeans so bleached from sunlight and washing that they looked the same color as the pale swirls inside blue marbles. Caleb sure wished his jeans looked like that.

Caleb had seen Samuel Conacher drive by their land in a pickup, but he'd never gotten a good look at him. This guy appeared to be old, pissed off, and mean. He was also riding a horse on Conacher land. Adding up the clues, Caleb decided the laws of probability dictated that it had to be Conacher. *Are there laws of probability?* Caleb wondered. *Even if there aren't, I'm making the call on this. That's Sam Conacher, and he just saw my dad touching his daughter's butt.* This wasn't good. In fact, Caleb couldn't think of much that could have been worse.

He needed to intercept his dad on Fox Hollow Road before he reached the gate and the private road. Only Caleb's truck wasn't at camp. He'd left it parked under a tree near the gate so Gram wouldn't hear him pull in. She would have popped out of her trailer to ask why he wasn't in class. He'd learned over time that she could be stone-deaf unless she wanted to hear something, and she had a nose for when he might be doing something wrong.

The old man swung off his horse. Caleb thought, *Wow, nice moves. He's the real deal.* And then he watched as Conacher walked in a tight circle, kicking up grass and cussing. Caleb was too far away to hear the words, but he doubted that a tall, sunbaked cowboy recited poetry to himself. Caleb jerked when the old fart pulled off his Stetson and threw it on the ground. *Yep, he's cussing,* Caleb decided. *And he's madder than a yellow jacket stuck to flypaper.*

Caleb really, *really* needed to intercept his father. He might come walking up the private road to camp and get waylaid by Conacher. Caleb knew for sure that his dad could hold his own against most men. Unfortunately, he also knew Cam McLendon wouldn't fight back if an old guy jumped him. He'd just take a beating and keep picking himself back up.

As if Conacher sensed someone or something watching him, he stared right in Caleb's direction. Caleb flattened himself against the damp weeds and held his breath. He couldn't do that for very long and finally let his breath out. Inching up his head, he peered through dancing green grass blades and saw that Conacher was riding away. His body went limp. When the old man had ridden far enough, Caleb tensed, sprang to his feet, and ran as fast as he could toward Fox Hollow Road. When he got there, he angled across the alfalfa field to gain the highway. Stopping to get his truck would have been a waste of time.

Chapter Four

CAM WALKED WITH HIS HEAD DOWN, WHICH WAS UNUSUAL for him. Normally he enjoyed the views all around him. But right now all he could think about was Kirstin. They could have been killed by that moose and featured in Missoula's news headlines tomorrow. Cam hadn't realized how much he'd come to care for her until he thought she might get hurt.

"Dad! Dad!"

Cam's head shot up. He saw Caleb racing toward him along the gravel shoulder of the asphalt. For a moment he feared something had happened to his mother. Cam picked up his pace to shorten the distance between them.

When Caleb reached him, he bent forward, planted his hands on his knees, and gasped for breath. Their camp was quite a ways off, but not a distance that would have winded a fit young man so badly. "What's wrong?"

Caleb gulped and said, "Sam Conacher saw you kissing Kirstin and touching her butt."

Cam winced. "How do you know that?"

"Because I was out there." He gulped for another breath. "Conacher didn't see me. But I saw him. He was totally pissed, Dad."

Cam's stomach clenched. He hated to think of Kirstin walking into a shit storm when she got home, unprepared for a huge fight with her dad. He jerked his cell from his hip pocket. "Hold on, Caleb. I need to text her."

"Good thinking," Caleb observed. "Someone needs to warn her."

Cam made short work of sending the message and could only hope Kirstin read it before she encountered her father. "Why aren't you in school?"

Caleb shifted his gaze to the field. "I came home for lunch hour and cut my next class. It's only woodshop, and I'm way ahead of everyone else on the project we're doing."

"Did you let Gram know? You didn't get in touch with me."

"No, I didn't let her know."

Cam felt a buzz of concern. "Son, you know the rules. If you aren't going to be where we think you are, you're supposed to give someone a heads-up. What if you were in an accident or someone kidnapped you? We'd have no idea where to start searching for you."

Shoving his hands in his pockets, Caleb hunched his shoulders. "I'm too big to get kidnapped."

"Grown men have been kidnapped, Caleb. Cut the crap."

"Okay. Fine. I didn't tell Gram because she wouldn't have approved. I was spying on you and Kirstin."

"You were *what*?"

"Spying." Caleb looked him straight in the eye. "Before you say anything, I'm sorry. I didn't feel like I was invading your privacy. It's state land over there, and anybody out walking the river could have seen you, too."

Cam made a snap decision to discuss this with Caleb later. He might lose his temper if he dealt with it right now. Without saying a word, he started walking again. At the gate, he saw Caleb's truck parked under one of the bordering trees. "Let me guess. You didn't drive in because you were afraid Gram would hear the engine."

"Yeah, and she would have asked a heap of questions." He toed the gravel on the side of the road. "I wanted to get out there fast so I wouldn't miss anything good. Then you took forever to come out into the open, and I missed another class waiting for you. I may as well skip the whole day now."

Cam clenched his teeth. Never in a million years would he have considered getting intimate with Kirstin in a place where passersby might have seen them, and thank God for that. He had a feeling that Caleb had been hoping to see something X-rated. Once they passed through the gate, he turned to his son.

"You should get back to school regardless of how short the day will be."

"Yeah. I really am sorry, Dad."

"We'll discuss this later. I can't let it slide. I love you. Drive safely."

Slouching and hanging his head, Caleb walked to his pickup, and Cam turned toward home. With each step he took, he wondered what Kirstin might be facing right now. Only one thing seemed certain to him, which was that her decision of when to tell her father about their relationship had been taken out of her hands.

Cam had just reached the cabin he shared with Caleb when a text notification sounded on his phone. He grabbed his cell and thumbed the screen. The message was from Kirstin. *I can tell Dad's upset, but he hasn't said a word to me about seeing us down at the river.*

Cam wrote back, *Maybe he's thinking it over and concluding that you did nothing wrong. You aren't a child. Going on a picnic with a man isn't an unreasonable thing for a woman to do.*

• • •

AS SAM CONACHER DROVE BACK TO THE GRAZING LAND, HE knotted his fists over the steering wheel. When he'd gone home to meet with the farrier for a follow-up call on a horse that had thrown a new shoe, Kirstin hadn't been there. When she failed to make an appearance after more than an hour, he'd gotten worried. He knew she sometimes liked to walk during her lunch break. Recently she'd been doing that a lot. If she'd taken the usual trail to stroll along the river, she could have fallen. She was nimble and sure-footed, but after the farrier left, Sam decided to saddle up and go check on her, anyway. Accidents could happen. He hadn't wanted his daughter to lie out there somewhere, unable to get home and possibly bleeding to death.

Now he felt as if he were in shock. Plain as day, he'd seen Kirstin tonguing the tonsils of their neighbor. Sam had never met the man and hadn't bothered to learn his last name. He knew just by looking at their damned camp that they were low-class. He couldn't believe Kirstin was swapping saliva with someone so beneath her.

Sam's chest hurt. He felt as if he'd been stabbed with a knife. His daughter hadn't been taking long walks. He'd only ever been a good father to her, giving her the best of everything. And this was the thanks he got, lies and deception? If his Annie were still alive, she'd be heartbroken.

Sam wished now that he hadn't granted an easement on his private road to the former owner of that acreage. The land wouldn't have sold so quickly to those hillbillies without existing ingress and egress.

Sam decided that he'd pay Kirstin's boyfriend a visit tomorrow. It would be better if he went toe-to-toe with the man and left his daughter out of it, considering the confrontation was going to be ugly. Sam had made more than one young fellow pay for messing with Kirstin, and not a single one of them had made out with her in an area frequented by hikers and fishermen.

The thought made Sam grit his teeth and then swear when a back molar panged.

MADDIE HAD BEEN WORRIED WHEN CAM STARTED SEEING KIRSTIN along the river on an almost daily basis. They'd thought they were being so clever, but when Maddie had suggested that location to Cam, she hadn't intended for them to go there again and again. She'd told Cam more than once that Conacher was bound to find out sooner or later. And today her warnings had been proven right.

She wasn't clear on exactly how Caleb knew that Samuel Conacher had seen Cam and Kirstin kissing. So far as she knew, her grandson had been in school all day, and Cam hadn't told her differently. *Oh, well, treat me like a mushroom,* she thought. *I'll be just fine.* Only she wasn't. Cam had been working so hard to build his business. Even while meeting with Kirstin so often, he'd still gone out in the morning and again in the afternoon to dig up clients. Now, before he'd even made a sale, Conacher might start gunning for him.

Might? She scoffed at herself. There was no question about it. The man had a fearful reputation in Rustlers' Gulch for destroying anyone who looked twice at his daughter. And Cam had done more than just look.

Angry and frightened for her son, Maddie saved the original draft of her book under a different title and began rewriting her work in progress, which would now feature Sam Conacher as her murder victim. Caleb had gotten home a couple hours after his father had, so she knew her grandson was safe and otherwise occupied.

She thought of this writing activity as a therapeutic foray, and she had no intention of sticking with it. When she got her resentment toward Conacher out of her system, she'd return to her first, well-drafted plot.

She envisioned Sam to look a lot like Gus, the wiry cowboy in the television series *Lonesome Dove*. She altered his appearance a little to avoid any accusations of copyright infringement, and as she revised the existing chapters, the hours flew by. Even better, she thoroughly enjoyed herself by making the killing gorier and more torturous. She left the fictitious name of her original victim the same, only now he was a cattle and land monger without scruples. Her readers loved when a victim had it coming, and Sam Conacher definitely deserved to suffer. Maddie couldn't help but wonder how many young fellows he had ruined.

Cam startled her half to death by tapping on her trailer door before opening it. "Dinner's ready, Mom."

Maddie saved her work, hurried to tidy up, and went to join her family for the evening meal. When she walked into the wall tent, she saw Caleb slumped in one of the swivel rockers. "Hi, darling. You didn't stop in after school for an afternoon snack."

"When I got home, I had to talk with Dad. For *hours*."

Maddie glanced at her son, who rolled his eyes. "Forget the drama, Caleb. Tell Gram what you did."

Caleb sighed. "I skipped lunch, woodshop, and Spanish, and I didn't notify you or Dad to let you know where I was."

"Oh." Maddie preferred to keep her nose out of it when Caleb got in trouble. It was Cam's job to be the disciplinarian. "I see."

"Probably not," Caleb said. "I came home, parked by the front gate, and walked way downriver to spy on Dad and Kirstin."

"Again?" Maddie wanted to call back the word the instant she said it, but she'd been taken off guard.

"What do you mean, *again?*" Cam sent his son a smoldering look. "Don't tell me you've done it before today."

"Okay, I won't." Caleb looked at his father and sighed. "Only once, Dad. It was the first time you met her over there. I had a half day at school, and I was bored. *Nothing* interesting happened. I was worried that you needed a how-to manual."

Cam met Maddie's gaze. "You knew about this and didn't see fit to tell me?"

"I didn't think it was a serious infraction, Cam. More just harmless curiosity."

"It's not your place to decide what's serious and what isn't."

This was why Maddie preferred not to be involved in disciplining her grandson. "Bad call on my part, I guess. I apologize."

Cam pinched the bridge of his nose and then waved his hand as if to clear the air. "Mom, I'm sorry. I shouldn't have said that. Of *course* you have every right to decide what's serious. You and Dad helped raise him. Maybe I'm the one blowing this all out of proportion."

"No." Maddie hated to take sides against Caleb. He was a dear, sweet boy. But she didn't want to sway Cam into thinking this was all just silliness. "Caleb skipped school today. And I believe he was trespassing on Conacher's ranch, and Montanans take that very seriously." She met her grandson's gaze. "I gave you a pass the first time, Caleb. I believed you realized that you'd done something wrong and wouldn't do it again. If I led you to think otherwise, I'm sorry. But I don't think I did. You wouldn't have gone to such lengths to hide the activity this time if you thought it was an okay thing to do."

"Now are you going to lecture me, too?" Caleb asked.

"Hmm." Maddie stepped over to the stove and saw that Cam had fixed a steak-strip stir-fry. "Do I need to?"

"No."

"Awesome. Then you can tell me why what you did was wrong, starting with skipping school and not telling me or your dad where you were."

Caleb groaned. "Our address isn't officially on the rolls yet. If I'd been in a wreck, the police might not have been able to locate where I live. You and Dad thought I was at school. If I had been kidnapped, you wouldn't have known where to start looking for me."

"What about spying on people?" Maddie asked.

"I didn't think it was really spying. They were on state land, where anyone could have seen them. It wasn't like I peeked through a window to watch them."

"Thank you for pointing out the difference between spying and spying." Maddie filled a plate and handed it to Cam. "Now explain why it was wrong."

"Well, Dad says it should have been his decision who he allowed to see him kissing Kirstin. A stranger is one thing, and his son is another thing. As my father, his job is to set a good example for me, so when he knows I'm watching him, he tries to be on his best behavior. But when he doesn't know I'm watching, sometimes he isn't perfect, just like I wasn't perfect today. He's never done anything really bad, but sometimes he deserves a break from being a father. I didn't think of it quite that way."

Maddie glanced at Cam. He inclined his head almost imperceptibly to let her know that he found his son's response satisfactory. "Nice way to put it," she told her grandson. "And I think it's wonderful that your father cares more about what you think of him than he does about a stranger's opinion."

"Yeah." Caleb stuck out one booted foot and studied it. "Dad and Kirstin also got chased today by a bull moose, which makes Dad even more upset about me skipping class and hanging out along the river." Before Maddie could ask questions, Caleb continued. "What if it had visited our side of the river and I'd had no tree to climb? Plus, some things are private, and everybody knows they are. Like when Dad and I first got here. We didn't have the portable toilet here then, and we had to hide out in the woods to go. If someone had spied on us, that person would have known we wanted privacy. It was implied by the nature of what we were doing, Dad says. So kissing a girl is sort of the same."

Maddie stuck a filled plate under Caleb's chin and then handed him a tall cup of milk. "Very nice, Caleb. I'm confident now that you have a firm grasp of what an invasion of privacy is." She winked at Cam. "I'm also sure your father now realizes that an implied need for privacy may not be enough when he's kissing a lady."

Cam snorted, sat down, and waited for Maddie to take the seat beside him. "Shall we say the blessing?"

AFTER CAM AND CALEB WENT TO THE CABIN FOR SOME MUCH-needed father-and-son time, Maddie did the dishes, smiling over Caleb's transgressions that day. The youngster had intended no harm, after all. She was grateful that Cam had gotten right on top of it, though. The boy needed to let her or his father know where he was. It was a courtesy to those who loved him. Both Maddie and Cam extended that consideration to each other and to Caleb as well.

Well, she thought, as she dried a skillet, she didn't always do that these days. When she went for chemo treatments or a consultation with her oncologist, she implied that she was going for physical therapy. She refused to feel guilty about that. She always had her cell phone so they could call her, and she didn't actually lie. A treatment was a treatment, and she was saving those she loved from hours of unnecessary worry about her health.

When the kitchen area was clean, Maddie went to feed her outdoor cats and lock them in their safe house for the night. Then she headed inside her trailer, eager to resume writing. She was enjoying this different slant on the story. It allowed her to vent. In the morning she'd put her professional hat back on, but for tonight, she would allow herself to play.

As the evening wore on, she felt deliciously evil as she revamped the plot, mentally applauding herself for this idea because it provided her with countless suspects, men who detested the victim because he had ruined them. *Heck*, she thought. *Maybe I'm really onto something with this.* Her fans would love it. And it had been months since she'd been so completely in her writing zone. The real world faded away.

Long after Cam tapped on the trailer door to wish her good night, Maddie continued to work. She didn't call it a day until her murderer needed to figure out how to dispose of the dismembered body. She had to come up with something extremely clever. That was her trademark.

After performing her nightly ablutions, she snuggled down in bed with two of her cats, one a fluffy black feline with white markings that didn't get along with the others, and Sissy, a mostly white kitty with black patches who weighed less than eight pounds, glowed eerily white after dark, and would be easy pickings for a raptor if there ever came an evening when Maddie couldn't get her into the cathouse. Maddie hoped to convert both felines to indoor living in order to keep them safe.

The two cats began to purr. Maddie, loving the silky push of fur against her fingertips, cuddled Sissy close and smiled as the cat's motor revved to a higher gear. Sasha, who apparently didn't like people much more than she did other members of her species, retreated to lie upon the unoccupied pillow. Maddie was exhausted. She was just now feeling better after her last treatment and had put in a long day.

She drew in a deep breath, slowly exhaled, and let her body relax. The next instant, she slipped into the blackness of slumber.

SHORTLY AFTER NOON THE NEXT DAY, MADDIE WAS MAKING herself a cup of aromatic ginger tea. She'd started drinking it to settle her stomach after chemo treatments, and now it had grown on her. She enjoyed at least one serving a day, if not two. She liked the ritual of bobbing the tea bag in the hot water and watching the ginger release its deep golden color and delicious scent.

Suddenly the trailer rocked violently. She froze and snapped her gaze to the front window. The striped awning, which provided her front yard with shade late in the afternoon, jerked skyward and then, just as suddenly, plunged onto the support braces. Hurrying over to the table, Maddie peered out the glass pane to see her welcome mat go airborne and flatten against the wire fence that Cam and Caleb had built to enclose her front yard. Then her cute yard table lifted, went sideways, and crashed into one of the matching white chairs. *High wind.* The awning was being whipped so violently in the strong gusts that it was in danger of being torn from the metal siding. Maddie knew she needed to roll back the canvas.

She grabbed a light jacket and drew it on as she went outside. The instant she gained the porch, the power of Mother Nature nearly knocked her off the step. Across the river, conifer and de-ciduous trees bent under the force one moment and then whipped erect. At the edge of her mind, Maddie recognized that the violent gusts followed by abrupt cessations were a storm pattern that could snap huge trees like toothpicks.

They had never experienced any high wind on this property, and that posed a problem for Maddie. Cam had never shown her how to operate the awning braces and retractable arms. *It can't be rocket science,* Maddie assured herself. Retired baby boomers, many of them suffering from early-stage dementia, traveled the whole country in massive RVs, and they used awnings. *If it was all that complicated, they'd forget how.*

Another violent updraft of wind prodded Maddie to do something instead of hold on to the railing. She grabbed an awning extender arm, and just as she did, another gust pulled the canvas upward, lifting Maddie off her feet. *Where is Cam when I need him?* she wondered. Unfortunately, he had driven to Missoula to pick up supplies and meet with a real estate associate. He probably wouldn't be back for hours, and Caleb was at school. It was up to her to figure out how the support mechanisms worked and rescue her little home on wheels. It was too darling to let it be destroyed.

When her feet touched ground again, Maddie lost her balance and fell on the gravel rump first. Upon impact, she knew Caleb was right. She'd lost a lot of weight and had little padding left. Pain shot through her hips. She couldn't move for a moment. Her short hair whipped across her eyes, blinding her as she struggled to stand. She'd no sooner regained her feet than the storage tent, a twelve-by-twenty carport canopy, caught an upward draft and went skyward like a gigantic kite. Horrified, Maddie watched it somersault and land on top of her trailer.

Afraid that the wind might damage Cam's extra-large wall

tent next, Maddie ran from her yard to check its tie-downs. They could make do without her trailer, but the cook shack was vital. She was glad to see that Cam had used sturdy rebar stakes and rope that wouldn't break under extreme tension. It was the shelter where they cooked, did dishes, washed laundry, and sat around the fire at night, so it was crucial to their comfort. Before trying to retrieve the storage shelter, she made sure the ropes that anchored the cook shack were snug. Each time she bent over, her backside hurt as she straightened. *I detest getting old*, she thought. *But the alternative is even worse.*

When she tried to walk against the wind, her legs trembled with the effort. She quickly ran short of breath. Chemo treatments did this to her. It took at least three days to feel better and a couple more to fully recover. How on earth was she going to get that heap of plastic tarp and metal framework off the roof of her miniature home?

Making her way toward the three-hundred-gallon water tank, she noticed that all the dogs had run for cover under the trailer. The wind was scary, and Maddie didn't blame them for hiding. At least they hadn't chosen to cower around her feet. If she could crawl up onto the tank, she might be able to grab a handful of tarp, but if she pulled on it, the whole works might come down on top of her. If she got knocked off the water vessel, she would fall to the ground. All she needed was to break a hip. She'd end up recuperating in a motel room and leaving Cam here to care for all her animals and his as well. That didn't sound pleasant for either of them.

As suddenly as the wind had struck, it died down. Relieved, Maddie did her best to climb up on the tank, but it was slick, heavy plastic, and there were no footholds. Just as she gave up and slid back down, she glimpsed a man on horseback to her right.

He'd ridden into their camp as if he owned the place. His smirk suggested that he found her predicament amusing.

Maddie turned to face him. He emanated strength, superiority, and arrogance. She knew who he was the instant she clapped eyes on him. *Samuel Conacher in the flesh.* He sat tall and formidable in the saddle and shifted his lean weight as his red horse sidestepped. He wore a tan Stetson that had seen better days. She noted that he'd anchored it to his head during the wind with a chin string. His sideburns had turned white, but his sooty eyebrows and mustache, peppered with gray, indicated that the original color had been black. His weathered features looked as if they'd been carved from granite, especially his mouth. Maddie wondered if he ever smiled.

What really upset her, though, was that he looked nothing like the character Gus in *Lonesome Dove.* In Maddie's mind, *this* was the man who would ruin her son's reputation simply because he had dared to meet Kirstin across the river. She hated him on sight.

"Looks like you have a problem on your hands." His voice rang deep and set her nerves on edge.

"How may I help you?" Maddie asked, endeavoring to be cordial.

"I'm here to powwow with the randy, useless, uneducated little fucker that's sniffing after my daughter."

Uneducated? Useless? Maddie had an Irish temper, and it ignited. She wouldn't give this man the satisfaction of seeing her try to defend her son, who had degrees in both fish and game biology and civil engineering. Planting her hands on her hips, she said, "When you say *daughter*, are you referring to that black-haired tart whose only talent is wiggling her hips to tantalize every decent man who gets within a hundred yards of her?"

Conacher stiffened his shoulders, which revealed, even with a shirt as camouflage, that he was well muscled. Maddie wasn't impressed. She'd detested him at first sight, and he hadn't risen in her opinion a hair. Even worse, now she would have to revise three chapters of her book to torture the right man.

She wasn't a woman who wilted during a confrontation. Instead she informed Conacher, "Only gutter slime uses the F word in a lady's presence, and only a lazy, good-for-nothing jerk sits on a horse while an old woman's camp is destroyed by a windstorm. How long were you watching me?"

"Long enough for it to get interesting." He leveled his steel blue gaze on her. "And you aren't *that* old. Just for your information, white trash isn't welcome in this valley. I was hoping all your shit would blow clear to Kansas."

Her blood roiled.

"It appears that your son isn't here, so I'll take my leave." He turned his horse and rode toward his ranch. "I'll catch the randy bastard another time. For his sake, you'd better hope I'm not as pissed off as I am right now."

Maddie was so furious that she wanted to throw things at him. *White trash?* She wouldn't take that lying down. She picked up a rock, knotted her fist over it, and imagined aiming it straight at the delineated depression of his spine. Maybe she could hit him with enough force to knock him out of the saddle. But no. She wouldn't stoop to his level. But oh, boy, was she ever going to get even with him somehow.

Just as Sam Conacher reached his own land, Maddie saw Caleb's battered old pickup careening down the gravel road that divided the two properties. When he screeched to a stop near the cabin, he jumped out as if the truck cab were infested with fire ants. "I *knew* it!" he yelled to Maddie. "When I saw trees about to blow down, I cut class to get here fast."

Maddie was still so angry that she wanted to stomp her feet like a child. Instead she forced a smile. "I won't give you a scolding for that. I definitely need help to set things right, and your father won't be back for hours."

Caleb, looking wonderful in a red plaid Western shirt and Wrangler jeans, stopped during his approach to gape at the storage carport on top of the trailer. "Oh, Gram, you must have been scared half to death. That was a mighty fierce blow."

"Actually," Maddie told him, "I didn't have time to feel afraid. I was just worried our whole camp would blow away."

"Something could have gone airborne and hit you on the head. You should have stayed inside where it was safe." He glanced around. "Where are the dogs?"

"Hiding under the trailer. The storm scared the wits out of them."

"It was smart of them to hide. I wish you had. We need you, Gram. What'd we do if you got hurt?"

Her grandson strode toward her. She'd noticed many times recently that he'd grown over the summer and was becoming a man, but now his loose-hipped saunter drove that home. "As long as the wind is down, you can gather stuff that blew away, Gram. I'll take care of the rest. But if the wind comes up again, will you please go in the house?" He moved closer to the trailer while Maddie turned to survey the land. Caleb was right; things had blown as far as their future building site. "Don't do any heavy work," he said. "I've got this."

As Maddie struck off to pick up lightweight items that had been lifted and tossed helter-skelter, her grandson put the awning up and then jumped on top of the water tank. He soon had the carport off the trailer. Feelings of inadequacy swamped her. Twenty years ago she could have done that herself, but time had passed, and now even her hands, the tools of her profession, were growing stiff and achy from arthritis.

They worked for two hours setting their camp back to rights. The items Maddie collected were *not* trash. She found gas cans, tarps, two buckets, a roll of paper towels that had unfurled over the field like garland, and various other things they had stored or set down outside. But *no* garbage. That made her feel slightly better. *White trash, my foot.*

Then the wind began to blow again. Maddie ran around stuffing things like buckets into the wall tent so she wouldn't have to pick up any more far-flung objects. Caleb assisted her. When their camp was battened down, he positioned two lawn chairs at the back of her trailer and said, "We've put away everything that may go airborne, Gram, so let's watch the storm. It'll be better than a movie."

"I thought you said for me to go hide." Maddie shouted to be heard.

Caleb grinned. "It's safe now," he hollered back. "I anchored that carport down with rebar stakes this time. It won't go anywhere."

CALEB HOPED HIS GRANDMOTHER WOULD ACCEPT THE INVITA- tion. Her legs quivered as she walked, and she was hunched over. He had a bad feeling that she'd gotten hurt somehow. He relaxed slightly as she forced a smile and eased herself down onto the chair he had provided.

"Are you okay, Gram?"

"The awning lifted me off the ground, and I fell on the gravel. I didn't break anything, but my rump aches."

That made Caleb feel better. Now he knew why she was walking funny and that she wasn't badly hurt.

He joined her in staring across the river where deciduous trees were being stripped of still-green leaves. Raising his voice to be heard, he asked, "What was that man on a horse doing over here? I saw him yesterday. Was I right? Is he Sam Conacher?"

"Yes. He just stopped by to introduce himself."

Caleb jerked his gaze to where he'd last seen the horse and rider. "Was he an asshole to you?"

His grandmother clicked her tongue, a sound she made to let him know she disapproved of his language, only now he could barely hear it. "He isn't the most pleasant person I've ever met. I'll leave it at that."

Caleb stiffened. "If he upset you, Gram, I'll go over and tell him to stay the heck away from here."

Gram laughed and shook her head. "You're becoming a young man, Caleb McLendon." She leaned closer. "You're not a little boy anymore who can retaliate against people in childish ways. I said he was a little unpleasant, not that he said or did anything bad." She went back to watching the storm. "I have to admit, this is magnificent." Lightning zigzagged across the blue sky just then. "I'm not even cold, and I can't think of anyone I'd rather watch this with."

The storm suddenly subsided again, and they no longer needed to raise their voices to be heard. Caleb was glad. He hadn't thought about Gram getting cold. He should have grabbed her a blanket.

Hoping to make her smile, he said, "Proper English, Gram. You should say I can't think of anyone *with whom* I'd rather watch this." He cocked an eyebrow at her. "Am I right?"

She relaxed and laughed. "No, but you are correct." She nudged him with her elbow. "Give your poor old gram a break, kiddo. I have to follow the rules of proper English every workday. Now I'm enjoying some unexpected downtime, and I don't want to edit myself."

"True. I'm just working hard on my English at school. Dad pulled good grades in college. I don't want to crash and burn before I even graduate."

"You have lots of time to prepare for college, and you *won't* crash and burn." She snuggled down in the chair and let her gaze follow the gentler breaths of the wind, its path marked by rustling trees, bending grass, and tall weeds doing a graceful dance. "Just don't miss out on all the fun of high school. It's a time in your life that you can never recapture. When you go off to college, the course work may be tough. Not a lot of time to play at that point in your life."

Caleb plopped a dusty boot on his opposite knee. "You sound kind of blue. Did you miss out on having fun during high school?"

"A little. But then I met your grandfather my senior year, and he reminded me how to have fun. And believe me, that's what we did. He moved away to attend a different college than mine, and we stopped seeing each other for a couple of years. Then we ran into each other at a university ball game, and the fun began again. If he didn't drive from his campus to see me, I drove to see him."

Caleb sighed. "I don't think my dad had much fun in high school. He met my mom, and heaps of responsibility was dumped on his shoulders."

His grandmother nodded. "He made some bad choices, but I don't think he'd change a thing. He got you out of the deal, and he's told me that you're the most wonderful gift he's ever received."

Caleb nodded. "He tells me that a lot. But I still wish it hadn't happened that way."

"If it hadn't, you wouldn't be here."

Caleb laughed. "You're right. Jeez, I'm so glad my dad messed up."

She surrendered to mirth, and he followed her lead. Then she said, "I'm very glad he messed up, too. You're a joy in my life."

Reaching over to clasp her hand, Caleb asked, "Are you missing Gramps today?"

"No," she said.

Caleb thought she answered a little too fast, and then he regretted asking. Of course she missed Gramps. All of them did.

"I'm in love with this place," she added. "I'm really excited that we can start building on this land soon. In my mind's eye, I'm already decorating my residence. I'm having a wonderful adventure." She turned her head to look at their camp. "Do you think it looks like white trash has moved in here?"

Startled by the question, Caleb gave their camp a solemn once-over. Gram was fussy about her house looking nice, and he couldn't remember her yard ever being junky. "Is that what Mr. Conacher said?" Caleb shook his head. "It looks like we're camping, Gram. And guess what. We *are* camping, so what's his problem?"

"Don't go off half-cocked," she warned.

"I won't," Caleb promised, "but he upset you, and I am going to tell Dad. He'll go over and set that old man straight."

"No," she said sharply. "I don't think that would be wise. Mr. Conacher knows now that your father has been meeting with his daughter. That would be like stirring a hornets' nest."

Caleb thought about that for a second. "Do you think Mr. Conacher is that pissed?"

Gram gave him another *stop that* look. "I think you can safely say that." Then she smiled at him. "And, yes, he upset me. But I'll get over it eventually, no damage done. Instead of stirring up trouble with him, I think our best plan of action is to politely teach him an important lesson."

Caleb just wanted to punch the old dude. "What's that?"

"That he should never judge people by how they look."

BEFORE HEADING BACK TO THE RANCH PROPER, SAM DECIDED TO enjoy the windstorm while he rode fence line. With fifteen hundred acres of grazing land, checking the perimeters and cross fences had become a frequent habit born of necessity. He figured that if he engaged in this activity for two hours a week, he might complete the job once a year, and then he could start all over again. The only problem was that he couldn't devote that much time. Most days he was on his grazing land, trying to round up cattle and haul them back here before winter hit. With only one man to help him, it was like trying to stab scattering ants with a toothpick.

Normally Sam enjoyed riding fence line. It gave him time alone, except for the company of his horse, which didn't talk much. Sam could clear his head, ponder life's twists and turns, or merely be and let his thoughts wander. Today he found no pleasure in the solitude. He kept thinking about that older lady next door and how badly he had treated her. Sam was starting to feel as if he'd become two different men, one sane and the other one meaner than a snake. Even worse, he couldn't seem to control the bad guy. That man was furious with the world. He wanted a pound of someone's flesh. He said things that Sam would *never* say. Cruel things. Nasty things.

That woman had nailed it on the head when she jumped him about using foul language in her presence. Every time Sam thought about it, he cringed. His parents had raised him better than that. At what point in his sixty-eight years had he stopped caring about the simple things, like practicing good manners? He never would have said such words to his wife, Annie.

As Sam rode into the ranch proper, he bypassed his sprawling post-and-beam home and stopped at the barn to unsaddle and groom his gelding before putting him out to graze. The wind came up again. He could hear it raging outside the enclosure. Then all went quiet. He led the horse out and turned him loose inside a roomy enclosure with shelter.

Angry with himself over his earlier behavior, he saw a five-gallon bucket sitting about five feet from the rail fence. The container had no business being there, and he was sick and damned tired of people leaving shit here and there, showing no respect for the land. In a fit of pique, he kicked the pail with all his might. Pain lanced from his toe to his shin, making him grunt and grasp his leg. Vile expletives streamed from his mouth. When he kicked something as light as a bucket, it normally went flying. He craned his neck only to see that someone had filled the damned thing with rocks.

Gimping into the barn, he decided the culprit had probably been the son of Miguel Alvarez, his employee. The boy, Rickie, was a cute kid who'd taken on a project bigger than he was. The family lived in one of the nicest employee houses on the ranch, and Rickie had been trying to build his mama a rock garden over the summer. Sam had been meaning to get a truckload of stone for the kid, but he hadn't had the spare time. *Fancy that,* he thought. *All I do is work, because all the lazy bastards I used to have on the payroll couldn't man up.*

He slumped down on a hay bale and pulled off his boot to check his toe. *Damned if it doesn't feel broken.* He shoved the boot back on and winced. *Serves me right. I've never in my life treated a woman so badly. That crack I made about white trash cut her deep.* He could barely believe that he had ridden away when an older lady needed his help. *She isn't the one who's screwing my daughter. It's her no-account son that I'd like to beat to a pulp. I had no right to act that way.*

Sam recalled watching his daughter smooch with that jerk on the riverbank yesterday, and his anger spiked again. How had Kirstin met the guy? He'd pegged their new neighbors as low-class the instant he'd seen their camp. Had she failed to hear a word he'd said? Surely she hadn't stopped by there to make friends with them. Even more mysterious to Sam, what the hell did she see in that man? She'd been going for walks in the afternoons, and at night she supposedly went to sit with her sick friend, Marcy, as often as she could.

Only now he wondered if Marcy actually existed. According to Kirstin, the woman had been near death for at least three years.

The thought that Kirstin had been lying to him in order to meet men struck fear into Sam's heart. He loved his little girl with every fiber of his being. If and when she fell for somebody, Sam wanted him to be worthy of her, someone close to her age, intelligent, and financially successful. The dope next door had to be ten years her senior. In his mid-thirties, Sam guessed. And he lived with his mother and a kid in a makeshift campsite featuring a vintage travel trailer, two tents, and a shed. By the time Sam turned thirty, he'd already owned his first sizable chunk of land. His Annie had worked at his side to make something of it.

Now that Sam came to think of it, they had camped on the property that first summer. Sam cringed at the memories of cooking over an open fire and sleeping in a tent, much like the new neighbors were doing now. Kirstin had been only a twinkle in his eye back then. He and Annie had been young and full of it, wildly in love, and excited about their future. They'd bathed in the river and slept on the ground. They'd made coffee in a beaten-up tin can.

Sam sighed. He'd been wrong to be such a jackass. *She isn't the one who's messing with my daughter,* he reminded himself yet again. It was just so hard for Sam to accept that Kirstin was seeing that fellow. She was special, so very special. She shouldn't waste herself on some loser. Sam would never change his mind about that.

Chapter Five

KIRSTIN SAT IN HER TRUCK IN THE PARKING LOT OF THE COWBOY Tree. Cam was running late. Even though they had both agreed last night that they could see each other only on occasion now, Kirstin had told her dad that her sick friend, Marcy, was having a bad spell and needed Kirstin to spend the night with her. Sam had been grouchy about it, but he'd finally granted her permission. *Permission?* She was a grown woman and so tired of pandering to him. Once she had an all clear to go out, she'd texted Cam, and he had agreed to meet her here. Their plan was to hide her pickup and go to Missoula, not to sleep together, but to spend another evening just talking and getting to know each other better. Cam said it was time they went out to dinner and maybe even danced to a live band.

When she saw his truck pull into a parking spot near hers, she was so excited to see him that she exited her vehicle and ran to meet him. Her steps slowed as she reached him. Something was wrong.

A worried scowl creased his forehead. His blue eyes blazed with anger.

She stopped in front of him. "What is it?"

He flashed a smile that didn't reach his eyes. "I'm really sorry, but I have to cancel."

"You could have just called me. I would have understood," she assured him.

He placed his big capable hands on his hips. "Too many ears. My mom had a rough day, and I didn't want her to know I was canceling a date to stay home with her and Caleb."

"Is she all right?" Kirstin asked. "What happened?"

"A neighbor took some shots at her. I need to stay home and cheer her up." He shrugged. "More important, I need to be around so Caleb doesn't get a wild hair up his butt and do something stupid. He gets hot under the collar when someone says mean things to his grandmother."

"A neighbor?" Kirstin's chest tightened. "Not my father. Please, tell me it wasn't my dad."

Cam clamped his lips together.

His reluctance to answer told Kirstin all that she needed to know. Her stomach churned. Her body snapped so taut with rage that she couldn't move for a moment. Then she squared her shoulders, pivoted on one foot, and headed back to her truck.

"Kirstin, don't do anything foolish! It'll only make matters worse."

Kirstin whirled on him. "I'm *sick* of this, Cam. My father has no right to interfere in my life!"

"I realize that, but—"

"You realize nothing!" she cried. "You have no idea what this is like for me! Now your mom will hate me, all because my father is a screwed-up mess and takes his pain out on everyone he encounters. It's showdown time."

As Kirstin got into her truck and closed the door, she heard Cam yell, "You need to get the cantankerous old son of a bitch into counseling!"

She rolled down her window and grinned at him. "Congratulations, Cam. You finally have Sam Conacher pegged."

SAM WAS ENGAGING IN HIS FAVORITE EVENING PASTIME, READING a Madeline McLendon murder mystery, her latest release. It was a particularly riveting plot. The killer had poisoned the victim by adding large quantities of potato sprouts to a flavorful smoothie, and now the lead character, a pretty female detective, was hot on the trail of clues. Sam had heard that the solanine in potato sprouts was poisonous, but he'd never heard of anyone dying from it. Regardless, he kept reading, confident that Madeline McLendon would pull it off. She'd never failed him yet.

Suddenly his front door flew open and slapped against something, emitting a resounding *thump*. Sam couldn't see who had come inside until Kirstin stepped from the entry hall. He couldn't resist saying, "Aw, Marcy must have taken a sudden turn for the better. Too bad. Now you're all slicked up with nowhere to go."

Fists clenched at her sides, she marched across the spacious living room to stand in front of his chair. Black hair tousled from the wind, she looked angry enough to chew nails and spit out screws. Her eyes were the same color as a rifle barrel, much like his, but for a moment he could have sworn his Annie had returned from the grave. Kirstin had gotten her coloring from Sam, but in every other way she was her mama all over again.

"You are an irascible, sharp-tongued, heartless, arrogant"— she broke off to drag in a deep breath—"impossible, cantankerous, bitter man and without any feeling!"

"Excuse me for pointing it out, but you're getting redundant." Sam laid his open book facedown on the arm of his recliner and released the footrest so he could stand. "What the Sam Hill did I do to get you so riled?"

Kirstin's face turned so red he worried for a moment that she might physically attack him. "You went over to visit our new neighbors and upset Cam's mother. You took shots at her!"

"I wasn't carrying a weapon."

"Your mouth qualifies! I don't know for sure what you said to her, but it must have been awful."

"So that's his name, Cam. Good to know. Next time I can add that to my long list of unflattering adjectives."

Kirstin jabbed a finger in the general direction of his nose. "There won't *be* a next time! You have no right to interfere with my life!"

Sam sank back down on his chair. "I admit I wasn't at my best this afternoon, Kirstin, but if I hadn't seen you swabbing that man's tonsils with your tongue on the riverbank yesterday and if you hadn't been going for walks so much before that, I might have been in a better humor."

"Like I'm responsible for your humor?" She bunched her muscles as if she might spring at him. Though she was a woman of diminutive stature, Sam didn't discount her strength. While doing ranch work, she held her own against most men. "My tongue and where I decide to stick it are nobody's business but *mine*. I'm sick-to-death tired of being monitored as if I'm sixteen. I'm twenty-six, soon to be twenty-seven. You act as if I'm still a baby. Well, news flash, Dad. My biological clock is ticking. I want to meet the right man, fall in love, and maybe have babies like nearly every other young woman on the planet!"

Sam rose from the chair again and jabbed a finger at her impertinent little nose. *"Not with that jackass next door, you won't!"*

She grabbed his hand and shoved it away from her face. "You

know nothing about him! And I'm finished with your nonsense. This is *my* life, and I'm going to live it *my* way. The way you treated his mother today is inexcusable. *Despicable!*"

Sam knew he had no ground to stand on. He'd already reached that conclusion and felt rotten about the way he had behaved. "Kirstin, I'm sorry, really sorry."

"Not good enough!" she shouted. And then she started jabbing his chest with a skinny finger. For the first time, Sam realized that she had inherited his temper. "From now on, you are not allowed at the ranch manager's house. I may be entertaining a gentleman friend there. If you crack open the door and stick your nose in my business, I'll smack it!"

"I will allow no such thing on Conacher land!" he yelled back. "A gentleman friend? Over my dead body! You'll honor the rules when you're living under my roof."

"I don't live here." She glared at him and squared her shoulders. "I work hard for my wages and my right to live in the ranch manager's house! It may sit on *your* land, but technically the house belongs to me for as long as I work here. Out in my yard or within my own walls, I'll do whatever I please. And if you so much as *try* to interfere, I'll pack my bags and leave. *Do you understand?*"

Sam's heart squeezed. She was his little girl. He had walked the floors with her when she was a baby. He had rushed her to urgent care when she ran high fevers. Night after night, he'd read her bedtime stories until she drifted off to sleep. If she left the ranch, he'd be alone. He'd have no one who gave a shit about him and no one to love.

Before he could think of what he might say to mend fences with her, she retreated a step and cast a scathing look at the paperback he'd accidentally knocked off onto the floor. Then a nasty little smirk peeled her lips back from her teeth. She left the house in much the same manner as she had entered, slamming the door so hard that the walls shook.

Sam sat down and stared stupidly at the floor. He was losing his daughter. The handwriting was on the wall. And whose fault was that? That horny bastard next door was responsible. Feeling older than he was, Sam turned off the lights and went to his upstairs bedroom. For years, he and Annie had used this suite. He'd been unable to sleep up here after her death, but he'd stuck it out until rest no longer evaded him. *Another win for Sam Conacher*, he thought. But in all honesty, he could admit, if only to himself, that he'd used alcohol as a sedative in order to pass out.

Before he stripped down to his briefs and undershirt, he couldn't resist stepping to the window and carefully parting the curtains to see if a second vehicle was parked in front of Kirstin's house. If that jackass showed up, Sam vowed that he'd kick his ass good and proper. He would allow no man to defile his beautiful daughter on Conacher land.

After peeling off his clothes, Sam crawled into his bed. He punched his pillow. He lay on one side and then on the other. Every time he nearly dozed off, he thought he heard Annie's voice. *Sam, sweetheart, you have to let her go. Set her free.*

Sam, lying on his back, pulled up each end of his pillow to cover his ears. But he wasn't hearing Annie with his damned ears. Her voice was inside his head.

"Of course it's all in my head," he grumped. "I stood over her grave. Dead people can't talk."

But as Sam finally drifted off to sleep, he knew in his heart of hearts that if anyone would come back to defend her child, it would be Annie.

• • •

THE NEXT AFTERNOON MADDIE WENT OUT TO THE CAT BUILDING to clean litter boxes, top off the food dishes, and freshen the water bowl. It was only a temporary home for her kitties. The water that Cam hauled in had to be used judiciously, making it necessary that she wash the cat bedding only rarely, and then it was so thick with fur that it plugged up the washer. She swept their shed as often as she could, but the floor was a scant eight-by-eight, leaving precious little room for anything but beds, blankets, bowls, and litter boxes. Cam insisted that the building was well insulated and the felines would be just fine even in winter with an electric heater. Maddie knew it was true. Many cats slept in barns and lean-tos, enduring freezing temperatures and even hunting for their own food. By comparison, her felines were pampered. But this building wasn't up to the standards of living to which her babies had become accustomed.

As she emerged from the shelter, she was half startled out of her wits when she found Sam Conacher outside, once again staring down at her from the back of his horse. Her first thought was that the dogs had gone to the slough again. They loved playing down there in the water, and she didn't mind that they went often. But while they romped, they weren't on duty to warn her of interlopers.

He inclined his head at the structure. "From a distance, I figured this to be your pump house, but it's obviously not."

"It's the cathouse."

He arched an eyebrow. "Hang a red light on it. Maybe you'll get some business."

Maddie's spine stiffened. "Why are you here, Mr. Conacher? If it's to nettle me, I'm in no mood for it today."

He rubbed his jaw. Then he took off his hat, revealing a thick head of white hair. "I—um—came to apologize for my behavior yesterday. I forgot my manners and was way out of line."

To her ears, his apology rang sincere even though she could tell that he'd struggled to push out the words. She said nothing. When a man came to eat crow, a smart woman made sure he swallowed it, feathers, bones, and all.

"It had nothing to do with you," he added. "My beef is with that jackass son of yours."

"Do you honestly think I'm willing to make peace with a man who's still calling my son names? And on *my* turf? I think not, Mr. Conacher." She lifted her chin. "Please, get off my land."

He looked at her as if he couldn't quite believe what she'd said. "Are you kicking me off your property?"

Maddie pointed toward his ranch. "That's how white trash people deal with obnoxious, foulmouthed neighbors. Make tracks, Mr. Conacher. If you trespass again, I'll call the cops."

"Let me remind you that this is a very small valley," he said. "And your son is just starting out here."

The implication to Maddie was that Sam was saying he had the power to ruin Cam professionally. And she saw red. "Yes, it's a small valley. But listen up, buster. You'd better think twice before you start slinging dirt, because I have a pretty strong throwing arm in this area myself. Your reputation will be just as tarnished as my son's before I'm done with you."

Maddie wished she could stomp away, but she was still recovering from her fall in the gravel. No grand exit for her. The same wasn't true for Sam. He nudged his gorgeous mount into a gallop. Maddie gazed after him, unable to decide which was more magnificent, the horse or the man. Then Sam suddenly wheeled the gelding around and rode back toward her.

Sliding hooves sent up dust as he brought the animal to a halt. "Who the hell are you?"

Maddie bit back a grin. "Nobody special, but if you mess with me or mine, you'll come to know me as your worst nightmare."

SAM RODE HOME SCRATCHING HIS HEAD. HE KNEW A BLUFF WHEN he saw one, and that feisty little woman wasn't bluffing. She'd looked him dead in the eye without a single twitch of her facial muscles. Who the hell was she? She seemed to think she was somebody important—important enough to go toe-to-toe with him in a dirt-slinging contest. Sam no longer spoke with many people. Other ranchers who'd once been his friends had abandoned ship after Annie died. All but one of his hired hands had quit. So he didn't hear all the latest scuttlebutt anymore. He hadn't known the land next to his had sold until he noticed squatters on it. Even then he hadn't cared enough to learn anything about them. His ranch proper rested clear at the end of Fox Hollow Road, a far piece from that hog-wallow camp. Sam had known he'd have to drive by their property regularly, but he'd had no intention of mingling with them or taking them a welcome cake. Hell, no. That had been Annie's specialty.

Curiosity nettled him, though. That woman had just thrown down a glove, daring him to mess with her. She *had* to be somebody. Otherwise she never would have issued that challenge. He needed to find out her name. Sam preferred to know everything possible about his enemies.

CAM WAS ACCUSTOMED TO TEXTING A LOT IN HIS BUSINESS, BUT he'd never texted as much as he was now with Kirstin. They didn't dare meet by the river again, and they felt cut off from each other. Over the last twenty-four hours, they had messaged each other close to a hundred times. Fortunately, Cam had Bluetooth and voice recognition in his truck, enabling him to listen to her texts and reply by voice while he drove around the valley to check out expired ranch listings.

Kirstin told him about her confrontation with her dad the previous night. She apologized profusely for Sam's behavior. Cam wanted to remain angry. But the man felt responsible for his wife's death, and in Cam's opinion, that would mess with anybody's head. The ornery old bastard needed counseling, but he'd probably never get it. He was too damned stubborn.

When it came to his mom, Cam was extremely protective, though, and Kirstin's father had made a bad mistake by upsetting her. Cam said nothing to Kirstin of his conflicted feelings toward her dad. It seemed better to keep their exchanges about him light.

But that was nearly impossible with Kirstin. Their texts were personal, and through them, he learned more and more about her, just as she did about him. He wished that she could call him. He wanted to hear her voice. But she was working with her dad, and she didn't want her conversations with Cam to be overheard.

Was it possible to fall even more in love with a woman while texting? Cam's first thought was no, but as the day progressed, his feelings for Kirstin deepened. She wrote to him about the dog she'd borrowed from her dad's place. He was a red merle Australian shepherd, and her father, unimaginatively, had named him Red. Red slept with her at night. When she needed a confidant, he was always there to listen. And, working with her dad, she had plenty of reason to vent her feelings on a regular basis. Her old mare, Marigold, had stepped in a hole that morning and strained her hock. Kirstin had wrapped the leg and put the horse in a stall until morning. If she still limped tomorrow, the vet would be called.

She seemed to adore every animal on the place. Cam admired her for that. And, as he already knew, she also loved nature. She wrote to him about what she saw and smelled: fluffy white clouds against an incredibly blue sky, craggy mountains tiered with variegated green, a yearling deer with gigantic eyes and a twitching nose, and the scent of freshly cut grass from the yard of a neighbor down the road. Cam, an incurable nature enthusiast, texted her back about sighting a bighorn sheep, getting caught in a traffic jam caused by cows instead of cars, and how crisp and clean the air smelled with his window down. He also asked why someone would mow a lawn so late in the season. She never replied. He suspected she got busy with work and couldn't use her phone.

Then she texted him again. *My friend Marcy is very sick. I'll be sitting with her all night, or at least I think I have my dad convinced of that. Going with you to Missoula calls to me. Can you possibly get away?*

Cam hated that Kirstin had been forced to pretend she was sitting with a sick friend in order to get away from her father. He seldom left his family overnight on the new land, but he had done it for business trips. Everything had gone well during his absences. Caleb had also had a day to get over his anger with Kirstin's father. It was unlikely that the boy would confront the older man now.

Sure, he texted back.

He and Kirstin agreed to meet, hide her pickup somewhere, and go to the city, where she could blend in with a crowd. They planned to go out for dinner and then find a nightspot with a live band so they could dance. That was something they hadn't done together yet. Maybe they'd even see a film before the evening was over. They both agreed that it was too soon for them to engage in physical intimacy. The situation with Kirstin's father was still unresolved. Cam hoped to establish some measure of peace with the man before making love to his daughter. Cam also wanted to be absolutely sure of his feelings for Kirstin, and hers for him, before they took their relationship to that level.

That night, Cam and Kirstin made their great escape. In Missoula they dined at a fabulous Thai restaurant. They both had so much to say that they talked around bites of food, listened intently to each other, and laughed at each other's stories. Cam enjoyed how easy it was to converse with her. There was no tense period when they saw each other again. Somehow they just picked up where they'd left off. He'd never felt so comfortable with a woman he found to be attractive. She echoed the same sentiment.

Conversationally they were all over the board, discussing their educations, their parents, childhood memories, and dreams for the future. Cam pictured himself becoming successful in real estate sales and raising cattle on a small scale. Kirstin wanted to take over the ranch for her dad, hire a large crew, and return the operation to its former glory. Their goals didn't conflict, Cam realized. If they built a life together, they could both be happy. He wondered if she was thinking the same thing.

When they finished their meal, they visited a nightspot renowned for hosting great live bands. It was too noisy for them to talk, so they danced to every slow song. While Kirstin went to the ladies' room, Cam approached the lead singer with a special request and offered a generous tip if the band could play it. When Kirstin returned, he led her straight to the dance floor.

Kirstin grinned up at him as they moved in time with the music. One number ended, and after only a brief pause, the lead singer said, "This next song is by special request for a lady named Kirstin."

Kirstin went motionless in Cam's arms as the man hummed

the opening refrain of "The Way We Were." Tears filled her eyes. Cam grinned, pulled her snugly against him, and murmured near her ear, "I hope we never look back with any regrets."

She pressed her face against his shirt, relaxed, and moved with him. At the end of the song, she again looked up. "No mistakes and no regrets. I hope we're together until we're old and gray, and that when we hear this song, we remember being young, happy, and madly in love."

After dancing almost nonstop for more than an hour, they adjourned to a quieter establishment to have a nightcap. The atmosphere there was cozy, with other couples all around them, yet their booth offered them privacy. After exhausting several topics of conversation, Kirstin asked for more details about Caleb's mother.

Cam smiled. "Becky was a sweet girl. We both thought we were in love, and in a juvenile way, I believe we were. Unfortunately, it's hard on a teenage girl when she gets a baby bump that grows bigger and bigger. She no longer felt pretty and swore that I flirted with other girls. I had to work at night, and that made things worse. She thought I was stepping out on her."

"The poor thing. I can only imagine how she must have felt."

Cam appreciated that response. It took heart to understand how hard life might be for a girl during an accidental pregnancy. He also admired Kirstin for not feeling any trace of jealousy. If their roles were reversed, Cam wasn't certain he could have been so magnanimous. "I have an older sister, Grace, who'd already gone off to college, so I didn't really understand younger girls and how sensitive they can be." He shrugged. "I tried to reassure her. I tried to be romantic whenever I could be with her, but my days were pretty crowded, and I had to work on weekends. My dad was willing to help me financially, but he wasn't willing to give me a full ride. He made sure I had time to study and time to sleep. But I had a wife and a baby on the way. I needed more time to be at home. But Dad refused to let me ignore my responsibilities. I had to man up."

Kirstin smiled and rolled her shoulders. "That sounds eerily familiar. I think men of that generation often set impossibly high standards, not only for their kids, but for themselves, too."

Cam nodded. "My mom tried to talk to Dad and present my young wife's side. How she was feeling. That she needed special attention from me that I didn't have time to give her. But Dad just said it was time for her to grow up, too, and accept her responsibilities just as I was. She'd chosen to take risks, she'd gotten pregnant, and she had to face the consequences. He was fond of saying, 'If you play, you have to pay.' I understood where he was coming from. I truly did. But sometimes I muttered under my breath that he was a heartless prick."

Kirstin giggled. "Well, Cam, in a way he was. But did you ever stop to think that, in his mind, it wasn't his responsibility to raise your wife? That maybe he was more concerned about molding you into the man he wanted you to become?" She pointed a slender finger at him. "I think he succeeded. You're a dutiful son and a caring father. You thought about the impact on Caleb if we got together tonight. Do you know how refreshing that is in a world where there are so many careless parents?"

"Caleb is my responsibility. At his age, I have a limited capacity to influence him, but I try to be a good role model. Tomorrow night is our flick night. Even my mother sets aside time for that. We take turns choosing movies. Caleb and I like adventure and action."

"Don't tell me! Your mom likes to watch *Forensic Files* or something like that."

Cam burst out laughing. "You're so right. Her brain is like a sponge. I tease her about it, but mostly I enjoy watching with her. I learn a lot, and so does Caleb."

Her expression went wistful. "Dad and I barely talk at night. Some nights I join him for dinner. We can't entertain each other over a meal with accounts of our day, because we experienced it together. Sometimes he'll mention something I missed out on, or vice versa, and we'll engage. But mostly our shared meals are silent. Sometimes the silence is deafening. I can hear him chew. He can hear me. Do you know how loud a swallow can be at a quiet table? I'm so frustrated and bored sometimes that I want to scream." She dimpled a cheek. "Listen to me, hogging the conversation and making it all about me again."

"You're speaking to a fascinated audience," Cam told her. "And of course you're frustrated and bored. You're young. You enjoy people. Your father is what? Sixty-eight, I think you said. After a hard day, he's content to go home, eat, and read. You want conversation, laughter, and excitement."

"Don't forget sex."

"Nope, I won't forget that. It happens to be on my mind right now a lot more than I'd like."

Her cheeks colored. "Mine, too. But you know what's nice? We have such great things to talk about that I don't think about *only* that."

Cam understood what she meant. Sexual tension was there, but with Kirstin, he got the whole package: great conversation, laughter, and a sense of friendship that had deepened each time they were together.

She finished her margarita. Cam signaled the bartender that they'd like another round. "We aren't driving. Why not?"

She grinned. "Can we get arrested here for walking under the influence?"

Cam chuckled. "God, I hope not. Although, as it pertains to my son, if I'm going to get arrested for any infraction involving alcohol, I prefer to be walking. I never want Caleb to drink and drive."

"So you limit yourself to one drink when you know you'll have to get behind the wheel." She nodded. "I like that. It's smart, safe, and admirable. And you're setting a great example."

After chatting for another hour, they walked to their hotel. Soft lighting illuminated the sidewalks. The night breeze, unlike in Rustlers' Gulch, smelled faintly of gas fumes, and cars moved busily past them, even so late at night. Occasionally couples emerged from nightspots or restaurants that were still open. Cam had rented two rooms on the same floor. They had already checked in. They held hands as they entered the lobby and went up in the elevator. Kirstin's suite was six doors down from his.

As much as Cam yearned to spend the night with her and even though he had picked up some protection, he didn't want to rush this. Kirstin led a pretty secluded life, and he didn't want to hurt her if he began to feel she wasn't right for him. Although, after talking with her so much, he couldn't imagine that ever being the case. Everything about her seemed to suit him.

At her room, he kissed her good night, a long slow joining of mouths that made him yearn for more, and he could tell by her response that she felt the same way. The sparkle in her eyes also told him she'd noticed his arousal. She leaned her back against her still-locked door. "You're a fabulous kisser. And I've enjoyed this evening so much."

Cam replied, "Not as much as I have."

She went up on her tiptoes to kiss his cheek. "Thank you. I'll be awake and ready to leave at six thirty as we agreed. Gotta get back to the ranch early so Dad doesn't get in a snit."

After she used her key card and vanished into her room, Cam

stood in the empty hall, wondering if he was certifiably nuts. She'd looked so beautiful all evening, wearing Montana's version of casual dressy: a flashy pink Western shirt that hugged her figure, boot-cut jeans, and riding boots. No man in his right mind could have failed to think about making love to her, and many would have followed her into the suite. He'd thought about it all evening, yearning to do just that, but Kirstin wasn't one-night-stand material. She deserved a man who considered her feelings, respected her, and moved cautiously forward. How many times had he told Caleb that girls weren't objects, but people with feelings? If he couldn't do as he preached, what kind of man was he?

Cam walked slowly to his room. He had a hunch that he was facing a very long night.

Nearly an hour later, he lay awake staring up through the darkness at a ceiling he couldn't actually see. He jerked when a light knock came at his door. Sighing, he sat up. He knew it was Kirstin, and he wasn't sure what to say when he answered her summons. That he was a father and had to live like a saint? Except he wasn't a saint. He'd been with women over the years, but none of them had worn their hearts on their sleeves. He was afraid Kirstin was, and he suspected that hers was a very tender heart.

He grabbed his jeans and drew them on. "Coming."

Not bothering with a shirt, he opened the door. She stood in the lighted hallway, looking adorable. She wore an overlarge buttoned-front nightshirt with an image of a red merle Australian shepherd on it. Her shapely, slender legs were encased in snug jeans. Her silky black hair was tousled from her pillow. Under the wash-worn top, her small breasts looked soft, except where her nipples pressed against the fabric. His urge to grab her arm and pull her into the room was so strong that he clenched his hand over the door handle.

She licked her lips. "I—um—can't sleep." Her blue eyes implored him. "Please don't send me back to my room. I understand that you'd like to move slowly, Cam, and I know that's probably wise. But my body isn't feeling very wise right now, and I—"

I can't let her stand out there, pleading with me, Cam thought. *Especially not when I want this as much as she does.* Cam clasped her hand, drew her inside his room, and closed the door. After he locked the dead bolt, she threw her arms around his neck, kissed him with hunger, pressing her body against his, and blew every rational thought from his mind.

AFTERWARD CAM FELT DELICIOUSLY EXHAUSTED AND CONTENT. Kirstin snuggled against him like a kitten, her bare skin igniting his. He smiled. Judging by the response of his body, the night wasn't over, and he had to admit that this was a hell of a lot better than taking a cold shower. He turned toward her. She tipped her chin back to meet his gaze.

"Please don't tell me you're sorry," she whispered. "I know this wasn't part of our plan."

"Kirstin, I'll never say I'm sorry for tonight. Being with you was the most beautiful experience of my life."

"Almost perfect."

His gaze sharpened on hers. "Not completely perfect?"

"Oh, no! Being with you was perfect, absolutely perfect." She let her eyes fall closed. "I just can't stop thinking about our parents. While we're falling in love, they're quarreling like ill-behaved children."

Cam stiffened. "What makes you say that?"

She punched her pillow. "Because it's true. I wish they'd both grow up."

"Can you make that singular? My mother has done nothing, absolutely nothing, to incur your father's wrath."

She pushed up on her elbow. "I'm not saying she invited him to go over and insult her. It's just"—she released a tight breath—"that today she kicked him off her property."

Cam blinked. "She did *what*?"

"You heard me, and then she threatened to call the cops if he trespassed again."

"What the hell would have possessed her to do that?"

"Dad says he went over to apologize for his behavior yesterday. He told her he was out of line, and she'd done nothing to deserve how he'd treated her. Or something to that effect."

"Good for him. Sounds okay so far. So what led to my mom kicking him off our place?"

Kirstin sighed again. "Apparently he said you were the one he wanted to beat to a pulp, and in the process he called you a less-than-nice name."

Cam's chest jerked. He couldn't help it. A laugh pressed hard against the base of his throat, and then it exploded from his chest.

"This isn't funny. For all my dad's faults, and they are presently legion, he's respected in this valley, and nobody—I do mean *nobody*—has ever dared to kick him off their property. And according to him, she also *threatened* him."

"My little mom threatened Sam Conacher." Heat rose up Cam's neck. "I'm sure he was frightened half to death."

Kirstin sat up. "Are we about to have our first fight?"

Cam pushed up beside her. "That depends on you, I guess. Your father has been obnoxious to my mother. And now you're defending him."

"I'm *not* defending him. He's been horrible to her, and I don't deny that. But he isn't used to being threatened. So now he's totally pissed. Your mom isn't in the wrong. He has no right to call you names when he's on *her* property. I totally get how she must have felt. But all that aside, Cam, my father is now gearing up to wage war, and *damn it*, for the first time in my whole life, I'm happy with a man. How do we have a chance in *hell* of building anything between us when our parents are at each other's throats? This isn't about them; it's about us."

Even in the dim light, Cam could see that her whole body was trembling, including her beautiful breasts. He yearned to pull her into his arms and comfort her. She had a point; this was about the two of them and not about their parents. But he found it hard to believe that his mother had been in the wrong. She always erred on the side of being polite. He couldn't imagine her kicking anyone off her property.

"Can we both calm down and talk about this? My mom isn't the sort of person to kick someone off her land for no good reason. I know her inside and out."

"Well, my dad has lots of faults, but lying isn't one of them. And he's very offended."

"Maybe he deserved to be offended."

"You know what, Cam? I didn't start this to place blame on anyone. In fact, it doesn't really matter to me who was at fault. What matters is that our parents are declaring war on each other, and that's going to make it really difficult for us."

"I understand. It just bothers me when you act as if my mother was rude to your father without good reason."

"I didn't say she had no reason. I only said that my father is unaccustomed to being kicked off someone's property, and he's furious."

"Yeah, well, he's always furious about something."

"I shouldn't have come to your room." She sprang from the

bed, flashing her bare bottom at him as she started grabbing her clothes.

"Kirstin, please, let's discuss this."

"Not when you're unable to discuss it rationally because you think your mother's a saint."

"Oh, ho-ho." Cam was starting to get really angry now. "Did you just imply that I'm a mama's boy?"

"If the shoe fits . . ." She bent to draw on red French-cut underwear; her lingerie was her one concession to *fancy*. Then she jerked on the tight jeans, doing a hip wiggle that made his mouth go dry. "Sorry, Cam. Sing your mom's praises to the wall. I can't handle hearing it. This isn't about what drove her to do it. It's not about how furious he is with her. It's about how their childish shenanigans are going to ruin things for us." She struggled to button her jeans and gave up. They slipped back down over her hips. "I'm falling in love with you. It's important to me that we get a fair shot at making this work. I wanted us to come up with a game plan."

Cam's surge of anger died quickly. "Kirstin, you're not alone. It's premature for me to admit it, but I'm developing deep feelings for you, too."

She straightened with her jeans still gaping open to reveal the swatch of lace that covered what he considered every man's gate to heaven. "Premature? Oh, great. I'm sorry if I rushed you into this."

Cam strove to keep a clear head. "You didn't rush me, not exactly. I simply know from experience that it's not wise to move forward too fast. Then you knocked on my door and all my good intentions to play this smart went out the window." *Wrong thing to say.* He knew it the moment he spoke. "Kirstin, please. Let's back up."

He saw by her stricken expression that he'd injured her pride. "I am so out of here!"

She'd barely gotten her shirt halfway on when she slammed out of his room.

CAM THREW ON HIS CLOTHES AND WALKED BAREFOOT UP THE hall to Kirstin's room. Her door was closed, but he could hear her inside, throwing things around. She was in a high temper. And Cam honestly couldn't blame her. No woman wanted to think she'd rushed a guy into going to bed with her. If the situation were reversed, he'd have been humiliated and hurt. Anger was sometimes the only defense a person had.

He knocked softly on the door. He doubted she'd answer, but in a moment, she jerked the portal open against the chain lock, sending a resounding *thump* up and down the hallway. It had to be at least one in the morning. It'd be just his luck that someone would place a domestic violence call to the cops.

"What?" she asked. Her pretty face twisted. Her dark blue eyes swam with tears. "Say it, and just leave."

Cam had never meant to hurt her. "I'm sorry. You're beautiful. I feel like the luckiest guy in the world to have been with you tonight."

"Yeah. And what about the premature part?"

He wished he could sit down and talk to her instead of baring his soul through the crack of a door. "I tend to be cautious in relationships, Kirstin, but that has nothing to do with you or how I feel about you. I'm the guy that knocked up his girlfriend when he was seventeen, and she divorced me before our baby was born. Remember? It was the shortest, most miserable marriage on the planet, and now she's messed up, treating husbands as if they enter her life through a revolving door." He passed a hand over his eyes. "I can't help but wonder if our brief entanglement damaged her somehow. So maybe I'm a little scared, not because you rushed me into anything, but because I'm finding it really, *really* hard to put on my emotional brakes. Does that make any sense at all to you?"

More tears sprang to her eyes. "Say you just acted like a jackass, and I'll let you in."

Cam shoved his hands into his pockets. "I just acted like a jackass."

A door opened down the hall, and an older man jutted his balding head out. "Hey!" he shouted. "I agree with her, buddy. You're a jackass! Go to a shrink. Call a help hotline. I don't give a shit, but let the rest of us sleep."

Kirstin clamped a hand over her mouth. Her cheeks went bright red. *Fabulous,* Cam thought. *Now she's laughing and crying at the same time.* She finally recovered enough to unfasten the chain. Cam pushed into the room, half afraid guys in blue uniforms would spill out of the elevator.

Kirstin closed the door softly behind him. Cam walked to the bed and sank down, noticing that she had almost finished packing her small overnight bag. He couldn't help but wonder how she'd planned to get home. They'd come in his truck.

"Where were we?" he asked, because he honestly couldn't recall how they'd gone so swiftly from passion to fighting.

Kirstin bent her head and said, "Oh, my *God.* I put my head through an armhole, one arm through an unbuttoned section of the front, and one boob is poking out the neck."

Cam started to laugh. Her breast *was* poking out. Angling an arm over the feminine protrusion, which did little to hide it, she started to laugh, too. Then she plopped down on the edge of the bed beside him.

Catching her breath, she said, "How did this happen? I'm almost certain it wasn't what I've heard people call 'the afterglow.'"

Chapter Six

CAM STARTED LAUGHING ALL OVER AGAIN. WHEN HIS MIRTH finally subsided, he said, "I think I'm way too protective of my mom, Kirstin. I'll work on that. And I'm sorry if she was rude to your father."

"I'm sure he had it coming," she replied.

"As for rushing into things," Cam said, "we are. Please don't get upset with me again for saying it, but we're just really getting to know each other."

"So you don't feel like I do."

"I didn't say that. I'm feeling way too much, way too fast. And I should know better. But for some reason, I can't seem to slow things down. I've paid for one mistake for more than seventeen years. This time I want to be absolutely sure."

"I understand." She shifted her shirt around to get it on correctly and then struggled to fasten the buttons. "I did rush things by going to your room. And I don't want to make a mistake, either. Only this doesn't feel like a mistake to me, and I think maybe, because you're older than me, you think having sex is like making a commitment. Only for people my age, it isn't necessarily that way."

"Are you implying that there's a generation gap between us?" Cam held up his hands. "I've had sex with plenty of women, and they weren't making a commitment and neither was I. It just feels different with you. And it also feels important."

She folded her arms. "It feels important to me, too. My first time with a guy, it didn't. Being with you was amazing."

Cam went still. "Um, wait a minute. Are you saying you've been with only *one* other guy? You said you'd dated several guys after the first one."

"Yeah, but I do have standards. All the others were duds."

"Well, hell." Cam leaned his head back to study the ceiling.

"It feels *right* with you. Please don't regret what we did."

"I don't regret it." He sighed. "It felt right to me, too. It *still* feels right. So maybe I'm thinking too much. When you get to be an old guy like me, you feel obligated to behave maturely."

She giggled and bumped his arm with her shoulder. "You can be as mature as you like."

"Do you see my concern? I should have known how many men you'd been with before I joined the lineup. And now I find out there isn't a line—or almost isn't one, anyway."

"You *are* thinking too much," she teased. "Dad put a lid on my social life, but he couldn't stunt my emotional growth. I'm a grown woman. I think we've found something special. If I'm wrong, I'm wrong. But why worry about it now? How do you stop feelings? I think we just need to go with the flow and see where we end up, enjoying each other as we go along."

Cam couldn't think of a better plan. "In order to do that, we need to figure out how to deal with our parents."

"Yes. Before I left, Dad was ranting and raving to Miguel, saying it's time to build a tall, sturdy barrier to keep the white trash next door off his land." Her mouth thinned. "How can we see each other if our parents are feuding? Dad was talking about a brick wall, for heaven's sake."

"Are you kidding me?"

"No, I'm *not* kidding. If he hauls in a big load of bricks, I swear I may bean him with one of them."

Cam shook his head. "It is a pickle," he admitted. "Funny thing is, Mom didn't say a word about all this to me before I left to meet you."

"Maybe she didn't want to spoil our evening. Also, she has no idea about the wall yet. She's new to the valley and may not realize how volatile Dad can be."

"Do you know any more details about what they said to each other?"

Kirstin focused on the wall, her expression thoughtful. "Well, when Dad was ranting to Miguel, he said he *would* ruin you, and then he asked how your mom dared to tell him that *his* reputation would be just as tarnished as yours before it all ended. Dad kept saying, 'Who the hell does she think she is?' Apparently she said if he started slinging dirt, she had a pretty strong pitching arm in this valley herself."

"Madeline McLendon," Cam said softly. "That's who my mother is."

"I know. At the Cowboy Tree that first day, I overheard you and Trish talking about her latest release."

"I don't think about her public persona much. But she has a gigantic Facebook following, and she wasn't talking smack. When we moved here, she had oodles of fans from the valley who posted about how excited they were to have her here." He paused and joined her in staring at the rug. "Shit, Kirstin. If Mom posts about your dad's behavior toward her, her fans will tell their friends, and their friends will tell their friends. We're going to get caught in the middle of a smear campaign."

"If it weren't so awful, I'd laugh. If anyone has that coming, it's my father." She met his gaze. "As always when it involves me, he thinks the worst and hates your guts for *defiling* his daughter. He said—his words, not mine—that I was 'tonguing your tonsils.' We got in a huge fight. I told him he wasn't welcome in my house anymore, that I'd smack him on the nose if he cracked open the door. That it's my life, and I may be entertaining a gentleman friend at night."

"You didn't give me these details in your texts this morning."

"It's difficult in texts to tell everything."

"And he now knows I'm the gentleman you might entertain."

"I don't think *gentleman* is one of his preferred nouns to describe you."

Cam chuckled. Then he sobered. "You're right. If we're going to take this relationship forward from here, we're faced with a hell of a mess."

Kirstin nodded. "And I really hope we do move forward."

Cam met her worried gaze. "When you texted about us meeting tonight, you didn't say a word to me about a brick wall."

"I know it was selfish of me. But with everything blowing up at the ranch, I was afraid I'd never get another chance to be with you. Dad was already furious and out to get you. I couldn't see how being with you tonight could make matters any worse."

He bent sideways to kiss her forehead. "True enough. He's already pissed off. And he was also already bent on doing his best to ruin me. At least we had tonight together before everything turns ugly." He trailed his lips down her cheek and gently angled his mouth over hers. The kiss turned long and deep. When he came up for air, he said, "We haven't used this bed yet, and I paid for both rooms. I think we should get our money's worth."

"Spoken like a true Scotsman. But first I want to tell you that I won't let him harm your career without a fight, Cam. No matter what happens between us, whether we can make this work or not, I'll use every weapon I have against him. You'll always be my good friend."

"Thank you for that, Kirstie. But this may end up being a battle between me and your dad. Unless, of course, my mother gets involved. Then Sam Conacher may find himself squaring off with a totally pissed-off Irishwoman. Trust me when I say I wouldn't envy him in that event. Madeline McLendon is a sweet lady, but she has one huge fault."

"Which is?"

"Do one of her loved ones wrong, and your ass is grass with her pretending to be a lawn mower." Cam frowned. "It's kind of scary when I think about it, actually. She could write a book titled 'One Thousand and One Ways to Commit Murder and Get Away with It.'"

Kirstin chortled. "Go, Madeline!" She no sooner spoke than she sobered. "She wouldn't *really* hurt Dad, would she?"

Cam grinned. "I'm guessing not." He glanced behind her at the untouched bed and wished he had her lying on it. He locked an arm around her and gently rolled her onto her back. "You're so damned beautiful, Kirstie. I can't keep my hands off you."

She smiled and bent a denim-clad leg over his hip. "Then don't try."

He cupped her face between his hands. "This old guy has one more thing he wants to say. In relationships, no matter how fabulous they seem at first, a smart woman holds part of her heart in reserve until she knows for sure that things will work out."

"Are you holding part of your heart in reserve?"

Cam kissed her and groaned against her lips. "No, damn it. And I know it's not smart."

She trailed a kiss along his jaw and then whispered in his ear, "Then just let go and be foolish with me."

• • •

MORNING CAME EARLY FOR CAM AND KIRSTIN. HE RETURNED TO his room to quickly shower and dress, then met her in the hall. Even with her hair still damp, she looked beautiful. She'd dressed for work on the ranch, her clothing less flashy than the previous night. In only minutes, they were in his truck and headed south toward home, both of them sipping lattes.

The moment Cam pulled the truck out onto Highway 93 and got up to traffic speed, Kirstin resurrected her concerns about their parents. "We didn't really solve much of anything last night, Cam. I can't help but be worried. I *think* I can bully Dad into backing off, but what if I can't? And what if he obliterates any chance you have? Your family is depending on you to bring in an income."

"I'm licensed in Idaho, too. And I can be there and back in a day. I suggest that we ignore your dad's threats. He can't hold a grudge against me forever." He sent her a reassuring grin. "And I've got my charming personality to fall back on. Ranchers may hear negative stuff about me, but I'll do everything possible to overcome that. I'm good at what I do, and this is a perfect place for someone with a background in both fish and game biology to sell ranches. I can show potential buyers land and knowledgeably point out its varying topography, along with the wildlife species it may attract."

She turned her cup in her hands. "And us? Or do you think there'll even be a chance for us?"

Cam fixed his attention on the road. "After last night, I sure hope we'll move forward from here, Kirstie. We'll deal with our parents somehow so we can see each other."

"Thinking positively, Cam, what if this is the real deal, and later we end up wanting to get married?"

"Whoa. Where did you tuck that part of your heart I asked you to reserve?"

"It's in my shirt pocket. Judging by how great things are between us, is it so crazy of me to think of the possibilities?"

"No, it's not crazy. You're like an unexpected miracle to me, Kirstie. A dream I had started to think might never come true. My next chapter. Remember? If neither of us starts to feel differently, getting married would be the logical outcome. In the event that we do make it official and eventually have a baby, we'll establish strict visitation rules for our parents. If they can't be civil to each other, they'll have to take turns visiting. If one of them misbehaves, he or she won't be invited again."

Kirstin sent him a surprised look. "You're hoping to have a baby? You're almost finished raising Caleb. Surely you aren't thinking about starting all over again?"

"I'm only thirty-five, and as much as I've loved raising Caleb with the unflagging assistance of my parents, it wasn't a normal situation. In college, I took a full course load and worked. I squeezed in all the time I could with him. My parents were wonderful, and he certainly didn't lack for attention or love. But I missed out on so many little things, coming home at night barely in time to rock him to sleep when he was small, to read a bedtime story when he got older. I missed seeing him take his first step. He lost his first tooth when I was working. I can't count the times I couldn't be with him when he got sick. I'd like a chance to be there for almost everything with my second child."

Her answering smile made her face glow. "I'm so glad. I really want a baby."

"Only one?"

"Well, I'd actually like three, but if you and I are together, we'll already have Caleb."

"Maybe we'll shoot for two, then—if we're together. Don't pull that piece of your heart out of your pocket yet."

She huffed under her breath.

"I'm only asking that you keep both feet on the ground," Cam told her. "I may have a load of bad habits you haven't discovered yet. Little things that will drive you crazy."

"I've already discovered one. You assume because of my limited experience and lesser age that I'm emotionally unprepared to deal with falling in love and getting my heart broken. I'll soon be twenty-seven. I've dealt with a lot of shit. I had to shoot a horse once. Have you ever done that?"

Cam swallowed hard. "I can't imagine having to do something like that."

"I'm not sixteen. Why does everyone treat me as if I am? First my dad, now you. It's starting to piss me off."

Cam glanced over at her. "You're right. I'm sorry." He turned his attention back to the road. "We've talked about so many deep subjects, and you never told me about having to shoot a horse."

"Trust me, if you ever have to do that, you'll never want to talk about it, either." She bent her head. "It was Dad's horse, his favorite one. We were way up in the mountains on one of our grazing parcels. A bank gave way under him and the horse, and they tumbled more than forty feet down a steep and rocky slope. The horse had open compound fractures in both front legs. It was in agony. We couldn't wait for hours until a vet could get there to euthanize it. We couldn't get it down the mountain to the trailer to take it in. Dad tried to shoot it. He'd put the end of the rifle barrel on its forehead, curl his finger over the trigger, and then lower the gun to his side. He loved the horse so much he couldn't do it, so I had to. Sometimes you do what you have to do and think about it later. My dad was bleeding and banged up. I had to get him off the mountain and to a hospital."

Cam wasn't sure what to say. "I'd have nightmares."

"Oh, yeah. They always end with a loud *bang* and me sitting straight up in bed with sweat pouring off me. My point is that I'm perfectly capable of living through a breakup. Stop trying to protect me. I know how to pick myself up and glue myself back together again."

Cam nodded. "Request granted."

NORMALLY MADDIE WENT STRAIGHT TO WORK IN THE MORNING, but Sam Conacher's implied threat yesterday to ruin Cam's future in the valley had her signing on to her Facebook page instead. Over the years, her fans had become her loyal friends, and since moving to Montana with Cam, she had discovered that several of them lived in the Bitterroot Valley. If Conacher went on a campaign to tarnish her son's reputation, would those people rally behind her?

Maddie took several sips of tea as she considered what, if anything, she should post. Sasha, the fluffy black cat, came to perch on the arm of Maddie's recliner and stared at the lighted screen as if she stood by to offer counsel. "So, my dear, I have to be careful here," Maddie said. "I shouldn't mention Conacher's name. People will guess who I'm talking about. Bitterrooters know their valley by heart." She gnawed her lip. "As long as I don't give any particulars, he can't sue me. Right?"

"Meow" was the cat's reply.

"I'm glad you're with me on that. So I'll give no details and only the bare bones of what I believe that evil man may do."

Maddie phrased her post to be a plea for help, heading it with WHAT SHOULD I DO? Her readers loved to be involved in her life and offer advice. When Maddie finished the brief draft, she read it carefully to be sure she'd included nothing over which Sam could file a lawsuit. Then she published the message, waited for a response, and refreshed the page every minute or so to load more replies. She was soon beaming a smile. Her Montana fans voiced concern, anger, and a willingness to do anything they could to help her. One male reader wrote, I don't know who this dude is, but he'd better understand the powerful reach of social media. He can't ruin your son's reputation in a lasting way, because we'll network to tell the truth, and before long, most people in the valley will have heard it. He'd better think before he shoots off his mouth.

Maddie grinned. She had a cyberspace army behind her. *Bring it on, Sam Conacher,* she thought. *I'm ready to nail you to a wall.*

SAM CAME IN FROM A HARD DAY'S WORK FEELING SO EXHAUSTED that he stood under a hot shower to get some of the soreness out of his muscles. Once dressed in clean clothing, he wandered downstairs to the kitchen, keeping his gaze fixed on the floor as he walked because the stairwell walls sported dozens of family pictures. Annie holding Kirstin as a baby. Annie and him standing next to a stream, their faces creased in smiles. Kirstin at all different ages. Looking at those photos brought back memories that nearly broke his heart. He'd tried once to take them all down, but he hadn't been able to erase Annie from his life.

"Evening, Mrs. Alvarez," he said to his housekeeper and cook as he entered the huge kitchen.

"Good evening, senor." A pretty woman with an attractive figure, she filled one end of the long plank table with his place setting, two serving bowls, and a small platter. Sam had tried to explain that he'd be just as happy with a filled plate and flatware, but she hadn't understood him and had stacked every dish in the cupboard in front of him. "Senorita Conacher?"

Sam knew she was asking if Kirstin would be joining him for dinner. He had been told the woman's first name, but he couldn't remember it. She was a pleasant person and a hard worker, and she seemed to enjoy her job. Sam wondered if his inability to communicate well with her contributed to the fact that she'd been with him for more than a year. He couldn't easily insult someone who understood only memorized English phrases. He guessed he should have thanked his lucky stars that he spoke no Spanish. He might have been left to clean the house himself and do all his own cooking. He had a talent for pissing off workers and making them quit. Trying to run his ranch with only Kirstin and Miguel to help him was already more than he could handle.

"Senorita not come," he said as he sat at the head of the table. He sounded like an Indian chief in an old black-and-white movie. Kirstin had loaded a translation app on his cell phone once. Sam had soon gotten rid of it. The first and only time he'd tried to tell Mrs. Alvarez something, he'd asked her in Spanish to do something disgusting. He couldn't remember for sure what, but he thought he'd told her to go outside and hump the horse. She'd run from the house in tears. To this day, Sam didn't understand *how* what he'd typed had turned into something awful. Fortunately, Miguel spoke fluent English, saw the text, and got his wife calmed down enough for her to laugh about it. Miguel had later explained to Sam that slang words didn't translate well. When he wanted to send Mrs. Alvarez translated messages, he had to write them in formal English. Hell, Sam wasn't sure he even *spoke* formal English.

The woman tidied up the kitchen, bade Sam good night in Spanish—at least he'd learned what *buenas noches* meant—and left the house. As Sam tucked into his meal—pot roast with gravy over mashed potatoes, and a salad on the side—his mind drifted back to yesterday when that woman next door had kicked him off her property. All he'd done was try to apologize and then mentioned that it was a small valley. What the hell was her problem? What really bugged him, though, was her threat to sling dirt back at him, the implication being that she carried more weight in this area than he did.

He had to find time to get on his computer tonight and learn her name. *Simple enough,* he assured himself. Land sales were undoubtedly a matter of public record. Only when Sam got on his system later, he was soon so frustrated that he wanted to throw the desktop out a window. *Fuck this*, he decided. He'd stop trying to dig up the information and just call a neighbor. Somebody along Fox Hollow Road surely knew who had purchased that damned land.

Sam looked at his phone contacts and rejected one rancher after another. *He's a prick.* Next one. *Hell, no. Screw him and the horse he rode in on.* The next name made him clench his teeth. *Oh, yeah, my onetime best friend, Frank. Where the hell were you after Annie died? Europe, that's where, celebrating your forty-fifth anniversary with your wife. Well, Annie didn't live long enough for us to celebrate that occasion, you jackass.*

Sam decided to call the only person he figured would speak to him, a little old lady whose house sat on the south side of Fox Hollow Road. Sam went over every summer to cut and bale her alfalfa. When he had time, he dropped by to fix things for her. She never failed to make him mint cookies as a thank-you and then call him to come pick them up. He fed them to his dogs because they tasted like toothpaste. Even the dogs had turned up their noses at the last batch. He needed to ask her to make chocolate chip, he guessed, but she was such a sweet old thing, as frail as a bird and thinking her husband was still alive sometimes. He didn't want to hurt her feelings.

Sam rang her number. When she picked up, he said, "Hi, Mrs. Pedigrew? This is Sam Conacher across the road."

In a shrill, shaky voice, she said, "Oh, Mr. Conacher, how lovely to hear from you. How are you?"

"I'm good." Sam wanted to get to the point, but for her, he'd be cordial. "How about you?"

"Oh, I'm very worried. Herman is awfully late getting home. I called the Cowboy Tree. He wasn't there. Knowing that silly man, he probably went to another bar."

Sam tried to think what to say. He didn't want the old lady to walk the floors half the night, waiting for her husband to get home, but at the same time, he didn't want to remind her that Herm was dead, either. She might fly into full-blown hysteria. Normally after spells like this, she woke up right as rain the next morning. He'd been through this with her before, and he'd gone over the following day to check on her. "Um, do you think he may be at a cattle sale somewhere? Bozeman, I believe, is having one this week. If that's where Herm went, he won't get home until tomorrow."

"Oh, my stars, you're right! I'm such a silly old lady. He probably told me, and I forgot."

Sam wished that he could sometimes believe Annie was still alive. Then again, maybe not. He didn't think he could survive losing her over and over. "Um—Mrs. Pedigrew, have you met our new neighbor who bought the acreage across the road from you?"

"Oh, shame that it is, I don't visit neighbors that much anymore, but I heard she joined our book club two weeks ago and gave an interesting talk." She went on to explain that she'd missed that meeting due to a doctor's appointment.

"A talk? About what?"

"Novel structure. She's a writer. I've read many of her books. Wonderful murder mysteries. Her name is right on the tip of my tongue. Madeline something."

The back of Sam's neck prickled. "Madeline? Is her last name, by any chance, McLendon?"

"Oh, yes, that's it! Her stories are amazing. Have you read any of them?"

Sam had read all of them except her latest, which he hadn't finished yet. He gripped the phone harder, but he let Mrs. Pedigrew rattle on. She hopped from topic to topic, and his ear was starting to ache before he could politely end the conversation.

SAM PACED THE LIVING ROOM, TRYING TO WRAP HIS MIND AROUND the fact that the woman who'd written the books he went through like candy was living next door in that damned trash heap. *No wonder she acted as if she was somebody,* he thought. *She's a famous author.* It riled Sam to no end that she actually might have the wherewithal to ruin his reputation in the valley. Then amusement replaced his anger. What Ms. McLendon didn't know was that he'd already ruined his reputation with no help from her. She couldn't do any more damage unless she murdered him. That was a sobering thought.

As he circled the room again, Sam came to the conclusion that he didn't care what people thought of him. Dying didn't scare him, either. He was a Montanan, born and bred. He'd come from poor folk and scrabbled his way up from nothing to own one of the largest operations in the area. People might not like him, but they respected him, and that woman had no idea whom she was pitting herself against.

Sam grabbed Madeline's latest release, *Death by Potato Sprouts*, from the arm of his recliner and tried to rip it apart with his bare hands. The damned thing felt as thick as a phone book. He strained so hard trying to break the spine that his stomach muscles panged. *Damn*. With a slump of his shoulders, Sam accepted that he wasn't as strong as he'd once been. Arthritis had taken up residence in his hands, and trying to tear a book to shreds made his thumbs hurt. Giving up, he tossed the paperback on the floor and stomped it with the heel of his boot. "If I can't get rid of you one way, I'll do it another. My name is Sam Conacher!"

Sam whirled away. Then he got a great idea. He could burn all his McLendon books.

CAM HAD GONE WITH CALEB TO A HIGH SCHOOL FOOTBALL game, and Maddie had been left for the evening to fend for herself. At first she had wondered what she would do. Normally her guys kept her company. Out of habit, she gravitated to the cook shack. Not wishing to dirty a bunch of dishes, she plugged in the George Foreman grill to make a melted cheese sandwich and heated a paper bowl of tomato soup in the microwave. For weeks they'd had no electricity except for that produced by her trailer generator. Now that temporary power had been installed, she felt like she was living in the lap of luxury.

She ate near the radiant heat of the woodstove, sitting in one of the upholstered swivel rockers with her feet propped on a log that would later fuel the fire. *This is the life,* she thought. When she finished her meal, she opened her e-reader and took a sip of chardonnay. All three dogs slept near her, their snores blending into a rhythmic sound that suited her mood. LED lightbulbs hung from the ceiling cross braces and illuminated the butter-colored canvas, creating a cozy golden glow. It made her think of being in a tipi. Maddie liked it so much that she was seriously thinking about replicating the effect when she painted the interior of her house. Natural. Earthy. Warm.

The eerie sound of a bugling bull elk came from the pasture. Maddie sighed and set her reading device aside. She heard the call again and smiled. Their camp was smack-dab in the middle of nature. Who wanted to read when they could listen to the creatures that lurked in the darkness? Next an owl screeched. Maddie suspected it was the great horned owl that liked to perch at the top of a dead snag standing just behind the tent. She'd seen him several times and marveled at his beauty. He was large enough to grab one of her cats and fly away with it. No worries about that right now. The felines were all safe in their house or the trailer.

Maddie finished her wine and decided, since her oncologist had said it was okay for her to imbibe in moderation, to treat herself to another glass while she enjoyed the solitude. Not that she felt alone. How could she with three sleeping dogs, an owl, and a herd of elk nearby? Working her way through the swivel chairs, she went to the side-by-side refrigerator and refilled her cup. Gone were the days of sipping from fine crystal—at least until their homes were completed. Here all drinking vessels were plastic. After resuming her seat, she listened to the fire in the woodstove snap and pop.

Minutes later, she realized that the wine, along with her daily quota of bottled water, had gone straight through her. Because it had grown pitch-dark, she collected her flashlight—a recent gift from Cam—which was encased in a thick rubbery substance that enabled it to float if she accidentally dropped it in the river or slough. Not that she would. Cam had searched high and low to find her a device with a fabulous cushioned grip.

Only Bingo got up to go outside with her. Bear and Boomer kept snoozing.

"I'll be fine, Bingo. If I trip on the rough ground and can't get up, I can call for help with my cell," she assured the dog, but Bingo followed her anyway.

Maddie could have gone to her trailer to use the restroom, but at night while she spent time in their community area, she found it faster to use Old Blue, a portable toilet a few feet away from Cam's cabin. It was regularly pumped and cleaned by the service provider, and periodically replaced with a freshly sterilized unit. Keeping the light trained on the ground, where large rocks, sticks, and other trip hazards hid in the shadows, she made her way to the enclosure. Bingo waited outside.

It grew chilly along the river after the sun went down. Maddie shivered as she laid her oversize flashlight next to the black toilet seat. After she finished her business and stood, the portable facility shifted slightly as she drew her jeans back up and fastened them. *What the heck?* She guessed that a new unit must have been delivered sometime that day, and the man hadn't made sure the replacement was sitting on level ground. She deliberately rocked sideways to see. With her back to the seat, the lid of which she hadn't yet closed, she heard a soft rumbling sound followed by a splash.

"Oh, no. Not my light!" Maddie whirled around, and sure enough, a glare beamed up through the hole. She tried never to look down into the collection tank. The company used a dark blue chemical in there to eliminate odor. As harmless as it might smell, looking inside was nauseating. "Oh, my poor light."

It bobbed and turned in the chemical waves caused by the splash. Maddie stared down at it, trying to think of some way she could fish it out of there. She groaned and leaned closer to measure the distance. In the trailer she had a reaching device that she used to pick things up off the floor. That might work, and she could clean it afterward. Cam had probably paid a handsome price for that light, and she hated to tell him that the gift he'd gotten her had fallen into what he called the shitter.

Just as she started to straighten, her cell phone fell from her shirt pocket. Maddie tried to catch it, but it followed the flashlight into the hole. *"Shit! No, no, no!"*

That phone had cost her a small fortune. She'd replaced her old one right before she moved here, and she'd chosen a device that supposedly could withstand submersion in water. She'd known she would be next to a river, after all, and she was a methodical person who thought ahead when she purchased things. Well, now she would put that phone to the test. Adding chemicals into the equation, she doubted it would last one minute, let alone the purported time, which, if she recalled correctly, had been an hour and a half.

"Damn it. Damn it. Now if I take a spill going back to the tent, how will I call for help?"

Bingo barked. Maddie heard a diesel truck approaching. The next instant, headlights washed over the wall of the outdoor toilet. *Maybe,* she thought, *Cam and Caleb are home early.*

SAM HAD RUN INTO TOWN FOR A SIX-PACK BEFORE HE STARTED HIS book-burning party. As he exacted his revenge on Madeline McLendon, he wanted to enjoy himself and have a couple of beers. Once he'd come through the automatic gate to get back to the ranch, he'd wondered if his vision had gone wonky. Out near the McLendon camp, a huge blue rectangle glowed in the dark. What the hell was it? Crazy things like spaceships flitted through his mind.

Curiosity got the better of Sam, and he drove onto the McLendon land, not caring if Madeline called the cops on him. Hell, if she got a rise out of the local police, he would just pay the fine. He angled his truck so the beams pointed straight at the object, which turned out to be a blue portable toilet similar to those used on construction sites. Without turning off the truck engine, Sam swung out of his vehicle. Just as he did, Madeline emerged from the enclosure. An aging black-tri Australian shepherd charged toward Sam with its hackles up. He liked dogs better than he did most people, so he stepped clear of the open driver door and hunkered down. The dog slowed its approach.

"Hello, old man." The dog advanced with caution, but it finally got close enough for Sam to give it a friendly scratch behind the ears. Smiling up at *Madeline the Horrible*, he said, "I saw that you're running a blue-light special. I just had to check it out. Thought maybe the cathouse was open for business, and you wanted to give first-time customers a special deal."

She rested her fists on her hips. "Sorry. I'm the only woman on this land, and I'm a dead unit from the neck down."

Awash in his headlights, she looked as if she wanted to go a few rounds with him in a boxing ring. Sam wanted no part of that. He'd had it ingrained in him by his father that no man worth his salt ever struck a woman. "Too bad. A whorehouse next door would be more entertaining than the Beverly Hillbillies."

"Do you go out of your way to be obnoxious? Or were you just born that way?"

"Well, now, Madeline, there's a good question."

"Maddie, please, if we're moving to a first-name basis. I'll point out, however, that it may be a bad idea. My son is Cam. You're Sam. It could get confusing."

"I doubt there'll be any confusion. No intention on my side to ever be that chummy with folks of your ilk."

"'Ilk'?" Her smile was more a sneer. "I'm surprised you know that word." She squinted her eyes against his headlights. "And how did you find out who I am?"

Sam felt off-balance, and he couldn't think why. As he watched her bend to pat her dog's head when the animal returned to her, he thought she looked more vulnerable than she had before, smaller, less sure of herself. Maybe that was because darkness had fallen and she was apparently out here alone. Anyway, he no longer wanted to zing her with nasty comments. "A little lady across the road, surname of Pedigrew, told me who you are. Her husband, Herm, died a while back. I try to look after her and take care of her place. She can't do the heavy work."

"Samuel Conacher taking care of an elderly neighbor? That's a new twist. Maybe there's something about you that I can find to like, after all."

"Don't count on it."

Just then Sam heard a ringtone. His phone made that sound, and in stores he'd heard other devices that mimicked it. He tilted his head. "What the hell is that? It's one thing to have a glowing shitter, but one that also calls you? You're getting pretty high-tech out here."

"Are you enjoying yourself, Sam?"

"I'm having a blast. How about you?"

"I'm wishing I had a shotgun."

"That'd be sweet. Maybe it would end up in the john with your flashlight and cell."

"I really don't have time for this. And we both know you're only guessing. I have electricity here. Maybe I ran a cord to the outhouse and installed a light. I also heard you pulling in, and I may have come out to see who was here and just left my phone behind me."

"Not bad, but I've heard more believable stories. For an author, it sucks." He inclined his head at the restroom unit glowing behind her. "What else but a high-powered flashlight could make that toilet look like a psychedelic phallic symbol?"

"Okay. So what if I dropped my flashlight down the hole? Things happen. It's an expensive device, waterproof, and it floats. I was trying to think of some way to fish it out before my son gets home. It's a gift from him."

"That the same son who can't keep his pecker in his britches?"

In silhouette, he saw her shoulders straighten. *Good,* he thought. *She's a worthier opponent when she's pissed off.*

"You're just nasty to the core, aren't you?"

Sam shrugged. "I'm like that John Wayne toilet paper in your glowing toilet: rough, tough, and don't take shit off anybody." He turned to get back in his truck and then hesitated. "I'll do you one favor, Maddie McLendon. Never expect another one. I'll stay parked here so you can use my headlights to make it safely back to camp."

"No, thanks. I have a flashlight app on my cell phone."

"Your phone is obviously swimming in the toilet tank with your flashlight. Pride comes before the fall. Don't be stupid. Walk back while you can see."

"I still need to fish out my flashlight. A gentleman would offer to help me."

He couldn't help but laugh. "Well, thank God, I've never claimed to be a gentleman. In my estimation, that's a flashlight that should be permanently retired."

Just as Sam started to swing back into his vehicle, she called out, "Hey, Sam! What is it that you don't understand about someone telling you not to trespass on her land?"

Sam laughed again, which he didn't do often. She was more fun than a barrelful of monkeys. "The warning you gave me wouldn't hold up in a court of law. It'd fall into the 'he said, she said' category. You ever heard of putting up no-trespassing signs? Take a picture of them with a camera that records the date. Then maybe, just *maybe*, you can actually prosecute me."

"Asshole!" she shouted after him. "As of tomorrow, this land will be posted with signs every ten feet!"

"Did I just hear you call me a bad name? Not nice, Maddie. You led me to believe that you wouldn't say shit if you had a mouthful. And, please, post your land every ten feet. I get a kick out of running over signs."

AS CONACHER DROVE AWAY, MADDIE WAS SHAKING WITH ANGER. "Asshole!" she yelled again. "You redefine the word!"

Bingo whined. When she looked down at him, she noticed that his black fur shimmered blue. She turned to study the portable toilet, wondering how long it would take for the battery in that floating flashlight to go dead. Their camp was already a topic of conversation among people who drove along Fox Hollow Road. Now gossipers would whisper about the john that glowed in the dark.

Turning toward camp, Maddie wished she had that stupid phone. Somebody had called her. She hoped it had been her sister, Naomi, or her daughter, Grace, and not Cam. He worried about her out here, and when his calls to her went unanswered, his imagination went into overdrive.

She used the faint illumination from the outhouse to pick her way past Cam and Caleb's cabin. She'd make it back to the cook shack without falling, she assured herself. There was no way in hell she'd ever let Sam Conacher say, "I told you so."

WHEN SAM GOT HOME, HE PREPARED TO HAVE A BOOK ROAST. HE went behind the barn to get the burning barrel. He placed it a safe distance from his front veranda, where he and Annie had once dreamed of sitting in rocking chairs when they got old to watch their grandchildren play. So many of their dreams had now turned to dust and left a sour taste in Sam's mouth. He was sixty-eight and alone. He and Annie had waited to have a family until he got the ranch operating in the black. He'd been over forty when Kirstin was born, and the other children they'd hoped to have had never come along.

Refusing to let himself think any longer about Annie and all the sadness, he went into his den to gather up every book he owned that had been written by Madeline McLendon. He tossed at least thirty into the barrel. Ever conscious of fire danger, even at this time of year, he hooked up a garden hose to a nearby spigot before he used his long-nosed barbecue lighter to set fire to the books.

"Take that, Madeline McLendon, with your high-and-mighty attitude. And this is only for starters!" He walked to his truck and opened the passenger door to grab a cold beer. "If you're half-way smart, you don't lock horns with Sam Conacher. You may be a hoity-toity writer, but you're small potatoes in this valley compared to me."

The fire went out. When Sam walked over and peered into the dark abyss, he could have sworn those smoldering books smirked at him. He pried off the bottle cap with his front teeth. *Shit!* His lower incisors felt as if he'd just pulled them out with a pair of pliers. *Ouch! Son of a bitch!* He tasted for blood. Checked the teeth with his tongue to make sure they were still there. Sam sighed, feeling older than dirt. As a younger man, he'd always snapped the caps off bottles with his teeth, and it had never hurt. Annie used to fuss at him over the habit, saying he'd ruin his smile and end up wearing dentures. Now he couldn't pop off caps anymore. Sam knew he no longer had the physical endurance he'd once taken for granted. He'd also noticed he wasn't quite as strong as he'd once been. His whole body was going to hell in a handbasket.

He took a swallow of beer to wash the metallic taste of pain away. His teeth panged. He shook his head, determined to drink at least three beers and enjoy his book roast. Only he'd need some diesel to get a fire started. That woman's books were as stubborn and difficult as she was. Why was it so hard for her to understand what an insult it was to him when her son diddled his daughter any old time the mood struck him? Possibly even in a public walking area, for Christ's sake.

Sam set his beer on the front fender of his truck and walked to the huge workshop that sat to the left of the barn. Without turning on a light, he located the can of diesel. When he got back to the barrel, he splashed in enough to incinerate a whole library. The next instant he felt himself flying backward. A loud *ka-boom* rang in his ears. *Holy shit!* Sam couldn't think what had happened.

From a distance, Sam heard Kirstin screaming. As her voice drew closer, Sam's senses cleared. He could tell he wasn't badly hurt, only stunned.

"Oh, dear God, Daddy, what have you done?" Kirstin ran around him in circles, her flashlight bobbing. "You used *gas*?"

"Thought it was diesel."

She shone her light on the fuel can. "It's *red*, Dad! Remember the rule—red for gas, green for diesel."

"It was dark. I didn't turn on the light. I guess I grabbed the wrong can. Damn it. I've lost my night vision, too." Sam closed his eyes. "Must have been the embers down in there. Diesel doesn't normally explode like that."

Kirstin circled him again. As he struggled to regain his feet, he felt as if a mule had kicked his tailbone. From the corner of his eye, he saw Kirstin pick up something from the ground. "Oh, Daddy, your favorite Stetson. The front of the brim is scorched."

Forgetting about his aching ass, Sam snatched the hat out of her hand. Annie had given it to him for his birthday years ago. In the play of the light, Sam saw that he had ruined it. Piece by piece, he was losing everything in the world that mattered to him. First his wife, now his daughter and his blasted hat. Tears he refused to shed stung his eyes. He clamped the Stetson back on his head. "No harm done. I can still wear it."

"Not in town, I hope." She went onto her tiptoes to look into the flaming barrel. "What are you burning at this hour?"

"Books."

She huffed like a disgruntled mare. "Madeline McLendon books, I'm betting. That's the most childish thing I've ever seen you do."

"Why childish? She writes pulp fiction. I don't like reading them anymore, and I don't want books I hate taking up space on my shelves, end of story."

"You lie like a rug," she snapped back. "You *love* her writing."

She turned away from the fire, her face cast into shadow with the flames dancing behind her. "Oh, dear God, Daddy."

Sam realized that she was spotlighting his face. "What?" Blinded by the brightness, he reached up to feel. "Am I bleeding?"

"No. But you did singe off your mustache and eyebrows."

Chapter Seven

SAM STOMPED INTO THE UPSTAIRS MASTER BATH AND STARED at his face in the mirror. *No real harm done*, he concluded. He'd just use his handy little nose trimmer to even up his brows and mustache. He grabbed the trimmer, which was black and about the size of a Magic Marker. He buzzed off a little here. He snipped more there. Then his hand jerked, and he nicked the lower edge of one brow, turning it into an upside-down V. He swore under his breath, avoiding the F word because this had once been Annie's bedroom, and she'd hated vile language.

"Now I look like Groucho Marx."

Then Sam remembered his six-pack. He had five more beers out in the yard, and he'd damn well guzzle every one of them while he waited for those books to burn. Sitting on the edge of the front porch, he plucked a longneck from the carton and drew his all-purpose tool from his pocket. He fumbled with it in the shadows, trying to find the damned opener. He found a little knife and a small set of pliers. By the time he drew out the tool he needed, he no longer wanted the beer. And he no longer cared about his face. Cows and horses paid no attention to such things.

. . .

WHEN HIS DAD PULLED HIS TRUCK UP BESIDE THE CABIN, CALEB, sitting in the passenger seat, peered out the windshield and said, "Holy shit, Dad. Our outhouse glows."

His father cut the engine and stared. "What the hell? Old Blue looks like a fat, squat laser torch."

Caleb started to laugh. "I know what it is. I bet Gram dropped her new flashlight down the hole. Her cell phone wouldn't be that bright."

With a groan, his dad got out of the truck and walked to the outhouse. Caleb followed, but he hung back at the door. It was a tight fit in there. "Sure enough," his dad said over his shoulder, "the gift I got Gram is floating in our shitter."

"You gonna fish it out?" Caleb asked from behind him. "It's got something like a thousand lumen hours."

His dad shut the seat lid. "Nope. It'll just have to go dead. Hopefully it isn't as waterproof as advertised, because I'm not reaching in there, not even with gloves."

They walked toward the cook shack, which shone golden in the darkness. Caleb saw his dad grin at him. "I know camping out here is difficult for Gram, but we've done everything we can to make her comfortable, and the truth is, I love it here."

"Me, too," Caleb agreed. "Gram has a nice trailer, too, and now that you ordered a big propane tank for it, she'll be able to run the forced-air heat twenty-four-seven when winter comes."

They found Gram in the wall tent. A roaring fire snapped and crackled in the woodstove. She sat in a swivel rocker with her feet propped on a log. Behind her was the stand-alone utility sink.

She glanced up from her e-reader, which sported a red book-style cover. "How was the game?"

"It was killer," Caleb told her. "The Rustlers were losing until the last quarter, and then they poured on the steam."

"We were on the edge of our seats, Mom." His father stepped around Gram to get a bottle of water from the stainless-steel fridge. "How'd your evening go? Did you get lonely?"

"Heck, no. I'm sure you noticed that my flashlight fell in the portable toilet."

"Hard not to notice. I told you the surface around the seat is slightly sloped so water will drain off when it's hosed down."

Gram chuckled. "Yes, but my smaller flashlight never rolled over the edge of the seat. Somehow the man who changed out the toilet today didn't set it on level ground. It rocks when you move in there. That monster flashlight you got me wasn't stopped by a quarter-inch rim of plastic." She sighed. "When I bent over, trying to decide how to get it out, my cell phone fell from my pocket and dived in after it."

"Not your phone, Gram!" Caleb didn't much care about the flashlight, but her new phone had all the bells and whistles that he wished his did. "*That* is a bummer. Will your insurance cover it?"

Gram nodded. "Otherwise the evening went fairly well. Except for the fact that the blue glow drew the attention of our neighbor."

"Oh, no," his dad said.

Caleb's ears perked up. "You mean Sam Conacher? What did he say to you this time? There's something wrong with that old man."

Gram sent his father a warning look. "Nothing's wrong with him. He's just a little . . ."

Her voice trailed away, and his dad jumped in with "Eccentric."

"Anyway," Gram continued, "he stopped to ask if I was running a blue-light special."

His dad laughed. Caleb frowned. He didn't know what a blue-light special was.

Gram smiled at him. "I rarely shopped at Kmart when you were little, honey. You've probably never seen a blue strobe light flashing inside a store. I'm not even sure Kmart still runs those surprise sales."

"Does our neighbor think we're selling things here?" Caleb asked.

His dad got a funny look on his face, the look that Caleb had come to realize meant that he was too young to hear about certain things. He hated that. He was sixteen, not a baby anymore.

"It may look like we're having a garage sale with so much stuff everywhere." His dad sat in a rocker across from Gram, searching her face as if to see if she was upset. All Caleb noted was that she looked a little tired. "Well, it's good to know you got some company while we were gone."

Gram patted her e-reader. "I don't need visitors. I thought about watching a film in the cabin, but I couldn't work up any enthusiasm. Movies aren't as much fun when you guys aren't here. I spent the first part of my evening listening to the wildlife. I heard a bull elk bugle twice."

"We saw them as we drove in, Gram. A whole herd of them. Dad guesses maybe eighty."

His father's phone vibrated. He withdrew it from his pocket and smiled when he saw who the message was from. Caleb suspected that it was Kirstin who'd just texted. His dad seemed to really like her. Caleb hoped it worked out between them—his dad needed someone special in his life. And no matter what Gram thought, the savings on fuel would be *huge* if his girlfriend lived next door. Guys *did* think about things like that.

His dad started to laugh. Gram asked, "What's so funny?"

Dad shook his head. "I shouldn't share this, but maybe it's a good lesson for all of us that God will somehow take us to task when we're ornery to others for no good reason."

Caleb hoped it was that mean old rancher who'd had a piece of bad luck.

"It's from Kirstin," his father revealed. "She wrote, and I quote, 'My dad burned all his Madeline McLendon books. Mistook gasoline for diesel. Minor explosion. His hat is ruined, and his facial hair took a hard hit.'"

Caleb gulped back a startled laugh.

"What?" Gram asked. "Why on earth would that stupid man burn all my books?"

Caleb noted that his grandmother didn't seem to care if Sam Conacher had singed all the hair off his face, only that he'd burned her stories. That seemed out of character for her. Most times she would have been worried that their neighbor might have been hurt. Caleb guessed she had a real hate case for Conacher. Caleb didn't blame her.

THE NEXT AFTERNOON, WHEN CALEB GOT HOME FROM SCHOOL, he saw Gram on their shared private road pounding stakes into the ground about ten feet apart. If it hadn't been for the NO TRESPASSING signs on each one, he would have thought she was building a crooked fence. Caleb stopped his beaten-up old truck and put it in park.

After jumping out of the vehicle, he cried, "Gram, what're you doin'?"

She pounded on the metal some more with a carpenter hammer. "I'm posting our land."

Caleb figured she needed a sledge to drive those stakes deep enough to withstand another windstorm. "Do you really need this many signs?"

She slanted him a surly look. "A certain trespasser may try to ignore them. I figure he can't if he trips over them."

Caleb hooked his thumbs through his belt loops. "You talking about Sam Conacher?"

"Go to the front of the class."

"I know you don't like him, Gram, but that's no reason to be mad at me."

She lowered the hammer to her side, pushed at her windblown hair, and turned to give him a weary smile. "I'm sorry, darling. I'm just in a bit of a grump." She gestured at the stakes. "This is a lot more work than I expected."

Caleb walked over and took the hammer away from her. "I'll finish for you. It'll go faster with a sledge." He gave the property perimeter a measuring look. "How far do you want them to go?"

"Clear to the bloody corner."

Caleb gave her a startled look. "This close together? Gram, that'll take a lot of signs."

"I bought more than two hundred. If that isn't enough, I'll get more."

For the first time in his life Caleb wondered if his grandmother had lost some of her marbles. "Okay. While I'm putting them in, why don't you go take a rest? I have something important I need to talk to you about, and I want you to be out of your grump."

"Give me a ride home, and we can talk while I get over my grump enjoying a cup of tea. You can pound in stakes later."

Caleb drove Gram back to her trailer. Once inside, he sat at her small table while she made them both ginger tea. She had rain spots on the outside of her window. He made a mental note to wash it for her. Gram was a clean freak.

When she finally sat across from him and gave him an expectant look, Caleb got the nervous jitters. "I have this problem," he began. "Dad wants me to participate in equine sports. I love horses, Gram—I really do—but I want to do other things."

"Like what?"

"I want to play string instruments." Everyone at school treated him like he had fleas. They'd roll with laughter if he competed in horse-riding events. He needed something he could do by himself without any friends. "It sounds fun."

"Like a guitar?"

"That's back to the cowboy stuff, Gram. I want to play the violin."

"Oh."

"I'm not sure why I suddenly want to do it, but at my high school, the music teacher offers private lessons. It'll cost sixty dollars to rent an instrument and thirty a month."

Gram smiled and shrugged. "I can finance the endeavor. It's no big deal."

"I think I can find a weekend job to pay for it," Caleb told her. "That's not the problem. I just don't know how to break it to Dad."

"Oh." Gram frowned and gazed out the window at the river. "He is very sold on the Montana dream. He hoped to see you engage in Western activities." She looked back at him and sighed. "Just tell him, Caleb. I think he'll understand."

Caleb wasn't so sure about that.

WHEN CAM GOT HOME, IT LOOKED TO HIM AS IF A GIGANTIC BIRD had flown the length of their property, depositing NO TRESPASS-

ING signs. What the hell? He couldn't believe his eyes. *Mom,* he thought. *Sam Conacher must have really pissed her off last night.* Cam wouldn't have minded her posting the land. It was the vast number of signs that blew him away. And the fact that they looked junky. She hadn't even gotten them in a straight line.

As he pulled up to park outside the cabin, Caleb circled the building and ran to the passenger door. As he climbed into the truck, he said, "Hi, Dad. I need to tell you something, and I don't want to be nervous about it all evening, because you're not going to like it. In fact, I'm afraid you're going to be really disappointed in me."

Cam had a flashback to when he'd been only a year older than Caleb and had said essentially the same thing to his father. His whole body tensed. "Okay." He tried to sound calm. "Hit me."

"Please try to understand and don't get mad," Caleb said. "I love you, and I respect you, and I want you to be proud of me. But I don't want to participate in equine sports. I want to play the violin instead."

Cam's lungs deflated. "Damn it, Caleb. I thought you'd gotten some girl pregnant."

His son looked at him as if he'd grown a third eye in the middle of his forehead. "I don't even have a girlfriend."

"Yes, well, I don't know if my dad knew I had one before I told him that news. I think he knew I was dating, but not that I was serious about anyone." Cam flexed his shoulders. "Whew," he said on another exhale. "The violin, huh?" He sent his son a questioning look. "Did I just get snookered? Because you playing a violin suddenly seems like nothing compared to a grandchild."

Caleb grinned. "I didn't snooker you. I just thought you'd be upset. You want me to do equine sports, and that isn't my thing now."

Cam digested that. "I never intended to push you into doing anything. If you want to be a violinist, I'm totally fine with it. Will you still go riding with me?"

"Sure. I like to ride horses, Dad. I just don't want to compete on them."

Cam nodded. "Gotcha." He hooked a thumb over his shoulder. "What's with the gazillion signs along our road?"

"Gram's making sure that Sam Conacher will trip over one if he tries to trespass on our land again. But if you think that's bad, you should see the brick wall Mr. Conacher started building today. It's six feet tall. Makes me wonder if he's going to install underground sensors and infrared cameras to make sure we don't tunnel under or try to crawl over."

Cam started to laugh. Caleb joined in. "Damn," Cam said with a punctuating sigh. "My life has gone crazy. A violin? One rule from the start. You practice out of my earshot."

SAM LAY LOW UNTIL HIS EYEBROWS GREW BACK AND HIS MUSTACHE looked like a shorter version of its former self. It took only a week, which surprised him, but he honestly didn't know why. At his age, he was thinning on top, and he could have sworn all the lost hair had moved to his face. As a young man, he'd had nice eyebrows. Now they sprouted like untended hedges over his eyes. Sometimes when he woke up in the morning, they waved at him when he looked in the mirror.

Kirstin's friend Marcy had had a few bad spells during that week. Sam knew damned well that his daughter wasn't sitting with a sick friend, and his heart ached over it. It wasn't only her seeing Cam McLendon that hurt him. What really drove the knife deep was that she was lying to him about it.

Sam tried not to think about his beautiful daughter rolling

around in bed with that jerk. He also tried to feel thankful that Kirstin hadn't followed through on her threat to bring the man to her house. Sam wasn't sure he could handle that. There was already enough tension between him and his daughter without her making it worse by engaging in nocturnal activities right next door. So he pretended that she actually *was* sitting with a sick friend. When they worked together during the day and he saw her texting on her phone with a dreamy smile on her face, he turned away.

KIRSTIN SPENT HER LUNCH BREAK ON THURSDAY WALKING MARMA-lade. The horse no longer showed the slightest sign of a limp. The wrap on her leg had done the trick, and it hadn't escaped Kirstin's notice that her father had been checking on the mare and changed the bandage a few times. The realization made her both happy and sad. At his core, her dad was such a caring person, but since her mother's death, Kirstin rarely saw that side of him.

A warm breeze wafted over the pasture grass, bringing with it the scent of trees. The people of Montana endeavored to be good stewards of the ecosystem and preserved as much forestland as they could. Since childhood, Kirstin had tried to differentiate between the smells of the tree species on the valley floor and in the surrounding high elevations. She caught whiffs of alder, birch, Douglas fir, spruce, and ponderosa pine. No perfume created by man could ever compare.

Her phone notified her that she had received a text. She stopped the horse to read the message. Pleased to see it was from Cam, she tapped on the screen to read what he'd written: *The builder broke ground today, so we'll be celebrating. I'd love to have you over for dinner tonight. Your father is included in the invitation.*

Kirstin grimaced. Her dad had ordered enough brick to build his own version of the Berlin Wall between their two properties. He wasn't likely to join the McLendon family for a meal. Kirstin felt her palms grow moist at the thought of going herself. Cam's mother probably disliked Kirstin on general principles because of her father's horrid behavior. It might be a very uncomfortable evening. On the other hand, she wanted to meet Caleb. Her feelings for Cam continued to deepen. If it turned out that Caleb didn't like her, it would be curtains for her and Cam.

Kirstin understood that—and if it came down to it, she would be supportive of Cam's decision to stop seeing her. Cam had to put his son first; that was a parent's duty to a child. Still, she needed to know, sooner rather than later, if what she and Cam were feeling for each other needed to be snuffed out.

Cam texted again. *It's time for you to meet Caleb.*

She smiled. *So,* she mused, *we're thinking along the same lines.* That was good. Teenagers had their own way of looking at things. Since his birth Caleb had been the most important person in Cam's life. He might resent the sudden intrusion of a girlfriend. If so, both she and Cam needed to know that now.

She messaged him back. *I'd love to come. What time?*

When you're done with your workday. That'll give you the whole evening to hang out with us. Don't dress up. We're pretty casual over here.

Kirstin shoved her phone back in her jeans pocket. She was glad she didn't have to dress up. At least she wouldn't find herself standing in front of her closet, trying to find the perfect thing to wear.

• • •

KIRSTIN'S PALMS WERE SWEATING WHEN SHE PULLED HER TRUCK IN beside Cam's at the McLendon camp. She'd just driven past what appeared to be hundreds of signs along the shared private road. It looked as if someone was holding a political rally. Only that wasn't the case. Each placard essentially sent a message to her father that he wasn't welcome here.

Three dogs raced out to meet her and barked ferociously as she exited her vehicle. Kirstin had never met a canine that didn't like her, so she wasn't alarmed.

"Bingo, Bear, Boomer!" A teenage boy appeared at the back side of the cabin. He looked like a younger version of Cam with his brilliant blue eyes and honey brown hair. He had a lanky build, but she imagined he would fill out with more muscle as he grew older. "Sorry," he called to her. "They're ill-mannered heathens, but they don't bite."

Kirstin hunkered down to fondle each dog as they jostled one another for position. "They're gorgeous, and we have Aussies at our place, so I'm used to the bluster." She straightened and held out her hand to the approaching youth. "You must be Caleb. I've heard a lot of good things about you."

Caleb grinned. "I've heard the same about you. I think maybe my dad wants us to like each other."

Kirstin wasn't sure how to take that. Did that mean Caleb had reservations?

He began telling her the name of each dog.

"Who named them?" she asked.

"Me. I was four when I named Bingo, ten when I named the other two. Sounded like great names to me at the time. But now all of us get confused sometimes and say, 'B-b-b,' without ever getting one of their names spit out."

Kirstin grinned. "They look so much alike that I'll never get them straight."

"Over time you'll be able to tell who's who."

Kirstin fell in beside him as he led the way. It was getting toward dusk, and golden light spilled from the cabin windows, the white canvas carport, and the large wall tent at the rear. She also noticed dimmer light coming from the trailer, which sat facing the river. Everywhere she looked, she saw evidence of how hard Cam had worked to make his family comfortable. The two tents had wooden floors.

"Dad's stirring the brandy sauce, and if he lets it separate, it'll be ruined." Caleb grinned. "*That* qualifies as a disaster around here. So let me show you around."

Kirstin went with him to admire his grandmother's yard. The wire fence was, at best, a temporary barrier, but they had extended it far beyond the front end of the trailer to give the dogs plenty of running room. Kirstin assumed Cam put the dogs in there while his mother was here alone. "Dad rented some equipment, so I put out gravel almost everywhere while he was doing something else. Some of the rock is big, though, and Gram isn't steady walking over it. So I spent a lot of time tossing away large stones. Still do. We don't want her falling."

Kirstin nodded her understanding and thought how lucky Maddie was to be so loved. The dogs joined them by the fence, bouncing around and playing with one another.

Caleb pointed at the trailer door. "I built the steps for her. Well, my dad helped."

That prompted Kirstin to stifle a smile. Building steps could be tricky, but someone had measured the angles and risers almost perfectly. She suspected that Cam had done more than just help.

"And I made her the handrail," Caleb said with pride. "Dad's going to paint the surface of the steps with that no-slip stuff before winter comes."

Kirstin noticed a lighted plastic pumpkin sitting at the front trailer window. Following her gaze, Caleb said, "I know. Halloween's more than a month away, but Gram gets into decorating for the holidays."

"Are you getting too old to enjoy it?" Kirstin asked.

Caleb's cheeks colored. "Nah. My dad still likes decorating for holidays, too, so maybe I'll never outgrow it."

Kirstin could tell that Caleb considered his father to be the gold standard of masculinity. If his dad liked something, Caleb didn't feel like a sissy if he did, too.

From there, he took Kirstin out into the field to show her where the building team had broken ground. To Kirstin, it wasn't too impressive, only disturbed earth and dirt piles, but Caleb seemed delighted.

"Our residences will be at this end, Dad's and mine upstairs, Gram's downstairs. She'll have nice views of the mountains, but from the upper deck, ours will totally kick butt."

Next he led her to the cabin at the front of their camp and opened the door. "This is where Dad and I sleep, and all of us watch television in here on movie nights. Sorry for the paper mess and all the boxes. It's my dad's office, too, and he has nowhere to store his stuff." Caleb stepped inside and kicked into a pile of what Kirstin presumed were his soiled clothes. "We stay cozy out here, and that's what counts." He picked up a long instrument case. "This is my violin. I'm just starting with lessons."

"I play the guitar. Someday maybe we'll jam together."

Kirstin wondered how Cam would feel when he learned she'd gotten a tour of his bedroom. Both he and his son had full-size beds. A huge flat-screen television took up the entire length of a table angled across one corner of the room. A canvas zip-up armoire sat against the wall in the opposite corner. The structure was crowded and cluttered but functional. She imagined joining the family in here to watch a movie and wished that she and her dad did things like that together.

Next Caleb showed her the carport that they used for storage. She was fascinated by the ingenious ideas Cam had come up with. Even though their camp was composed of four different shelters, it felt homey to her. She noticed yet another cabin farther out in the field, only it was much smaller.

"That's for our cats. Gram had a great big house before, and it was surrounded by forest. The cats kept rodents away. She's got six."

"We have barn cats," Kirstin shared. "I know how important a feline population can be."

The wall tent flaps had been tied back. She and Caleb stepped inside. Kirstin swept the room with her gaze, noting that the McLendons had everything necessary to cook, wash dishes, and do laundry. The walls of the tent were lined with a woodstove, appliances, tables, and food storage. The center of the room boasted comfortable rockers, and camp chairs for extra seating leaned against one end of a table. She could picture the McLendons sitting in here for dinner, sometimes with guests. On one table, she noticed stacks of heavy-duty paper plates and bowls protected by plastic.

Cam turned from the propane stove. "You made it!" He stepped over to hug her. "I heard Caleb showing you around."

"I even got a tour of your sleeping quarters."

Cam threw back his head and guffawed. "Oh, well. We're roughing it, remember."

He looked so handsome. He wore a bibbed apron over a plaid Western dress shirt, which she suspected he'd worn for work that day. The shiny toes of his riding boots shone beneath the hems of his jeans.

"If you think this is roughing it," she scoffed, "you need to go camping with me and Dad sometime."

"I'll look forward to it."

Just then Kirstin heard a woman speaking to the three dogs that had lain down between the storage room and tent. She turned to see an older woman with reddish brown hair stepping up onto the plywood flooring. She had merry blue eyes and a beautiful, friendly smile. In the brighter light, Kirstin could now see a light dusting of silver in the strands of her hair, suggesting that Maddie hadn't been to a salon for coloring in a while. Or maybe she chose to age naturally, which was what Kirstin planned to do.

"I'm sorry for not coming out sooner, Kirstin." Maddie thrust out her right hand. "I'm under a deadline, and I had to finish disposing of a body. I keep thinking of better ideas."

Taken aback by that, Kirstin chuckled. "At least the writing life must be interesting."

Cam, already stirring the sauce again, glanced at his mother. "Mom, I'd like you to meet Kirstin. Kirstin, this is my mother, Maddie."

Since they'd already shaken hands, Kirstin fluttered her fingers in a wave. "I'm pleased to meet you, Mrs. McLendon."

"That's a tongue twister. Just call me Maddie if you don't mind. And may I call you Kirstin?"

"Of course."

Cam moved the cast-iron skillet away from the heat. "I've got our sides ready—all except for the asparagus, anyway." He rubbed his palms together. "It'll be roughly fifteen minutes for the steaks. Another five to let them rest. Caleb, would you like to take Kirstin with you to walk the dogs? She might enjoy seeing the slough."

"Sure!" Caleb said. "You want to come, Kirstin?"

"I'd love to."

KIRSTIN REALIZED THAT CAM WANTED HER AND CALEB TO SPEND more time alone together, which would give the boy a chance to take her measure. That made her nervous, but with the dogs to provide comic relief, she soon relaxed. Like his father, Caleb was a talker. He told her about how he'd created the trail they walked. He gave her a rundown on each of the dogs and pointed out identifying marks so she could tell them apart. It was a challenge for Kirstin to keep up with him, let alone get a word in edgewise. But she enjoyed every second of the young man's company. He was so very like his dad, open, friendly, and relaxed.

When they reached the slough, he said, "We got permission to lay thick planks over the water here so Gram can walk the whole half mile to the bridge, but we haven't gotten around to doing it yet."

"It'll be a lovely walk for her once you get it done."

"Yep. But winter's on its way, and she may not be able to walk up here if we get deep snow. We have other projects that Dad says are more important to worry about right now."

Kirstin admired the surroundings. "It's lovely here, so peaceful, with the wonderful smells of nature."

"I like it here," he said. "On this land, I mean. Not so much at school."

Kirstin nodded. "I've heard it can be hard to switch schools."

"Yeah, it kind of is." He bent his head and toed a rock. "I—um—know that you and my dad have been seeing each other."

Kirstin wasn't sure how to respond. "Yes. He's a great guy, and I like him a lot."

Caleb lifted his gaze. Kirstin noted that he already stood a half head taller than she did. He would soon be a grown man. "My dad got my mom pregnant when he was only a year older than me. Has he told you about that?"

"Yes, he mentioned it."

Caleb nodded. "Good. I'm glad I'm not telling you something he hasn't. Ever since I was born, Dad has focused on me. My mom wouldn't let him take me out of California, so he stayed there even though he dreamed of living here. My mom didn't want me. She tried to give me up for adoption. My grandparents helped my dad get custody of me. But that didn't mean she lost all control. Nobody ever said, but I think my grandfather told my mother that she'd never have to pay child support if she gave me to my dad. So far as I can tell, she grabbed that deal and ran. After that she never called or even sent me a card. She's been an invisible mom, except when she got a chance to stop my dad from moving where he wanted."

"How do you feel about that?"

"When I was little, my dad would call her and try to let me hear her voice on the phone, but she always refused to talk to me. He thought I needed to have some kind of relationship with her, I guess. He only did it a few times, though, before he decided not to put me through that again." Caleb shrugged. "So I'm fine with the way she wants it. I don't need her in my life. Gram and Dad say she's a nice person, but I wonder. She's been married something like four or five times. I've got half brothers and sisters, and I don't even know their names or how old they are."

"That's too bad."

"I don't really care. Not that I wouldn't like having brothers or sisters, but the ones I've got are strangers. My point is that my dad has been my only parent. He had to work to help support me, even when he was still in high school and then going to college. He didn't have much time for a social life. Dating women, I mean."

Kirstin let her gaze stray to the river. The view resembled those from the ranch. Where was Caleb going with this?

"Anyway, I think it's great that he's met you," he said. "I just want to say that I'd really appreciate it if you would try not to hurt him. I think he likes you a lot."

Kirstin's eyes stung with tears. What a wonderful job Cam had done raising this boy. He wasn't worried about how Cam's relationship with her might impact him. His only concern was his father's happiness. "I like your dad a lot, too, Caleb, and I'd never hurt him on purpose. But relationships can be tricky, and we're still in the process of making sure we're right for each other. Things could go wrong this early on." She gave him a smile. "For instance, you may decide you don't care for me."

"No, I like you fine."

She nodded. "I like you, too. But if your dad and I start to get *really* serious, you may have second thoughts about me being around all the time. If that happens, your father will base his decisions on what he feels is best for you. You're the most important person in the world to him."

Caleb sighed. "In two years, I'll go away to college. He shouldn't worry about me. After college, I'll have a job. I don't have a girlfriend or anything yet, but someday I might get married. I'll have my own family."

"True." Kirstin hadn't known teenage boys had such serious

thoughts. "I'll try my best not to hurt your dad. Honestly I will. Right now it's hard to predict what may happen tomorrow or the next day. It could be your dad who backs out."

He grinned. "I doubt it."

"Ah, but people surprise each other. For instance, I don't like asparagus."

His eyebrows shot up. "Are you shit—kidding me? It's my dad's favorite vegetable."

Kirstin laughed. "So, there, you see? We still have a lot of things to learn about each other. Asparagus could be a deal breaker for him."

They turned to walk back toward camp. Caleb called to the dogs, and when they bounded up, they were covered with mud from romping in the slough. "My dad won't dump you over not liking asparagus. If you hated steak, it might be a real problem, though."

KIRSTIN ENJOYED BEING WITH THE McLENDONS. UNLIKE AT HOME, where meals with her father were eaten in silence, this family joked around, laughed between bites of food, and talked, the topics of conversation drifting from one thing to another. They sat in chairs and balanced paper plates on their knees. Kirstin's red wine was served to her in a red Solo cup. Paper towels were provided as napkins. The flatware was plastic.

"We aren't fancy here," Maddie said. "We use our soiled plates and bowls to start fires. We wash the plasticware about three times for reuse, and then it goes in the trash. I cringe, but the garbage company offers no curb service for recycling."

"We're a little behind the times here," Kirstin replied. "It's a small town. We can haul recyclable material to a collection center, but many people don't do it because it's so time-consuming."

"Our steak and brandy sauce is fancy," Caleb pointed out.

"And delicious beyond belief," Kirstin added.

Cam turned to say something to Maddie. When he wasn't looking, Caleb snatched the asparagus from Kirstin's plate and put it on his own. She nearly choked on a sip of wine as she gulped back a laugh. Grinning, she gave him a thumbs-up.

"What are you two up to?" Cam asked.

"Nothing important," Caleb said.

Kirstin met Cam's gaze. "Caleb is trying to cover for me. I love every vegetable on earth—*except* asparagus. So he's eating mine. I *hate* the stuff."

"You should have said something," Cam told her. "I'm sorry I put it on your plate."

"It's one of the hazards when the chef dishes up." Maddie winked. "You get some of each dish."

"I'm enjoying everything else." Kirstin smiled at Cam. "Can you teach me how to make brandy sauce? It's fabulous with beef."

All too soon, it seemed to Kirstin, the meal ended. She helped tidy up, oiling the cast iron after Cam scrubbed it, and then teaming with Caleb to dry the cooking utensils and plasticware. When she thought of driving the short distance home, she wished she didn't have to leave. As basic as the McLendons' living conditions were, they had created a warm and welcoming home here, and she could feel the love that they felt for one another as if it were something tangible. Kirstin loved her father, and she knew he loved her, but there was little laughter or sharing under his roof.

When the work was finished, they sat in a circle, enjoying the warmth of the fire and one another's company. The three dogs came in and lay on their respective beds under the tables.

"Who's up for a game of canasta?" Cam asked.

Caleb rubbed his palms together. "I am. You whipped me last time. Now I can get even."

Kirstin couldn't imagine how they could play cards, but Cam brought a small folding table from the storage area and set it up.

Before he could get the cards out, Caleb grabbed a large roll of white paper off a wire shelf and said, "First, let's show Kirstin our house drawings!"

"Oh, how fun," Maddie agreed. "I love to look at them and dream."

Kirstin enjoyed being shown the floor plans for each residence, which would each be around fourteen hundred square feet. "I like the open-living concept," she told them. "And the designer wasted little space."

Maddie talked about wall colors and her stamped-concrete floors downstairs. She even pointed to where she would put her Christmas tree if her residence was finished prior to the holiday. "We decided to have in-floor heating. I think we'll all love that."

After Caleb rolled up the blueprints, Cam pulled a chair up to the table and began shuffling the cards. They spent the rest of the evening *boo*ing over bad hands and shouting with glee when they prevailed.

Before Cam walked Kirstin to her truck later, he turned to Maddie and said, "Mom, I'm going to see Kirstin home, and I may stay to visit for a while."

Maddie's expression tightened. "Are you going to climb over the wall and risk being shot by border control? Or are you going to drive in like a normal person?" She smiled apologetically at

Kirstin. "I have no doubt that your father is a wonderful man, honey, but he can be a handful when it comes to you."

"I'm sorry about that wall he started," Kirstin told her. "I think Dad has gone over the edge."

Maddie shrugged. "It would have been a lot less money if he'd gone with signs like I did."

Chapter Eight

KIRSTIN HADN'T EXPECTED CAM TO CHOOSE TONIGHT TO ENter the lion's den, but after she thought it over, she could see how it made sense, at least to Cam. She had just met his family, and now he intended to meet her father, no matter how badly that might go. She'd been nervous when she first arrived at the McLendon camp, hoping to win over Caleb and possibly make some inroads with Maddie. But now her stomach felt as if she had swallowed a quart of live pollywogs.

As she and Cam walked out to their vehicles, she said, "I think this is a bad idea, Cam. Dad isn't ready for this yet."

He slipped an arm around her shoulders. "I understand, but will he ever be?"

Kirstin honestly didn't know. Her stomach still quivered as she turned to lean against him. "Maybe he'll never be, but, please, try to see this like I do. I just met your son and mom. I think the evening went really well."

"How could it fail? You're a wonderful person."

"They won't continue to like me if you tangle with my father tonight," she replied. "My dad will do everything he can to destroy you, and if he succeeds, they'll go down with you. Can't we just coast along a while longer before we stir the pot with Dad?"

Cam tightened his embrace around her. "Ah, Kirstie. I'm really uncomfortable with sneaking around. You've made a valid point, but I think it boils down to two things. Am I falling in love with you, and are you falling in love with me?"

"You know what my answer to that question is."

He sighed. "It's the same for me. That's why I wanted you to meet Caleb sooner rather than later. I don't think it's wise for us to continue to invest in each other emotionally until we're sure we can eliminate any possible obstacles. For me, Caleb is one of them, and like it or not, your father is another one. Do you really want me to postpone meeting him?"

Kirstin tipped her head back to look up at him. Golden light spilled through the cabin windows to illuminate his face and sparkle in his eyes. She'd come to care for him in ways she hadn't expected, and now she couldn't imagine how awful it would be to move forward without him. "Dad isn't an obstacle for us. I won't allow him to be. I'll move off the ranch first."

"What if he puts a gun to his head after you walk out? That night when you found him on his knees in the living room and what he said to your mother about putting a bullet in his brain troubles me. People sometimes threaten to commit suicide to manipulate people or get attention. But your dad said it when he didn't realize he had an audience. That leads me to think it wasn't a threat and he actually considered it."

Kirstin's stomach muscles coiled into knots.

"He loves you, Kirstie, and you love him. It will be better for everyone involved if he can wrap his mind around this and come to accept it. We can't keep sneaking around like two kids. My guess is that he already knows we're together. With everything out in the open, he can stop imagining worst-case scenarios and deal with reality."

"Which is?"

"That our feelings for each other will have no impact on him. That you love him and the ranch, and you'll never leave."

Kirstin finally nodded and moved from his arms. Aloud, she said, "Okay. Let's do this."

Silently she said a prayer. *Please, God, don't let Daddy be a complete jerk.*

BORED OUT OF HIS SKULL BECAUSE HE HAD NOTHING GOOD TO read, Sam sat in his recliner, trying to concentrate on a news broadcast. Kirstin had left hours ago without even bothering to say where she was going. He was getting damned tired of her lack of common courtesy. That irked him to no end, and it also terrified him. When she grew so bold that she no longer lied to him about her whereabouts, he had to accept that he was inches away from watching her pack her belongings and drive away.

He knew she was with that useless jackass who'd moved in next door. Every time Sam drove by that sprawling camp, he marveled at the guy's stupidity. Who in his right mind would subject his mother and kid to a campout during winter in the Bitterroot Valley? Sam didn't have to trespass on Maddie's property to see what was happening over there. He had a great set of binoculars.

Sam briefly lost his train of thought, sidetracked by the memory of glimpsing Maddie McLendon in the buff through a window of her trailer early one morning. He prided himself on the fact that he'd been a gentleman and quickly looked away. But he'd seen enough for the sight to be branded on his brain. For an old broad, she was still put together pretty nice.

He forced his thoughts back to her son, the king of dumb. The idiot might not know it, but that drinking-water tank he'd put next to the trailer would freeze like a gigantic ice cube if the temperatures dropped low enough. And that fancy washing machine wouldn't work with a frozen waterline. All his crazy notions of how to care for his family were going to blow up in his face.

Just then Sam heard vehicles go by his house. Punching downward with the heels of his boots as he released the recliner footrest, he stood and crossed over to the living room windows. Through the glass, he saw the taillights of two pickups glowing red in the darkness as they pulled up in front of Kirstin's house. The next instant, all went dark, and then dome lights illuminated both of the passenger cabs.

He glimpsed Kirstin's black hair as she piled out of the ranch truck. He stiffened when he recognized Cam McLendon as the driver of the second vehicle. Rage, hot and sudden, roiled through his veins. He'd hoped Kirstin wouldn't do this. He'd been pretty damned clear with his wording when he told her that he wouldn't allow her to consort with men on his property.

Sam flipped on the outside lights and slammed out of the house to stand on the porch. He glared as his daughter and her worthless boyfriend met in front of their respective pickups. He fully expected the weasel to hurry inside Kirstin's residence. Instead he turned to walk toward the main house—and Sam—as if he'd been invited to a late supper. *That'll happen when hell freezes over.*

Kirstin ran after her friend and grabbed his arm. Sam couldn't hear what she said, but she was clearly trying to convince him to turn back. *Smart girl. She knows just by looking at me that I'm ready to go after him like a mudhole I'm stomping dry. If that jerk keeps walking, I'll give him what he deserves.* As the two drew closer and Sam could see his daughter's face, his heart squeezed. The way she looked at McLendon told the story. He'd lost his little girl. She'd gone and fallen in love with the asshole. Sam wished he had more time to think this through. He needed a plan to make Kirstin see how worthless the dude really was. Only Cameron McLendon kept walking.

Once at the porch, he dared to look Sam directly in the eye. Blue eyes. No hesitation. He stood on Conacher land as if he had every right to be there. "Mr. Conacher, my name is Cam McLendon. I believe you've met my mother. We live next door."

Kirstin moved closer to hug McLendon's arm. "Daddy, please, stay calm."

Calm? Sam felt his pulse hammer in his temples.

McLendon patted Kirstin's hand before gently prying her fingers loose from his shirtsleeve. "This isn't the way I wanted to do this," he said as he took one step closer to Sam. "I would have preferred to talk to you long before now, Mr. Conacher. I wanted to ask your permission to court your daughter, but given your feelings about her dating, Kirstin didn't think it was a good idea. She feared that you would just say no and then try to destroy my reputation so I couldn't sell ranches here in the valley. It seemed to her a premature thing for me to do until we knew for sure our personalities meshed. Now I'm falling in love with her, and she's falling in love with me. I don't like sneaking around to see her, so I'd really like to have your blessing."

My blessing? This asshole had had sex with his daughter in a fucking park. Sam felt like a champagne bottle that someone had just uncorked. Without weighing his options, he went down the steps, taking them two at a time. "I'll destroy a hell of a lot more than your reputation, you bastard!"

Sam swung and planted his right fist in the center of McLendon's face. The younger man keeled over backward. Kirstin screamed.

After he moved to stand over his daughter's fallen lover, Sam's voice shook with rage as he said, "Get back up and fight me like a man."

"No, sir," McLendon said through bloodied fingers that he'd

clamped over his mouth. "You're Kirstin's father, and I respect her too much to behave that way."

Sam thought Cam McLendon was a lying coward and just putting on a show for Kirstin. "Any man will fight back if he has a lick of sense."

Reaching down, Sam clamped his hand over the younger man's arm and jerked him back to his feet. Then he hit him again.

Kirstin jumped in to intervene. "Stop it, Dad!" Her voice rang shrill. "Just stop it!"

"Get out of my way, girl."

"The hell I will," she yelled. "Just *look* what you've done! I love this man! He's my guest here!" She knotted her fists. "I never realized until now just how much I've come to hate you! I'm leaving the ranch for good in the morning. You can wallow in your anger and misery for the rest of your life as far as I care."

She turned to help her pansy-assed boyfriend to his feet. Sam watched as she led McLendon back to her house. A sinking sensation attacked his belly as his anger ebbed. What had he just done?

Feeling as if each of his feet weighed a thousand pounds, Sam made his way back up the steps. Once inside the house, he sank down on the living room hearth and held his head in his hands. For the life of him, he couldn't think what to do or how to fix this. He'd worked his whole life to build an empire, and now he'd driven his daughter away from everything he had to offer her. God, he missed Annie. As delicate as she had been, she'd always kept him in line and made him stop to think before he acted.

WHILE KIRSTIN NURSED CAM'S FACE, HE COULD SEE THAT SHE trembled with anger. "I can't *believe* him. He's gone way too far this time."

Cam grabbed her wrist to stop her from dabbing at his mouth with the cool cloth. "You need to calm down. You can bet he's regretting his actions right now. He'll realize how wrong he was and apologize."

"Apologize? As if that will make up for his behavior?"

Cam pressed the now-bloody rag against his nose, which still trickled. "Kirstin, we all do and say things at some point that we can never take back. It's not as if he seriously hurt me. And of *course* an apology will make up for his behavior. And after he apologizes, everything will be good between him and me."

"Nothing will ever again be good between him and *me*. That's the problem you're failing to see."

"That's just plain silly, Kirstin. I'm not hurt that bad. A banged-up nose, a split lip, and a sore cheekbone. Trust me, your father could have done far worse, but he held back."

She looked at him as if he were crazy. Cam tossed aside the rag, grabbed her arm, and drew her forward to sit on his knee. Once she was settled, he slipped his arms around her. "Women think differently than men. I needed to make a point, and so did your father. Both of us were successful. Did you think your dad would suddenly back down from a lifelong battle to protect his daughter without throwing a punch or two? Hell, no. I encroached on his territory. We're like a couple of male dogs, pissing to mark the bushes. Whether Sam is right or wrong doesn't matter. In his mind, he was establishing his footing with me and staking his claim on you."

Kirstin shook her head. "I don't understand my father, and now I'm not sure I understand you, either. How can you be so cavalier about getting punched in the face?"

Cam tightened his arms around her. "Taking a couple of blows to the face is a small price to pay for a peaceful relationship with your dad. And it will be peaceful from now on. Whether Sam likes me or detests me, there will be no more punching. He has established himself as the top dog, and it's only right that he should be. I respect that, just as I would have with my own dad. Now you and I can explore the possibilities of our relationship without interference from him. I showed him deference. Things will be okay."

Kirstin sighed, and some of the tension eased from her body. "All right, if you say so. But I think I know my dad a lot better than you do."

"You certainly do. But this is a guy thing." Cam cupped her chin in one hand and forced her to look at him. "I'll remind you again of that night when you found him in the living room. After he hit me, you told him you hated him and would leave forever in the morning. Can you imagine how he's feeling right now? I think you need to go talk with him."

"Talk with him?" She squirmed to get off his lap. "I meant what I said."

"That you hate him and you're never coming back."

Her face crumpled. "I hate him right now."

"You don't hate him, Kirstin. You're just furious with him. I don't blame you, but please, don't leave those words ringing in his mind all night. They were a lot more hurtful for him than those punches were for me."

Her shoulders slumped. "Oh, all right. I'll talk to the mean old codger, but I'm not going to like it. After acting like that, he deserves to suffer a little."

KIRSTIN'S WALK TO THE MAIN HOUSE SEEMED LIKE ONE OF THE longest journeys of her life. When she reached the door, she stood on the mat and rubbed her palms back and forth on her jeans. She didn't want to go in. Anger bubbled within her like hot water in the stem of a percolating coffeepot. She *loved* Cam, and she had every right to be with him. She was tired of being monitored. Tired of plotting and lying to lead a normal life. She wanted nothing more than to go inside and scream at her father some more.

She opened the door and quietly stepped into the entry hall. She expected to find her dad halfway through a jug of whiskey. Instead he was sitting on the large hearth with his head in his hands. Kirstin paused in the archway. In that moment he looked so old—old and tired and defeated.

As if he sensed her presence, he suddenly looked up. His expression was tortured, and tears trailed down his cheeks, pooling in the creases that age and exposure to the elements had carved into his face. It hurt her heart to see him like that.

"I love you," he pushed out. "I don't want you to leave without knowing that."

"Oh, Daddy." Kirstin ran across the expansive living room to sit beside him and throw her arms around him. "I'm not leaving."

He hugged her close. She felt his chest jerking. Then, as he struggled to control his emotions, his whole body stiffened, and his embrace tightened until it was almost painful for her. "I handled that all wrong," he confessed. "I don't think highly of your boyfriend, but I'll never hit him again. I'll swear it on the family Bible, if that's what it takes to keep you on the ranch. I'll even walk over and apologize to the pansy-assed son of a bitch."

Kirstin ran her palm over his back, which was still padded with steely muscle. "I was furious with you, Dad, and I said things I didn't truly mean. I don't hate you. I love you. It's just that sometimes you're so impossible that you drive me clear over the edge."

"I know," he admitted. "I think I've got one of them damned split personalities. The real me stands there shaking his head while the other me does and says stupid things."

Kirstin patted his shoulder. "Dad, if you really feel that way, maybe you should consider seeing a counselor."

He dropped his arms from around her and turned to face outward from the fireplace. "You can forget that shit."

The response was so typical of her father that Kirstin almost smiled. "Well, if that is beyond the realm of possibility, you and I need to reach a few understandings. I'm no longer a child. I can't lead a satisfying life under my father's thumb. As I'm sure you already know, my sick friend, Marcy, doesn't exist. I lied about that so I could go out and have fun without you pitching a huge fit."

"I don't pitch fits."

Kirstin wasn't about to argue with him about that, so she ignored the denial and plowed forward. "Cam isn't the first man I've been intimate with."

"Dear God. Bite your tongue, girl. I can't stomach hearing about your sex life."

Kirstin sighed. "As I just said, Cam isn't the first man, but I have feelings for him that run deep, and I hope he'll be the last. You don't have to think highly of him."

"Well, that's a damned good thing, because I sure as hell don't."

"You don't even have to like him."

"Now you're talkin'."

"What matters is that I *do* like him, Dad, and you need to back off if you really want me to live on the ranch. That's not a threat. I can live elsewhere and still be here every day. This land is my heritage. You worked your whole life to build this place for me."

"Damned straight."

Kirstin sighed. "I think your split personality is taking over again."

"Don't get sassy. I apologized. I admitted I did wrong. That doesn't mean I'm not entitled to feel however the hell I want to feel."

"I'll grant you that privilege. But if I stay in that house next door, I'm going to need my space. I need my freedom. I need to come and go as I please. And if I want a man to stay the night with me, it'll be none of your business. I'm a grown woman. If you can't allow me those liberties, I can rent a place in town and still work the ranch with you."

"You're driving a hard bargain."

"It's the only bargain I'm offering, Dad. Take it or leave it. I love you, but I deserve to have my own life." Kirstin studied his profile. His expression had gone rigid. "You act so self-righteous. Do you realize that? Answer me honestly. Did you have sex with my mother before you married her?"

His steel blue eyes, so much like her own, shifted to meet her gaze. "Leave your mother out of this, and don't dishonor her memory by asking me such a question."

Kirstin patted his knee. "Thanks, Dad. I now know the answer to that question. You did have sex with her before you exchanged vows. And I'll bet she was still a virgin as well. Yet you curse Cam for daring to touch me. He's one rung above you on the honorable ladder, because I *wasn't* a virgin." She stood up. "You may be Sam Conacher, but that doesn't give you the privilege of living by a different set of rules than you expect Cam to follow. I hope you'll think about that." She turned to face him. "Do we have a bargain? Or should I start looking for a place to rent tomorrow?"

He raked callused and scarred fingers through his nearly white hair. It was as thick and straight as a polar bear's coat. "How nice do I have to treat him?"

Kirstin struggled not to grin. "Sugar better melt in your mouth."

"Sugar doesn't melt in my mouth when I talk to anybody."

She allowed her smile to break through. "I know. That's why I'm setting the bar high."

He pushed to his feet. He loomed over her, a rangy man with a muscle-roped body. He looked deceptively slender, but Kirstin had seen him in only an undershirt that summer and knew he still had the body of a man half his age. His skin had gone a bit wrinkly on his neck and upper arms, but he was still a force to be reckoned with.

"Don't push it, Kirstin."

"I won't. And from now on I expect the same from you." She turned and walked toward the door, feeling much lighter of heart than she had when she entered. "Good night, Dad. I love you."

His deep voice rang out behind her. "G'night, baby girl. I love you, too."

Kirstin nearly stopped to tell him she wanted him to quit calling her his baby girl. But she decided that would have been silly. She'd finally held her ground with her dad, and she needed to leave it at that.

WHEN KIRSTIN GOT BACK TO HER HOUSE, SHE FOUND CAM IN THE kitchen and threw herself into his arms. "I did it! I told him I love him and that I'll never leave the ranch, but I also stood up to him and held my ground."

Cam hugged her waist and executed a dizzying twirl. His warmth and strength enveloped her, feeling absolutely delicious. When he set her on her feet, he managed a lopsided grin with his puffy and split lip. His cheek had gone deep red, indicating that he'd sport a nasty bruise along the bone. But to Kirstin he was still irresistibly handsome.

"Did you yell?"

Kirstin frowned, trying to remember. "I don't think so."

He gingerly kissed her forehead. "Congratulations. Second question: did he yell?"

She sighed. "No, but he was difficult. And very sorry. Admitted he was wrong. He even offered to come over and apologize to you, but I chose not to press him on that."

"Wise decision."

Kirstin felt curiously lightweight, as if the pull of gravity had lessened. "I feel so free, Cam. I laid down rules that he has to follow if he wants me to live on the ranch. I made it clear that I could live elsewhere and still work here, but that I wouldn't stay here without absolute license to live my life however I want." She couldn't resist grinning. "That includes having you stay for the night."

Cam chuckled. "Now all you need is a footloose and fancy-free boyfriend, especially if you mean tonight."

"Oh, right." Her heart sank. "Caleb. Setting a good example."

"Don't look so disappointed," he said. "I can text him and Mom that you got into a nasty squabble with your dad, and I'm going to stay over to be with you. It's not the absolute truth, but it's not a lie, either."

Kirstin splayed her hands over his chest, loving the hardness and heat of his body. "Will Caleb buy that?"

"Sure. He knows your dad is difficult and doesn't want us seeing each other." He retreated a step to pull his phone from his hip pocket. He quickly sent the message. "Group text." He winked at her. "I'm all yours for the night."

She smiled and grabbed his hand to lead him to her bedroom. Cam stopped inside the door and gave the suite a long study. "Nice."

"I'll give you the grand tour tomorrow."

She reached behind him to turn off the wall switch and blanket the room in moon silvery shadows. Then she began unbuttoning his shirt, eager to run her hands over the mat of hair on his chest and feel his bare skin. His breathing quickened.

When his upper body was bare, he slowly unsnapped her shirt. After drawing the garment off her, he carried her to the bed.

IN THE MORNING CAM AWAKENED BEFORE KIRSTIN DID. AFTER grabbing a quick shower and dressing, he studied his battered face in the mirror. *Not too bad*, he decided. But his mother would still come unglued when she saw him. He went into Kirstin's kitchen, learned his way around, and put on a pot of coffee. As the rich aroma filled the room, he heard Kirstin getting up. The sound of the shower reached him. Minutes later, she appeared, dressed for her workday in a shirt, jeans, and boots. Hair still damp from the shower, she looked so beautiful that Cam wanted to carry her back to the bedroom.

Instead they took their coffee outside and sat on the covered paver deck in Adirondack chairs to enjoy the morning sunlight and fresh air. In the distance he heard ducks calling. Then he heard an eagle cry. The varied scents of a working ranch drifted on the air, a pleasant blend of alfalfa, grass hay, grain, and the ever-present scent of pine. It was the kind of day that tempted a man to sit still and admire the beauty of nature, how the leaves of cottonwood trees danced in lively patterns while evergreen boughs swayed in a lazy waltz.

About an eighth of a mile away, Cam saw a small herd of

Black Angus cows milling in a pasture with one of the biggest bulls he'd ever seen.

"That's Satan, our cleanup bull," Kirstin explained. "Dad brought cows in from a grazing parcel, and some of them didn't test positive for pregnancy. When the main breeding bulls fail to cover some of the cows, Satan takes care of them."

"In California I rented a bull once. It cost me so much money that I attended a school to get certified in bovine artificial insemination, so I could save money by inseminating the cows myself the next year."

"Careful with that," she said with a laugh. "It sounds like you're getting way too friendly with your cows."

He rewarded her with a slight smile. "Good one, but I can't really laugh. My lip still smarts. Before I got the job offer here with Long Barrel Ranches, I planned to start a business doing the same for other small operations. So many people run a few cows and don't have a bull."

Kirstin nodded. "I tried to convince Dad to get rid of Satan and just hire someone to artificially inseminate the cows that get missed, but he's old-school about that. He prefers getting the job done the natural way. Plus Satan sires high-quality calves, and they run small for the heifers."

Cam took a careful sip of his coffee, acutely aware of the woman who sat beside him. She didn't look sturdy enough to work with bulls that size, yet he knew she did. "Is Satan's name indicative of his nature?"

"Yes, which is why I think he should have become ground beef a long time ago. Sometimes, like right now, he's placid, and then for no apparent reason, he goes berserk. That's why Dad pastures him on the ranch. If we put him on grazing land, he'd be too hard to catch during the roundup season."

"Has Sam finished rounding them up yet?"

"No. Dad is so shorthanded that there aren't enough hours in the day. Things that need to be done are piling up on us." Still gazing at the bull, she savored another sip of coffee. "Satan's one of them. He's done his job with those cows, and for well over a week Dad's been meaning to move him into the bull pasture, but he hasn't had time."

"Is it important to get him moved soon?"

"Satan gets territorial when he's left with cows. It makes it difficult, if not impossible, for us to vaccinate, worm, and test for pregnancy."

Cam glanced at his watch. "I can help move him. I have a meeting at one in Missoula, but otherwise my day's wide-open."

She gave him a questioning look. "Do you know what you're doing?"

Cam didn't want to overstate his experience, but he didn't wish to sound totally ignorant, either. "I'm a decent rider, and I've entered some cutting competitions. I won't say I'm an expert, but I'm not a greenhorn."

She raked her nearly dry hair back from her face. "Dad would probably appreciate the help."

Cam stood and tossed the dregs of his coffee over the edge of the patio onto the lawn. "Let's whip up a quick breakfast and then take on old Satan."

BEFORE KIRSTIN AND CAM REACHED THE FRENCH DOORS THAT LED into the dining room, Sam appeared at the back corner of the house. He wore his scorched Stetson, a blue chambray shirt, Wrangler jeans, and beat-up Western boots, his usual attire for a workday. He touched the ruined brim of his hat.

"Good morning, Cam," he said.

From just behind Kirstin, Cam replied, "Good morning."

To Kirstin, Sam said, "Miguel and I are heading up to the grazing land. I'd like to line you out with a couple of chores before I leave."

"I'll go ahead and get breakfast started," Cam said.

Kirstin heard the door click closed and knew Cam had gone inside. Her father pursed his lips, which had been his version of a smile for almost seven years now. Arching an eyebrow at her, he asked, "How'd that rank on your sugar-melting scale?"

Fully aware that her father had no business to discuss with her, Kirstin fixed her gaze on his. He'd heard their voices and walked over specifically to greet Cam. "On a scale of one to ten, about a two, but I'll take it."

"Good." He touched the brim of his hat and turned to leave. "If Miguel and I find a few bunches of cows, we'll have to make several hauls back here and won't call it a day until after dark. We've got a section of fence in the east pasture to fix first. Getting a late start."

Kirstin knew it would be a long and trying day for the two men. Pushing cattle out of gulches and thick copses was a slow process for only two people. She wished she could go along and help, but someone had to remain behind to care for the animals already at the ranch.

"Be safe," she called.

The delicious smell of frying bacon drifted from the range vent to tantalize her. She hurried inside to join Cam in the kitchen for breakfast, wishing she could kiss the daylights out of him, because he'd been so right about her father. Sam was accepting Cam's presence, not only in her life, but also on the ranch.

She burst into the kitchen and grinned at him. "You are so

lucky that you have a split lip. Otherwise I'd drag you to the bedroom and make love to you all day."

"Other parts of me are in fine working order." He quirked a golden eyebrow at her. "What's the occasion?"

"Dad is behaving himself!"

AFTER A QUICK MEAL, KIRSTIN AND CAM SADDLED UP TWO horses. Kirstin chose to ride her gelding, Moses. She selected Major, another excellent cattle horse, for Cam. It was a perfect morning for a ride, and she wished that she and Cam could spend the whole day playing. Sunlight warmed her shoulders. The rippling sound of the river drifted to her on the air like a symphony played by woodland fairies. Unfortunately, as was the case most of the time, she had work to do.

As they approached the cow pasture, Cam asked how she wanted to handle Satan.

"I'm more familiar with the shenanigans that he pulls, so I'll have Moses cut him from the herd. You can stand ready to help if Satan gets nasty. Otherwise, be prepared to open the gate for me to run him out, and then follow me, closing the gate behind us." She pointed to another pasture about a quarter of a mile away. "That's the bull pasture."

"Boy, that fence looks stout," Cam remarked.

"It has to be. Otherwise he'll break out and get back in with the cows."

At the gate, Cam remained in the saddle and leaned down to disengage the latch. As he drew the panel open, Kirstin rode her horse into the enclosure. Cam followed, pulling the barrier closed behind him.

As Kirstin walked Moses into the clutch of cattle, Cam knew

he was watching a master. She moved fluidly with the horse, her slender body relaxed, legs lightly hugging the animal's barrel. He'd done enough cutting to know that going in slowly was critical. The cattle lowed, but none of them got spooked. Satan seemed to know Kirstin was coming in specifically for him, however. He swung his head from side to side and pawed the ground; then he began to dart one way and then another. Kirstin kept Moses pointed at the bull, which required the gelding to go down on its haunches and swing his front legs back and forth to remain hooked on.

Suddenly Satan panicked, lunged right, and made an incredibly quick U-turn. Kirstin, caught off guard, now had her mount broadside to the bull. Moses was fast, but as he tried to execute a lightning-quick shift, he wasn't quite fast enough. Full force and head down, the bull plowed into him. Moses, normally solid on his feet, took the blow at his center of balance. He screamed, craning his neck as he plunged to the ground.

Cam saw Kirstin struggling to get up, but her left leg appeared to be pinned under the saddle. The bull wheeled to charge again, and Cam thought, *No! Dear God, no!*

KIRSTIN SAW SATAN COMING AT HER. MOSES HAD STRUGGLED FOR an instant to get up and then stopped. Though she pushed against the saddle with all her strength, she couldn't pull her leg free. With a flash of icy terror, she knew that her foot was tangled in the stirrup. Everything went into slow motion. The bull lowered its head, pawed the earth, and dug in with his rear hooves to lunge. She could have sworn her whole life passed before her eyes. This was it. She would be trampled to death.

But then, seemingly from out of nowhere, Cam rode in, pushing his mount between Kirstin and the bull, deliberately letting Major take the full impact of the charge broadside. *Crazy, so crazy,* she thought. But it was all Cam could do to protect her.

Major was knocked off his feet, but Cam was ready for that and leaped off the horse instead of going down with it. While Satan circled to regroup for another onslaught, Cam grabbed Kirstin by the shoulders and tried to pull her out from under the horse. Panicked cows, bunched up in a corner of the enclosure, were bawling, the noise deafening. Cam's mount, still regaining its feet, protected her and Cam, but only for a moment. As soon as the horse got up, it galloped away to get out of the line of fire.

"My boot's twisted in the stirrup!" Kirstin cried. And then she yelled, "Watch out, Cam! He's coming at you from behind!"

Cam whirled, waved his arms, and roared like a bear to get the bull's attention. When Satan focused on him, he ran. Kirstin knew he was trying to draw the dangerous animal away from her. But at what cost? That bull might kill him.

SAM HAD LEFT MIGUEL TO WORK ON THE FENCE WHILE HE RE-turned to the ranch to get a fence stretcher they'd forgotten to take. As he rode into the ranch proper, he'd seen everything that happened in the pasture from start to finish. The young man he'd called worthless had deliberately put himself in danger to save Kirstin, and now the bull, hot on his heels as he tried to escape, rammed McLendon so hard in the back that he was thrown at least twenty feet.

"Goddamn it!" Sam yelled.

He dug his heels into his sorrel's flanks. Barron exploded into a run toward the pasture. Over the gelding's head, Sam saw Cam roll to his feet, turn to face the bull, and take another head butt to his upper abdomen that threw him backward so hard against the fence that two boards snapped under his weight.

Sam felt as if he were riding against a headwind. He jumped his gelding over the pasture rails and headed into the fray, swinging a coiled rope at the bull while yelling at the top of his lungs. Once he got the beast away from Cam and his daughter, he raced toward the gate, threw the latch, and pushed the panel wide open.

"Ha! Ha!" he shouted as he circled Barron behind Satan.

Slapping the bull's ass with the rope, he drove the bovine from the enclosure. When he got the gate closed again, he raced back toward Cam, knowing he had to be badly hurt. McLendon had regained his feet and was now holding his ribs as Sam closed the distance between them. Blood trickled from the corners of the younger man's mouth. His blue eyes were unfocused and looked blank.

Sam leaped off his horse. "How bad are you hurt, son?"

Cam crashed to his knees. By the time Sam reached him, he lay prostrate on the grass and was out cold. Sam jerked his cell phone from his belt and called for an ambulance before doing anything else. When he knew help was on the way, he knelt over his daughter's lover. *This is bad, really bad,* Sam thought. He was afraid to move Cam. He might do more harm than good. Sam suspected that McLendon had fractured ribs and a punctured lung, at the very least. A spinal injury couldn't be ruled out, either. Sam had built that rail fence to stand sturdy for years against bovine abuse, and Cam had hit those thick planks with such force that they had snapped like toothpicks.

"Is he all right?" Kirstin called.

Sam could barely hear her over the bawling of the cows. "He's out cold, but he's still got a pulse and he's breathing," he hollered back. "An ambulance is on the way."

Sam could do nothing for McLendon without rolling him over, and his gut told him that would be a mistake. Instead he went to help Kirstin get out from under her horse. Moses had stopped trying to get up, but he didn't appear to be injured. Sam's throat went tight when he realized the horse knew Kirstin's foot was tangled in the stirrup and that she might be injured or dragged if he stood up.

Sam crouched facing the horse's belly, where his daughter's trapped leg was visible. "Well, your boot went through the stirrup, honey," he told her. "Does your ankle feel broken?"

"No," Kirstin said. "It got twisted, and it hurts to have so much weight on my leg, but I don't think anything's broken."

Sam gently straightened her foot, and with some careful maneuvering, he worked her boot back through the stirrup to free her leg. He patted Moses's shoulder. "You're a damned fine horse, Mose."

He circled the gelding to grab Kirstin under the arms. As Moses rolled to get his hooves under him, Kirstin cried out. Sam tensed to pull her clear the moment the horse got up. The instant she was free, Kirstin scrambled to her feet and hopped on her uninjured leg to reach Cam. She dropped to her knees beside him.

"Oh, God. Oh, God," she cried.

Sam went to crouch beside her. Just then he heard a siren. "There's the ambulance, honey. You stay with Cam, but don't touch him. Okay? I've got to get Satan in the bull pasture so he doesn't hurt anyone else."

"What about all the cows?" Kirstin cried.

"They're bunched in the corner. I doubt they'll move from there unless they're pushed."

Sam mounted his gelding, left the enclosure, and found the bull in the barn, munching on alfalfa hay. Satan offered no resistance as Sam herded him from the building and got him relocated. "Stupid beast," Sam said as he fastened the gate. "I should've shot you the first time you caused trouble."

Just then he heard the ambulance pulling in. He nudged his sorrel into a trot so he could guide the paramedics to where Cam lay. Upon seeing Sam, the driver slowed down to follow the horse. Seconds later, three paramedics spilled from the vehicle. Sam dismounted and tied Barron to a fence rail. Kirstin still knelt over Cam. Even at a distance, Sam could tell that she was sobbing. He went to get her out of the way so the attendants had access to their patient.

As Sam drew Kirstin back, he noticed that she still couldn't put weight on her injured leg. A female EMT hurried over. Sam gently lowered his daughter to the ground so the woman could examine her.

"He distracted the bull to save me!" Kirstin cried over and over.

In Sam's mind an answering refrain rang loudly. *I know. I know. I know.* He had seen the whole thing, and he knew how bravely McLendon had acted to save Kirstin's life.

When the EMT tried to ask questions about the injury to Kirstin's leg, the only answer she got was "It's my fault, all my fault. He put himself in danger to save me!"

Sam finally intervened and explained what happened. "Unless you feel that she needs to be transported by ambulance, I can take her in."

The woman nodded. "That would be great." She gestured toward her teammates, who had strapped Cam onto a spinal board and were carefully moving him onto a stretcher. "They'll be busy in the back." To Kirstin, she said, "You can follow us in. I know you're very worried."

Sam saw Miguel ride into the ranch proper. His horse sidestepped, unnerved by all the commotion. Sam left Kirstin to meet the ranch manager at the fence. He quickly explained what had happened, asked Miguel to unsaddle Barron and tend to the other horses, and then returned to his daughter. The female EMT was giving Kirstin an injection. She finished and glanced up.

"A little something to calm her down and lessen her discomfort," she said.

Sam crouched by his daughter, scooped her into his arms, and carried her to his truck.

Chapter Nine

BY THE TIME SAM GOT KIRSTIN TO THE MISSOULA HOSPITAL, fondly called St. Pat's by the locals, he felt fairly certain her leg wasn't fractured. The injection given to her by the EMT had calmed her nerves, and although she still kept saying that Cam had put his own life at risk to save hers, she no longer trembled and wept. Sam parked under the wide portico and helped her into the ER. Apparently the ambulance attendants had called ahead that another patient was coming, because two nurses met them with a wheelchair and swept Kirstin away before Sam could even say he was her father.

He went to admissions to fill out all the paperwork. Afterward, he wanted to check on his daughter, but instead he drove clear back home, kicking himself every mile of the way because he didn't have Madeline McLendon's cell phone number. *You idiot,* he berated himself. He should have been a better neighbor from the start, giving Madeline his number and asking for hers, just in case of an emergency. But, oh, no, he'd been a world-class asshole instead.

As Sam drove onto the McLendon land, he saw two cement trucks on-site and realized the builder was finally pouring the construction footings. After parking his truck behind Maddie's gray SUV, he tried to think how in the hell he should handle this.

Worst-case scenario, she might think he had put her son in the hospital and try to tear his eyes out. He opened the gate to her yard. Three black-tri Australian shepherds awakened from their naps behind a table and charged out at him with their hackles up. Sam crouched down to meet them.

"Go ahead. Rip my throat out. Save your mistress the trouble."

He gave the oldest dog a couple of extra pats. They'd met the night Sam had driven in to check out the glowing toilet, which was still a light feature in the neighborhood.

Sighing, Sam stood and climbed the steps to knock on the trailer door. He heard movement inside, but it took Maddie a second to open up. She wore jeans and a long-sleeve T-shirt the same shade of blue as her eyes. Her reddish brown hair glinted bronze in the morning sunlight. Her face, bare of makeup, looked a little pale.

"To what do I owe this honor?" she asked. And then she apparently noted Sam's grim expression. The slight color in her cheeks drained away. "What happened? What have you done to my son?"

Sam winced, but he couldn't blame her for thinking the worst. "I didn't do it, but your boy is hurt. I'll give you the details on the way to the hospital. The ambulance took him to St. Pat's. I needed to come back and tell you, so I couldn't hang around long enough to get any details about his condition."

A CURIOUS NUMBNESS HAD OVERTAKEN MADDIE'S BODY. IF THEY had transported Cam by ambulance, she knew he must have been badly hurt. She wanted to ask a dozen questions, but her desire to reach her son as soon as possible forestalled her from voicing them.

"I need my purse."

She left the door standing open. Sam stepped inside as she

rifled through her bedroom closet. "A light jacket, too," he suggested. "If you get home after dark, it'll be chilly."

Maddie tugged a heavy corduroy shirt from a hanger. In the evening, she wore it around camp. Then she grabbed her purse. When she returned to the kitchen, she felt as if all the oxygen had been sucked from the trailer. Little bright flashes dotted her vision. A big, firm hand grasped her arm.

"Don't faint on me," Sam said.

"Don't be absurd. I don't faint." But for the first time in her life, she felt as if she might. "How badly is he hurt?"

Sam's deep voice curled around her. "St. Pat's has fabulous trauma care, and Cam is a strong young man. I'm betting that he'll be fine."

Maddie noted that he hadn't answered her question, which meant that Sam didn't know the extent of Cam's injuries—or that he believed they were severe and didn't want to upset her by saying so. She blinked and drew in a bracing breath. Then she fished in her bag for her car keys.

"I don't think it'd be smart for you to drive yourself. You're upset. You're also new to the area, and traffic in Missoula can be heavy." He released his hold on her arm. "I'll be happy to take you. And, please, don't be stubborn about it. Cam will need you. I don't want to tell him you were involved in a car accident trying to reach him."

The last person on earth from whom Maddie wanted to accept a favor was Sam Conacher. But her hands were shaking and her knees felt wobbly. "I suppose you're right," she conceded.

He glanced at her office area. "Do you want to turn off the lights and shut your computer down?"

Maddie cared about nothing but her son. "No. Just leave it."

She stepped out onto the porch. Sam followed her out. She

didn't bother to lock the door. There was nothing in the trailer she cared about.

She felt as if she were moving through a fog. Dimly she registered that Sam checked to be sure the three dogs had food and water before he enclosed them in the yard. Then, holding her arm, he escorted her to his pickup, helped her onto the passenger seat, and slammed the door. When he climbed in on the driver's side, Maddie was still struggling with the seat belt hasp. The mechanism refused to cooperate with her numb fingers.

"Here." Sam pushed her hands away and buckled her up. Then he did the same for himself before he started the diesel engine. "Just so you know," he said over the rumble, "I'll be driving fast. My daughter's hurt, too, and I didn't stay long enough to find out if her leg's broken."

"Oh, dear God." Maddie glanced over at him. "What happened?"

Sam shifted into reverse and backed out; then he floored the accelerator, peeling out on the pasture grass to reach the private drive. Once he turned onto Fox Hollow Road, he began telling her the story.

"That bull is huge and one mean son of a bitch. I don't know what Kirstin was thinking when she tried to move him without me being there."

Maddie had a picture in her mind of Cam being thrown by the animal with such force that his flying body broke sturdy fence railings. She couldn't think beyond that.

"Anyway, I'm damned grateful that Cam was with her. He saved her life. There's no question in my mind about that."

Maddie finally found her voice. "How badly do you think Cam is hurt?"

Sam took a moment to reply. "I'm no doctor, but my guess is

that he's got broken ribs, a punctured lung, and possibly a spinal injury." He glanced over at her. "I'm sorry for not prettying it up, but you strike me as a woman who wants it straight."

"Yes." Maddie caught herself fiddling with her hair and straightening her shirt. Nerves, she guessed. Or maybe she was in a mild state of shock. "I can't lose him," she blurted. "My husband died nearly two years ago. I'm still not over it. I don't think I can survive losing Cam, too."

"I hear you on that."

"Oh, dear heaven, my grandson." Maddie strained against the seat belt to fish in her hip pocket for her new cell. "I need to call the school."

Sam switched lanes and glanced over at her. "I don't think calling his school is a good plan."

"But I need to let Caleb know his father is hurt!"

"And then have him drive to Missoula like a bat out of hell? He could have an accident. You've already got one boy hurt. It might be better to find out more about Cam's injuries before you notify his son. If it's real bad, I can drive back down to pick Caleb up and make sure he reaches St. Pat's safely."

Maddie put the phone on her lap. "I'm not thinking clearly, am I?"

"I don't know about that. But I do know that being notified by the school office that his dad has been hurt might scare the daylights out of the kid."

As little as Maddie liked Sam Conacher, she was grateful for his presence and his levelheadedness.

ONCE AT THE HOSPITAL, MADDIE STILL FELT AS IF SHE WERE MOVing through a fog. An ER doctor came out to speak with her. They sat in a corner for privacy. Sam, though uninvited, remained at Maddie's side. Before the conversation was over, she was glad he'd stayed. He asked questions that she might not have thought to ask. The news was grim. Cam was undergoing emergency surgery. One of his broken ribs had punctured his lung in two places. There was also a possibility that Cam might have a back injury, but that was a concern for later.

After the physician left, Maddie couldn't stop shaking. "It's really bad," she whispered.

Sam curled a hard arm around her shoulders. "Not that bad. He's built like a brick shithouse. He'll pull through this and be right as rain. If the punctured lung doesn't fix itself, the surgeon can do it. And in this day and age, back injuries are repaired every day. It's amazing what they can do."

Maddie clung to those predictions. They were all she had.

SAM WANTED TO GO CHECK ON HIS DAUGHTER. SHE HADN'T seemed to be seriously hurt as he drove her in, but she'd gone down with a horse and had her leg pinned under its body. Kirstin was a slender, slightly built woman. That was a lot of weight, and not all injuries were immediately apparent after an accident. He couldn't bring himself to leave Maddie alone, though. He could tell just by looking at her that she was clinging to her composure by a thin thread.

Just when Sam thought he could bear the waiting no longer, Kirstin hobbled out on crutches into the ER waiting room. When Sam leaped to his feet, she gave him a groggy smile and said, "I'm fine, Dad. My leg is badly bruised and my ankle is sprained, but nothing is broken."

Maddie jumped up. "Oh, you poor thing. Are you in a lot of pain?"

Sam appreciated that Maddie could feel concern for his daughter when her son might be in serious peril.

Kirstin shook her head. "The doctor gave me a shot to take the edge off and told me to baby the leg for a few days." Struggling with the crutches, she lowered herself onto a seat cushion next to where Maddie had been sitting. She grasped the older woman's hand and drew her down beside her. "I'm dying to know how Cam is. They wouldn't tell me anything because we're not related."

Maddie's voice trembled as she repeated what the doctor had told her. Kirstin started to cry. Maddie hugged her close and cried with her. Sam felt like a tree that had put down roots in the glossy waiting room floor. He waited until both women got their spigots turned off and then went to stand in front of Maddie.

"I think I should drive back to Rustlers' Gulch and get Caleb out of school."

Maddie glanced at her watch. "Yes," she agreed in a shaky voice. "I'd offer to do it, but I'd have to use your truck." Looking up at him with tear-swollen eyes, she asked, "Would you like me to write you a note? They're pretty strict about allowing someone to take a kid out of class."

Sam mustered a smile. "Everyone knows me, and Caleb is old enough to speak for himself. I won't need a note."

WHEN CALEB WAS CALLED TO THE OFFICE, THE LAST PERSON HE expected to see was their mean neighbor. Inside a building, Sam looked bigger than he did at a distance. He wore a faded blue shirt, jeans, and dusty riding boots. His hat, once a beige color, had a ragged and charred front brim, dirt smudges all over it, and a sweat ring above the leather band. Caleb figured he'd probably been wearing that Stetson, day in and day out, for years.

He wanted to ask why a man with all his money didn't buy himself a new hat. Instead Caleb asked, "What do *you* want?" He had no intention of being friendly to someone who'd been rude to his grandmother. "You pulled me out of geometry class, so make it fast."

Conacher drew off his Stetson. His hair was thick and as white as a motel room towel. "I'm afraid I've got some bad news, son. Your dad got hurt this morning, and he's in the hospital. St. Pat's in Missoula. Your grandmother sent me to pick you up."

Caleb's stomach dropped. His father had gone home with Kirstin last night, and his grandmother had been afraid there might be trouble. "Hurt? What did you do to him?"

Conacher thrust his fingers through his hair. "I didn't put him in the hospital. He got charged by a bull. He's busted up pretty bad."

A funny, quivery feeling attacked Caleb's knees. "A bull? *Your* bull?"

"Yes, my bull, but I didn't sic it on him. It was an accident. If you'll come with me, I'll tell you about it on the way to Missoula."

Caleb's heart started to pound. "I've got my own rig. I can drive myself."

The rancher pursed his lips. He had deep wrinkles on his face, and his bushy black eyebrows looked like they'd been salted with a generous shaker. "Well, son, you could do that, I suppose. But your grandmother doesn't want you behind the wheel. She's afraid you'll be too upset to drive safely and might have a wreck. She's mighty upset about your father right now. Do you really want to give her something more to worry about?"

Caleb loved his gram almost as much as he did his dad. He always tried not to worry her. Ever since Gramps had died, his family fretted about one another too much as it was. To them death was like a contagious disease that might strike again at any moment. "No," he said. "I don't want to make her worry."

Conacher put his hat back on. "Do you need to get anything from your locker?" When Caleb nodded, he said, "I'll wait here for you. Make it fast, though. If your dad wakes up, he'll want to see you."

Heart still racing, Caleb ran to his locker and returned minutes later with his jacket and backpack. As he and Conacher exited the front doors into a shaded breezeway that bordered the campus parking lot, Caleb said, "Just because I'm letting you give me a ride doesn't mean we're friends."

The rancher chuckled. Caleb didn't think he did that often. He sounded like a rusty hinge being forced open. "Good to know we understand each other."

SAM WAS GLAD HE'D DRIVEN BACK TO COLLECT CAM'S SON. THE boy tried to act tough, but his face had paled and his hands were trembling, telltale signs that he'd taken the news about his father pretty hard.

"I'm sorry your dad got hurt," Sam said. "I know it can't be easy to hear the news from a stranger."

Caleb nodded. Sunlight slanted through the windshield to make his brownish blond hair glisten. He was a handsome kid and resembled his dad. Sam cut that thought short. Since seeing Cam risk his life to save Kirstin that morning, his estimation of the man had inched up, but he wasn't ready to credit him with being good-looking.

"Is my dad going to die?" Caleb asked.

Sam considered his answer. "He's in good hands. Some of the best doctors in the state are caring for him."

Caleb gave Sam a sideways glare. "I'm not a baby. Give it to me straight. How bad is he hurt?"

Something tugged inside Sam's chest. He was starting to like this kid. "He's in pretty bad shape. But my money is on him pulling through."

"Where is he hurt?"

Sam took Caleb at his word and gave it to him straight. The boy tensed his shoulders and lifted his chin. "A punctured lung won't take my dad out. He's tough, and he's a fighter. We lost my grandpa not that long ago. Dad knows we can't lose him, too."

Once again, Sam felt glad that Caleb wasn't driving.

IT SEEMED TO SAM THAT HIS ASS HAD BEEN GLUED ALL DAY TO THE driver's seat. During the trips back and forth between Rustlers' Gulch and Missoula, he'd had a lot of time to think about his recent behavior. And he wasn't proud of himself. He recalled all those nights when he couldn't sleep because he imagined Annie berating him for hanging on so tightly to Kirstin. He'd never been a fanciful man, but now he suddenly wondered if that voice inside his head had been only his imagination. A burning sensation settled at the base of his throat when he thought of Annie. She'd been more than just beautiful; she'd been his everything. When he'd gone off half-cocked, she'd always helped him calm down and find his center. She'd also been a wonderful wife and mother, thoughtful, wise, and loving. If anyone would come back from the grave to protect her daughter, it would be Annie.

And now, with sudden clarity, Sam realized how much Kirstin had needed her mother's intervention. Sam's whole world had fallen apart when Annie died, so he'd turned to Kirstin to be his support post. Once he'd made that transition, he couldn't bear the thought of losing Kirstin and being alone. He hadn't wanted her to love another man because that would have weakened his hold on her.

As if a recording played inside his head, he recalled Kirstin saying that she was nearly twenty-seven and running out of time to fall in love and have babies. Sam had nearly destroyed her life with his possessiveness. Even worse, if she'd found true love with Cameron McLendon and the young man ended up dead, her life *would* be destroyed. Nobody knew better than Sam that true love came along only once in a lifetime.

Sam was still mulling that over when he delivered Caleb to the hospital. While Sam parked his truck, Caleb ran through the automatic doors into the ER waiting room. By the time Sam got there, only Maddie remained.

"We've been assigned a new waiting area," she told Sam as he sat beside her. "Caleb is so upset he can't sit still, so Kirstin took him up. It's where the doctor will go to talk with us after he finishes operating."

Sam had always held his thoughts and emotions close to his chest, so he felt as surprised as Maddie looked when he blurted, "I've been a horrible father to my daughter these last six years."

He expected a sarcastic comment from Maddie. He sure as hell hadn't been pleasant to her. Instead she made a low sound in her throat and touched his arm as if to comfort him.

"It's never too late to change, Sam."

Even to Sam's ears, his voice sounded strangled when he replied, "I'm not sure I know how to change."

Maddie sighed. "Talking with someone about it may help."

"I hate counselors. Hate the whole idea of baring my soul to someone whose only knowledge comes from a textbook."

She surprised the hell out of him by saying, "I'm not sold on counseling, either. Sometimes, though, a good friend who has also made mistakes can give sound advice."

Sam couldn't resist asking, "Have *you* made mistakes?"

Tears welled in her eyes. "Haven't we all? It's those of us who don't realize we've made mistakes that can't change our ways."

"Yeah, well." Sam removed his hat and hung it on his knee. "I no longer have any friends to advise me. After Annie died, I ran all of them off."

Just then Caleb came racing into the waiting room. "The doctor's upstairs waiting to talk to us."

MADDIE'S CHEMO TREATMENT ON MONDAY WAS STILL PLAYING heck with her body. Sam flanked her, setting the pace with long strides as she followed Caleb to the elevators. Sweat beaded her brow. She got short of breath. Her legs felt as if they might buckle. It seemed to her that the hallways were miles long. She normally had several good days before a treatment. Then, afterward, she felt nauseated and her energy bottomed out. Now was one of those times.

"Are you all right?" Sam asked, looking down at her with concern.

Maddie was panting and could barely reply. Sam grasped her arm and drew her to a stop. "This isn't a footrace. Let's stop for a second."

She cast a frantic glance at Caleb as he turned a corner into yet another hallway. "No," she managed to say. Cam's doctor waited upstairs. If she took time to catch her breath, she might miss speaking with him. "I—have—to—get there."

She struck off again, and Sam followed, setting his strides to match hers. A wave of gratitude swamped her. *Sam Conacher isn't all bad,* she decided. Buried under that crotchety exterior lurked a man with at least some goodness in his heart.

After walking for what seemed forever, Maddie saw that Caleb was holding the elevator door open for them. She entered the cubicle with a sigh of relief and grasped the handrail to steady herself. When Sam stepped in, he seemed to loom over her. The car gently bumped its way up to the correct floor. As the panel slid open again, Sam grasped her elbow with a firm grip. Maddie realized that he was lending her his strength. It was as if he sensed she had no reserves of her own.

She was shaking almost uncontrollably when she spotted Kirstin sitting in a nicely appointed waiting alcove. Flanked by her crutches, she looked pale and frustrated. She'd tied her long black hair into a knot at the back of her neck, and her forehead was deeply creased with worry. Maddie surmised that the physician, a young fellow wearing blue scrubs and a surgical cap that concealed his hair color, refused to divulge any information to Kirstin because she wasn't a member of the family. Sam helped Maddie sink onto a chair beside his daughter. Again, his actions struck Maddie as being out of character for the irascible man she'd come to know. Caleb perched on the edge of a cushion next to Maddie.

The doctor leaned forward to shake Maddie's hand as he introduced himself. "You must be Mrs. McLendon."

"Yes."

"I'm a great fan of your books," he said with a smile. "I know writing is the last thing on your mind right now, so I'll get to the point." He glanced at Kirstin and Sam. "Do I have your permission to speak freely in front of your friends?"

Maddie never would have thought that Sam Conacher would be referred to as one of her friends, but she nodded nevertheless.

Somehow their brick walls and signposts had gone the way of the wind. "Please. My son would also grant you permission."

The doctor, already sitting on the edge of his seat after shaking Maddie's hand, braced his elbows on his knees. "First, let me say that your son survived the surgery, but he's still in critical condition. He arrived with severe traumatic pneumothorax, which is air that escapes from a punctured lung and collects in the chest cavity. Often a lung puncture will clot and repair itself, but in this case, with a double puncture, that didn't occur. The lung remained collapsed. We had no choice but to go in to do surgical repair, and we almost lost him on the table. The uninjured lung had a lot of pressure on it as well, so he couldn't breathe efficiently."

Maddie winced. Kirstin grabbed her hand and squeezed it hard.

"We performed thoracentesis, a procedure done with a short-bore needle attached to a syringe. We go in between the second and third ribs to draw out the air and fluid crowding the lung. In this case, there was so much fluid and air in the pleural space that it was doubly difficult for us to get all of it. The lung punctures were too large to quickly close by themselves, so I went in to repair the damage by putting a tube down the throat and into the bronchial passage. Now it's a wait-and-see game. In the morning, if he remains stable, we'll get some images of his spine. He was unresponsive to stimuli in his right leg. Let me stress that it could be due to swelling around the spinal cord."

He said nothing more. Maddie understood what he'd left unsaid, that her son could be partially paralyzed. She wanted to scream, *"No!"* She choked back the word. Cam was so active. He loved to hike and ride horses. He enjoyed working on the land. His life would be changed forever if he came out of this unable to walk.

"Right now Cameron is out of recovery and in intensive care," the surgeon continued. "Only one close family member is allowed to see him at a time and for only ten minutes per hour. He's asleep, not unconscious. Rest is the best thing for him right now, so I really don't want anyone talking to him, because he may feel obligated to respond. I want that injured lung to rest as much as possible."

Maddie knotted her hands on her lap. "You said 'if he remains stable.' Can I take that to mean he's in stable condition right now?"

"He is. At the moment. We'll be keeping close tabs on him. One possibility, which we hope doesn't occur, is pulmonary edema, fluid in the lung instead of outside of it. Another is a recurrence of traumatic pneumothorax. He endured blunt trauma to his chest. The bruising was extreme. But if those things happen, we will be ready to deal with them."

"What about his broken ribs?" Caleb asked.

The surgeon's blue eyes focused on the boy. "You must be Caleb." He grinned. "I read your dad's admittance chart, which your grandmother filled out after she reached the hospital. And you've asked a good question. Your father has three broken ribs, two simple and one complex. A simple rib fracture is where the rib is broken but stays in alignment. A complex fracture means that the fracture is slightly out of alignment or completely disconnected from the chest wall. The complex fracture left a piece of your dad's rib disconnected. It's rare with complex fractures for only one rib to be involved. Normally three or more adjacent ribs are disconnected, each of them broken in two or three places.

"Your dad got off lucky. Somehow that one rib broke away from the chest wall, punctured the lung, and sprang back into place after the blunt trauma. Because the lung was punctured twice, I believe your dad was butted two times. The rib is still disconnected, but I hope the healing tissue and muscles will slowly reconnect it."

"How could only one rib get broken clean in two?" Caleb asked shakily. "That doesn't seem possible."

The surgeon grinned. "You should become a doctor, because you're absolutely right. It's an anomaly. This is only my guess, but your dad's chest above the broken ribs is severely bruised, so I think the bull butted him at a slight angle, hitting the upper chest with its forehead and the ribs with its nose, striking with more force on that upper rib than the ones below it. It's the only explanation I can come up with."

"Can you fix the disconnected one?" Caleb asked in a thin voice. "If it just dangles in there, it might poke more holes in him."

"In some cases we will go in and repair the ribs with a metal plate, but in your dad's case we prefer to track it with imagery. Sometimes the rib will realign itself and heal, and I think your dad's may do that. In the meanwhile, we'll administer good pain management and supplementary oxygen to make it less painful for him to breathe. We'll also use pulmonary toilet treatments. That sounds pretty awful. A better term might be pulmonary hygiene. That means keeping fluid and mucus off the lungs. We can do that with breathing treatments and by raising the foot of his bed."

The physician stood up and smiled. "I believe the prognosis is good. He's young and strong. He's also in the hands of very concerned and talented caregivers who will watch him around the clock." He glanced at Maddie. "After seeing him, you should go home. Walking the halls and sleeping in chairs will exhaust you, and tomorrow he may be awake and wanting to see you." His cheek creased in another smile. "I know you'll probably decide to stay. If you do, ask a nurse for pillows and blankets so you can be halfway comfortable."

After the surgeon walked away, Caleb dissolved into tears. Maddie, recovered now from the footrace in the hospital hallways, gathered him into her arms. He'd soon soaked the shoulder of her top. It broke her heart to feel his body jerk with each sob.

"Now, now," she murmured. "You heard the doctor. Your father is going to be fine."

"Maybe paralyzed, Gram. He'll never be fine if he can't walk."

Maddie mustered her strength and refused to cry with her grandson. "Don't be silly. People can walk with one paralyzed leg. But let's not get ahead of ourselves. The doctor said the lack of response to stimuli could be due to swelling. He was thrown against thick fence rails. I'm betting that his back is pretty swollen and feeling will return to his leg as soon as the swelling goes down."

Maddie didn't believe a word she was saying, but she had to be upbeat for Caleb's sake. He needed to feel optimistic.

"Oh, Gram. I love him so much. He's the best dad ever. I wish I could go in there and fix him."

"So do I, sweetie, but we'll have to leave that to the doctor."

Just then a nurse came into the waiting area. "The surgeon says Mr. McLendon can have visitors now." She held up a finger. "One visitor per hour for only ten minutes, and the person must be an immediate family member. He's still asleep, so please don't wake him. Who would like to go in first?"

Maddie gave Caleb a nudge. "You go. I know he'd like it if you came first. I can go next time."

As the boy walked away, Maddie sent up a silent prayer that Caleb would feel better after seeing his father.

"That was good of you, Maddie," Kirstin said. "I know you're dying to see him yourself."

"I'm sure you are, too," Maddie replied. "I'll see to it that you get your turn."

"I'm not a family member," Kirstin said.

"I guess I know better than a nurse who's related to him and who isn't." Maddie forced a smile. "You'll have your turn."

Sam shifted in his chair and crossed his ankles. When Maddie glanced at him, he looked relaxed, but she sensed that he was unaccustomed to sitting and doing nothing. Unlike her, he was active all day. She went for walks on her good days, but it was difficult to find enough exercise time to make up for the hours of inactivity when she was behind a keyboard.

As if he heard her thoughts, he said, "I detest hospitals. When my wife was dying, this place became my second home."

Maddie could relate. How many hours had she spent in hospitals while Graham lost his battle with cancer? "I hate hospitals, too. Unfortunately they're a necessary evil."

The conversation, if it could be called that, ended there. She had a feeling that Sam could be a man of few words.

The ten minutes that Caleb was gone seemed like a small eternity, every second dragging by. When he finally emerged from the bowels of the ICU, he looked calm and more hopeful. Maddie's taut muscles relaxed as he walked toward them.

"He's sleeping good," the youth said. "And his breathing is even. Except for his back, I think he's going to be okay. It's scary to see him, though, Gram. He's got a needle in the back of his hand with a bag of stuff dripping into him. And he's on oxygen. He's really pale, too."

Striving to keep her voice steady, Maddie said, "Well, of course he's pale. He's been through an ordeal."

Caleb sat next to Sam. Within seconds the boy was tapping his toe on the floor. Then he started popping his knuckles.

"Keep doing that," Sam said, "and you'll have arthritis when you get to be my age."

Caleb looked at Sam as if he couldn't imagine ever being that old. Maddie bit back a smile. Beside her Kirstin yawned and then sat straighter.

"That pain shot is making me sleepy. I need to move around." She pushed up on her crutches. "Something to drink sounds good. Does anybody know the way to the cafeteria?"

Because Sam had just mentioned that St. Pat's had become his second home during his wife's decline, Maddie figured that Kirstin must have spent a good deal of time in this hospital as well. Surely she knew where the eatery was.

Caleb jumped up. "I saw the signs. I can show you where it is."

Kirstin winked at him. "Lead the way."

As Maddie watched the unlikely pair go up the hallway, she mustered a smile. Caleb walked with exaggerated slowness while Kirstin hobbled along beside him. "She's a sweet girl, Sam. She knew Caleb needed a distraction." She glanced over at him. He had removed his hat and hung it over his bony knee again. Except for here in the hospital, she'd never seen him bareheaded. "It's just my observation, but it appears to me that you did a fine job of raising her."

Sam held the brim of his hat to keep it on his knee while he crossed his ankles again. His boots, poking out from the legs of his jeans, were scuffed and dusty. She guessed that he'd started his day working on the ranch. "That was her mother's doing. Ever since Annie died, I've botched the job."

Maddie glanced at her watch, thinking two things—that what remained of the hour before she could see her son would seem like forever and that Sam could say a lot with an economy of words. Silence settled between them. Normally Maddie felt a need to keep a conversation going, but she didn't really like Sam well enough to bother with the effort. Thirty minutes passed without a word being exchanged between them. Maddie was watching the minute hand on her watch.

Suddenly Sam asked, "What was his name?"

Startled by the sudden question, Maddie gave him a curious look. "What was whose name?"

"Your husband's."

"Why do you want to know?" She was wary. If this man said a derogatory word about Graham, she'd come unglued. She was in no mood for more of his snarky comments.

"He did a damned fine job of helping you raise Cam. He's a fabulous young fellow. I know your husband's dead and gone. And maybe I'll sound crazy, but I'm starting to think there's some weird kind of link between this world and the next. Just in case I'm right, I'd like to know the man's name so I can tell him his son is really something in my book."

Maddie could scarcely believe her ears. "Are we talking about the same randy little fucker you hate so much?"

He scowled at her. "I thought you never used the F word."

"On special occasions that warrant it, I can curse right along with the best of them."

Watching him in profile, she saw one corner of his mouth twist up in a reluctant smile. "How long are you planning to rub my nose in it?"

"I just started. You hated my son. Now you hold him in high regard. Why the change of heart?"

"I saw it all, like I said. That damned bull would have killed my daughter. Cam ran interference, knowing when he did that he was putting his own bacon on the plate. He didn't think about himself, only about her. Of course I hold the man in high regard."

Maddie smiled. She doubted that Sam often said a good word about anybody, and he'd just given Cam a rare compliment. "Graham."

"What?"

"My husband's name was Graham."

"Like the damned cracker? Who the hell would name their son something like that?"

Maddie almost chuckled. The reaction was so typical of the Sam she'd come to know. With a start, she realized that the better she came to know him, the closer she came to liking him. "It's a wonderful Scottish name for a boy."

"Your husband was a Scot?"

"Yes."

"I'll be damned. Are you Scottish, too?"

Maddie folded her arms. "No, I'm Irish. Mess with me too much, and you'll find out how red my hair should have been."

He flicked her another halfhearted smile. "I should've known when I counted those damned no-trespassing signs. Don't you think two hundred and thirty-nine was overkill?"

"I don't know. Compared to a brick wall, it's not so crazy. If I went onto your property, what did you think I might do, anyway?"

"Contaminate it?" He looked at her straight on, and his weathered face creased in so many places it looked like a road map. Regardless, Maddie noted that he was one handsome fellow when he actually smiled. "I didn't want any hillbilly germs to rub off on my dirt."

Maddie stifled a laugh. "Go to hell, Sam Conacher."

He sighed and settled back in his chair. "I'm already there, Maddie. Have been for a long, *long* time."

"I lost the love of my life, too," she told him. "You're right. It's hell."

"Annie meant the world to me. It's been six years, and I still miss her with every breath I take."

"Oh, God. I was hoping I'd feel better after that long."

"It no longer hurts quite as much," he admitted. "You get to thinking you've moved past it, because you don't think of the person for a few hours. Then, bang, it blindsides you." He released a long breath and fiddled with his hat. "She was my other half in every sense of the word, my guiding light, my adviser, and my comfort during the storms."

Maddie smiled sadly at her own, similar memories. "I don't think everyone feels that way after losing a spouse. You and I were blessed to have found that kind of love."

Sam nodded and then wondered aloud, "Does anyone ever totally recover from the loss?"

"I doubt it." And the thought filled Maddie with dread, because she had to face an unknown number of years feeling pain. "All a person can do is keep moving forward."

Just then she realized the hour was up. "Oh! I can go in now and see Cam."

As Maddie made her way into the ICU, she braced herself after Caleb's warning. Her body quivered as she stepped to her son's bedside. He did look awfully pale. She checked the clock so she wouldn't overstay her visit and then fixed her gaze on Cam. His golden brown hair lay in tousled waves over his forehead. The oxygen cannula had slipped slightly in his nostrils and canted to one side. She noticed that his nose was swollen and his lower lip was split, injuries that struck her as odd. If a bull had butted him in the face, surely the damage would have been worse.

She wouldn't allow herself to touch him for fear of disturbing his rest. He breathed evenly and seemed to be sleeping peacefully. Those were good signs. *Dear God,* she prayed, *don't let him come through this partially paralyzed.* Sam had described the bull's attack, so she knew her son had been butted on the back and sent flying against thick fence rails. Could a man have sustained such severe blows *without* having spinal damage?

Even as Maddie asked herself that question, she saw Cam's right foot move. She released a taut breath. Had it been a nerve twitch? She desperately hoped not. She wanted her son to go home with the use of both legs.

Chapter Ten

LEFT IN THE WAITING AREA ALONE, SAM SAT FORWARD ON THE chair, using his knees as an armrest as he stared at the floor. *Poor Maddie,* he thought. He couldn't blame her for being so worried. Cam had taken some solid hits.

It had been a long time since Sam prayed, but he did so now, sending up a silent plea that Cam McLendon would completely recover. He remembered how Cam had walked to his porch last night and faced him. He also recalled how the younger man wouldn't get up and fight back after Sam busted him in the chops. When Sam died—and he hoped that didn't happen soon—Kirstin would need a man who'd protect her with his life, and Cam had proven today that he would do that without thinking twice. Sam wasn't a person who changed his mind easily, but he'd done a turnaround in his estimation of Cam McLendon. Sam hoped he would fully recover to stand at Kirstin's side.

Maddie emerged from the ICU. Sam took careful measure of her expression and thought she looked less drawn and sad. She resumed her seat beside him, sighed, and smiled slightly. "I saw his right foot move."

"That's a good sign."

She nodded. "It could have been a nerve twitch, I suppose. But it gave me hope that his back is okay."

Kirstin and Caleb returned from the cafeteria. The boy's arms were filled with food cartons and a drink tray. "Lunch," he said. "Kirstin paid for everything."

Maddie murmured a thank-you, and Sam, remembering his manners, followed suit. Caleb handed out sandwiches, small bags of chips, and soft drinks.

As Kirstin unwrapped her BLT, she said, "You know, Maddie, you could go home. I plan to stay the night."

"Oh, no. Even if I left, I wouldn't be able to sleep."

"Me, either," Caleb said. "I don't want to go home."

"Well, I have the only vehicle," Sam inserted, "so I reckon I'll hang out here, too."

Sam was secretly glad to have a reason to stay. He no longer wanted to be a badass, but a sudden about-face wasn't easy, either. As soon as he'd finished eating, he walked up the hall to call Miguel and ask him to rustle up some help for the following day. Neither Kirstin nor Sam would be around to work, and the McLendons also had livestock and pets that needed care.

"But, senor," Miguel said, "how will I find anyone to help? No one wishes to work here anymore."

Sam's heart sank, because he knew it was true. He had burned too many bridges over the last six years. His once-loyal friends avoided him now. He had hired and fired so many ranch hands that people no longer applied for work at the Conacher Ranch.

With a sigh, Sam said, "Then just take care of the animals, Miguel, and let the rest slide."

He went on to speak with his manager about other concerns before returning to the ICU waiting area. Caleb had wolfed down his meal, and now, like a satisfied pup, he was nodding off to sleep. As Sam sat beside Maddie, he saw Kirstin draw the boy's head down on her shoulder. Relaxed by the pain shots the ambulance attendant and the ER doctor had given her, she soon fell asleep herself.

"Well," Sam said, "I think we'll be keeping this vigil by ourselves."

Maddie looked up at him. "There's no reason for you to stay. If we need to go somewhere, I can always hire a cab."

He stretched out his legs and set his hat on the empty seat beside him. "I've driven back and forth so much today that I'm not excited about doing it again." He glanced at her uneaten sandwich, perched atop her purse, and the glass bottle she held. "Ginger tea? My wife drank that to settle her stomach while she was getting chemo treatments."

She shuddered. "God save me from that. I've just developed a taste for it."

Sam studied her face, remembering how exhausted she'd become while walking in the hallways. "You're not sick, are you?"

"Heavens, no." As if she guessed that he was recalling her lack of endurance earlier, she added, "I just get winded easily these days. I chalk it up to age. I also feel off my mark sometimes." She shrugged. "It may be something I eat every once in a while that disagrees with me. I feel nauseated and shaky."

"Are you feeling that way today?"

"A little."

"That explains the ginger tea," he noted. "It's supposed to soothe the stomach. Maybe you should get a wellness check."

"I had a complete physical last spring."

GROWING UNCOMFORTABLE WITH THE CONVERSATION, MADDIE was relieved to see that an hour had passed, allowing her to check on Cam again. She considered waking Kirstin to give her a turn, but the young woman looked so exhausted she decided to let her snooze. Cam looked much the same when she went in. She was disappointed not to see his right foot move again, but someone had straightened his cannula, and the monitors showed that his heart rate and blood pressure were normal.

Maddie's visits to see Cam each hour set the pattern for the remainder of the afternoon, with her and Sam making small talk to pass the time in between. Around six, Caleb woke up as if he had a built-in dinner bell. Maddie gave him her credit card to go to the cafeteria for his evening meal. Kirstin continued to sleep. When Caleb returned with his hunger appeased, he slumped beside Kirstin and nodded off again.

SAM DIDN'T KNOW WHAT IT WAS ABOUT MADDIE McLENDON, BUT he found himself telling her things he never dreamed he'd admit to anyone.

"Were you angry after Graham died?" he asked.

"Oh, yes," she confessed. "Not with Graham, but with the world in general. I still find it hard to see couples my age who are still together. I wonder why I had to lose my husband and other women get to keep theirs."

"Oh, yeah," Sam said. "I still think like that. It doesn't seem fair, does it?" He sighed and ran a hand over his eyes. "Only I was referring to real anger, the kind that burns in your gut and pushes you into a rage at the tip of a hat."

She sent him a questioning look.

"I was envious of my rancher friends who still had their wives, and I hated them because they did. I guess you could say that anger and sadness festered inside me and turned me into someone nobody likes. Hell, Maddie, I don't even like myself."

"I'm sorry it's been such a difficult road for you."

"If it hadn't been for Kirstin, I might have popped myself."

"With a gun?"

Sam huffed. "How else can you pop yourself?"

"Oh, Sam. Having suicidal thoughts isn't good. I know you hate counselors, but maybe it would help if you saw your doctor and got on an antidepressant."

He shook his head. "And be like a zombie? Everyone I've known who took that junk was flatlined."

"Flatlined is better than dead. Do you still think about killing yourself?"

"No. I focused on Kirstin and found a reason to live. But I still have other feelings I can't dump. Guilt is the big one for me."

"Guilt?"

"For arguing against Annie getting a hysterectomy after Kirstin was born. We both wanted another child. But she started getting ovarian cysts. When Kirstin was around seven or eight, the doctor recommended a complete hysterectomy, and I asked Annie to try to get pregnant for another six months before she had the surgery. If I'd been more supportive of her having the operation, she would have had it done and couldn't have gotten ovarian cancer."

"Did Annie have ovarian cancer at the time?"

"Only cysts back then. But what if it was there, and the doctors didn't find it?"

She laid a hand on his arm. Her touch comforted him. He felt as if she had put salve on a raw wound deep inside of him. "Sam, I'm sure she had yearly exams. A good gyn would have noticed abnormalities when he palpated her ovaries. There's also a blood test that can be run."

"But she had an exam not that long before she was diagnosed.

She was having pains in her side. The gyn found nothing and thought she was having flare-ups of chronic appendicitis."

"I've never heard of chronic appendicitis," she said.

"Most people haven't," Sam told her. "For whatever reason, sometimes an inflamed appendix builds enough pressure to shift the blockage that causes the appendix to get infected, allowing the appendix to drain. Then the crisis is over. Chronic appendicitis can happen again and again in some people. But eventually they will have an acute attack, requiring immediate surgery."

She kept her hand on his sleeve. "How old was Kirstin when Annie passed away?"

"Twenty."

"And you think Annie lived with ovarian cancer for more than twelve years, Sam? I don't believe that's how it goes."

"She was diagnosed when Kirstin was eighteen. In a little less than two years she was gone."

"You can ask a doctor, but it's my guess that your wife had no cancer until Kirstin was in her late teens." She withdrew her hand from his arm. "I'm not saying you're crazy for blaming yourself. In fact, I think it's normal. Graham loved bacon, eggs, and fried potatoes for breakfast. I knew high-fat meals weren't good for him, or for me, but I cooked the food anyway. When he was diagnosed with colon cancer, I wondered if I caused it."

Sam gave her a sharp look. "Do you still think that way?"

She scrunched her shoulders. "It goes through my mind. But I try to chase it away, Sam. As humans, we want to believe we're in charge of our own destinies, but the truth is, most of us aren't. In fact, I doubt that any of us are. Cancer strikes people in all walks of life, people who ate healthfully and exercised, people who never smoked or drank. We can do everything right and still be victims. I think life is too short to blame ourselves for the death of someone we dearly loved and never would have deliberately harmed."

Sam said nothing.

"I felt robbed of my golden years with the only man I'll ever love," she went on. "But at some point, I realized that Graham left me a fabulous legacy, my son and my grandson, who love me and support me and watch out for me. I also have a wonderful daughter back east with two beautiful girls. She would leave work and temporarily abandon her family to be with me if I needed her."

"In other words, you count your blessings."

"I try. I still feel as if something precious was stolen from me, but if I mean to move on with my life, I need to get past that." She smiled up at him. "The ugly truth is, Sam, our kids can't fill the emptiness inside us. I don't know how people move beyond the feeling of loneliness. I could have gone to grief counseling, but those resources often offer only group sessions, and I'm uncomfortable with spilling my guts to strangers."

"Me, too. But we seem to be doing a fine job of it with each other."

She grimaced. "I guess we don't feel like strangers anymore." She picked at a fingernail. "Graham's hospice company had a counselor. She was a lovely young woman with little kids. I liked her immensely, but I couldn't help wondering how she could possibly understand how it feels to lose a spouse." She shrugged. "For some reason I feel better just talking about it with you, though. I know you've experienced a loss equal to mine and many of the same feelings."

Sam heard an echo of his own sentiments in every word Maddie said. He appreciated her honesty and wished that he'd tried to get to know her sooner. She had a low-key sense of humor that could catch him off guard.

"How can I wean myself away from my daughter?" he asked.

She glanced at her watch, reminding him that she eagerly awaited her next chance to check on Cam. "Why do you need to? Kirstin seems to love you dearly. I don't think she sees your need of her as an imposition. It's also natural for you to turn to her. You've lost your wife, your best friend, and your life partner. And remember that she lost her mother. She was very young when it happened. Together, you can form a new core that gives you both a sense of familial strength without limiting each other's personal freedoms."

Sam felt that barb. He had ruthlessly limited Kirstin's personal freedom, clinging to her like a child. But he didn't believe Maddie had meant the comment to hurt. She was a woman who spoke her mind, but she'd done so thoughtfully, and she'd given him some things to mull over. In a strange way, he felt as if they had become friends. How in the hell had that happened?

MINUTES LATER, AS MADDIE STOOD OVER CAM, WHO STILL SLEPT, she thought about Sam Conacher. During their shared vigil, she'd gotten glimpses of who he really was: not the cold, heartless man she'd believed he was, but more an old warrior who'd survived the death of his wife the only way he knew how. Maddie had never had to cling to Cam after Graham died, but Cam had been older and more mature than Kirstin was at twenty. He'd been generous with his time and support, always there for Maddie to lean on. She'd never needed to so much as ask. He'd just been there.

"Mom?"

At the sound of Cam's weak, raspy voice, Maddie jumped with a start. Then she leaned over her son, taking care not to touch his chest or jostle his bed. She settled for smoothing his hair. "Oh, darling. What a fright you gave me."

His smile was more a grimace. "Kirstin," he pushed out. "Is she hurt?"

"No, sweetheart. Her leg got bruised up, but she's otherwise fine. Sam arrived just in the nick of time to get the bull away from you."

"Will you t-tell her I love her?"

"Maybe you should tell her yourself." Maddie had been keeping an eye on the clock and knew six minutes of the allotted ten per hour still remained. "Let me go get her."

Dashing from the cubicle, Maddie encountered a nurse, told him that Cam was awake, and then said, "He's asking to see his fiancée. She was involved in the accident, and he's terribly worried about her. Can she come in to see him?"

The man smiled. "A fiancée qualifies as immediate family in my book. Of course she can come in."

Maddie raced to the waiting room, shook Kirstin awake, and then sank down beside Sam. He studied her for a moment. "You're out of breath again. A woman smart enough to write murder mysteries that keep me guessing should have the good sense to see a doctor. That's not old age creeping up on you."

Maddie could not tell Sam that she was recovering from a chemo treatment. Right or wrong, she had decided to keep her colon cancer a secret from her son and grandson, and she couldn't risk that Sam might let the cat out of the bag. She locked gazes with him. "I'm told that you burned every one of those books."

Sam emitted a laugh. The sound had a rusty edge, but it nevertheless surrounded her with warmth. "I bet I have my daughter to thank for you knowing about my book-burning party."

"No, you have yourself to thank. It was foolish to start a fire in a barrel with explosive fuel."

He rubbed his jaw, looking chagrined. "The gas was a mistake. I didn't turn on a light, and my night vision has gone to hell. I thought I grabbed the can of diesel."

It was a long vigil. Kirstin grew more alert after the shots wore off and she went to ask for pillows and blankets. Caleb, still asleep, nestled down with a murmur when he was covered and had something to support his lolling head. Maddie went in once more to see her son, and afterward she, too, succumbed to exhaustion. In her sleep, she gravitated toward Sam. He didn't mind lending her an arm to rest her head against. Kirstin draped a blanket over her and then moved Sam's hat to another chair so she could sit beside him.

"Well, Dad, it's been quite a day."

"How was Cam when you saw him last?"

She studied him with the same steel blue gaze he saw when he shaved each morning. "You sound like you might really care."

Sam dipped his head to kiss her forehead. "I was wrong, Kirstie. I was wrong, and I'm sorry. I'll say it as many times as you need to hear it."

Surprise crept into her expression. "You really mean it."

With a sigh, Sam said, "I do. With no thought for his own safety, he saved your life. I totally misjudged him. I said and did a lot of things I regret now. More than anything, though, I'm sorry for how I've treated you. I wanted you to remain my baby girl. I didn't want to be alone."

Her eyes went moist. "How could you think I'd ever leave you?" She blinked. "If I did, you might cut me out of your will."

Startled by her sassiness, Sam chuckled. "Who else would I leave my millions to?"

It was her turn to laugh. "Other people may believe you're a multimillionaire, but I know you're only rich on paper."

Sam gave her a long study. "You really want to spend the rest of your life looking at cows' asses and mending fences?"

"What else would I want to do? I'm a Conacher."

"You're also your own person. Maybe you want a cottage, a picket fence, and a litter of kids."

"How would you feel if I did?"

"Disappointed, but I'd get over it. I'm trying to turn over a new leaf. I need to let you follow your own dreams. The ranch is my dream, not yours."

Kirstin looped an arm around his neck and kissed his cheek. "I'm sorry to ruin your leaf turning, but I love the ranch, Dad." She drew back to smile up at him. "I rebelled. I probably went about it wrong. All I ever really wanted was to be my own person and break my eleven o'clock curfew."

"Was I *that* bad?"

"Worse," she quipped.

"Well, if I act that way again, tell me."

Maddie stirred awake. "Is it time to see Cam again yet?"

Kirstin glanced at her watch. "Go back to sleep, Maddie. I'll wake you when it's time."

THE FOLLOWING MORNING, A DIFFERENT DOCTOR, THIS ONE A neurosurgeon, came to the waiting area to speak with Maddie and Caleb. Imagery studied that morning revealed no sign of Cam having a spinal injury, but the doctor had seen evidence of nerve impairment and Cam still had little feeling in his right leg. The doctor hoped that most of the trouble was due to severe bruising and swelling, and Cam would be kept in the hospital for at least forty-eight hours for observation.

"The pulmonologist wants to keep a close eye on his lung as well. A setback at this point could be devastating."

After the doctor departed, Kirstin was the first to speak. "Caleb needs to get back to school, and, Maddie, you should probably get back to your writing. The two of you can come to the hospital to visit in the evenings. I can stay with Cam here at the hospital."

Maddie protested. "You're hurt. You should probably be elevating that leg."

"The ER doctor didn't say a word to me about elevating it. He just told me to baby the leg for a few days. I'll be useless to Dad at the ranch. At least by staying here, I'll be doing something."

Maddie relented. "If you're here, I won't worry. I know you'll call me if anything goes wrong."

"Absolutely," Kirstin assured her.

Maddie raised an eyebrow at Caleb. "Well, what's your vote?"

Caleb nodded. "If Kirstin is going to be with him, I should probably get back to classes tomorrow. Geometry is kicking my butt."

All the adults laughed. And so it was decided that the McLendons would go home and Sam would return to the ranch.

AS PICKUPS WENT, SAM'S WAS ROOMY. MADDIE HAD BARELY NOticed the interior as she rode into Missoula, but now, although she was bone weary and feeling nauseated, she wasn't beside herself with worry about Cam. Buttery soft gray leather hugged the seats, and it still had that faint "new car" smell that Maddie liked. Caleb rode in the backseat and made a halfhearted attempt to study geometry while Sam and Maddie maintained a peaceful silence up front.

When they reached camp, Maddie was delighted to see men

working on what would be their new homes. "Caleb, look! They've poured our cement slab!"

Caleb sat forward to peer out the windshield. "Holy smokes, that happened fast."

"Oh, to be in by Christmas!" Maddie dreamed aloud.

"Do you think we'll make it, Gram?"

Though Maddie had little hope, she said, "Possibly."

Caleb touched her shoulder. "Well, if we don't, Gram, don't you worry. I've got a plan, and we'll have the best Christmas ever."

When Sam pulled up behind Maddie's SUV, the three dogs greeted them at the fence. They bounced and twisted in midair, as Australian shepherds were prone to do, and it was difficult to distinguish any separation between them. They appeared to be one writhing mass of black, curry, and white fur.

"Miguel put them in last night in case it got cold," Sam said. "I'm glad to see that he came back over early to let them out. All the same, I'll make sure the horses have been fed and have plenty of water before I leave."

Caleb grabbed his backpack and exited the truck. "I'll come with you."

In no hurry to move, Maddie watched them take off together toward the horse pasture. She felt like a folding chair with rusty brackets. Her cozy trailer bed called to her. She'd have some ginger tea followed by a quick shower and then rest for a few hours before she attempted to work. Sleeping in a chair had left her knees achy and stiff.

She'd barely climbed out of the truck when Sam and Caleb returned.

"Is there anything else I can do that Cam usually takes care of?" Sam asked.

Maddie felt uncomfortable. She and Sam had been enemies

only yesterday, and now they'd forged a friendship of sorts, albeit a wary one. It seemed all wrong to let him do chores here when he probably had mountains of work to do at his ranch. "Thank you for offering, Sam, but I can't think of a single thing."

Sam touched the charred brim of his hat in farewell and swung back into his truck. "I'll keep in touch," he said through the lowered driver's window. "If you need anything, just let me know."

Maddie didn't have his phone number, but she refrained from reminding him of that. She and Caleb watched him drive away. Then Caleb beamed a pleased grin at her.

"Sam says I'm a good hand with horses!"

Maddie suspected that Sam rarely dished out compliments, so she dredged up a smile. "That was nice of him to say. I don't think he gives pats on the back very often."

Caleb, book bag in hand, took off for the cabin he shared with his father. Watching him go, Maddie was struck with a sudden and very worrisome thought. Cam might come home in a wheelchair. How on earth would he be able to get around out here? Exhaustion forced her to shelve that worry. Caleb would be fine while she grabbed a few hours of sleep, and oh, how badly she needed to stretch out.

THE NEXT MORNING, AFTER CALEB LEFT FOR SCHOOL, MADDIE heard a diesel truck pull up. She knew without looking that it had to be Sam, but she watched through a window anyway as he methodically cared for Cam's livestock. Maddie had intended to go out and do it. She felt much better today and hoped she would quickly regain her strength before she was due for her next treatment.

She was surprised when Sam left without tapping on her door. She shook her head. Most men would have at least stopped to receive a thank-you. But not Sam. He'd done something nice for a neighbor, but he clearly wanted no recognition for that. In fact, Maddie suspected that he'd have felt mortified if anyone else found out. Being kind to others didn't fit with his image as the local hard-ass.

She was smiling as she settled down to work while she could. Later that day, she had an appointment for a consultation with her oncologist, which she always dreaded. What if her cancer had returned? What if he wanted to change her chemo drug or administer it in stronger doses? Graham's course of treatment had called for chemo for a week, followed by three weeks of rest. He'd been sicker than a dog afterward, and toward the end, he'd had no good days.

Because she felt so much better, Maddie decided to leave early so she could drop by the hospital to see Cam and get some necessary shopping done. While in camp, she wore only jeans, knit tops, and hiking boots, but she had a nicer top for trips to town. After she dressed, she styled her hair and put on a touch of makeup. She liked what she saw in the mirror. Well, she guessed at her age a woman never really *liked* how she looked. Maddie was more inclined to study her reflection and wonder when that old gal had sneaked in and taken over her former self. But the foundation she'd lightly applied made her chemo-ravaged skin glow with artificial good health, and the mascara enhanced her eyes.

She enjoyed the drive to town. It was now early October, and the valley was getting another day of Indian summer. The mountainsides offered a variety of color to offset the evergreens, and the sky was so blue it took her breath away. Traffic was heavy in Missoula. Maddie jockeyed from lane to lane to reach the hospital and spent a quarter hour with her son, who could now have two visitors for thirty minutes at a time.

Cam seemed to be in good spirits. He complained about the rib pain, which was, he said, horrific when he used crutches to reach the bathroom. The hospital food was, in his opinion, better than average, and he was counting the hours until he could go home.

"Has any feeling returned to your leg?" Maddie asked.

Shadows dimmed the twinkle in Cam's eyes. "The neurologist took more pictures of my spine. He feels certain there's no actual nerve damage, but he says it may take weeks before the deep-tissue bruising and swelling go down. I may go home in a wheelchair."

"Permanent paralysis would be a much grimmer prognosis," Maddie reminded him. "And we'll figure out the wheelchair issue. Maybe Caleb can make ramps so you can move around the camp."

"I'm more worried about how I'll work."

Kirstin hobbled in, bearing a fresh pitcher of ice water. After greeting her and giving her a gentle scolding about not using her crutches, Maddie took her arrival as her cue to leave. "Well, sweetie," she said to Cam. "I have physical therapy at one, and I'd like to pick up a few grocery items on the way. I'll be back tonight with Caleb. We'll have a longer visit then."

Maddie went to the store and was heartened when she was able to hurry up and down the aisles without feeling breathless and weak. Chemo made her feel as if all her blood had been drained from her veins. Hungry for the first time in days, she stopped at the deli and enjoyed a cup of creamy pumpkin soup, a pleasant reminder that Halloween would soon be upon them. Maddie loved holidays, and somehow, by hook or by crook, she would decorate their camp to make it look festive. Caleb kept saying he had a plan for Christmas, but she had no intention of leaving it all up to him.

Soon she was sitting in front of a desk, facing her oncologist.

He was a stout, older man with a bald pate that shone like a beacon in the overhead lights. His sharp, humorless blue eyes told Maddie that he'd learned to distance himself emotionally, and she didn't blame him a bit. The success rates for curing many kinds of cancer had risen, but this man still faced failures in his profession, and it had surely taken a toll.

"I'll put your mind at ease right away. Your cancer hasn't returned. The images we took last week were absolutely clear."

Maddie relaxed in the leather swivel chair. "That's good news."

"It's all good news today. Low doses of this new drug every two weeks seem to have worked beautifully. I admit that I had reservations when your former oncologist in California suggested this approach to treatment, but at this juncture, I'm a believer. It's been more than six months since your surgery. After nine months of treatment, I won't have a qualm about reducing the frequency of your infusions or stopping them altogether."

Maddie felt as if she floated out of his office after the appointment. Her big Christmas gift this year would be having treatments only once a month from there on out, or possibly being finished with them.

Maddie took a short nap after she got home and put the groceries away. Then she went to work in her small kitchen to fix an early dinner. She hoped to get Caleb home from visiting his dad at the hospital tonight at an early enough hour for him to get a good night's sleep.

The meal was almost ready when Caleb came in, jabbering a mile a minute with Sam, who followed him into the trailer. Sam took off his hat and inclined his head to say hello.

"Gram, we've got plenty of food. Right? I invited Sam to have dinner with us."

Inwardly Maddie groaned. Outwardly she smiled. She'd fixed

a ground beef version of stroganoff. It wasn't exactly haute cuisine, a one-skillet offering created to fill hungry stomachs while not necessarily appealing to one's taste buds. "It's not fancy, but there's plenty," she settled for saying. "We'd both love to have you."

"Normally I wouldn't intrude on such short notice, but I'm hoping to go with you to the hospital tonight. Kirstin called. Cam can have friends or family visit him now, and I'd like to thank him for saving my daughter's life."

Maddie wasn't so sure that Cam counted Sam as a friend, but she wouldn't argue the point. She dished up the stroganoff and set it on the table, and each of them sat down on space-saving stools to eat. Caleb wolfed down his food and then put his plate and plastic flatware in the trash.

"I gotta go do my math assignment, Gram. It won't take me that long, and then we can leave to go see Dad."

Sam, still eating, gazed after the departing youth. "He's a nice young fellow, Maddie. You've done a fine job of helping to raise him."

Maddie swallowed and wiped the corners of her mouth with a paper napkin. "It definitely was a joint effort. Cam went to school and worked when Caleb was little. It fell to me and Graham to be stand-in parents. It was nice, actually. We were at an age when we could really enjoy him."

"Maybe I'll get to experience that with some grandchildren." Maddie had made coffee and served them both a cup. Sam took a slow sip of his. "Kirstin and I talked a little at the hospital. All she really wants is some freedom. I'm going to try my best to give her that."

"I don't think you have a choice. I could be mistaken, but I believe she and Cam love each other."

"I haven't a doubt," he agreed.

They ate for a moment in silence. Maddie, whose appetite was on and off again, finished first and excused herself to dispose of her plate and utensils. While she was bent over the trash receptacle, Sam asked, "Since your husband died, have you ever considered having a relationship?"

She straightened and turned to look at him. "I'm not interested in anything but friendship." Palm turned downward, she marked a spot just under her chin. "From here down, I'm a dead unit, just as I once told you."

Sam chuckled. "That's a dangerous thing to tell a man. He may want to recharge your batteries."

"Trust me, Sam, my batteries are well beyond being recharged. I wouldn't pass on an offer of friendship, though. You and I have some important things in common, and each of us can understand how the other one feels. Since losing Graham I've felt so alone. Cam and Caleb grieve for Graham, but that's different."

"Can mere friends go out to dinner and maybe take in a film?" he asked.

"I'd love to do dinner and a movie. I used to go out with Graham, but after his death, I felt conspicuous. Eating out alone is no fun, and neither is watching a film on your own."

"Isn't it awful?" Sam shook his head. "I felt like people were staring at me and never went again."

They were still discussing the topic when Caleb finished his homework. When they climbed into Sam's truck for the drive to Missoula, the boy said, "Can I go with you guys and help pick the movie?"

Sam shrugged. "I see no reason why not."

WHEN CAM CAME HOME, MADDIE HAD NO TIME FOR FRIVOLOUS things like dining out or seeing a movie. She barely found time to write. With only a trailer, a cabin, and two tents, she had no area large enough to accommodate the needs of someone in a wheelchair. She went online and desperately searched for a home she might temporarily rent, only none that she found accepted one pet, let alone three dogs and six cats. She even offered an absurdly huge security deposit and still couldn't negotiate a rental agreement.

Cam's right leg wouldn't support his weight, and his ribs pained him horribly when he attempted to use crutches. Caleb missed a day of school to build his father wheelchair ramps, which worked beautifully, but the moment Cam got on the gravel, his chair got stuck.

"This is ridiculous," Kirstin cried when she came to visit. "The nurses said he should use the crutches only to reach the restroom. Swinging his weight on his arms may prevent that detached rib from healing properly."

Maddie knew the younger woman was right. But she had no solution.

"While Cam recovers," Kirstin went on, "I want your whole family to stay at my place. The house is huge, with three empty bedrooms. And I'd love to have you."

"I appreciate the offer," Maddie said, "but I don't feel comfortable with that idea."

Cam seconded Maddie's vote. "We aren't moving in on you, Kirstin. I wouldn't feel right about it."

Maddie was left to walk back and forth between shelters, carrying meals to Cam, gathering his laundry, and taking it to the cook shack to wash it. That didn't include checking on him countless times in between. By the end of the third day, she was so exhausted that she groaned as she fell into bed, and the next morning she could barely force herself to get up. She felt weak and sick to her stomach. Normally once she had a good day after a chemo treatment, she felt fine until she had another infusion. She had physically overdone it, she guessed, but what choice did she have? Cam couldn't fare on his own yet.

She was in the cabin, helping her son get up to greet the day, when Sam made a surprise visit. He took one look at Maddie and asked, "Are you sick?"

She'd never been comfortable with lying. She preferred to be evasive. But if she looked half as bad as she felt, Sam would see right through her. "I'm just feeling under the weather."

He studied her with a sharp gaze. "You need to go back to bed. I'll take care of Cam until Kirstin can get here."

"I can't let you do that. It's a huge imposition."

"I insist," Sam replied. "If you have something contagious and Cam catches it, it won't be good. With broken ribs, coughing or vomiting hurts like the devil, and the strain of either one may do a lot of damage."

As reluctant as Maddie was, and as certain as she was that Cam wouldn't catch anything, she went back to bed. She fell asleep almost instantly.

SAM GRABBED A CAMP CHAIR AND SAT BESIDE CAM'S BED. CAM eyed the older man warily. They'd never spoken to each other when only the two of them were present, and Kirstie's father looked like a man with a lot on his mind. He wasn't sure what to expect.

What he didn't expect was for Sam to say, "This is too much for your mother, son. She looks like death warmed over."

Guilt stabbed through Cam's chest. "I know. I never saw this coming. The problem is, there's not much I can do to make it easier on her."

"Yes, there is," Sam replied. "You can swallow your pride and move your family to my place. It's even larger than Kirstin's house. I have five extra bedrooms, three on the ground floor. Miguel and I can build you a ramp so you can get down the front steps. It'll be a much better place for you to recover, and it'll make things far easier for your mother."

"I can't do that. Mom won't agree to it. She doesn't exactly like you."

Sam's face creased in a grin. "Actually, while you were in the hospital, we talked for hours and became friends. Only friends, but we've agreed that it would be nice to do dinner and a movie some night. Maybe more than once. We're about the same age, and we've both lost our spouses. Each of us needs someone to do things like that with."

"You're kidding. What about the six-foot brick wall and all those no-trespassing signs?"

Rubbing his jaw, Sam replied, "I've changed my mind about the wall. I didn't get far with it, and I've decided to build a nice ranch entrance instead. As for your mom's signs, she hasn't had time to remove them, but I'm sure she will."

Cam had difficulty grasping all this. "She still won't want to stay in your house."

"She will if you convince her it's the best thing for you."

"I can't even convince myself of that." Cam didn't consider himself to be prideful, but the McLendons didn't like feeling obligated to anyone. "That being the case, I won't have much luck convincing Mom."

Sam spread his hands palm up and studied the lines on them. "You wouldn't be in this shape if you had let that bull trample my daughter to death. I owe you a debt I'll never be able to repay.

At least let me make you and your family comfortable in my home until you've recovered."

"It wasn't some huge act of courage," Cam clarified. "Things happened so fast I didn't even have time to think. I didn't try to save her so you'd feel obligated to me in any way. That's for sure."

"But I do feel obligated, and I don't like owing anyone."

"I don't either."

"Then accept my offer so I can feel that we're halfway even. What I first said still stands. This is too much for your mother."

"I know that."

"Then for her sake, accept my offer."

Cam thought about it for a moment. Then he locked gazes with Sam. "Do you always get your way?"

"Mostly."

Cam laughed and regretted it when pain tore across his rib cage. It took him several seconds to recover enough to speak. "Mom might agree if we pay you a hefty amount in rent."

"Don't insult me, young man."

Chapter Eleven

MADDIE AWAKENED TO THE SMELL OF FOOD COOKING. HER stomach rolled, reminding her of when she'd had morning sickness years ago. She had no idea why she felt nauseated. Exhaustion must have been taking its toll on her weakened body, she guessed. Still fully clothed except for her boots, she sat up and saw Sam standing in front of her tiny gas range. He glanced up the short hallway that housed her bathroom sink on one side and a toilet-shower combo on the other.

"I'm making lunch—nothing fancy, only grilled-cheese sandwiches."

Even though her stomach still pitched, Maddie felt rested. "That's good of you. How long did I sleep?"

"Around five hours. I checked to make sure you were breathing a couple of times." He sent her an amused look. "You snore."

Maddie arched her brows. "No, I don't. I stayed awake one night to see."

With the easy grace of a man at home in a kitchen, he flipped the sandwiches. "Ah, well, it's a soft snore, not a wall shaker."

Maddie bent to put her boots on. Then she finger-combed her hair as she entered the kitchen. "Thank you for the break. I needed it."

While Sam moved the sandwiches onto a waiting platter, she

gathered paper plates, napkins, and cutlery. Then they walked together to Cam's cabin. "You should have worn a pedometer over the last few days," he said. "I bet you clocked in some miles running around this camp."

Maddie nodded. "It's not a convenient situation. Before Cam got hurt, we made it work, but now it's impossible for him."

Sam switched the platter to one hand and rapped on the cabin door.

"I'm decent," Cam called out.

They entered the room. Sam set the platter on the table Cam used for work and then positioned two chairs beside the bed. Maddie assisted him in serving, declining any food for herself. That turned out to be a good thing, because the men had just started eating when Kirstin showed up. She had fully recovered from her leg injury and no longer limped. Maddie found another chair and offered Kirstin lunch.

"Dad cooked?" She laughed. "At home, he has Mrs. Alvarez for that. I'm surprised he remembers how."

"I give the woman weekends off when she wants them. Mostly she prefers to get the hours, but I do cook for myself now and again."

Cam finished most of his sandwich before setting his plate aside. "Mom, I reached a decision while you were asleep. Staying in camp isn't working for me. Please don't get upset, but Sam offered to let us stay at his place until I'm recovered, and I've accepted the invitation."

Kirstin protested, "How is that fair? You refused to stay at my place, but you're willing to stay with Dad?"

"I have three spare bedrooms on the ground floor," Sam pointed out.

"And your dad isn't my girlfriend," Cam inserted.

"You can say that again," Sam told him.

Maddie felt suddenly claustrophobic. "Um, Cam, I think I should have some say in this."

Cam met her gaze. "Mom, you can argue the point, but can you try to think about what's best for me? In the last X-rays, my detached rib was back in place and starting to heal. But the doctor warned me against using the crutches any more than absolutely necessary, because I could pull it all loose. Look at this room. In these cramped quarters, I can't maneuver a wheelchair, and I'm not getting a patient commode you have to empty. It'd be disgusting."

Maddie knew her son was right. And she did have to think of him. "All right. If Sam is sure about this, you and Caleb can stay at his place. I'll remain here with all the animals."

"I have a barn for your cats," Sam informed her. "Your dogs will fit right in with my three. When we feed our livestock, one of us can swing over here to tend the horses. You staying here won't work. You need to be at my place so you can care for Cam."

Kirstin, who'd apparently resigned herself to the suggestion, said, "That would be best, Maddie. Now that my leg is healed, I'm working long hours again. I can't take care of Cam without letting Dad down."

"Will the horses be okay over here alone?" Maddie asked.

"They should be fine." Sam met her gaze. "In fact, they'll probably be happier in a familiar place. We can always move them later if it becomes necessary."

Maddie felt outnumbered. And Cam had made a good argument. This situation was impossible for him, and it certainly wouldn't speed up his recovery.

"One neighbor helping another neighbor is common in Montana, especially on ranches," Sam said. "I know you've tried to find a place to rent, Maddie, and you've found nothing. Staying at my place is the only solution." He waited a beat. "When I first met you, I behaved horribly. This gives me a chance to make up for that. Are you going to deny me the opportunity?"

Maddie held up a hand. "Enough. I'll agree to do it. But I've got to say I never thought I'd live to see the day when Sam Conacher invited a bunch of white trash to live under his roof."

Even Sam laughed.

BEFORE CALEB GOT HOME FROM SCHOOL, THE McLENDONS WERE settled in at Sam's house. All they had needed to move were personal things, and that went quickly. Sam got Cam settled on a reclining seat in the living room sofa with his wheelchair close at hand. Kirstin made him some iced tea and sat beside him. Maddie chose for him the most spacious downstairs bedroom, which had an adjoining bath. She put away his clothes and toiletries, making sure they'd be easy for him to reach.

Maddie had owned a gorgeous home in Northern California, but Sam's house was even more spacious and lovely. She admired the rustic ambience with its quality slate floors and massive beams in the open ceilings. The room she selected for herself was next to Cam's and also had an adjoining bath. The Jacuzzi tub had her name written on it, she decided. Only a midget could soak in her trailer tub, so she hadn't enjoyed that luxury since moving here. When she saw the walk-in closet, she made plans to visit the local storage units they'd rented to avail herself of more clothing. Not a lot, because they surely wouldn't be here for long, but she looked forward to having more choices in her wardrobe for a while.

She'd barely finished unpacking her things when she glanced at her watch and realized Caleb would be getting home from school in only minutes. If he found no one there, he might panic, thinking his dad had been taken back to the hospital. Maddie hurried to the front of the house to tell Sam she needed to fetch her grandson, but both he and his daughter had vanished. Cam explained that they'd gone out to work.

Maddie drove to camp and was there when Caleb pulled up to the cabin in his pickup. "Hi, Gram! What's up?" he asked as he walked toward her.

"The camp isn't working out for your father."

"I know. I thought the ramps might help, but they didn't."

"Well, Sam generously offered to let us stay at his place until your dad is able to get around better, so we moved our stuff over there. I packed for you, too. I even remembered your violin."

"Awesome!" Caleb said with what appeared to be genuine delight.

Maddie guessed that her grandson was one of the few people who saw through Sam's cranky facade and appreciated him for who he really was. He piled back in his truck to follow Maddie's SUV to their temporary home.

THAT EVENING GABRIELLA ALVAREZ MADE A FABULOUS DINNER and removed one chair so Cam could sit at the table with everyone else. Cam had taken Spanish in high school and knew just enough words to communicate with her. He thanked her for her thoughtfulness and praised her for preparing such a wonderful meal. Looking pleased by the compliments, she beamed a smile. Cam wondered if all Sam did to recognize her efforts was grunt. He sat at the head of the table. No one sat at the foot. For all his many rough edges, the man had clearly loved his wife.

Kirstin met his gaze. For a moment Cam got lost in her eyes, and he would have forgone eating for a chance to be alone with her. Unfortunately, he was in no shape for any bedroom calisthenics.

"I'm still bummed that you chose to stay with Dad instead of me," she said.

Sam got up to pour Maddie some merlot before he filled his own glass. "Quit your whining," he scolded his daughter. "As soon as Cam's able, he can start sneaking over to your place so I can stay in shape kicking his ass."

Cam saw his mother's gaze sharpen. Then anger flared in her eyes. "I *knew* it wasn't a bull that messed up his face."

"Mom," Cam said quickly, "it's a long story. Now isn't the time to discuss it."

Maddie looked up at Sam. "Did you, or did you not, strike my son?"

Sam at least had the good grace to look slightly embarrassed. "I did, and now I'm sorry for it. I don't know what came over me."

"A hot temper?" Maddie suggested.

Gabriella departed via the front door just then, and all three of the McLendon dogs raced into the house. Sam had an equal number of Aussies—a black tri, a red merle, and a blue merle— and they rose from their places around the dining room to bristle and growl. Sam yelled for them to knock it off, and even Bingo, Maddie's old dog that was starting to grow deaf, heard his deep voice and stopped the nonsense.

As Sam resumed his seat, he lifted his wineglass to Maddie. "Did you see how my dogs just reacted? That's a perfect example of what occurred when I hit your son. I was protecting my turf. Then my daughter yelled at me and set me straight."

"My thanks to you, Kirstin." Maddie smiled at Sam with saccharine sweetness. "Did she by any chance smack you on the schnozzle? Please say yes and make my day."

"Mom," Cam inserted, "we're guests here. Let's mind our manners and let bygones be bygones."

Maddie grimly cut into her steak. Sam said, "Your mother doesn't have to mind her manners under my roof. I never do."

Even Maddie couldn't help but laugh.

THE NEXT DAY MADDIE WENT TO SPEAK WITH THE BUILDERS WHO were erecting the large building that would house her and Cam's residences. The progress update was dismal. If everything happened on schedule, which Maddie knew seldom occurred during construction, they would be in their homes February first.

Maddie didn't really mind staying at Sam's. Even though he'd struck her son, and she'd done a slow burn for a few moments last night when she'd found out, she enjoyed sparring with him. For reasons she didn't clearly understand, he brought out her feisty side, and she felt at liberty to say whatever was on her mind, whether it was polite or not. Since Graham's death, she'd found nobody who could really comprehend how lost she felt without him. But Sam did. Admitting to him how devastated and lonely she often felt didn't make her feel weak, because he had experienced the same feelings and had no problem saying so. In an odd way, she thought they were good for each other.

She did have one worry, though, and it was a big one. How would she slip away for her chemo treatments and follow-up consultations? She decided to stick with her original story about going for physical therapy. She would tell Sam she was working on her balance and doing pool exercise therapy for her back.

Over the next few days, Maddie determined that she'd worried for nothing. Sam didn't hang around the house at all during the day. He had Kirstin and one hired hand to keep the ranch running when he actually needed a whole crew. On a daily basis, the two men drove into the mountains to round up cattle from Sam's grazing land. Kirstin remained behind to work at the ranch, which kept her busy from daylight to dark.

Maddie wished Sam had more help, but she guessed it was his own fault and shook her head. He had made his bed, and now he'd have to sleep in it. As a result, he left the ranch before first light, rode all day to herd cows from their hiding places in thickets, and came back home just before dark with only a few cattle. Kirstin worried aloud daily that her father would go broke if he couldn't find all the cows.

It made no sense to Maddie. If cows were so hard to find, why did Sam graze them in the summer where they could hide? Kirstin explained that the grazing land provided free food for the cattle, increasing the ranch's profits. Maddie accepted the explanation with a shrug.

Gabriella came in daily to clean, cook dinner, and prepare field lunches for Sam and her husband to eat in the mountains the following day. Kirstin came to the house for lunch and spent more time cuddling with Cam on the sofa than she probably should have. Except for on weekends, Caleb attended school. This left Maddie free to write in her bedroom, stopping only when Cam needed something. And half the time Gabriella even took care of that.

The woman was lovely and efficient, but she spoke little English. Maddie struggled to communicate with her and resorted to using Google Translate to message her. Maddie received some garbled texts, and she felt sure Gabriella did as well. She wondered if Sam had provided the Mexican couple with a nice home and if he paid both of them well. She knew that many ranchers and farmers across the country paid Mexican workers pennies on the dollar of what they'd pay an American, and Maddie was sickened by the practice.

One afternoon Maddie encountered Gabriella's son, Ricardo, on the front porch. Nicknamed Rickie, he was a handsome, nicely dressed kid, and she was delighted to discover that he spoke fluent English. Maddie guessed him to be ten or eleven, and he was extremely proud of his parents.

"My mom and dad have work papers," he explained, "and they're trying to get citizenship."

Maddie learned that Gabriella was studying English at night with her husband, but Miguel wasn't a good speller, so Rickie had to help her with that.

"She's very smart, though," he boasted. "She'll learn the language. Sometimes at night I won't speak Mexican to her, and she gets really upset with me. But I think it's the fastest way for her to learn."

When Maddie asked why he called the language Mexican instead of Spanish, he said, "Because the languages are different. Spanish is, um—more proper, I guess is the word. Mexican has lots of words and phrases from our country."

"Do you like your house here on the ranch?" Maddie asked.

"Oh, yeah. When we send pictures to our relatives in Mexico, they text back that we are very rich." He laughed. "My dad makes good money here—thirty-five dollars an hour, plus overtime—and my mother is paid well, too. They send money home every month to help the family. It is hard in Mexico."

A tightness in Maddie's chest eased. She was pleased to know that Sam showed his appreciation of Miguel and Gabriella's hard work by paying them good wages. She liked this boy—he was as cute as could be, open and friendly. His parents had done a good job with him.

A mongrel pup loped up onto the porch just then. Rickie introduced him to Maddie. "This is Jasper. He's my dog. That's why I came over here. He ran off, and I was looking for him." He snapped his fingers and said, "Come on. You need to go home before you eat another pair of Mr. Conacher's boots."

Maddie's mouth curved in a smile as she watched the boy and dog run side by side toward their house, which lay hidden somewhere on a vast reach of the property.

CAM'S PHYSICAL LIMITATIONS GAVE HIM AND KIRSTIN EVEN MORE time to talk. After dinner each night, Maddie retired to her room to write, Caleb went upstairs, and Kirstin sat with Cam on the sofa. They spoke softly to each other as Sam read in his recliner on the other side of the large room. Both of them refrained from teasing him when they realized he had replaced all of Maddie's books that he had burned. He was now about two-thirds of the way through *Death by Potato Sprouts* and so engrossed in the story that very little got his attention, the one exception being the shriek of Caleb's string instrument, which he said sounded like two tomcats fighting over a female in heat.

Cam and Kirstin talked about silly things sometimes, telling each other their pet peeves, sharing their most embarrassing moments, and comparing how much coffee they'd consumed while studying for college finals. Kirstin was quick to laugh, and Cam loved the sound. Other times their conversations drifted to more serious topics. Could they raise their kids in the house Kirstin now occupied? Would Sam infringe upon their privacy or interfere in their business? They moved beyond saying, "If we get engaged," to saying, "When we get engaged." They had already settled on having two kids, but Cam knew Kirstin actually wanted three. He told her one night that he was open to that, which brought tears to her eyes.

Cam realized now that he hadn't ever truly loved Caleb's mother. He'd possibly been too young to comprehend what love was. He knew only that he'd never had feelings that ran as deeply as the ones he had for Kirstin. She was sweet, warm, and understanding. He felt good about himself when he was around her. When he worried aloud about making his first sale and starting to bring in some money, she bolstered his confidence and told him he was going to exceed all his own expectations and surprise everyone with his success.

He came to admire her work ethic. At nine thirty every night, she went home to go to bed. Saying good-bye was always difficult. Cam wanted to hold her in his arms while he slept, and he knew she wanted him to be with her. But she always kept to her schedule, asleep by ten and up before five so she could put in a full day on the ranch. She labored like a man in Cam's estimation, and he worried about her hurting her back or having an accident. Satan's sudden attack remained fresh in his mind, and he knew some of the things she did each day could be dangerous.

SAM CONSIDERED TELLING CAM AND HIS DAUGHTER THAT HE wasn't deaf, but being around Maddie had mellowed him somehow. Cam's only comfortable roost was the reclining chair of the sofa, so that was essentially the only place he and Kirstin could talk. Sam didn't want to spoil their nightly visits. He'd forgotten about those long-ago times with Annie, when they could chat for hours and then just listen to each other breathe when they ran out of things to say. The kids were falling in love, and listening to them reminded Sam of how magical a time that was in people's lives. He bit back smiles when they discussed him. Could they raise their children in the ranch manager's house? Sam thought they should. The ranch was a fabulous place for a kid to grow up. Would Sam infringe upon their privacy and interfere in their business? Hell, yes. That was a father's job.

Only, of course, Maddie would bend his ear and tell him he was wrong about that. Sam wouldn't mind. She was brimming with good old-fashioned common sense, that lady, and he knew he was falling under her spell. He refused to think of his feelings for her as love. He'd never love any woman but Annie. But he had grown fond of Maddie, he enjoyed her company, and he respected her.

Yesterday Sam and Miguel had worked all afternoon to build Cam a wheelchair path with packed gravel. It would come in handy soon, when Cam was recovered enough to *sneak* over to Kirstin's house. Sam had learned that Cam was old-fashioned about intimacy outside of wedlock. Caleb knew about the birds and the bees, but Cam didn't want to set a bad example for the boy by being open about his arrangement with Kirstin. Sam figured the joke was on Cam. Kids were savvier than their parents gave them credit for, and he was pretty sure Caleb knew the relationship wasn't platonic. Even so, Sam silently congratulated Cam for trying to be a good father.

Sam had joked once about kicking Cam's ass if he sneaked over to Kirstin's place, but he hadn't been serious. It was no fly-by-night relationship. Sam had realized that the moment he saw Cam draw Satan's attention to save Kirstin's life.

One evening Cam had already vacated his place on the sofa and turned in when Maddie emerged from her room. Sam closed his book and smiled at her. She had taken a break for dinner and then returned to work. She had that sleepy-eyed look she always had after a long day of writing.

"Hey," she said, "did we outlast the kids?"

"Yep. Caleb sacked out at a little after eight, Kirstin left at nine thirty, and Cam just called it a day."

She yawned and took the seat Cam had just vacated. In the dim light, Sam could imagine how lovely she had been when she was younger. She was still a beautiful woman, and he liked to think he was still a handsome man for his age. He found himself wishing that they could be more than just friends, but he was wise enough not to press his luck. Judging by the derogatory comments he'd heard Maddie make about herself, he had a feeling that part of the reason she claimed to be a dead unit from her neck down was that she believed her body was ugly. When a woman felt that way about herself, a man had his work cut out for him to convince her otherwise.

"So how's the book coming?"

"Awful. I've written myself into a corner and can't think of a way out. Maybe if I sleep on it, I'll wake up with a bright idea."

Sam loved difficult mysteries. "Tell me about it. I'm good at plot twists."

She smiled slightly. "Um, it's difficult to explain."

Sam got up and went to the kitchen for a cold beer. Maddie said she would join him, so he popped the caps from two bottles, handed one to her, and sat at the opposite end of the couch. "Just talk. I'll try to make sense of it."

"I honestly can't." She sighed. "The truth is, Sam, I'm in a mess. My murder victim is a real person, and I realized today that despite the fact that I've given him a fictitious name, he's still recognizable. If I publish the book, I could be sued for libel."

Intrigued, Sam asked, "Who's the victim?"

She took a pull from her beer. After swallowing, she said, "You."

Sam thought he'd misunderstood her. "Come again?"

"You, Sam. You're my murder victim."

Sam nearly choked on his microbrew. "Me?" he squeaked.

She lifted her shoulders and then went back into a slump. "I disliked you before I ever met you, because I knew Cam was seeing Kirstin and I feared you'd start saying horrible things about him to destroy his reputation."

Sam almost said, *Guilty as charged,* but he decided this wasn't a good time to confess those transgressions.

"Then, after I met you, my dislike turned to hatred. You called us white trash, if you'll recall. I was so mad I wanted to throw rocks at you. Instead I got even by murdering you in my book."

Sam couldn't help it; he burst out laughing.

"It's not funny!" she cried. "I went back to the beginning to do some editing today, and I was horrified. I can't turn that mess in to my editor. I nailed you almost perfectly. Anyone who knows you, meaning anyone in the Bitterroot Valley, and reads the book will realize almost immediately that you're the victim."

Sam wiped under his eyes, amazed that he'd laughed so hard that his sides hurt. Maddie was good for him. "What if I sign a waiver promising not to sue?"

"It's sweet of you to offer, but that won't work. Writers aren't supposed to pattern main characters after real people. You can entertain readers by using their names for unimportant, secondary characters, but only with their written permission, and then you have to change things about those characters to make them mostly fictitious. But my victim in this book is unmistakably *you*! If this piece of work goes to publication, it will destroy my reputation and credibility as a writer."

"Maybe you can just change the guy's appearance."

She shook her head. "You're featured throughout the plot. The things you've done or said to ruin other people, mostly young men who dared to look twice at your daughter. The killer's reason for offing you. Suspects out the yang who also had motivation to kill you. In order to erase you from the book, I'll have to revamp the entire story."

"I have to read this. I've never been featured in a book before. What a kick."

She pressed the cold beer bottle to the frown lines above her nose, a sure sign that she had a bitch of a headache. "You have no idea how much trouble I'm in. My publisher is counting on me to deliver this work. I'm contractually obligated to send it in on a certain date. There's no way I can revise the whole thing now and get it to them in time."

Sam saw how upset she was and no longer felt like laughing. "I'm sorry, Maddie. If I hadn't been such a jerk, you wouldn't have vented your anger at me in a story."

"It's my own fault. I should have been more disciplined." She lowered the bottle to her lap and smiled slightly. "You were awful at first, though, and it was so much fun to torture and dismember you. When I first got the idea, I imagined you to look like Gus in *Lonesome Dove.* Then I met you and had to change you entirely. Stupid, stupid. I can't believe I just kept writing this whole time."

Sam tried to think what he might say to make her feel better. He stood and sat down again right next to her, something he rarely did because he was afraid of spooking her. To hell with that. She needed a friend right now who could think outside the box.

Slipping an arm around her shoulders, he drew her against his side, pleased when she didn't resist. "Maddie, all during the creation of this book, you've either been angry or worried. And on both counts, you had good reasons. I kept stopping by your place to pour fuel on the fire. Remember the night you dropped your flashlight in the portable toilet?"

She started to laugh. "Oh, God, what a night. You were at your obnoxious best."

Sam contributed a chuckle. "I was angry, too. The way I saw it then, Cam was busy demolishing what was left of my world. When I stopped by your place, hoping to light into him, I only ever found you, so you took the brunt. I was at my obnoxious best right up until the morning he got rammed by the bull.

"But even though I backed off from my war on Cam that day, you didn't get a break from the stress. Your son nearly died, and you were worried that he might never walk again. When have you had a moment to really analyze the book you're writing?"

She took a shaky breath. "I should have gone back prior to today to give it a read from start to finish, but I didn't. I was racing against time and writing in a dead heat."

"So you weren't stupid, only stressed out and under the gun. You are in a pickle, though."

"I should just call my editor and face the music. He'll be upset, and it will hurt me financially if I bunch the story, but it's the only way I can see out of this mess."

"This may be the best murder mystery you've ever written. You worked on it with passion. Several emotions drove you. Giving up on the book may be the worst mistake you've ever made."

She went limp and rested her head against his shoulder. Then she sighed. "I'm so screwed. I did a great job of portraying you, and I incorporated flashbacks of you in the minds of suspects who had as much reason as the killer did to do you harm. So you're everywhere in that story!"

Sam pressed his cheek against the top of her head. She smelled like carnations. Sam was no expert on flowers and normally couldn't tell one kind from another. But as a young boy, he'd loved to stick his face in clusters of carnations to take in their scent. Luckily for him, his mother had liked them, too, and had peppered her garden with them every year. "I know I'm not a writer, but as a rancher I am a good strategist. I have an idea."

"What kind of idea?"

Sam enjoyed having her nestled against him, so he was loath to move. But he gently set her away from him, stood, and turned to help her up. "Can you bring your laptop to the kitchen? I'll find a tablet so we can take notes."

"I really, *really* don't want you to read the book."

"I don't need to read it, Maddie. Your problem can be resolved by tackling only one thing, setting. We're going to relocate me to somewhere in another state with similar terrain and topographical features."

"But the victim will still be recognizably you."

Sam grabbed her hand and drew her to her feet. "I'm not the only ornery and cantankerous rancher on earth. I'm sure every state has more than a few. Change my hair and eye color, stick me in Wyoming, Idaho, or Utah, and your problem may be solved."

"Oh, Sam, that's *brilliant*!"

GOING TO THE KITCHEN WITH SAM TO SAVE HER BOOK WAS REMI-niscent to Maddie of times past when Graham had helped her develop a plot. She'd missed that. Sam got her settled at the table with her laptop, brought a tablet and a pen, and then unearthed a bottle of Crown Royal Apple Whiskey. It was Cam's favorite alcohol, and Maddie loved the taste.

Sam poured a measure in tumblers for each of them. "This'll chase your tension away and get your creative juices flowing."

Maddie sipped as she surfed the Internet. Sam sat beside her so he could see the screen. "There's terrain in Wyoming that's similar enough to ours that we could make it work," Sam told her. His deep voice soothed her raw nerve endings. "Can you just make up fictitious places, like valleys and rivers and towns?"

"Yes," Maddie replied. "I have to remain true to the topography of an area, but I can create a town, businesses, and people who have nothing to do with reality in that locale."

Maddie was soon laughing. Sam came up with the crazy idea of calling her fictitious area the Ole Codger Valley.

"Why not? The victim's an old codger," he said.

Maddie shortened the name to Codger Valley. That sounded more realistic to her. When she checked a valley registry for the United States, she found no place with that name.

"It's a go," she told Sam.

He sloshed more booze in their glasses, they clicked the tumblers together, and Sam made a toast, saying, "Here's to saving Maddie's ass."

When their session ended, Maddie had three pages of notes. She would need to slightly change the flora in Codger Valley, but the scenery could pretty much remain the same because her valley was fictitious. Gratitude welled within her.

"Oh, Sam." She went up on her tiptoes to hug him and still couldn't reach his neck. He drew her in close and told her to stand on his boots. When Maddie did so, the embrace was perfect—and physically stirring. "Oh, shit," she said. "We shouldn't do this."

Sam tightened his arms around her. "We're old, remember. And I'm fresh out of my little blue pills."

She buried her face against his shirt and giggled. "My book is saved."

"It is, and I'm glad I could help."

Dimly Maddie realized that she might have been a little bit tipsy. Otherwise she would never remain pressed full length against Sam Conacher for this long. But it felt so good that she stayed where she was. His body radiated warmth and strength. The taut muscles in his chest and arms made her feel safe—and feminine. She hadn't felt like a woman in far too long. He made her wish that she wasn't a totally dead unit from her neck down. Then it occurred to her that not every hard place she felt on Sam was a muscular bulge.

She leaned her head back and fixed him with an accusing look. "You don't need little blue pills."

He gave her one of those Sam Conacher grins that she'd come to love without realizing it. "Guilty," he said. "But in my own defense, I haven't tried out my equipment in more than eight years. I've got snow on my roof. How was I to know I still had a fire in my stove?"

He loosened his hold on her, and Maddie drew away from him. Low in her abdomen, her insides felt all funny. She wouldn't kid herself. Being in his arms had turned her on. How could that be? Even before Graham's death, she'd had to see her gyn about vaginal dryness.

Sam touched the tip of her nose. "Don't take it personally, Maddie. Jack just reacts. I learned a long time ago that he's got no brains."

"Jack?"

Sam bent over her laptop to shut it down. "Oh, yeah. At seventeen I named it the Jackhammer, but I shortened it later to Jack."

"Well, that's really more than I wanted to know." Maddie began gathering up her things. "But thanks for sharing."

He winked at her. "With friends, I practice full disclosure. We can still be friends. Right?"

"Of course. Just keep Jack well away from me."

Sam chuckled. "If it's any comfort, I didn't know until just now that he had any life left in him."

On the way to her room Maddie was laughing quietly.

Once she was in her suite, her euphoric sense of floating on air underwent a crash landing. Sam had helped her save the book so it could be published, but what if he bought a copy after it hit the shelves? She had described him as handsome and used romantic terms to bring him to life on the page. If he read the story, he would know she thought he was handsome and, even worse, attractive. He might start thinking of ways to recharge her batteries. She'd gotten certain proof tonight that his hadn't gone dead.

She liked their friendship just the way it was, merely friends. Okay, they were starting to become really *good* friends, but she wanted nothing more. *Well,* she thought as she sank onto the edge of the bed, *sometimes I feel a little charge when I'm near him. And I occasionally yearn to feel his arms around me, or to have mine around him. But he's still in fabulous physical shape. I sag here and hang there. My thighs have turned to crepe and look like they need ironing. The chemo has aged my face even more. Never will I be with a man like Sam in an intimate way. It would be the most humiliating experience of my life.*

BY MID-OCTOBER, CAM WAS GETTING PHYSICAL THERAPY THREE days a week, and he quickly mastered driving himself. His vehicle had an automatic shift, and he could tuck his right leg back against the seat to operate the accelerator and brake with his left foot. By balancing on his one good leg, he was able to fold and lift his wheelchair into his truck with a battery-powered hoist, then reverse the process when he got where he was going.

The therapist lifted Cam's spirits considerably. He was starting to wonder if he'd ever be able to walk again. Had the neurosurgeon missed something in his MRI? Was there nerve damage in his spine after all? The therapist had a lot of letters behind her name, and when she talked, Cam knew there wasn't as much as a tiny bone in the human body that she hadn't studied. By cautiously palpating his ribs, she could tell that the detached piece of bone had remained in alignment and was healing. She cautioned Cam not to use the crutches too much. That put stress on the muscles in the chest wall and might hinder healing. Cam, accustomed to seeing people with fractures mend in six weeks, couldn't understand why his rib was taking so long. The therapist said that it wasn't only bone involved. Muscles and tendons had been damaged, and they took much longer to not only mend but also become strong again.

She was somewhat mystified by his back injury, but she assured him that eventually the bruised tissue would heal, the swelling would go down, and he'd be able to use his leg again. During sessions, she made Cam stand on the leg and execute certain movements to *wake up* the nerves in his spine to start sending out signals again.

"When I was a kid," she told him, "I fell from a tree house, and on the way down, I hit a huge, gnarly oak limb. I landed so hard on my thigh that I limped for weeks, and it took six months for the bruising to go away. Your back is still black-and-blue. Get a gander of it with a hand mirror when you get home and give your body the time it needs to recover."

Cam felt like a horse gnawing at the bit. His career was at a standstill. He'd been in Montana since last spring and still hadn't made a dime. He'd give his body all the time it needed to heal, but in the meantime he had to work. If he could get himself to therapy sessions three times a week, he could work on those days as well.

After therapy he began driving through ranchland, watching for large parcels that were for sale by owner. At home he spent hours on his laptop, combing through properties with expired listings. After a week, he'd snagged two clients. That excited him, but it didn't last long. Having his own listings was great, but he'd make no money off them until they sold.

ONCE CAM RETURNED HOME AND SHARED HIS NEWS, KIRSTIN INsisted on a celebration. "In order to make great money, you need listings, Cam. You're building a path toward that first big check. I believe in you, and you have to start believing in yourself."

She went directly to the kitchen to ask Gabriella to cook something special for dinner. Then she ran to the store to buy two bottles of Cam's favorite red wine.

Maddie silently applauded Kirstin for making a big deal out of Cam's successes. She began to feel confident that Kirstin would be a fabulous wife for her son. If the young woman could stand by him during a time like this, she would support him during the good times as well.

Chapter Twelve

WHILE CAM STRUGGLED TO GET WELL AND REENTER HIS PROfessional field, Sam struggled with his conscience. Early on he had bad-mouthed Cam whenever an opportunity arose—at the hardware store when he bought feed, and even when the farrier came out to shoe the horses. Word of mouth traveled fast in the valley. Sam needed to undo any possible damage he'd done to Cam's reputation, but he wasn't sure how. He'd said some pretty shitty things. It would be awkward to start singing the young man's praises. Only Sam had a bad feeling that was exactly what he needed to do.

He was busy, though. He still had cattle on grazing land, and if he didn't get them rounded up, they'd perish once the higher elevations got snowed in.

One morning Sam got up at three in the morning to start his day, which gave him time to drive to town. He sought out every person to whom he'd spoken about Cam McLendon. He had a memorized speech so he wouldn't screw it up. His story now was completely honest. He'd hated Cam, considered him to be a loser, and wanted to ruin him. Then the young man had shown Sam what he was truly made of by putting his life in danger to save Kirstin. Sam left nothing out, even telling people that Cam had been so badly injured by Satan that he still couldn't walk, that he needed prayers, and if anyone needed a cow covered after Cam got well, they should call him, because he was certified in bovine artificial insemination.

Sam didn't know if his efforts would do any good. That made him feel horrible, so horrible that he couldn't keep it to himself any longer. One night when Maddie emerged from her writing nest after the kids had gone to bed, Sam asked her to sit with him on the sofa. Because of what he had to tell her, he didn't slip an arm around her, which had become his habit of late when they ended an evening talking.

"I've done a terrible thing, Maddie."

She took a sip from her glass of white wine. "So what else is new?"

Sam couldn't even dredge up a smile. "This was more terrible than most things." Looking over the last six years, Sam wondered if that statement was true. Maybe what he'd done to Cam wasn't all that much worse than what he'd done to others. He remembered the young guy who'd flirted with Kirstin on the Chevrolet sales lot. Sam had caused him to lose his job. "I deliberately ruined Cam's chances to sell ranches. I'm glad he's gotten two listings, but it's a miracle that he did."

Maddie turned her goblet, studying the sparkles in her wine as the liquid swirled.

"Did you hear me?" Sam asked.

She settled her blue gaze on him. He saw sadness in those depths but no recrimination. "I heard you, Sam. I'm waiting for you to tell me what you've done to fix the situation. That's the answer for you, you know, the only way you can redeem yourself. It's the only way any of us can."

Sam told her about driving all over town to undo the damage. "I felt ridiculous, and it was embarrassing, but I deserved it."

Maddie smiled. "Yes, Sam, you did deserve it. Have I mentioned that I belong to a book club? We meet at the Rustlers' Gulch Library, and there seem to be a goodly number of wannabe writers here. We only get together every two weeks, and I can't find time to read the selected books, but I enjoy the camaraderie I find there with avid readers, and I've been asked to teach writing afterward. I limit my talks to an hour, and the next time we meet, they bring in their assignments."

"What's that got to do with Cam?"

Maddie took another sip of wine. "I see people, and they love to talk. I was told at the last meeting that you had said some awful things about my son to key people. I was also told that you used to be one of the nicest ranchers in the valley. When people needed help, Sam Conacher was always one of the first to offer it. They say you attended services every Sunday. You volunteered for parish fund-raisers, and you donated lots of money to different good causes. Then your wife died, and that nice, generous man became bitter, hateful, and vengeful."

Sam closed his eyes. His stomach felt as if someone was threading a knitting needle through it. Voice gravelly with regret, he said, "I figured you'd get mad when I told you, and I'd be wearing that wine."

"I am angry," she replied. "But I'm angry with the man you were, not the man you're trying to resurrect. I'm very glad you attempted to restore Cam's image. I'll pray that you succeeded."

"What if I didn't?"

Maddie sighed. "My son will win people back over. Your verbal assaults on his character will become distant memories. He'll have a rough start, but he'll build his business and become very successful on his own merit." She paused. "And if he doesn't, I'll kill you in another book and relocate you to Nevada."

Caught off guard, Sam chuckled. "Put me in one of the beautiful parts of the state."

"No way. You'll be surrounded by flat desert."

He sighed. "A fitting punishment, I suppose. I'm sorry, Maddie."

SAM CONTINUED TO SPEAK HIGHLY OF CAM EACH TIME HE HAD reason to drive into town. He told people that the young man was no run-of-the-mill Realtor and knew his stuff. He was good on a horse and could cut cattle like a pro. He stressed that Cam could knowledgeably guide potential buyers to find the property that would best suit their needs.

In late October, Cam came in late with a beaming grin on his face. "I just sold one of the ranches I listed!" he shouted. "My listing, my sale. Except for my company broker's percentage, I'll get both sides of the commission."

Kirstin came bouncing from the kitchen, where she and Caleb had been carving pumpkins. She leaned over to hug Cam, still in a wheelchair, and then danced circles around him. "That is so awesome, Cam! How much will you make? I *knew* you could do it!"

Caleb joined them, his exuberance equal to Kirstin's. "Way to go, Dad!"

Cam pulled out his phone to use the calculator. "Beats me how much I'll make. A lot, though. I was too excited to get home and share my news to think about the numbers. The buyer offered three-point-five mil, and the owner accepted it."

While the younger people eagerly tried to figure out Cam's profit, Sam met Maddie's gaze. She smiled and inclined her head slightly to give him a barely noticeable nod of approval. Sam felt as if a burden had been removed from his shoulders. His attempts in town to salvage Cam's reputation had worked. He still needed to apologize, though. *Damn it to hell,* he thought. *Trying to be a nice guy again totally sucks.*

THAT THURSDAY MADDIE WENT TO MISSOULA FOR ONE OF HER physical therapy sessions. She came home in a festive mood and, in Sam's opinion, glowing with good health. She'd stopped at a store and loaded up on trick-or-treat candy and Halloween decorations.

"Most of ours are in storage," she explained to Sam, who gazed with mounting amazement at all the witches, goblins, and cobweb stuff she drew from the bags. "I love holidays!" she exclaimed when she saw his expression. "You did say to consider this my home while we're here, and I normally decorate."

"I'm a man of my word. Decorate to your heart's content."

Sam took refuge in his recliner. A deluge of grief had flooded through him. Annie had been like a kid during the holidays, and few surfaces inside or outside the house had escaped her enthusiasm. Maddie had caused dozens of beautiful memories to slam into his brain—only they didn't feel beautiful because of the pain that accompanied them. He didn't want to spoil Maddie's fun, though, or the kids', either. They were as excited as she was.

Tears glazed Sam's eyes. Visions of Annie standing on the stairway banister to string Christmas lights around the stairwell flashed through his mind. She could have fallen so easily. Sam had been so afraid for her that he'd pulled her down and into his arms, telling her he'd skin her alive if he caught her up there again. Then he'd gone to get a ladder and put up decorations he didn't think they needed.

Maddie must have noticed his sudden withdrawal, because she left the kids to sort through her purchases and sat on the hearth near him. "I'm sorry. I hit a raw spot, I think. I can forgo decorations this year. I misspoke a minute ago. This isn't my house, not even temporarily. It's Annie's, and I was disrespectful of that."

Sam stretched out his arm. She took his hand. He gave her fingers a squeeze. "You weren't disrespectful. Annie would be right in there with all of you and cheering you on. She loved the holidays, too. One Easter she hid plastic eggs filled with surprises for Kirstin and left one on the stairs."

Maddie stifled a laugh. "Oh, no, don't tell me."

Sam worked up a smile. "You guessed it. I found the egg. I fell halfway down the stairway."

"I hope you weren't hurt."

"Banged up, mostly. And there stood my little girl over me. I couldn't even scold Annie for being foolish enough to leave an egg where it could cause an accident. Kirstie still believed in the Easter Bunny. Shit, Annie did such good snow jobs on the kid that she believed in Santa Claus until she was at least fourteen."

Again Maddie laughed. "I'm sure she'd heard at school that Santa doesn't exist. But some kids want to cling to the magic of it all."

Sam sighed. "Go have fun." He gave her hand a second squeeze. "Make me believe in the magic again."

Sam remained in his chair, emotionally and mentally floating between the past and the present. Until Kirstin moved into her own residence, she had decorated on a small scale for the holidays, but Sam hadn't participated. He'd gotten Kirstin a gift at Christmas, forgetting to wrap it half the time, and called it good enough. It was yet another crime against his daughter that he could add to the list.

Sam forced himself to get up and move toward the kitchen. It hurt when he saw the glow of happiness slip from Kirstin's expression when she saw him. She was clearly afraid he'd spoil the moment by ranting about the foolishness of Halloween. Sam hadn't changed his opinion about that, but unless he wanted to rain on everyone else's parade, he needed to pretend that he had.

"What all have we got here?" he asked.

Cam answered. "Heaps of candy and decorations. We've taken up the table with all of it, so Gabriella is serving us dinner buffet-style. We're going to decorate before we eat. I say *we* loosely, because I obviously can't help much. And then we thought we'd take our plates to the living room to watch a Halloween movie. If it's all right with you, that is."

Sam never allowed a television to be on during dinner. He glanced at Kirstin, who looked as if she were holding her breath before the explosion. "Can we vote on the movie? I don't want to watch some damned idiotic cartoon."

ALL DAY FRIDAY SAM REFLECTED ON THE PREVIOUS EVENING AND had to admit he'd had fun. They had ended up watching *The Monster Squad*, which Sam had judged to be stupid, but he'd laughed in spite of himself. And as he moved from room to room inside his home, he had to admit that the decorations were cheery and bright. He'd gotten a little pissed first thing that morning when his hair was entangled in fake cobwebs hanging above the kitchen sink. He determined that a short person had hung them, possibly Maddie. Even if she stood on a step stool, he doubted she'd be tall enough to get her hair caught in that shit.

As usual, Sam and Miguel loaded their horses into the stock trailer and headed for the grazing land.

Despite working at a disadvantage, they had a good day and made two trips to bring in forty head. After getting the bovines safely pastured, they tended to their horses and then went to their respective homes. Sam looked forward to seeing Maddie. She'd become like an addiction to him, and he needed his nightly fix. Only Maddie was nowhere to be seen.

"She's feeling a little off tonight," Cam said.

"Not again?" Sam was starting to get worried. Maddie would go for nearly two weeks feeling fine, and then she'd be sick, sometimes for as long as three days. "She sure gets sick a lot."

Kirstin, sitting beside Cam on the sofa, pushed to her feet. "Gabriella left your dinner in the warmer and went home to make sure Miguel gets fed. I'll get yours out on the table. You guys are really late tonight."

"We brought in forty cows," Sam told her. "Found three groups bunched up in thickets surrounded by rugged terrain. We had to herd each clutch down, one at a time. Otherwise they'd have bolted, and we'd have to start rounding them up all over again." Sam shed his jacket and hat, depositing both on the entry hall coat-tree. Then he made a quick trip to the hallway bathroom to wash up. "I appreciate you putting out my dinner," he said to Kirstin as he entered the kitchen.

As he thanked her, he realized that he seldom acknowledged her efforts anymore, and he resolved to fix that. *I need to make a list. I've got so many failings I can't keep track of them.*

The kids were watching another movie tonight. Sam thought about going to his downstairs den for some peace and quiet, but he was tired and opted to go to bed instead. He'd no sooner settled in for the night than he heard a lowing sound. For a second he thought he and Miguel had missed a cow down at the pasture and left her running loose. But this noise was coming from somewhere inside the house.

He slept in his briefs and an undershirt, not appropriate attire in which to wander around the house when he had guests. He fished through his side of the walk-in closet to find a robe Annie had gotten him for Christmas years ago, a plaid flannel thing he'd always hated. But at least it would cover him up. Well, mostly, anyway. He was tall, and the hem hit him above the knees. Annie had intended to return it, but she never had. That had been so unlike her.

Then, out of nowhere, Sam's memory sharpened. Annie hadn't taken the robe back to exchange it because she'd been sick that Christmas. Sam froze and gripped the closet doorframe. How could he have forgotten that? It had been such a sad holiday season, with Annie receiving chemo infusions that had made her as sick as a dog. His heart had bled for her.

And it bled for her again now. Sam leaned against the interior wall of the closet and passed a hand over his eyes. Why were all these memories suddenly blindsiding him? He'd done his time with all this grief stuff. It had been more than six years. He should be over it now.

Only he guessed he wasn't. Looking back, he recognized that he'd spent most of that time feeling numb or pissed off. He'd turned his back on everything that reminded him of his wife, especially the holidays. At least he'd thought of it as turning his back, but maybe the truth was that he'd run from everything that broke his heart. Sam's life as a rancher had never been easy, and he'd learned the hard way that a man couldn't overcome something until he faced it.

Had he ever really faced Annie's death?

• • •

MADDIE HAD AWAKENED THAT MORNING FEELING AS IF SHE'D been run over by all sixteen tires of a semitruck. The aching exhaustion had stayed with her all day and had been followed this evening by vomiting. Now she had the dry heaves because she'd been unable to hold anything down. Never in her memory had she gotten this sick from an infusion.

Trembling with weakness, she barely managed to get back in bed. Then she huddled under the covers, shaking with cold. *Please, God, don't let the kids hear me upchucking. Don't let Caleb come to check on me.* She had to get through this without them knowing how violently ill she was. She was too sick to think clearly and might reveal too much if they questioned her.

She'd locked the door to her room. Or had she? She'd meant to, but now she couldn't remember for sure. Just then someone knocked. Maddie clutched the covers to her chest and stared at the ceiling. *Just pretend you're asleep,* she thought. *Whoever it is will go away.*

"Maddie, it's Sam. Are you okay in there? I heard what sounded like a cow lowing, and it came from your room."

Sam. Maddie groaned under her breath. If she didn't answer him, he would come in whether the door was locked or not.

"I'm fine," she managed to call out in what she hoped was a steady voice. "I've come down with something. I don't want anyone to catch it."

"I won't catch it. Let me bring you some juice or something. Maybe some crisp toast and a broth-based soup. Does that sound good?"

Maddie gagged at the mere thought and covered her mouth with the extra pillow until the spasm ended so Sam wouldn't hear. Then she said, "I've got water, Sam. All I really want now is to sleep."

She heard him sigh. "Okay, then. But if you need me during the night, I'm a light sleeper. Just holler for me."

"I will."

Only Maddie knew she wouldn't. She yearned for a heating pad and a cold cloth on her forehead. She didn't think she was feverish, so how would she explain the chills? She couldn't let Cam and Caleb discover that she was battling this disease. They were only just now getting their feet on solid ground after Graham's death. Caleb had brought no friends home and had started playing the violin instead of socializing. Maddie feared that he wasn't settling in well at his new school. The building that would hold their future homes was progressing slower than molasses running up a hill. Everything was a mess. A complete mess. She wouldn't add to their troubles by springing cancer on them at this late date. She only had to make it through Christmas, and then, if everything went well, she'd receive no more treatments. She could do this. She had to.

"I hope you feel better in the morning," Sam said through the door panel.

"Me, too," she pushed out.

Then she rolled out of bed onto her knees and crawled back to the toilet.

SAM LAY AWAKE UNTIL AFTER MIDNIGHT. HE COULDN'T STOP worrying about Maddie. She claimed that she'd had a complete physical last spring, but she'd never specifically said that she'd passed it with flying colors. What if she was sick? What if it was something serious? He was coming to have feelings for her. He'd already lost one woman. He didn't think he could survive losing another one.

Sam realized how awful that sounded, even if only inside his head. This wasn't about him, and it was wrong to be so self-centered. Maddie might be sick. He needed to be concerned for her, not for himself.

He rolled onto his side and tried to sleep. Tomorrow would be another long day.

ON SUNDAY MADDIE FELT STRONG ENOUGH TO FACE HER FAMILY, Kirstin, and Sam, with her dread rating highest for Sam. He was a sharp man and missed very little. Maddie felt weak. Vomiting almost ceaselessly for two days had left broken capillaries on her eyelids and cheeks, which she tried to cover with makeup. She added blush to her cheekbones and then wiped as much of it away as she could, because it stood out against her pallor like Rudolph's nose on a dark night.

As she tottered out to the kitchen, she was relieved to learn that Sam and Miguel had already left to round up more cattle. Gabriella was getting better with English. She smiled at Maddie and said, "Men gone." Maddie hated that Sam and Miguel were up against such a big job alone, but she was inexpressibly glad that she wouldn't be under scrutiny from those laser-sharp steel blue eyes until evening. She could drink some ginger tea or maybe a glass of juice, and try to regain her strength without being grilled as if she were a criminal.

She had just gotten settled on a chair at the long dining table when Cam rolled in. She'd forgotten about him being mostly stuck in the house and bored out of his mind. He parked beside her and wrinkled his nose. "God, Mom, I don't know how you choke that stinking stuff down."

Maddie really didn't feel like talking yet. "You use ginger in cooking and love it."

"That's different." Cam bent his head for a moment to study his lap. When he looked back up, his blue eyes were filled with worry. "We need to talk."

"About?"

"Your health. Something's wrong. I'm sorry it's taken me this long to realize it, but you were gone for so long to Missouri visiting Aunt Naomi, and then when you got back to California, I was here in Montana looking for land. After I got you moved here, I was busy, either working on the land or just plain working to find some real estate leads. I didn't notice. But Caleb's right. You've lost a ton of weight. And your color isn't good. You're getting sick every couple of weeks as well, but I never hear you cough or sniffle, so I know you haven't caught something that's going around."

Maddie put forth a cough. Then she plucked a napkin from the wooden holder and blew her nose. "I did get something, Cam. What is it with all this detective stuff?"

"I'm worried about you. You've always been so healthy, hardly ever catching a cold, let alone a stomach virus."

Maddie took a much-needed sip of her tea, which she hoped would be the first fluid she would be able to hold down in forty-eight hours. "Well, I'm not made of iron, Cameron, and I'm getting older. Of course I catch stuff easier than I used to."

He shook his head. "You've dieted off and on all your life, trying to be slender. Name me one time that it ever worked."

Maddie patted his knee. "I'm just naturally plump, I think. Thank goodness your father liked me that way."

"But, Mom, you're not plump now. What's up?"

Maddie felt as if he was backing her into a corner. "I saw a doctor week before last, and he said I'm in perfect health." That wasn't a lie. The oncologist was a doctor, and he'd pronounced her to be cancer free. "Maybe the weight loss is due to me getting more exercise." Maddie felt so tired. She didn't want to waste her already depleted strength on a needless conversation with her son. "In California I had household help. All the animals were taken care of by others. Here I'm forced to get my butt up out of my writing chair and walk all over that property we bought. I also take the dogs for jaunts every day."

"You walked in California," he argued. "You were always worried about your sedentary profession and got outside to exercise. If the weather was bad, you worked out in the home gym."

Maddie angled for some levity. "Yes, I spent an hour on my exercise bike every single day. Sometimes I even pedaled."

Cam's mouth thinned into a grim line. "You're stubborn, Mama. And you're one of the strongest women I've ever known. I remember when you finally told me Dad was dying of cancer. You bore the worry and sadness of that all alone until you absolutely had to tell me, because it couldn't be hidden anymore."

"Your father didn't want you to know, Cam. He wanted all the time with you and Caleb that he could have without you fawning over him and feeling sad. He wanted things to be normal for as long as possible. I didn't make the decision to wait and tell you when we had to. Your father did."

"Well, whoever decided, I didn't like having things kept from me."

You don't want to know about this, she thought. *My chemo run is almost over. If I have my way, you'll focus on that young woman you love and your son.* That last thought reminded Maddie of her concerns about Caleb. "If you're going to worry about someone, Cam, worry about your son."

"Why should I worry about Caleb?"

"Hello? He's been uprooted from friends he's known all his life and moved to the northern reaches of our country. Has he mentioned a single *new* friend to you? He has apparently lost interest in horses and cutting, which used to be his mainstays, and now he's passionate about playing violin. Do you see nothing off-center in that picture?"

Maddie felt awful the moment she spoke. Cam's eyes reflected even more worry. "Do you think he's having a hard time at school?"

She thought carefully before she spoke. "Possibly. He seems like the same happy boy he's always been, and he hasn't said a word to me about problems at school. But where did his sudden desire to become a string-instrument maestro come from?" Maddie truly was concerned about Caleb, so she pushed away her feelings of guilt. If her son was going to fret about someone, Caleb was the needier candidate. "You've always spent so much time with him, and now you can't. He loves Christmas, and this year he may have to celebrate in a tent. He's young, and he's faced so many changes. Maybe tonight you can involve him in a game of canasta. Here he goes upstairs to do his homework, and you can't go up. Start asking him to work down here so you can join him at the table. You were always so good about doing that."

Cam gestured around them. "We're in Sam's house, Mom. He cements himself in his recliner every night. I feel guilty about even watching a show with Caleb. We shout and carry on when we play canasta. Sam reads. We'd disrupt his life if we carried on as usual."

Maddie could see Cam's point. "Sam has isolated himself for more than six years. Maybe, for whatever reason, God planted us here so we can disrupt that cycle. He's a very lonely and sad man. He needs life to buzz around him. He needs to hear laughter and shouting. This gigantic house became his badger hole after Annie died, and whenever he emerged he was snarling."

"It's not my place to save Sam from being a mean old recluse."

Maddie shook her head. "Leave Sam to me. If he gets out of sorts, I'll ask him to move his recliner to the den. He doesn't have to sit out here in the living room like a rock and make everyone tiptoe around him."

"It's *his* house, Mother."

Cam never called her *mother* unless he was upset with her. Maddie would take it, and with gratitude. At least now he was worried about his son and not her. She needed fluids in her body, most important her ginger tea, which was now cold.

CALEB CUT CLASSES FOR THE DAY AND WENT HOME, NOT TO SAM'S house, but to their camp. His gram loved the holidays, and Caleb worried that she'd have to celebrate Christmas in this helter-skelter mess of tents and dwellings, with no one place they could call home and decorate. Normally Caleb didn't mind the camp living, but it wouldn't do for December. Sam's house was beautiful, and he'd made them feel at home there, but it was temporary. Caleb's father would surely be recovered enough by Christmas to come back to their camp again.

An ache filled Caleb's chest as he went from Gram's trailer to the cook shack, the storage tent, and then to the cabin. Without his family here, it all seemed so dreary and lifeless now, kind of like a ghost town. They'd never decorate for Christmas again at Gram's big house in California. All the friends he'd grown up with were lost to him unless he made the long drive home to see them. *Yeah, like that'll ever happen,* he thought.

He set off from camp to their building site. It was changing every day. The framing was finished, so he could try to imagine what the rooms would look like. He could also see how big the workshop was now, which would eventually be where he and his dad would weld and do woodworking. The building crews had been hurrying so that they could move into the garage area after it was insulated before the snows came. They'd pull Gram's trailer inside and move the cabin to sit next to the building.

Caleb stood inside the cavernous room, wondering how long it might take for everything inside to be finished so they could pretend it was a house while the interiors of their actual residences were completed.

"Hello, Caleb!"

Caleb jumped at the loud voice. He turned to see Murphy, the construction crew boss who kept all the teams coordinated and working. He was a big redheaded man with crinkly green eyes, a coppery beard and mustache, and shoulders almost as broad as Caleb's dad's. According to Gram, she'd never seen a building go up with such attention to detail, so apparently Murphy was good at his job.

"Hi," Caleb replied. "I was just trying to picture everything."

Murphy walked around with Caleb in what would be Gram's residence. "Here's where her work island will be," he said. Then he pointed to a framed-in window that didn't have glass in it yet. "Under that will be her kitchen desk."

It made Caleb feel better just to imagine it all. "I'm mainly worried about the workshop area."

Murphy nodded. "So am I, son. So am I. We're racing against time to get you folks inside out of the weather before the snow comes."

"Are you going to make it?"

"Not as fast as we hoped," Murphy replied. "We were aiming for before Thanksgiving. But you should be in a few days afterward."

"Will we have electricity and walls?" Caleb asked.

"You sure will, and your dad's installing a propane heater as well, so it'll be toasty in there." Murphy led the way back out to the workshop area. "It'll be one big space, and once you get all set up, it should be pretty comfortable."

Because of his dad's injury, Caleb didn't know if they'd come home to live on their land until almost Christmas. Gram had said that she'd like to provide Christmas dinner for some of the friends she and Dad had made in Rustlers' Gulch and other nearby towns. Gram had joined a book club and was teaching writing classes, so she'd met lots of people who would be alone over the holiday. In California she had entertained a lot, so they had heaps of folding tables and chairs in the storage units that he could set up. He could find all Gram's china and glassware. He could dig out all their decorations and make this place look awesome.

Caleb started to feel excited. Maybe they had left home for good, but he could re-create it here. Gram would be able to see all the decorations that Caleb, his dad, and his aunt Grace had made for her over the years. He could get a permit and cut a mile-high blue spruce that would outshine every Christmas tree they'd ever had.

SAM GOT IN LATE THAT NIGHT FROM ROUNDING UP COWS TO FIND Cam, Kirstin, and Caleb playing a card game at his dining room table. They were laughing and playfully slugging one another's shoulders. As he walked to the coat-tree to hang up his jacket and hat, he spotted Maddie reclining in Cam's spot on the sofa. She looked like a rag that had been wrung dry. He couldn't help but be worried about her. Now that he'd come to know her better, he suspected that she hadn't been feeling well the day of the windstorm that nearly destroyed her family's camp. And she'd still been under the weather when Cam got hurt, barely able to walk in the hospital hallways without collapsing.

Since coming to stay at his place, she'd been sick twice more. It seemed to hit her in a cyclical pattern. For days on end, she'd be fine. Then without any warning, such as signs of a virus, she'd be weak, pale, and trembling again. It took at least two days for her to recover. She'd lost weight since he first met her, and he had no doubt that all the vomiting she'd done Friday and Saturday would trim a few more pounds off her.

Why did no one else notice that something was going on with her? Sam wanted to sit down and ask one more time if she was ill. But he knew she'd only say she was fine. So instead he greeted her and adjourned to the kitchen to eat his dinner, which Mrs. Alvarez always kept warm for him.

He sat at the unoccupied end of the table to eat. Gabriella had made meat loaf, creamy mashed potatoes with gravy, and corn with Mexican spices. It was all delicious.

Cam stood up to gather the cards. Sam observed aloud, "Well, it looks like your leg is doing better."

"It is. I get a little more feeling in it every day. I still don't trust it to hold me up while I walk, though."

Sam guessed that Cam had more than all the usual reasons for wanting to be completely recovered. He was in love with a beautiful young woman, and he undoubtedly felt like he was half the man he needed to be for her. So far as Sam knew, Cam hadn't used the wheelchair path to visit Kirstin after his son went to sleep at night, but realist that he was, Sam knew that would start occurring soon.

He finished his meal, got his dishes into the machine, and went to visit with Maddie until bedtime. An electric jack-o'-lantern sat on the windowsill behind her, illuminating her head with an orange glow.

"Feeling better?" he asked as he sat beside her.

"Very much so, and I hope nobody else gets sick. The big day is almost here, you know."

Sam tried to think what big day she meant.

"Halloween, Sam." She smiled, but her eyes didn't light up with warmth as they usually did. "It falls on Tuesday this year. I hope we still get oodles of trick-or-treaters, despite it being a school night."

There'd been no kids on Sam's porch since the Halloween after Annie died. But he was ashamed to tell Maddie why. Better to pretend that children would come and let her guess as to the reason why they didn't.

The sound of laughter erupted from the dining room again. Sam sighed and relaxed against the cushions. It was nice to have his home echoing with voices and good cheer again. There had been a time when that was the norm. The sense of family. Coming in from the land at night, knowing good company, food, laughter, and closeness awaited him. Having the McLendons under his roof wasn't the same for him as when Annie had been alive, but it was a damned close second. Sam cared for Maddie, and he had come to like Caleb. The boy was smart and respectful, and wasn't afraid of hard work. On weekends he had been trying to help Sam and Miguel move cattle back to the ranch. As for Cam—well, Sam still struggled with that. He liked the young fellow and never fell asleep now without thanking God that Cam had been there to protect Kirstin from Satan. But—and for Sam this was still difficult to accept—Cam was becoming Kirstin's everything. Sam saw it in her expression. Saw it in the way she smiled when she looked at the younger man. He wanted to be happy for her. He truly did. But a part of him still wanted to latch onto her with both hands and never let go.

AFTER THE HOUSE FELL QUIET AND CAM FELT PRETTY SURE EVERY-one was asleep, he put on his jacket and quietly slipped from the house. He had often used the wheelchair ramp to go for physical therapy or to work, but he'd never used the path that led to Kirstin's house. He felt like a teenager sneaking out after curfew. About halfway there, he stopped pushing, not to rest, but to ask himself if he should really do this. His leg was better. Though he still used his crutches only occasionally, he could tell that his ribs were healing well. But what if he started to make love to Kirstin and had to give up halfway to the finish line?

He nearly turned back, but he yearned so badly to hold her in his arms that he forced himself to keep going. The grounds lighting guided him to her place without mishap, and he was incredulous when he saw that Sam had added a ramp for him on Kirstin's porch so he could scale the steps. *Hmm.* Maybe Sam really was coming to accept their relationship. Or maybe, Sam being Sam, he was hoping that Cam would come here too soon and make a fool of himself.

Before he could change his mind and turn back, the huge hand-carved entry door opened. Kirstin stood on the threshold wearing the Australian shepherd T-shirt he remembered so well. In the dim illumination, he saw her lips curve in an impish smile that dimpled her cheek. "Well, miracles will never cease. I was starting to think you'd never come see me."

Cam couldn't help but grin. "My heart and other parts of me have been yelling at me to come for a solid week. But the coward in me kept chickening out."

"*Why?*" She sounded completely bewildered.

"I'm not fully recovered yet, Kirstie. When we're together again, I don't want to be a big flop, and I mean that literally."

She jutted out one hip and planted her hand on it. "Get your sexy ass in here. You won't be a big flop. I promise."

Cam pushed forward and ascended the ramp. She stepped back to allow him entry. He was glad the opening was wide enough for a wheelchair. Kirstin closed the door behind him and sat on his lap to kiss him. The melting sweetness of her mouth nearly took his breath. He had forgotten how delicious she tasted. And how fabulous her soft body felt beneath his palms.

Between kisses, she whispered, "I love you." Then, "All I really, *really* need is to have your arms around me, Cam."

He felt confident that he could deliver on that request. He wheeled them both into her bedroom. After she scrambled to her feet, he was able to stand by himself and get on the bed, where the covers were already pulled down. Kirstin slipped in beside him and sighed with a sound of contentment that resonated within him, because he felt the same sense of rightness.

Chapter Thirteen

FOR KIRSTIN, BEING IN CAM'S ARMS AGAIN WAS THE MOST BEAU-
tiful moment of her life. She'd loved him before his accident,
but during his recovery those feelings had deepened, making her
understand what *true* love actually meant. And for her, it was no
longer only about physical attraction or having incredible sex
with him. Even if Cam never completely recovered, she would
love him, and they would find ways to be intimate that pleased
both of them. With Cam, it would be fabulous, no matter what.

He turned on his side to face her and gathered her close
against him. She placed her head in the hollow of his shoulder
and breathed in the scent of him. "I want one of your T-shirts
after you wear it so I can keep it under my pillow."

She felt him smile against her hair. "How about a T-shirt with
me in it every night, and you don't keep it under your pillow?"

"Even better."

He kissed her then and ever so slowly began making love to
her. Ribbons of pure delight coursed through her body. *Cam.* His
name became a song in her mind. She floated with him on cur-
rents of desire that soon crashed over her in waves. When the
moment came, she took the top position, something she'd never
done, and along with the indescribable pleasure of being one with

him again, she experienced a feeling of feminine empowerment, no longer only a recipient of physical pleasure, but also giving it.

Afterward they lay tangled together, utterly spent and absolutely content.

"Ah, Kirstie, that was amazing," he whispered. "Can I come back tomorrow night?"

She kissed his shoulder. "If you don't, I'll come find you."

As they both recovered from their exhaustion, they began to talk, Kirstin about the rigors of her day, and Cam about her father.

"Things are so much better between us now," he murmured. "We're *almost* there, man to man, no more bullshit between us. But Sam still has a wall up that prevents me from feeling as if we're actually friends."

Kirstin rubbed his chest lightly, loving the way the mat of hair curled over her fingertips. "In my opinion, you've scaled the equivalent of Mount Everest with my dad. Just hang in there, Cam. I think he still feels a little threatened by you. He'll get over that in time."

"I think so, too," he told her. "And I'm really happy about that. I've moved way beyond thinking of you as a mere possibility in my life. My son likes you—if he doesn't already love you. And I know my mom thinks highly of you. She also seems to get along fine with your dad. I see no more hurdles in the way for us."

Kirstin heard a troubled note in his voice. "That's a good thing. Right?"

Cam sighed, his expulsion of breath stirring strands of her hair. "I'm just worried about my mom's relationship with Sam. They seem almost *too* friendly for my peace of mind."

Kirstin tried to read his expression in the dimness. "Why is that a bad thing? I think it'd be perfect if they got together."

Cam stiffened. "Together? I'm not sure I can handle that. I guess I'm not ready for another man to take my father's place. The whole idea gets my back up. Sam's a strong, honest, hardworking man. But I'm not sure I want my mother to be with him. No offense, Kirstie, but I know he can be impossible sometimes."

"He can be, yes," she admitted.

"And nobody can fill my father's shoes, not in my mind. Yet I can sense that my mom is softening toward Sam, maybe even needing him in some way I can't fulfill. It bugs me." He kissed her forehead. "I know it's probably silly of me. It's just that I've worked so hard to be her rock. I haven't made her the absolute center of my life, but I sure as hell have been a pillar of support for her. Why does she need anyone else?"

Kirstin tucked her face against his shoulder and smiled. With her voice muffled against his skin, she said, "Cam, I hate to say this, but you're starting to sound a lot like my father."

"*What?*"

She couldn't help but laugh at his horrified tone of voice. "Possessive, a bit jealous, and afraid of being usurped." She patted his shoulder. "I don't mean it's a bad thing. I guess it's a natural way to feel when you've loved someone faithfully and that person suddenly turns toward someone else. Can I tell you a story?"

"Oh, man."

She chuckled again. "It's a good story about when I was a little girl. Mom would cuddle me up and say that she loved me more than she loved anybody else in the whole world. I loved hearing that, but one day when I grew a little older my heart jerked, and I asked my mother how she could love me more than she loved Daddy. Mama laughed and jostled me. And I'll never forget what she said. 'My heart has beautiful corners, and on each of them is a name. One of them is named Kirstin, and in that corner of my heart, I love you more than I love anybody else in the whole world. Another corner of my heart is named Daddy, and in that corner of my heart, I love him more than I love anyone else. So you don't need to worry about that. I love both you and Daddy more than I love anyone else in the whole, wide world.' At that age, I was comforted by that answer, and I still am. Love has no boundaries. You need to understand that your mom can love another man in his corner of her heart. That will never diminish how much she loved your father, or how much she loves you and Caleb."

Cam wasn't so sure. It still irked him somehow that his mom seemed to be falling for Sam. But as Cam fell asleep in Kirstin's arms, he thought about the corners of his own heart. Caleb had complete ownership of one, and in that corner, Cam loved that kid with every fiber of his being. Nobody could ever take any part of that love away from his son. Cam had assigned another corner of his heart to Maddie. She reigned as queen there. And now he had opened up yet another corner for Kirstin, where she was becoming the most important person in the world to him.

How could that be? How could he love three people so completely? As he drifted off, Cam realized that Annie Conacher had been right. Love had no boundaries.

Now Cam just had to learn how to love Sam.

SAM TREASURED THE LATE NIGHTS WITH MADDIE EVEN THOUGH sitting up with her deprived him of much-needed sleep. He felt as if he could talk with her and say almost anything. She often challenged him to think about things differently. They'd developed a habit of sitting together on his sectional at night to talk after all the kids had gone to bed. Tonight Sam had invited her to join him in his den on the sofa, a conscious decision on Sam's part so that Cam would think everyone had gone to bed and feel free to slip away to visit Kirstin. He liked to think that meant that he'd *grown as a person*, one of Maddie's favorite things to say when she was praising him.

Sam enjoyed draping his arm over her shoulders and pulling her close while they chatted. She never failed to remind him that she wasn't looking for a physical relationship. He always laughed and said he knew all about her dead unit and wasn't angling for intimacy. Friends could go out to dinner and see a film. Friends could also be physically close without sex being part of it.

And tonight Sam realized that he meant it. Cam and Kirstin were young, and it was natural for sexual activities to be at the heart of their relationship, but Sam had already enjoyed that part of his life. At his age, he could still go for some sparks, but he could also be satisfied with mere physical affection. Maddie was as soft and warm as a pillow. When he looked into her wise gaze, he knew she understood him in a way no one else did. And he also understood her. She wasn't a twentysomething bikini girl anymore. She was embarrassed about her body. He was good with that, because Maddie had so much more to offer him than sex. She had become his friend, his sounding board, and his voice of sanity. He couldn't help but think Annie was in heaven clapping her hands, so glad that Sam had found this woman. Not the love of his life, he reminded himself. He'd never love anyone again the way he'd loved Annie. It hurt too much when you lost someone you cared about that much. But somehow he'd come to care about Maddie in a way he'd never expected.

Sometimes while he was with Maddie he felt as if he were being unfaithful to Annie. He wished he could ask Maddie if she ever felt that way, but it was a taboo subject. The last thing she wanted was for Sam to love her that way.

Only Sam was starting to. She was nothing like Annie. Maddie never came on to him. When they talked, she never fussed with her hair or seemed to worry about how she looked. When she was under the weather, she didn't even bother with the usual touches of makeup and looked as if a vampire had just drained her dry.

Sam had asked repeatedly if she was sick. She always denied it, saying she was absolutely fine, but his heart always squeezed when she claimed that. He wanted to believe her, but a part of him still worried. Maddie wasn't a liar, though. In fact, she was one of the most honest people he'd ever met. So Sam had forced himself to set aside his concerns about her health. She was getting up there in years. As was he. Some mornings he wondered how he would make it through another day of working like a man half his age. Getting older wasn't easy. Maddie had bad days, and so did he. It went with the territory.

"Have I mentioned that tomorrow is Halloween?" she asked him.

After she'd been so sick over the weekend, Sam had no clue how she could dredge up excitement about a commercialized holiday that hadn't been on his radar since his wife's death. "Yep. You mentioned it." *About a dozen times.* "Don't overdo it tomorrow, though. That virus kicked your ass. I've seen white pillowcases with more color than you have right now."

She smiled and leaned her head against his arm again. "By tomorrow I'll be full of vinegar. Can you come home a little early? We always have a family party on Halloween night, and if you don't mind, I'd like to continue with our tradition."

Sam could have gotten more excited about a root canal. "Sure. What kind of family party?"

"Well, it's always nice to have a lovely early dinner before the little kids start ringing the doorbell. I like to have the kitchen all tidy before they come so I can enjoy how cute they look. And I think Kirstin wants to officially celebrate Cam's big ranch sale." She looked up at him with those guileless blue eyes. "Thank you for that, by the way. I know it wouldn't have happened for him if you hadn't done damage control. I haven't properly expressed my appreciation."

Sam felt uncomfortable for more than one reason, but he focused on the damage control. "All I did was tell the truth about him, Maddie. I honestly thought I'd done that the first time around, but eventually I realized that he was a lot better man than I'd believed him to be."

"And it takes a good man to publicly admit he was wrong." She lightly punched his ribs. "Don't spoil my thank-you with a bunch of your macho bullshit."

"There you go again, cussing like a sailor. How is that fair? I cleaned up my language, and now you're cussing."

She smiled. "What's good for the goose isn't always good for the gander."

"Ah, I see. So you live by a double standard."

She flapped her hand. "Get out of here, Sam Conacher. I rarely use bad language. Only when it gets my point across."

"But you led me to believe you're as pure as new snow."

She laughed, and a hint of color came into her pale cheeks. "At *my* age? What were you smoking?"

"Now you're telling me you know about smoking dope?"

"Anyone alive in our country hears about that. It doesn't mean I've ever done it."

"Thank the good Lord. I've fired so many damned potheads that I've lost track."

"From what I've heard, you fired a lot of good hands who weren't potheads."

Sam sighed. "Yeah, that, too."

"Have you ever thought about calling them and trying to make amends? You could plead temporary insanity."

"Stop trying to fix me, Maddie."

"Why? From where I'm standing, you need some reprogramming."

SAM MADE IT A POINT TO GET HOME EARLY THE NEXT DAY EVEN though he'd lose his ass if he couldn't get all his cattle off that damned grazing land. He'd thought about it all day, and he did need some reprogramming. He hadn't celebrated Halloween with his daughter in seven years. Annie had been at death's door when Halloween came just days before she took her last breath. The next year, he had been in no mood to celebrate holidays, a pattern he had established the prior Christmas, when he'd wanted to hang a black wreath on the door and shake his fist at God.

This year he would celebrate Halloween and smile if it killed him.

When Sam walked in the door, he found Kirstin and Maddie in the kitchen making popcorn balls and packaging individually wrapped candies. He doffed his hat and jacket to sit at one end of the table. He enjoyed watching the preparations. The large house seemed smaller and cozier somehow, and the air was redolent with a mixture of the rich smells of caramel and Gabriella's cooking, the most mouthwatering of those the yeasty sweetness of homemade dinner rolls. He felt as if the Conacher Ranch was coming alive again.

When the large wicker basket was filled with goodies to later be distributed to children who wouldn't come, Kirstin and Maddie jumped in to help Gabriella finish dinner, and Cam, using only one crutch to help stabilize his leg, commandeered the stove to create a brandy sauce for the steaks. It fell to Caleb to set the table. Sam decided to help the boy and noted that there were too many plates. Seconds later, the mystery of that was solved when Miguel and Rickie arrived for the party. Sam hadn't thought to invite the Alvarez family to join them, but apparently someone else had. Miguel was a good man, and his loyalty had been a godsend to Sam. He and his family were welcome at Sam's table anytime.

The mood was festive as they gathered to eat. Kirstin smiled at Miguel and said, "Would you do us the honor of leading us in the meal blessing?"

That had always been Sam's job, but he'd pretty much stopped praying. It wasn't that he no longer believed, but more that he was still mentally shaking his fist at God. So he was happy to have Miguel take charge.

Everyone raved over Cam's steak sauce and laughed when Caleb said, "Just don't distract Dad when he's reducing it. The world comes close to ending if it separates."

Kirstin lifted her wineglass and proposed a toast to Cam for breaking into the ranch market in such a huge way. "Congratulations, Cam! May this be your first sale of many!"

After sharing good food and conversation, the latter of which felt odd to Sam because he now mostly ate in silence, all the diners helped to clean up the kitchen. Sam and Caleb, armed with dish towels, dried all the pots and pans.

When all was tidy and shiny again, Caleb turned on the porch light to welcome little goblins. He and Kirstin put on simple costumes: Kirstin's a witch's robe and hat, Caleb posing as a warlock with a black mustache and bushy eyebrows that reminded Sam of his own. Rickie had nothing special to wear, but he seemed excited to participate. They sat at the small breakfast bar near the basket, ready to greet children.

Sam occupied his recliner. He didn't miss that Kirstin kept glancing at the entry hall with a worried look on her face. He guessed that she knew the doorbell might not ring. His mind went back in time to when little raps had come on the door and Annie and Kirstin had fussed over the kids in their costumes. Mentally, Sam started to squirm. He knew damned well that no visitors would show up, and his daughter probably did, too.

Midway through the evening, everyone began to realize that the following school day would prevent any grade-schoolers from arriving so late. Caleb, apparently disappointed that he hadn't been able to play his role as a warlock, rubbed his hands together and grinned wickedly at the basket.

"Come on, Rickie! All this means is that there's more for us!"

Gabriella, sitting beside Miguel on the love seat and sipping warm cider, called, "Rickie, no too *mucho*. You be *náuseas*."

Sam was impressed. He was starting to understand the woman. "Gabriella, how you say, go outside and hump the horse?"

"Sam," Maddie said from her place on the sofa. Her tone was scolding.

Gabriella laughed and flapped her hand. "Senor Conacher bad, bad, bad *español*."

Miguel curled his arm around his wife. "She's doing good at her studies."

Rickie called out from the bar, "I'm helping with her spelling. Dad's mostly teaching her how to cuss."

Maddie got up to raid the basket. Cam went over in his wheelchair so he wouldn't miss out. Kirstin playfully slapped his hand aside to pick her treat first. The popcorn balls were a favorite. Maddie beamed because it was her recipe.

Sam wanted nothing. The main activity of the evening, giving out candy, had been a total flop, and it was entirely his fault. He didn't wish to remember why, but his brain worked despite his reluctance to allow the thoughts in. The Halloween following Annie's death had come only a few days after her passing, and he'd been angry at the world. When parents drove up with their kids to let them knock on his door, Sam had totally lost it. He yelled at the children and told them to get the fuck off his porch. Now no parents brought their youngsters onto his land, and for good reason. He'd acted like such an ass that night. Kirstin had cried and run to her room, and she'd barely spoken to him the next day.

Feeling ashamed, Sam watched Maddie unwrap her popcorn ball and take a huge bite. He'd screamed at little kids and driven them off his porch. He'd hated them and their parents for being happy when his heart was breaking. A part of him still understood that man. But he'd also moved forward now and made progress.

The Alvarez family thanked Sam for having them and then bundled up in their winter wear to head home. After they left, Caleb went upstairs to practice on his violin. The awful noises still reminded Sam of two cats fighting. Kirstin helped tidy up the treat mess and left. Sam knew Cam would probably throttle his wheelchair to high speed and follow her. But first he'd dream up a reason so Sam wouldn't know he was boinking his daughter.

"I think I'll go over to Kirstin's for a while," he said. "She made mulled wine and asked me over for a nightcap."

Sam shifted in his chair. "That sounds delicious. Do you like mulled wine, Maddie?"

His eldest houseguest gave him a look that could have pulverized granite, and Sam, biting back a grin, settled against the cushioned leather. "Um, I guess not. We'll settle for a boring glass of white wine."

Cam looked vastly relieved. He glanced at his mother. "Will you tell Caleb that I'll be back in a bit?"

Maddie nodded. "But take your time and enjoy yourself. Caleb no longer needs his father to tuck him in."

When Cam had made his way out onto the porch and the entry door closed behind him, Sam vacated his recliner to join Maddie on the couch.

"You did that on purpose," she accused as he sat beside her.

"Hell, yes. I'm allowing him to have sex with my little girl. That doesn't mean I have to make it easy for him."

"Actually, you paved his way by making that pathway to her house."

Sam huffed under his breath. "You're right. What in blue blazes was I thinking?"

A brief silence fell between them, and then Maddie observed, "Tonight was interesting. One of the largest ranches in the valley, and you didn't get a single kid at your door."

"Do we have to go there?" he asked.

"Yes." She narrowed her eyes at him. "What did you do? Come on, don't be shy. I'm waiting to hear with bated breath."

Though it was difficult, Sam told her the whole ugly story.

"Oh, Sam," she said softly.

"I feel bad about it," he confided. "But when Annie died, I wanted the world to stop turning."

"And it didn't." She settled against him. "I felt that way, too. Everyone else went on with life while mine had come to a stop."

Sam appreciated her understanding. Maddie had a way of cutting through all the bullshit to put his feelings into words.

"I'd like to fix it," he told her. "Halloween, I mean. But I can't think how. Protective parents don't want their kids hearing the kind of language I used that night."

"A grand gesture is called for," she said. "Next year you should set up a haunted house in your barn and throw a Halloween party in here. Heaven knows this house is big enough for that. Kids love to bob for apples and win prizes for half drowning themselves."

"Nobody would come, Maddie." Sam shrugged. "Why would they?"

"Because people, by nature, have forgiving hearts. You can hang posters all over town, inviting people to come. And they will come, Sam. You used to be well thought of in this valley."

"I have no idea how to create a haunted house or throw a party for a bunch of kids," Sam said. "It sounds like you do. Would you help me?"

She nodded and smiled. "I'd be pleased to be a part of that. By then I'll be in my own place on our land, but we'll still be neighbors."

A heavy, tight feeling entered Sam's chest. He didn't want Maddie to move back onto her own land. Without her, he'd slip back into the anger that had darkened his world for so long. He needed her in his life.

CAM HAD BEEN OBSERVING HIS SON EVER SINCE HIS MOTHER talked to him the day before Halloween. It was true that Caleb brought home no friends, and he didn't appear to be meeting with other kids away from the ranch. The boy had never been a whiner, but Cam sensed that all wasn't right in Caleb's world since they'd moved to Montana.

As the early days of November passed and Cam saw no change, he took Caleb aside to have a talk.

"I'm fine, Dad," Caleb responded when Cam asked what was

wrong. "I still like horses. It's just that you can't ride with me right now, so it isn't as fun."

Cam recalled that Caleb had asked to take up playing the violin prior to the incident with the bull. "Caleb, man to man, no BS, what's going on with you at school? You don't seem to be making friends, and you've always done that easily."

"It's different in California," Caleb replied. "I've known all those kids most of my life. Here I'm like—I don't know—the odd one out." He gestured at his clothes. "I'm all Western. The kids dress this way sometimes. But most of the time, they dress normal, wearing athletic shoes and T-shirts with stuff on them. When you and Gram took me clothes shopping, you went all cowboy, like Montana is a totally different world and everyone's a full-time wrangler."

Cam's heart sank. "Why didn't you come to me and say something?"

"Do you know how much a stupid T-shirt costs? And ball caps. Lots of the guys wear those, and they're expensive. We need to watch our budget. I couldn't ask you to buy me a bunch of regular clothes."

"And the violin thing?"

"It's something I can do by myself. I don't need a friend to do it with."

Cam felt horrible. He'd worked hard to have a good relationship with his son, and now they'd had a huge communication gap. "How's woodshop going? Surely you've made at least a couple of friends during that class."

Caleb shrugged. "I wear Western shirts with pearl snaps or buttons. Dress shirts, Dad. And have you ever tried to wear a Stetson backward? The guys in shop have the bills of their caps backward."

"Okay," Cam said. "We're going shopping. Do you need different jeans, too?"

"Dad, what if I buy a bunch of stuff and it isn't right? What do you think I am, an expert shopper?"

CAM DUMPED THE PROBLEM IN KIRSTIN'S LAP. "CALEB NEEDS NEW clothes, and I can't ask Mom to help us shop," he told her. "She'll take a radical swing toward her idea of normal and have Caleb dressed like a rapper."

Kirstin hugged him and kissed his cheek. "I'll be happy to help. Buying ordinary clothes isn't rocket science, Cam. Most of the parents dress their kids as inexpensively as possible." A frown pleated her brow. "They grow like weeds. Think sparing and cheap. Remind me that we need to find a few Griz shirts."

"What?"

"Griz shirts," she repeated. "The University of Montana's Griz athletics teams? Football, for one. We're big on the Griz here, and don't let Caleb call them the Grizzlies. Here we say the Griz, singular or plural."

Cam had never shopped for his son in a wheelchair, which made him doubly glad that Kirstin had gotten off early to go with them. Sitting down, Cam couldn't see what lay on the display tables, and after about the thirtieth time he stood up, his leg started to ache.

At first Caleb acted as if he'd rather be anywhere than in a department store, but Kirstin's enthusiasm was contagious, and the kid was soon wearing a backward Griz ball cap as they shopped.

"Wrangler jeans are fine for school," she pronounced. "Half the population of Montana has a *W* branded on each cheek of his or her butt. And Western belt buckles are fine, too. But you need to mix things up."

She found some awesome T-shirts for Caleb. Cam didn't get how Western belts and sloppy T-shirts went together, but when he voiced his opinion, Caleb politely told him to stay out of it. Kirstin, whose words were now apparently the Holy Grail, knew what worked.

When Caleb was fully decked out for school all over again, Cam took his shopping partners out for dinner at the Cowboy Tree. Caleb ordered fifteen chicken wings and devoured them all. Cam ordered ten to Kirstin's five, and pretty soon all three of them looked like they'd been dining on fresh roadkill, with red sauce ringing their mouths and smeared on their hands. They soiled a mountain of napkins and poked fun at one another while cleaning themselves up.

"No more chicken wings," Kirstin pronounced. "They do serve lots of other good stuff here."

"Nah. My favorite when we go out is wings," Caleb argued. "And we don't go out that often because Dad always cooks. He makes homemade wings that are the bomb, but Gram says they're high in fat."

"Well, fatty or not, I'll make wings once a week. If you think your dad's are good, just wait until you lock your lips on mine. Maybe on those nights, we can eat at my place so Gram doesn't have to indulge."

Caleb gave Kirstin a long study. "*You* make *wings*?"

Kirstin guzzled Coke from the straw in her glass. "What? Do you think your father is the only person in this family who cooks?"

In that moment, Cam knew he'd gotten it right this time. Kirstin not only suited him perfectly, but she suited Caleb.

When they got back to the ranch, Caleb came up missing. It

had already grown dark, but when Cam rolled his chair out onto the porch, the yard lights helped him see his son, who was crouched down and doing something in the dirt.

"Caleb, what the Sam Hill are you doing?"

Caleb peered up at him through the gloom. "I'm getting my hat good and dirty."

That made no sense at all to Cam. "That's a brand-new hat. It cost me twenty-five bucks."

"I know. That's the problem. Brand-new will stick out like a whore in church."

Startled, Cam asked, "Who taught you that saying?"

"Sam. He says it all the time."

Cam watched his son walk toward the porch, rubbing dirt onto the cap as he stepped. "Well, don't say it at school."

Caleb rolled his eyes as he scaled the steps. "What do you think the guys at school say, 'shucky-darn'?"

Cam sighed. "Have we just reached the horrible sixteens?"

AS NOVEMBER SPED BY, CAM'S LEG GREW STRONGER. WHEN HE went into Missoula for another MRI, the neurologist studied the film as if he were looking for a flea on a shaggy dog's back. Cam sat in the wheelchair beside him, waiting for a verdict.

"So?" he asked. "What do you see?"

"Almost nothing." The doctor, a tall, slender man with dark hair and striking brown eyes, flashed Cam a grin. "And that's exactly what I hoped to see. Your spine is fine. The numbness and pain in your leg were caused by nerve swelling, and in these layered images, I can see that the nerve impairment from that is almost gone."

"So why is my leg still weak? I went shopping with my son

the other night, and after repeatedly standing up and putting weight on it, it ached like no tomorrow."

"Lack of use. There's still a little swelling and slight nerve impairment from the injury, but mainly I think the muscles have atrophied. Turn the wheelchair back in to the rental company and get a cane. Start using the leg." He wrote a script, tore off the sheet, and thrust it at Cam. "Continue with physical therapy for another month. If you aren't at one hundred percent after Thanksgiving, come back to see me, but it's my educated guess that you'll be dancing a jig by then."

When Cam got back to the ranch after exchanging the wheelchair for a cane with the medical equipment rental company, he tried to go up the porch steps and cursed the doctor. His leg nearly buckled, and pain radiated from his lower back to his ankle. "Lack of use, my ass." By the time he made it into the house, he was sweating bullets. He collapsed on the sofa, raised the footrest, and stared at the open-beam ceiling, feeling sorry for himself.

Caleb burst into the entry hall wearing a black Montana Grizzlies jacket topped by his dirty ball cap. Cam glanced down and saw that his Wrangler jeans had been cut at the hems and dangled faded threads. "What happened to your pants?"

"I just remodeled them a little."

Cam almost said that he'd ruined perfectly good jeans. But then he remembered Caleb's deliberate soiling of his new hat and kept his mouth shut. Being a dad had always seemed so easy— until now. "Oh," he said, hoping to sound cool. "Looking radical, man, looking radical."

"Nobody says 'radical' anymore."

"What do they say, then?"

"All kinds of things. Just listen to people talk, Dad." Caleb went in to grab an apple from the fruit bowl. His cheek bulged as he reentered the living room. "A guy talked to me in woodshop today."

Cam's heart lifted. "That's awesome, Caleb! What did he say?"

Caleb shrugged. Around a bite of apple, he replied, "'Would ya pass me that chisel?'"

Cam stared at his son. The youth looked happy and triumphant. "Well, that's a start."

"Yeah. I'm fitting in."

THAT EVENING MADDIE HAD HER HANDS FULL WITH SAM. HE GREW agitated because Kirstin was fixing dinner at her house for Cam and Caleb, and Maddie and Sam weren't invited.

"Now do you see why I was so afraid for her to fall in love?" Sam, wearing a limp gray shirt with long sleeves, paced back and forth in the living room. "She gets a man in her life, and now I'm about as popular as horseshit on Sunday boots."

Maddie, sitting on the sofa, smiled at him. "Sam, Sam, Sam. It isn't like that at all. Gabriella is fixing us a perfectly fabulous meal right here. Kirstin is making chicken wings, which are high in fat and really not good for you and me to eat."

"Oh! So now I'm a geriatric who has to have menu planning? Next, she'll mash up my food and spoon-feed me."

With a sigh, Maddie pushed to her feet. "All right, then. I'll call and have her issue you an invitation, but I think you're being absurdly sensitive. If she and Cam get married, are you going to expect them to make you the center of their lives?"

"Married? WTF?"

"That's progress!" she said cheerfully. "Vile language reduced to an acronym. I'm proud of you. As for marriage, isn't that the logical next step when young people fall madly in love? You and

Annie got married. Graham and I got married. Would you feel better if Kirstin and Cam had babies out of wedlock and gave them the hyphenated surname of Conacher-McLendon?"

"Babies?"

"Yes. I believe they're commonly referred to as grandchildren. And luckily for them, I'll live on adjoining land so I can ride herd on you. Otherwise you'll glower and teach them how to cuss before they go to kindergarten."

He plowed his fingers through his hair. Maddie had a strong urge to give him a comforting hug. "I just feel like I'm losing her."

"You'll never lose her, Sam. Unless, of course, you continue to behave like an insecure and spoiled child."

He sank onto the hearth and held his head in his hands. "Damn it, Maddie, you've got a barbed tongue."

"I'm sorry. I don't mean to hurt your feelings, but it's the truth. So what if the kids have an evening together without us old fogies present? Caleb needs to have a sense of belonging. Kirstin and Cam have developed a relationship, and now it's time for them to include him as part of their unit." She arched a brow at him. "We'll continue to have dinner with them most nights."

"I hope so. I enjoy ending my day with everyone over a good meal."

"Personally, I was looking forward to dinner alone with you tonight. I wanted to tell you how my revisions are coming and get your advice on the slight differences in terrain." She folded her arms. "Dinner for two. A lovely wine. Adult conversation. For one evening, it sounded to me like a nice change of pace."

"Put like that, it does sound nice." He drew in a deep breath and looked up at her. "I really am acting like an insecure kid, aren't I?"

Maddie joined him on the hearth. "For the most part, I think you've been awesome. Don't blow it all now by trying to cage your daughter again." She toyed with the crease in her slacks, glad she'd finally carved out time to get some dressier outfits out of storage. Sam didn't seem to notice, but she felt more like her old self. The only problem was that she'd had to use a safety pin to make the waistline fit. "Here's how I see it. The three of them need to forge bonds as a family, and we need to give them the space to do that. We won't be abandoned in the end. Instead our lives will be enriched."

"You're right. I just—I don't know—panicked, I guess. And deep down, maybe I do want her to make me the center of her life." He looked over and smiled grimly. "That's wrong. I'd better straighten up my act, or I'll have two women yammering at me, you during the day and Annie when I try to go to sleep at night."

Maddie crossed her ankles and admired her Dansko clogs. It felt so good to be wearing actual shoes instead of hiking boots. "I envy you. Graham hasn't let out a peep. I'd love to hear his voice again, even if he was yammering."

"You don't think I'm crazy?"

She laughed and elbowed his arm. "Crazier than a loon. But aren't we all? I definitely don't think you're nuts because you sometimes hear Annie's voice. Maybe it's only your imagination. Many people would think so. But I'm inclined to think that she's worried about you, and she's even more worried about Kirstin. Some people believe heaven is somewhere far away, but I picture it as being just beyond a curtain we can't see, another plane of existence."

He nodded and reached over to clasp her hand. "You're a good friend, Maddie. You make me sound halfway sane."

"Don't beat up on yourself. I've been told that it's much harder for men to lose a spouse than it is for women. We're the nurturers, and men are geared more toward being providers. Hunters, if you will, who focus less on emotions and more on the hard realities. We gals practice all our lives at dealing with emotion. We worry that one of our kids will be killed in an accident, and in our minds, we can imagine how painful that would be. Men get blindsided when their wives die, and they're swamped with a sudden rush of emotions that they never imagined and aren't able to handle.

"I'm not saying losing Graham was easy for me. It was horrible. It's still horrible. When I try to understand how anyone could survive anything worse, I take my hat off to men. Did you know that a large percentage of widowers remarry within a year? They can't deal with being alone. You didn't do the rebound thing, Sam. You've toughed it out. Learn to admire yourself for your strength. Forgive yourself for your mistakes. And pat yourself on the back."

Sam laughed. "For caging my daughter? I realize now that I did do that, and I feel as if I've moved beyond it. Then some little thing happens, and I freak out again."

"Yes, but this time, instead of freaking out in Kirstin's presence, you vented to me. She'll never even know you got upset, so no harm has been done. And we'll enjoy a great dinner. I'm trying to plot my next book as I polish this one up. At the end of the evening, would you like to help me come up with an evil way to murder someone?"

Another laugh rumbled up from Sam's chest. "I'd love to."

As it turned out, the kids left Kirstin's after dinner and came to the main house for some of Gabriella's apple crisp. Maddie locked gazes with Sam after he received a particularly affectionate hug from his daughter. She wished she could say, *If you love her, let her go. If she loves you, she'll always come back.* But instead she reached up to ruffle her grandson's hair and asked if Kirstin's chicken wing recipe was as good as his father's.

Chapter Fourteen

CALEB LOVED THANKSGIVING. AS THE DAYS OF NOVEMBER passed, the main ranch house started to look like a harvest display. A horn of plenty decorated the huge dining room table. An autumn wreath hung on the front door. A scarecrow surrounded by dry corn husks stood guard on the porch. When Caleb thought about the huge meal they'd have on the big day, his mouth watered. Gram made the best pies ever, and he could almost taste the flaky crusts. Hot apple pie with ice cream melting over the top was his absolute favorite.

At school he'd made a friend named Hank Pierce who had horses. Caleb asked his dad for permission to use the horse trailer and transported his gelding, Latigo, to ride with Hank in his family's indoor arena. They practiced riding patterns, and Hank went on and on about how well-trained Latigo was. Because he had watched plenty of trainers work with equines, Caleb offered to show Hank how to teach his horse, Sylvester, some stuff. Before Caleb drove home, they exchanged cell phone numbers, and Caleb finally had group texts coming in again. The other guys sent dumb stuff, video clips that were good for a laugh. Caleb reciprocated, and the next day he had guys waving at him in the hallways between classes.

Just like that, he had some buddies. He was no longer the weird guy from California.

• • •

IN MID-NOVEMBER, MADDIE HAD ANOTHER CHEMO TREATMENT. Once again, she woke up sick the next morning. She did her best to hide it, layering on extra makeup and smiling when she wanted to escape to her room and hang her head over the toilet. She managed to stay under the radar until Sam came in that night for dinner. He was a man who didn't miss much. He took one look at her and pounced.

"If there's something wrong with you and you don't tell me," he said with a glower, "I'll never forgive you. I can't survive losing another person I love."

Maddie sat at the table, sipping her chemo mainstay, ginger tea. "Are you saying that you love me, Sam?"

He jerked his charred hat off his head and raked his fingers through his hair, making it stand up in tufts that resembled freshly whipped meringue. "What if I do? Are you going to sue me for breach of agreement?"

Maddie not only couldn't think what to say but also didn't feel well enough to examine her own emotions. *Sam.* They'd started out as enemies, and then they'd become the most unlikely of friends. Now she had no idea how to define their relationship. *Love* seemed too strong a word, and yet she'd come to care for him in ways that ran so deep it frightened her.

"May I take a rain check on this conversation?"

"No, ma'am, you may not. I just told you that I love you, and I expect some kind of answer back. Do you care for me, or not?"

It was so like Sam to bypass romance and go right to the nuts and bolts. "I care for you," she admitted. "But quite frankly, Sam, it goes against my better judgment."

"Well, Maddie, it scares the bejesus out of me, too. Especially when I suspect that there's something bad going on with you. You'd tell me, right?"

Maddie had become an expert at conversational evasion, but she yearned to tell Sam the truth. Only how could she do that when she hadn't been honest with Cam? "I went to the doctor again. He says I'm in perfect health." That was true. Her heart was strong. Her lungs were clear. There was no sign that her cancer had returned. She was sick only because she had received an infusion. "That said, Sam, I'm sixty-seven years old. I've had friends, both male and female, who were younger than I was, and they died of one thing or another. Cancer, heart attacks, diabetes—you name it. I can't give you an ironclad guarantee that I won't die, too."

"I don't expect a guarantee, only assurance that there's nothing wrong with you now."

"So your feelings for me are conditional?"

His eyes turned the color of a hot rifle barrel. "Don't twist my words. I'm an all-or-nothing man, always have been and always will be. Tell me, flat out, are you sick?"

She hesitated to answer. An awful ache settled in her chest and then inched up her throat. Sam had shared so many personal things about himself with her. She longed to do the same in return. But with the holiday season upon them, how could she do that to her kids? With a mere slip of the tongue, Sam could unveil the truth. Cam would be frightened half out of his wits. Caleb would panic. This should be a happy time for both of them. She didn't want them to be focused on her and worried that she might die. "Obviously I'm not feeling well, Sam. I have bad days, and I have good days."

He spun on his boot heel and left the dining area. Maddie sighed and pushed away the cup. Feeling wobbly on her feet, she went to her room, locked the door, and made it to the commode before the tea vacated her roiling stomach. The effort left her so weak that she kicked off her clogs and climbed into bed fully clothed.

BY THANKSGIVING, CAM WAS WALKING WITH LESS OF A STRUGGLE, but he still needed a cane for support. Even so, he could stand in one place well enough, so he was able to do one of the things he loved most, cooking. Gabriella came to help, because Maddie had once again invited the Alvarez family to share the holiday meal with them. At her home Gabriella took charge of snacks, and she arrived with corn chips made from scratch, a scrumptious guaca-mole with authentic Mexican flare, fresh salsa with a touch of heat, cookie rings called *galletas Elena*, and pecan drops. Cam focused on preparing dinner. Sam wanted a traditional meal, so Cam had gotten up early to get the turkey dressed and in the oven. Then he made all the sides, thankful that his host had a gourmet kitchen with two food warmers.

At three in the afternoon, they gathered around Sam's table as a family—or at least what felt like a family—to enjoy a fabulous meal. This time Sam led the blessing, confessing beforehand that he hadn't uttered the words in years. Caleb and Rickie had eaten so many cookies that Cam feared they'd have no room left for dinner, but both kids made a big dent in the offerings.

Cam looked across the table at Kirstin. She wore a bronze dress with a V-neck. Her long hair lay in a heavy jet braid over her shoulder, and little gold balls gleamed on her dainty earlobes. She looked so beautiful that she almost took Cam's breath away. He imagined future Thanksgivings when they would eat at their own table as man and wife. Sam and Maddie would be present, of course, humoring their grandchildren while Cam and Kirstin criticized their manners.

Kirstin smiled dreamily at Cam, and he had a feeling she was envisioning the same scene he was. It would happen, he promised himself. He could no longer imagine his future without her in it.

KIRSTIN HAD ENJOYED EVERYTHING ABOUT THE HOLIDAY, FROM working in the kitchen with Cam to the sense of family that had been absent for far too long in the house. Even her father had taken part. She was so accustomed to his silence at the dinner table, she'd nearly fallen off her chair when Sam had led the meal blessing. She hadn't seen him make the sign of the cross or bow his head in prayer since before her mother died.

Caleb had come to her house with Cam after the Alvarez family went home. Kirstin deeply appreciated the way that Caleb had befriended the much younger Rickie. A lot of teenage boys would have felt put upon if expected to *play* with a *little kid*. But Caleb had gone out with Rickie to toss a baseball, and together they'd groomed Latigo. Then they'd come in to help in the kitchen, which had mostly involved hovering over the breakfast bar after Gabriella laid out all the snacks. They'd eaten so much that Kirstin feared they'd be stuffed to the brim before mealtime, but she had underestimated the appetites of growing boys.

Kirstin didn't want the festivities to end, so the moment she entered her house, a smaller version of her father's, she went to the kitchen to reheat the cider she'd made. Cam didn't seem like his usual relaxed self, which troubled her. He sat with his son at the table and kept rubbing his palms on his khaki pants as if he was nervous about something.

"Caleb," she said over her shoulder, "I want to thank you for being so nice to Rickie. I think he had a great time today."

"He's a good kid," Caleb replied. Then he tacked on a long "Um-mm-m. Kirstin, can you lower the heat on the cider for a while? My dad and I need to tell you something."

Kirstin's stomach knotted. She turned down the flame under the pot and turned to face Cam, who'd completely stolen her heart, and the young man she hoped to call her son someday. She'd been praying that might happen soon, but now she wasn't so certain. Had Cam decided that their relationship wasn't working out for him or possibly his child? She searched Cam's expression as she went to sit with them at the table. Only last night he'd held her in his arms and told her he loved her very much. She couldn't grasp why he might pull the rug out from under her now.

After she was seated, Caleb said, "My dad is kind of weird about family."

"Caleb," Cam said with a warning tone.

"Anyway, he thinks I should be a part of this. I think it's totally dumb. I like you, and I think you like me, but Dad has to make sure I feel like I'm part of all this." Caleb took a deep breath and grimaced on the exhale. "Sorry. I've never proposed before." He gave Kirstin a twisted grin. "Would you consider being my stepmom? Actually, since my own mother never wanted me, I'd rather that you just be my mom. But I'll understand if you don't like the idea."

Normally Kirstin had no difficulty with knowing what to say. Words were always on the tip of her tongue, a trait she suspected she had gotten from her dad, and she wasn't sure it was a good one. After sitting in stunned silence for what seemed to her an awkward length of time, she pushed out, "I'd be honored, Caleb.

And I'd prefer being a full-fledged mom. Thank you for giving me the opportunity."

Caleb pushed back his chair and stood. He curled a hand over his father's shoulder. "Okay, Dad, do your thing. I didn't sign on for the mushy stuff, so I'm out of here."

The boy sauntered from the room. A moment later Kirstin heard the front door close. She fixed her gaze on Cam. He quirked a burnished eyebrow at her. "On a scale of one to ten, I know I don't get high marks for being romantic, but I want my son to feel that he'll always be a part of our life together and that his vote will always count."

Kirstin realized she was looking at him through a rush of tears. Voice tight, she said, "Cameron McLendon, any woman who didn't think that was awesome would have to be out of her mind."

He circled the table, pulled her up from the chair, and drew her into the warm embrace of his muscular arms, which had even more hard bulges now from using a wheelchair for so long. "Good, because now it's time for the mushy stuff."

Kirstin started to laugh, but the tenderness in his expression stifled her mirth. "I'm ready."

He bent to press his forehead against hers. "I love you. In fact, I love you so much that I can't believe it. From the first second I saw you, I was a goner. I don't just want you in my life, Kirstin. I *need* you in my life."

"I love you, too," she whispered.

He kissed her then, a long, slow, deep kiss that made even her toes tingle. Then, before she realized what he intended to do, he drew away and sank down onto his right knee.

"No, don't!" she cried. "What if you can't stand back up?" Then she saw tears glistening in his eyes. It was so perfectly beautiful that her legs went weak, and she sank to her own knees in front of him.

"Kirstin Conacher, will you marry me?" he asked, his voice thick and gravelly. "Will you be my wife, the mother of my son, and stand beside me for the rest of my life?"

"Yes," she whispered. "Yes, yes, *yes*!"

He reached into his pocket and withdrew a small blue velvet box. When he lifted the lid, she gasped with delight. The most beautiful set of rings she'd ever seen twinkled up at her. Cam tugged only one from the slot, returned the box to its former hiding place, and then slid the diamond onto her finger. The large center stone was set in a cluster of smaller chips, the whole design resembling a flower.

"Oh, Cam, you shouldn't have! This must have cost a fortune. You've only made one sale!"

He grinned. "I've got another client lined up. Besides, I figured that, for a once-in-a-lifetime purchase, I should go for fabulous. You're very special to me, and nothing less than spectacular should be on your hand."

"How did you know my size?"

"I guessed. I've felt your fingers so many times, it wasn't that difficult."

Without difficulty he stood and pulled her to her feet. Then he swept her up into his arms and carried her to the bedroom. In the light of the moon coming through the windows, he made love to her in a way that felt like a promise for the future, his every touch light and cautious, as if she were made of spun glass.

Afterward they lay with their limbs intertwined and talked about their wedding. Kirstin shared her girlhood dreams of that day. She had imagined every detail many times. When she finished telling her future groom what she wanted, he stiffened and said, "You want to get married *when*?"

• • •

AFTER HAVING TWO PIECES OF MADDIE'S DELICIOUS PIE, SAM cleaned up his dessert mess and retired to the living room with a piping hot mug of coffee spiked with cream and whiskey. Maddie hadn't been sick again, so he had real reason to be thankful today.

He'd chosen to sit on the sofa in hopes that Maddie would sit beside him. When she wandered in from her bedroom wearing a blue robe and slippers, she smiled as she went into the kitchen to get her own drink. Carefully balancing a cup of coffee, she joined him on the adjacent cushion.

"You're looking thoughtful," she observed.

Sam nodded. "That meal blessing was the first prayer I've said in more than six years. I'm thinking I need to return to church."

Maddie breathed in the aroma of her drink. "I've been slacking off myself. Living in the trailer, I had nothing nice to wear, and I was embarrassed to attend mass."

Sam was glad she shared his Roman Catholic beliefs. They wouldn't muck up their relationship with differing ideologies. "Would you consider going to church with me? That way, if the roof caves in, you can pull me clear of the debris."

"I'd love to as long as you don't mind if I bring extras. I've let my family fall away from our usual worship routine since the move." Her blue eyes twinkled up at him. "And although you haven't noticed, I now have some nice things to wear. I went to the storage units and did some gathering."

"Oh, I've noticed." He took a careful sip of coffee. "You look great. Judging by the way your clothes fit, though, I think you've lost more than a heap of weight."

A flush of pink flagged her cheeks. "A good thing. I was getting grandmother plump. At camp I exercised off the calories. I walked the dogs two or three times a day. I was afraid to just let them run loose for fear my cantankerous neighbor might shoot them."

"Never that. I like dogs even more than horses, and for me, that's saying something."

Sam also thought highly of her, and he'd as much as told her so. Yet neither of them had broached the subject again. Odd, that. Young people who fell in love couldn't wait to proclaim their feelings and plan their futures. He and Maddie, who had no guarantees of a future, as she'd so clearly pointed out when they quarreled, were moving forward slower than two tortoises. It made little sense when they both understood that their time together could be limited. With a sigh, Sam decided that there was really no need to be in a hurry. Maddie had made it clear that there would be no intimacy in their relationship, so maybe they didn't need rings and promises. They could be best of friends, married or not.

MADDIE HAD CAREFULLY PLANNED HER NEXT CHEMO TREATMENT around Thanksgiving and had scheduled an appointment for the following Monday. Prior to receiving an infusion, she spoke at length with her doctor over the phone about how ill she'd recently been after receiving the drug. He agreed to lessen the dose, as she was very near the end of the course of treatments. He also prescribed something to settle her stomach, assuring her that she wouldn't feel so sick again.

Maddie had reservations. She didn't want to be on her knees at the commode for another forty-eight hours, and the doctor hadn't lied. When she awakened the morning after her infusion feeling queasy, she immediately took the stomach medication.

Within a half hour, she felt good enough to have a cup of ginger tea and two pieces of dry toast.

As she enjoyed her breakfast, she breathed a sigh of relief when her stomach didn't rebel. She didn't know how other people survived receiving full-strength chemo treatments with harsher drugs going into their bloodstreams. She decided to be upbeat. She had only one more treatment to go, in mid-December. Even if it laid her out flat, she'd be feeling better before Christmas.

ON SUNDAY EVERYONE SLICKED UP AND WENT TO CHURCH. CALEB grumbled, and Maddie scolded him, saying that they'd become a bunch of heathens. Caleb retorted that he'd liked being a heathen. He still prayed every day, so why did he have to do it in a building?

Sam drove his truck with Maddie and Caleb as his passengers. He enjoyed listening to Caleb complain. It took him back in time to when he'd been a teenager and said similar things to his parents. His mom and old man had been honest, hardworking people with strong core values that they had drilled into Sam from early childhood. He'd clung to those tenets all his life, taking only a six-year vacation after Annie died.

It uplifted his heart to once again practice the religious rituals that had been a part of who he was for so long. It was especially wonderful to have Maddie on one side of him and Kirstin on the other. With Caleb and Cam tossed in, they took up nearly a whole pew. Though he hadn't been to confession in way too long, Sam went up to receive the Holy Eucharist. He figured that God would give him a pass this time, and he'd do his soul cleansing later.

As always, Father Merrick stood on the front steps after the liturgical procession from the church. He liked to chat with all the parishioners as they departed, and no matter how ugly the weather, he never shirked that duty. Sam knew the priest well. He'd been at St. Anne's for years, far longer than was usual. Sam guessed that he hadn't been relocated because of his age. Normally priests were shifted at least every ten years. Maybe the Church made exceptions for elderly clerics. Back before Annie died, Sam had considered the priest to be one of his best friends and had invited him to the ranch for dinner frequently.

When Sam stepped out onto the porch, Father Merrick beamed a grin at him and shook his hand with a strong grip that belied his advanced years. "Well, hello, Sam!" he said jovially. "It's so good to see you again."

Sam sensed that his daughter and the others had bunched up behind him. "Don't rub it in, Father. I just took a sabbatical."

Father Merrick laughed, the sound deep and jovial. "Priests take sabbaticals. Laymen fall away from the Church. But never mind that. You've come home now, and you've been sorely missed."

Kirstin stepped forward. "Hi, Father. How are you feeling after that bad cold?"

"Great!"

Sam sent his daughter a questioning look. She smiled and leaned toward him to whisper, "One of the places I sneaked off to behind your back was mass."

Once in the truck, Maddie raved about the old mission church. "It's not only beautiful, like a chapel of old, but there's a fabulous sense of community in its small confines, a feeling of neighbors praying with neighbors, which was not the case in the big church we attended in Northern California."

Sam thought to himself that none of his Catholic neighbors would bear him any goodwill, but he'd be attending mass anyway. People could glare at him all they liked. As Father had said, Sam had come home, and he believed it was high time.

Caleb piped up from the backseat. "You were right, Gram. It felt good to attend mass."

Maddie reached back to pat his knee but couldn't reach it. "It always does, honey."

When they got home, everyone gathered in the kitchen to make a big breakfast. Fasting before Communion had a way of sharpening appetites. Sam peeled potatoes and got them diced for the skillet. Cam put the bacon on to fry. Sam kept yelling at the dogs to find a place, saying they were trip hazards. Soon all the humans were gathered at the table, stuffing their faces. Caleb downed three large glasses of cold milk, making Sam consider getting a dairy cow. He quickly pushed aside the idea. His ranch already required a full crew, and he could barely keep it going with only Kirstin and Miguel to help him. He sure as hell didn't need to add milking a cow morning and night to his list of chores.

Toward the meal's end, Kirstin announced, "It's time to get Christmas trees up!"

"Trees?" Sam frowned at his daughter as he doled out bacon to the canines. "You mean more than one?"

She nodded. "One for here, and another one for my house. Stop glowering, Dad. We'll have decorating parties, and it'll be a lot of fun."

Sam remembered how *fun* decorating a tree had been, with Annie and Kirstin complaining that he hung Christmas balls any old place and never stepped back to look for balance. In his opinion, it was only a *tree*, not a science project. The quicker the damned thing was laden with sparkly shit, the better.

He tried to remember the last time he had erected a tree in

his home. Then he immediately ceased in his attempt. The memories were too sad, and he didn't want to feel gloomy today. He'd been to church, received Communion, and was turning over a happy leaf.

ON TUESDAY NIGHT AFTER THE TREE-DECORATING PARTY AT SAM'S house, which Cam was able to participate in sans cane, Cam asked Sam to take a stroll with him to the barn. Sam had no clue what Cam needed to speak to him about privately, but he suspected that the younger man, bent on doing things the respectful and old-fashioned way, even if it meant he'd get the shit kicked out of him, meant to ask Sam's permission to marry his daughter.

Instead Cam surprised him after they got situated on the hay bale that Sam had sat on after he hurt his toe kicking Rickie's bucket of rocks. He said, "As you can probably see, I'm strong enough now to take my family back to our Hillbilly Village, Sam."

Sam's heart caught. That meant Maddie would be leaving, and he wasn't ready for that yet. Maybe he never would be.

"Anyway," Cam continued, "as ready as I am, I hate to do that to my mom and Caleb. It's dropping to below freezing every night, and sometimes it's plummeting to well below twenty. The water lines in the trailer, our only place to shower, are probably solid ice by now." He raked a hand through his pretty-boy hair. "You were right, Sam. I was a dumb ass. But in my own defense, there were multiple delays in construction, and I never planned to be camping out in the dead of winter."

Sam felt a rush of relief. "You and your family are more than welcome to stay at my place until your homes are finished, Cam, if that's what you're about to ask."

THE CHRISTMAS ROOM · 321

"It is. We won't have real places to live in until possibly the first part of February, and I can't help but feel that the holidays will be more fun for my family if their living conditions aren't so rudimentary." He splayed his hands. "I'm no longer broke now that I've closed that first sale. I can pay you rent and help with groceries. Utilities, too. Three extra people living in a home cost a heap."

Sam shook his head. "I can't take your money, Cam. It'd be like charging family. I've enjoyed having you guys. I've grown fond of you all."

Cam looked Sam directly in the eye. "I've noticed that. You seem to be particularly fond of my mother. So I'll ask straight out. Do you have designs on her?"

Sam chuckled at the old-fashioned way Cam put that. "I sure would have liked to meet your old man. He must have been a pistol."

Cam didn't get sidetracked that easily. "I asked you a question. I shot from the hip with you about Kirstin and got my face messed up for my trouble. The least you can do is level with me."

Taking his time before he answered, Sam bent forward to give Bingo a scratch behind the ears. The Aussie had taken a liking to him and followed at his heels whenever he wasn't inside with Maddie. "Okay, straight from the hip. Your mother isn't in the market for a romantic relationship, but she and I have become good friends. And I won't shine it up for you. I wish she'd offer me more, so I guess I do have designs on her. But unless I can convince her otherwise, I'll settle for friendship." Sam gave the dog a final pat on the head. "At our age, having a companion is comforting. Would I marry her? If she'd have me, absolutely. But even in that event, we have both had the great loves of our lives.

Now having someone to talk to and do things with is more important than anything else."

Cam's shoulders relaxed. Then he gave a self-derisive laugh. "I've been feeling off-balance. I tried so hard to be a good son and be there for my mom. Now she acts as if everything I did wasn't enough, and I guess I'm feeling a little jealous of you. I don't want to lose her or have to hand her off to some ornery old codger who'll be difficult more times than not."

It was Sam's turn to laugh. "Oh, shit. Do I hear a familiar echo in that? Don't go there, Cam. It's a nasty trail to walk." He shook his head. "I understand exactly how you're feeling. Maybe it's a man thing, and we're wired to protect our womenfolk. I've felt jealous of you, too. That's my baby girl you've fallen in love with." He sighed. "You're treading on my turf."

"And you'd like to tread on mine."

Sam nodded. "You've got two free shots coming. I'll let you punch my lights out."

"I'll never act like you did that night. I love Kirstin too much to make her unhappy. Otherwise you would have a bloody nose and a busted lip." He winced and then frowned. "I'm sorry. Forget I said that. It wasn't very respectful."

Sam guffawed. When his mirth subsided, he said, "You're still shooting straight from the hip, and I'll be damned if I don't respect you for it. Never thought I'd say this, but you're a good man, and I couldn't do better for my daughter if I'd handpicked you myself."

"Thank you. That's a fine compliment."

"Yeah, well, don't get a big head. It took me a while to appreciate your fine points. I'm sorry for the way I behaved that night. I was upset and angry and feeling threatened. I was afraid I was losing my girl. That's no excuse, I know, but it's where I was, seeing red. You were the no-good bastard who was stealing her away from me."

"I knew that. And you won't lose her, Sam. For one thing, she loves you dearly, and for another, I was raised to respect family ties."

"Right back at you. I'll never come between you and your mom. Couldn't if I tried. From where you're standing, you may think what you've done for her wasn't enough. But your support meant everything to her, and it still does. If you walked out of here tonight, she'd be right behind you."

Cam took his turn petting the dog. "So, Sam, you going to kick my ass if I tell you that I've proposed to Kirstin without asking for your blessing?"

"Nope. I was about to ask when you meant to make an honest woman of her."

"Done. She's been hiding the engagement ring from you so you don't go ballistic again."

Sam pursed his lips. "I won't say I'm above it. I'm still learning my way back to sanity with a lot of help from your mom. But if you popped the question and she accepted, it's okay by me."

"Good, because she's dead set on getting married on Christmas."

"You're shitting me." Sam gaped at his prospective son-in-law. "Not *this* Christmas, surely. Isn't that rushing things?"

"I think it's a little quick, too," Cam confessed. "But she has always dreamed of being married on Christmas, and waiting a year won't work. She's afraid to take the pill because of her mother's ovarian cancer. I don't know if she has any reason to worry about that, but I sure as hell don't want to put her at risk. Even though we're using other protection, I don't think you want to take the chance that your grandchild could be born out of wedlock before next Christmas. I think every woman should experience the wedding of her dreams, even if it's tough to pull off.

Don't you? It'll be her big day, and she'll treasure the memories for the rest of her life."

"If you knock her up and wait until next Christmas to marry her, I'll—" Sam broke off and grunted. "That's the old me talking. I won't smack you, but I sure won't be happy."

"I pretty much figured that, Sam. But she says it's Christmas this year or Christmas next year, no other options. I had protected sex with Caleb's mother one time when I was seventeen, and the condom tore. What were the odds that she'd get pregnant? I'm older now, but I don't think my sperm count has diminished much. The same thing happened with Kirstin, and I was worried sick until her period came."

"Dear God, are we bonding?"

Cam rolled his eyes. "Can you stay on track and not be an obnoxious smart-ass for once? Will you support a Christmas wedding? Simple question."

"Yes." Sam took over the job of petting the damned dog. "But how will we pull it off? We've got very little time for all the trimmings I'm sure she's wanting. Shit. I need a magic wand."

Cam stretched out his legs and crossed his ankles. From the corner of his eye, Sam saw him rubbing his right thigh. "She isn't asking for big. She says the church is decorated every Christmas with three beautiful trees on each side of the altar. Only family and friends will be invited, and she's keeping the list really small."

Sam squinted to see the other side of the barn. It was getting dark. "The list of friends will definitely be short. Nobody will come. I don't have any friends left. There's another sin to add to my account when I go for confession. I drove them all away."

"Some of them will come, Sam, not because they give a shit about you, but because they love your daughter. Can I limp back to the damned house and tell her she can take the engagement ring out of her shirt pocket and wear it in front of you, or not?"

Sam didn't answer the question. "It better be a big chunk of ice. I know how much money you made on that sale. If you got her something I need a magnifying glass to see, I'll kick your ass."

KIRSTIN FELT AS IF SHE WERE FLOATING ON AIR. BEFORE LEAVING to feed his horses on his family's land, Cam had informed her that her father had given his blessing for them to get married. She could finally wear her beautiful ring in front of her dad without endangering her fiancé's life.

She quivered as she slipped it onto her finger. A few minutes later, Maddie, who had retreated to her bedroom to work for a short while, returned to the kitchen. Kirstin said nothing about the ring as she visited with the older woman over a glass of wine at the dining room table. Fluttering her hand as she talked, she waited for Maddie to notice. It was such a beautiful setting, and it glistened brighter than midnight stars on a clear night. How could anyone fail to notice it flashing on her finger?

Finally, Kirstin shoved her fist toward Maddie's face and held it steady until Maddie focused. "Oh, my!" the older woman exclaimed. "Does this mean what I think it means?"

"I'm sure Cam meant to tell you, but we had to keep it a secret until he talked to Dad, and then he rushed over to feed his horses."

"Wise decision about your father, and I completely understand." Maddie got up to wrap her arms around Kirstin. "I'm so happy, not just for you, but for myself as well. I can't think of anyone else I'd rather have as a second daughter!"

As they resumed their seats, Kirstin said, "Caleb proposed

first. It was the sweetest thing, Maddie. He asked me if I'd be his mom. How fabulous is that?"

Maddie looked bewildered. "My son. Doesn't he know kids should be left out of the equation when a man proposes? It's supposed to be the most romantic moment in a woman's life."

"He's such a devoted father, and he wanted Caleb to feel included. And, oh, Maddie, it *was* the most romantic moment of my life. So far, anyway. With Cam, I'm sure there will be others. It was all so perfect that I cried."

They heard someone come down the stairs, and both of them turned, expecting Caleb to appear. Instead Cam came into the room. "When did you get back?" Kirstin asked.

"A few seconds ago. I went upstairs to check on Caleb before joining you two." He hugged his mother and then circled the table to kiss Kirstin. "My son is still up there texting. I'm afraid he'll get radiation poisoning on the end of his nose."

Maddie chuckled. "I'm as pleased as punch that he's made friends, so leave the boy alone."

Cam poured himself some wine and joined them at the table. "I take it that Kirstin told you our news. I'm sorry for leaving you out of the loop, Mom, but I was afraid Sam might be difficult."

The sound of the front door opening and closing drifted through the dining area. Kirstin knew it must be her father entering the house. She reached across to squeeze Cam's hand. In a low voice, she said, "It was so brave of you to talk to him for me. I was scared to do it."

"Did I hear someone say my name?" Her father followed the bellowed question into the dining area. With his usual straight-to-the-point manner, he circled the table to study her ring. Then he looked at Cam. "Barely on the right side of chintzy, but it'll do."

"Sam!" Maddie cried. "It's a beautiful engagement ring."

"I measure rings with dollar signs," Sam replied, "and he didn't break the bank on that one."

Cam winked at Kirstin. "Why am I so happy that I've signed on for a lifetime of this?"

"Daddy, this is a special time for me. Can you try to be nice, just once?"

Sam bent over to hug her. She loved the feeling of her father's strong arms around her. "Okay, for you, I'll be so sweet it'll make your teeth ache. Congratulations, honey." He bent his head to whisper in her ear, "If he ever lays a violent hand on you, I'll hog-tie him in Satan's pen and kill a jug of whiskey while I watch him get trampled to death."

He opened a second bottle of wine, poured a measure into a goblet, and sat beside Kirstin at the table. She rested her head on his shoulder, enjoying the blend of scents that emanated from his worn and faded blue shirt. He smelled like her childhood memories of hay, horses, and cows, with a faint touch of equine sweat. He reached up to settle his callused palm over her hair. His touch conveyed the words that he didn't seem able to say.

"I'm happy for you, Kirstie mine. You found yourself a good man. I only have one question. How in the hell do you think I can pull off a wedding on Christmas?"

Kirstin curved her lips in a smile. "Father Merrick has posted the banns. He talked with Cam, who was raised in the church, so he waived premarital counseling. I already ordered my gown, Dad. I found a place online that makes them to order. I sent them a drawing, and I paid extra to rush things along. Cam and Caleb have an appointment to be fitted for tuxedos as well."

"What about me?" he asked.

"I figured you'd just walk me down the aisle with horseshit on your boots."

• • •

SAM MENTALLY GNAWED ON ALL THE COMPLICATIONS OF A RUSHED wedding. He wanted the day to be perfect for his daughter. "Kirstie, is there any possibility that we can wait and have the wedding next year on Christmas?"

Kirstin shrugged. "Fine, Daddy. We'll wait until next Christmas. But don't get all ticked off if I present you with a grandchild born out of wedlock before then. Gossip will fly, and everyone in Rustlers' Gulch will be whispering."

Sam kissed her forehead. "Nah. I'll send you to Europe, and when you come home with a kid, we'll tell everyone it's adopted."

"I'm going to work on this ranch until the day I give birth, just like my mother did. I can't do that in Europe, so I'll refuse to go."

Sam really wished she'd give him a year. As it was, nobody would show up on her big day. He might be able to mend fences with some of his friends if he had a whole year to make up with them. "You drive a hard bargain," he told his daughter. "Shit. I'll have to hire one of those wedding planners, and it'll cost me a damned fortune."

"I work, Dad. I can pay for my own wedding."

"Over my dead body. You're my girl. You deserve the best, and it's my place to make sure you get it." Sam thought of Annie, who had set such store on being a part of this community. She would have been so disappointed in him right now. "How will I find time for a wedding? By my rough calculation, I figure I've still got a hundred pair hiding up there on that mountain. If I don't find all of them and get them to lower ground before the first snowstorm, my losses will be astronomical."

"I'm able to ride again," Cam said. "I can help you and Miguel round them up."

"You have your own business. I don't expect you to partner up with me and do ranch work."

Cam gave him a long look that glinted with mischief. "The ranch will one day go to my wife. The way I see it, it'll be in my best interest to help. If she ever divorces me, I'll get half of what it's worth."

Sam glared at him. "Again, that'll happen over my dead body."

Maddie spoke up. "At your age, that's not only a possibility, but almost a certainty."

"Then I'll accept your offer," he told Cam. "I may as well work your ass off for every dime you might get."

Caleb came downstairs, bypassed them at the table, and stood in front of the open refrigerator. "What's everybody arguing about?"

Sam said, "We're not arguing. We're having a discussion."

"Oh." Caleb shrugged. "At our house, nobody yells unless we're arguing."

KIRSTIN LEANED AGAINST CAM AS HE WALKED HER HOME WITH HIS arm around her shoulders. For her, this was a beautiful ending to a perfect day. "I am so happy."

Cam hugged her closer. "I'm glad. But why? I feel as if I just dodged machine-gun fire."

She giggled. "I loved when you flipped him shit about taking your half of the ranch proceeds if I ever divorce you. That was priceless."

"Kirstin, I don't mean to burst your bubble, but I was trying to piss your father off."

"I know. But, Cam, you need to tread carefully with Dad. He played you."

"I'm not following."

"Daddy *hates* to ask people for help. He wasn't that way before Mama died, but now it's as if he has to prove to the world that he doesn't need anybody. This way, instead of accepting your generous offer, he can flip you crap about working for your half of my inheritance. Don't you get it?"

Cam thought about it for a moment and then chuckled. "And he'll never once shake my hand and thank me."

"Exactly."

"He's impossible, you know. Your ring is just on the 'right side of chintzy'? I'm telling you, the man terrifies me. Plus, he's in love with my mother. He admitted that he'd marry her if she'd have him. Can you imagine what her life would be like if she said yes?"

Kirstin smiled up at him. "Yes. Next to me, she'd be the most loved and spoiled woman on earth." In the illumination of the yard lights, the creases on his forehead from his frown looked black. "Why do you think your mom likes him so much?"

"I don't have a fricking clue."

"Because he reveals to her a side of himself that you never see. Around you, Dad's a negative old grump. I suspect he's just the opposite with your mom."

"Maybe so," he conceded. "It's the only rational explanation there is. To me, he's a constant rerun of Jekyll and Hyde."

"When I was growing up, there was no Mr. Hyde, Cam. He was the greatest dad ever, and he pampered my mother beyond belief. Except for during the lean years, whatever she wanted, she got. She loved him just as much as he loved her, and I wasn't exaggerating when I said that she worked on the ranch until the day I was born. She told me that he wouldn't allow her on a horse, even though she was an expert rider. He refused to let her clean stalls. No heavy work, period. But she'd sneak behind his back, because she knew he was stretched thin. She said when he caught her doing something she shouldn't, he'd yell and kick dirt. It was the only time during their marriage when he actually got mad at her."

"Hmm."

Kirstin studied his chiseled features, trying to read his expression. "You can't picture that man. Can you?"

He sighed. "Let's just say it takes a stretch of my imagination."

"He truly is worried about his bottom line this year if he can't find all the cattle."

"Why can't he just say that and share his concerns with the rest of us?"

"Because then he'd look weak. I don't completely understand my dad, but I have watched him struggle with grief. Never once did he come to me and talk about it. He just kept putting one boot in front of the other one."

"I don't understand him, either," Cam told her. "But I'll try my best to get along with him."

Chapter Fifteen

MADDIE WORRIED ABOUT SAM. EVERY MORNING HE HIT THE stable well before dawn to load the horses into the trailer. And even on those days when Cam could go with him and Miguel to search for cattle, he came in late, so exhausted that he had gray shadows under his eyes. Miguel and Cam were younger than Sam, Miguel by two decades and Cam by three.

One night when he walked in particularly late, Maddie met him at the door to help him shrug out of his jacket. He gave her that half grin that she'd come to love. "You're fussing over me."

As she hung his outerwear on the coat-tree, she said, "Yes, I suppose I am. You're working yourself into an early grave."

"I can't argue the point. If I had another ten men, I might be able to find all those cows and drive them off the mountain. Thank God there hasn't been any snow to speak of yet. It's rare in this country. Normally the surrounding mountains have deep accumulation by now."

Earlier, when Maddie had heard the diesel truck pull in, she'd made him an Irish coffee. She fetched it from a table and handed it to him. He thanked her before continuing. "Miguel and I have tried everything. We've ridden together, hoping that the two of us can bunch them up and herd them down. But each time, they scattered, so we always lost a good half of them, if not more." He sank onto the sofa and took a sip of his hot drink. "This is fabulous, Maddie. I swear I'm frozen to the marrow of my bones."

"Why do the cows run? I don't understand it. Don't they realize they'll starve to death up there?"

"They're stupid," Sam told her. "We got lucky today with a lead cow that has a few winters under her belt. She took off down the mountain like someone below was ringing a dinner bell. The others bawled and followed her. We caught fifteen. Almost filled the damned trailer. But that isn't enough. I have at least a hundred and eighty-five still up there somewhere."

Maddie went into the kitchen to make herself an Irish coffee. The doctor said she could drink in moderation, and she was moderating every ounce that she swallowed. It relaxed her at night and took the worries off her mind. Her book. Dying on Cam while she still owed a fortune on their building. Missing out on Caleb's graduation, when he went to college, and someday got married. She wanted to live long enough to hold her first great-grandchild in her arms.

When she returned to the living room, she sat beside the man who had baffled her and yet fascinated her ever since she'd first crossed swords with him. "Don't you have the capital to pay everything off, Sam? Sell all the cows. Then you could enjoy life."

"And do what?"

"Travel? Read to your heart's content. Sit on the porch and watch the sun go down, maybe?"

"If I did that, the ranch would die. I've worked all my life so I could pass it on to Kirstin."

"In other words, you plan to work until you die."

"Don't you? Are you ever going to retire from writing?"

Maddie couldn't imagine not writing. It wasn't just what she did for a living. It was who she was. "Probably not. I'll be pecking at a keyboard even if I get dementia, and Cam will set me up with a fake editor's e-mail address so I can send my manuscripts that make no sense off into a black hole."

"Well, I want to die in the saddle. My luck, I'll have a heart attack and do a face-plant in cow shit, but I'll never know it."

"I'm worried about you, Sam. You can't go on like this. These are supposed to be your golden years."

He sighed. "The only thing golden about getting old, Maddie, is peeing in a cup at the doctor's office."

"You're a stubborn man."

He smiled. Deep creases angled down from the outside corners of his eyes to line his cheeks. She yearned to trace every crevice with her fingertips. "Yep. But you care for me anyway."

Maddie's throat went tight. "I love you, Sam. And I don't know what to do with that."

He draped his arm around her. "Ah, Maddie. You worry too much. Act like it's one of your tea bags, and just let it steep."

TWO DAYS AFTER THEIR TREE-DECORATING PARTY AT KIRSTIN'S, A snowstorm struck after the three men left to go to the grazing land. Maddie had gotten up early to make sure Sam ate a decent breakfast. Then she'd added some energy bars to their lunch cooler so he would have something on hand to raise his blood sugar after he'd worked for too long on empty. She didn't worry much about the younger men, but Sam was a different story.

After they drove away, she went in to clean up the kitchen before Gabriella came. Maddie wasn't sure how long she puttered. She only knew that the next time she looked out the window, white stuff swirled through the cold air and sprinkled the ground. *Snow*, she thought with a squeeze of her heart. Had Sam checked the weather report on his phone?

Maddie guessed that he had, and she knew for certain that Cam would have. He complained about his son constantly using his phone after school, but that was the pot calling the kettle black. She pulled her own phone from her pocket and checked the report. *Damn it*, she thought. *The meteorologist needs continuing education*. No precipitation had been predicted.

How deep would the snow get at a higher elevation? Maddie stared out the window with growing dread. Gabriella appeared, a vague shape in a red coat until she reached the porch. Maddie heard her stomping her rubber boots to rid them of frozen clumps.

A moment later the woman entered the dining room divested of her outerwear and joined Maddie at the window to stare out at nothing. "This be bad," Gabriella said.

Maddie knew then that her concerns for the men's safety weren't unfounded. "How bad?"

Gabriella fixed a frustrated gaze on Maddie, flapped her hands, and jabbered something in Spanish. Maddie didn't understand a word, but she got the gist. Lives could be at risk.

Her son was out there. Gabriella's husband, Rickie's father, was out there. And so was Sam. Maddie wasn't a rancher, but she knew a horse could go down on slick, steep slopes. Those men needed assistance.

Maddie wished she were an accomplished horsewoman who could ride up the snow-covered grades to find huddled bunches of cattle. Sam had been a godsend to her family during Cam's recovery, and now when he needed her help, she was useless. *Or maybe not.*

Sam had once had many good friends in this valley, men who *could* go into the high country to help him. She was aware that

Sam had driven them all away, but in her opinion that was no reason for them to turn a blind eye to his predicament now. Cam had told her that many of the valley ranchers gathered for breakfast or lunch at the Cowboy Tree. She remembered the place well after a visit there once.

As if on cue, Caleb emerged from his bedroom, freshly showered, wearing tattered jeans and a shirt that had the shape of Montana on the front, with the counties all filled in with red. It read, WE'RE FULL UP. GO BACK HOME. A drawing of a hand with the middle finger uplifted strengthened the message. Maddie didn't think the sentiment was appropriate for school, but she was too concerned about the guys to say so.

"Hi, Gabriella," Caleb said. "I can drive Rickie to school if—" He broke off when he looked out the window. "Uh-oh, maybe only to the bus stop. It might be slick out there."

Gabriella replied, "He go bus."

Maddie cut in. "Caleb, can you look at your weather app? Mine says no precipitation today, and yet it's snowing."

Caleb pulled his phone from his pocket and thumbed the screen. "Same on mine. Oh, well, Gram. Sometimes the forecasts are wrong."

"No, you don't understand. Sam, your father, and Miguel left to gather cows not knowing a storm would move in."

Caleb's relaxed expression tightened. "That's not good, Gram. The terrain up there gets pretty rugged. It could be dangerous."

Maddie reached a decision. "I'm going to the bar."

"*What?*"

"The Cowboy Tree, where your father says many of the ranchers gather for breakfast. I need to round up help."

Caleb switched his weight from one foot to the other. "But, Gram, nobody in the valley likes Sam. Why would they even try to help him?"

"Because at heart they're good people, and also because I'm going to shame them into it."

"Uh-oh." Caleb looked worried. "I'm going with you, then. Dad's told me stories about what you're like when you get pissed."

Maddie had no time to critique her grandson's language, either. She hurried to the bedroom to throw on nicer clothes, slap on some makeup, and find nice shoes suitable for walking on ice. As she quickly examined herself in the mirror, she tried to see herself as others did. She wanted to look like the successful author she was, not a worn-out old lady. Her efforts had improved her appearance, but she was still a long way from making a statement.

Caleb left the house at her side, quickly stuffing jellied toast into his mouth so he could help her down the slick steps. A blob of sticky purple goo fell on his shirt and slid over several red counties on the western state line, turning them blue. The boy's chest now looked like a copy of last year's election map. He wore his new Montana Griz jacket hanging open and the dirty ball cap on backward. Maddie stifled a sigh. So much for making a good impression when she stormed the bar. She had what appeared to be a homeless teenager riding shotgun.

When she was safely in the car, she remembered that she'd taken the SUV to book club a few days ago, and while she was out, she'd picked up groceries for Gabriella. Only she'd forgotten to check the gas before she came home. The needle was on empty. If she stopped to fuel up, she might miss the breakfast crowd.

"Fuck," she whispered.

Caleb gave her a sharp look. "I can't believe I heard you say that. If I said it, you'd rub soap in my mouth."

"Caleb," she said with exaggerated patience, "I will be your polite grandmother again when your father, Sam, and Miguel are safe at home. For right now I do not need you to monitor my language. We may run out of gas."

"We could take my truck," Caleb offered.

"I can't get in it. It's too high off the ground and you have no running boards."

"Fuck," Caleb said.

"Don't push your luck, buster."

MADDIE FEARED THAT HER VEHICLE WAS RUNNING ON ONLY fumes as she pulled into the Cowboy Tree parking lot. She shut off the engine and hauled in a deep breath with her eyes closed. She heard Caleb unfasten his seat belt.

"Gram, are you praying?"

She lifted her lashes. "Lives may be at stake, Caleb. We got here on the strength of prayer. Now I'm asking for help to convince those ranchers to load their horses up in trailers and go to Sam's land to help our guys get the cows out of there."

"There's plenty of people here," Caleb observed, scanning the many cars and rigs in the vehicle slots. "Lots of ranchers, I hope."

Maddie sighed and got out of her vehicle. Caleb met her at the front fender, grabbed her arm, and said, "Hold on to me, Gram. This snow is slicker than greased owl shit."

"Where did you hear that expression?"

"Sam said it."

"We've both been around him too much."

Maddie was happy to cling to Caleb, and together they climbed the wooden steps. A covered, slatted walkway led to the double front doors. Nervous trembles attacked Maddie's body as she advanced on the entrance.

"It'll be okay, Gram. I've got faith in you."

That was all well and fine, but Maddie didn't have a clue what she meant to say. Once she was inside the building, a feeling of friendly warmth, the aroma of hot food, and a low thrum of both male and female voices surrounded her. She felt Caleb press close to her side.

"A tree in the building is weird," he whispered. "But I've decided I like it."

"Maddie!" a woman cried.

Startled to be recognized, Maddie followed the sound of the voice with her gaze and was doubly bewildered to see Emma Pedigrew climbing off a tall barstool at one of the high tables near the windows. Maddie had come to know Emma at book club. She was a delightful old lady who was now able to read again, thanks to her son, who'd recently gifted her with a Kindle that allowed her to enlarge the fonts.

As tempting as it was, Maddie couldn't very well ignore the tottering geriatric, so she walked over to greet her in front of the bar, where traditionally garbed cowboys of varying ages sat on stools that lined the footrail. Grasping Emma's fragile, veined hand, Maddie said, "Dear heaven, Emma, you should sit at a lower table so you can use a chair."

Two other book club members waved at Maddie from their lofty perches. Verna, a reading enthusiast with bright pink hair, said, "We walk on the wild side when we do breakfast. We even have caffeine."

Her sidekick, Martha, nodded and further explained, "We don't get many opportunities to practice our balance, dear."

Maddie noted that Caleb had the blank expression of a deer caught in the glare of headlights. She guessed that her grandson had rarely seen a lady with cherry blossom pink curls.

Emma kept hold of Maddie's hand. "You must join us! Verna, grab two more barstools." She smiled at Caleb. "And who is this handsome young fellow?"

Maddie, feeling like a bit of flotsam caught in a current, made the introductions. Emma finally let go of her hand to shake Caleb's. "I'm delighted to meet you. My husband, Herm, has been looking for someone your age to help out at our farm. Would you be interested in meeting with him to discuss the details?"

Maddie figured that would be a difficult interview for Emma to arrange. Herman Pedigrew was six feet under in a cement vault. At book club meetings, Emma sometimes told Maddie sad stories about Herm's illness and eventual demise. Other times, Herm was alive, at least in Emma's mind, and she was as happy as a little clam in its shell.

"Sure," Caleb said. "I need a job to help pay Gram back for renting me a violin."

Maddie wanted to follow through with her plan to recruit roundup volunteers, but Verna had already stolen two barstools from another table. She and Caleb had no choice but to take a seat.

Martha handed them menus. "This is perfect timing. We were just about to order."

"Oh, no, we can't stay for a meal," Maddie explained. "I've come on an urgent mission, I'm afraid."

Martha reached over to pat Maddie's hand. "Oh, dear, what kind of urgent decision are you trying to make?"

Verna slanted a snarky look at her friend. "Martha, for God's sake, did you forget your hearing aids again?"

Maddie quickly explained the situation. "The weather forecast was dead wrong, and Sam Conacher, along with two other men, is up on his grazing land, caught in this storm."

Emma clutched the sleeve of Maddie's wool coat. "Did you say Sam Conacher? He's been so devoted to me since Herm passed away! Of *course* the men in here will go help him."

Maddie vaguely remembered Sam saying that he did the heavy farm chores for a little old lady along Fox Hollow Road, but she'd never dreamed the recipient of his kindness was her new friend Emma, whose husband was dead one moment and resurrected the next.

Emma shifted on her seat, gripped the edge of the table, and started to climb off her stool. Caleb reacted like a jack-in-the-box that had just had its button pushed. He was steadying Emma in a blink. The elderly woman collected her composure, turned toward the bar, and clapped her hands.

"Attention!" she yelled, her normally crackly voice booming like that of a stevedore. Maddie decided Emma must have once been a force to be reckoned with. "We've got neighbors in trouble!"

The cowboys at the bar swiveled around in unison. Maddie was surprised to see that three of them were women. The heads of people sitting at the many tables jerked up, and all gazes became trained on Emma.

"Who's in trouble?" a man sitting near the ponderosa pine asked.

Maddie's mouth had gone dry. "Sam Conacher, along with his ranch manager, Miguel Alvarez, and my son, Cam McLendon. They trailered horses up to Sam's grazing land on the east side this morning. This storm wasn't forecast on the weather apps, and Sam still has a lot of cows at high elevations."

From somewhere else in the room, a man said, "If Sam hadn't treated his hired hands so awful, he'd have his cattle out to pasture by now."

"Regardless, the job is too much for only three men," Maddie argued. "If Sam can't bring those cows in, he'll take a huge financial loss. More important, all three men are risking their lives out there. They could even be trapped by the snow. Sam needs the help of his friends."

Seven extremely tall men got up from different dining places around the bar. Bundled in heavy jackets with insulated gloves poking up from the pockets, the ranchers looked huge to Maddie, and she wondered what on earth the mothers in Montana fed their boys as they grew up.

"Sam Conacher no longer has any friends in this valley," a fellow off to the left bellowed.

"Yep," another man agreed. "He's a mean-hearted, selfish, foul-mouthed bastard!"

Someone else cried, "Don't forget that he's also a hopeless drunk!"

"Why should we be friends to him when he abandoned all of us?"

"Yeah, where was he two summers ago when wildfire leaped onto my alfalfa fields? He didn't give a shit if I went broke."

Maddie felt sudden heat zap her bloodstream. "Sam Conacher is no longer a drunk!" she cried. "He quit the heavy drinking more than four years ago! And you're forgetting that he lost his wife. Have you ever stopped to think how angry you would be if the same thing happened to you? Is it beyond the realm of possibility that one of you might have drowned your sorrows in a whiskey bottle for a while and avoided former friends who still had their wives? Are you completely unable to recall the man Sam used to be—the friend who always came to help you?"

Emma tottered forward. "Frankie Johnson, I'm ashamed of you! I'll bet you still can't remember the spelling rule 'I before E except after C.'"

Maddie saw one of the angry ranchers bow his head and suspected she'd located Frankie.

"And *you*, Mary!" Emma cried. "Get up from that chair and elbow your husband a good one in the ribs. He always did talk when he shouldn't and disrupted my classroom." Emma took two more unsteady steps forward. "I hear all of you damning Sam for not coming when you needed his help. Well, now I'll ask where all of you were after Herm died. After his funeral, you vanished, and the only man in this whole valley who consistently stopped by my farm to offer me help was Sam. From where I'm standing, all of you are big on talk. Three men could die up there on that mountain today. If none of you go to help, I'll be ashamed of every last one of you."

The ranchers fell quiet, and all of them hung their heads. Maddie knew then that, with Emma's help, she had delivered her message. The rest was up to them.

She guided the older woman back to the table, resumed her own seat, and said, "Thank you, Emma. You were a godsend."

Emma got herself situated on her stool and said, "They're all wonderful boys. They just need to be bopped on the head every once in a while."

THE STORM HAD GAINED IN FURY, AND THE WIND, AS COLD AS DRY ice, pierced Sam's jacket to burn his skin. Even with the protection of gloves, his hands had gone numb, and though he could see that his legs were pressed tight against the sides of his mount, he couldn't feel them anymore. It wasn't yet noon, and they'd gathered only ten cows. Sam could fit twenty in the stock trailer. He kicked himself now for selling the double-decker attached to a semitruck. Hindsight was always better than foresight. He'd needed the money last spring, and he'd wrongly believed that he could get all his herds off the grazing parcels by making trips back and forth.

None of that matters now, he realized. The safety of Miguel and Cam weighed heavily on his shoulders. Sam reined his mount in a slow circle, whistling three long notes, the agreed-upon signal that would let the two other men know it was time to bunch up. Sam was afraid they might freeze to death in the saddle. Hell, he was even fearful for his own safety. It was time to get the hell out of here.

It saddened Sam deeply that the cattle he left behind would perish. Sam whistled for his companions again, and then he sent up a prayer that his cows would die quickly. He'd been meaner than a snake to other people for the last six years, but one sin he'd never committed was cruelty to animals. The stupid bovines would huddle up and starve to death, though. Sam hated for them to suffer, but he'd done his best by them.

He glimpsed a large shape moving toward him through the blowing snow. His eyes stung as he tried to determine who it was. Finally he recognized the buckskin horse and knew it was Cam.

"My reins are frozen stiff!" the younger man yelled.

Sam held back a smile, afraid his cheeks might crack. "Where's Miguel?"

"Beats the hell out of me! We lost each other about an hour ago, when we found some cows. They spooked and scattered." Cam lowered his voice as he pulled his mount to a stop near Sam. "Miguel went one way, and I went another, hot on their heels. I couldn't gather them up."

Sam knew how that story went. The cattle had gone wild over the spring and summer. They spooked easily and then ran blind. He whistled through his teeth again, emitting three sharp blasts. An instant later, he heard Miguel whistle back, but only once.

"He's coming in," he told Cam. "Soon as he gets here, we need to get off this damned mountain while we can still see. I should have brought flashlights and survival blankets, damn it."

"This storm must have sneaked in," Cam replied. "I checked this morning, and there was nothing in the forecast for the next seven days."

"Yeah, well, the saying is, 'Only a fool or a meteorologist predicts the weather in Montana.'"

Cam laughed. "People claim the same in Northern Cal."

Sam tugged up his coat collar to protect his neck. "This is the last hurrah. The snow will be so deep in the gullies by morning that a horse won't be able to safely make it up here. Chances are, even the quads could get stuck." Sam used ATVs only as a last resort, because they spooked the cows even worse than equines did. "You win some, and you lose some, I reckon."

"I'm sorry, Sam."

Miguel rode up just then. "I'm still good to go, Senor Conacher."

Sam couldn't allow that. "No, Miguel. We're calling it quits."

"But the losses, seor. They will hit you hard."

Sam couldn't let himself think about that. Maybe Maddie would get her wish, and he'd be sitting on his porch next summer to watch the sun go down. "You've got Gabriella and your boy to think about, and Cam is my daughter's future. Let's head down."

Sam had never expected semidarkness to descend so early in the day. Without electric lanterns or flashlights, the way down would be treacherous. Suddenly he saw golden orbs bobbing in the swirls of white just downhill from them. Bewildered, he drew his mount to a halt.

Riders entered the clearing, three abreast. Sam recognized Frank Johnson, one of his former best friends. Eleven men accompanied him. A lump settled at the base of his throat. He heard the unmistakable voice of another rancher named Sparky. The next thing Sam knew, all twelve riders drew in around him and his helpers. Sam knew they had spread out from his truck and ridden up until they saw horse tracks in the snow.

"I don't deserve this from you," Sam told them.

Frank said, "Not a man among us would be here if it weren't for Madeline McLendon and Mrs. Pedigrew. They shamed all of us into coming."

Sam almost told them to get the hell off his mountain then. But the truth was, he knew he'd earned their scorn. He had no idea what Maddie had said to them, but they had come. Even though he couldn't let them make this grand gesture at the risk of their lives, he'd be a fool if he acted like an asshole, even if it was one of the things he did best.

"I appreciate that you've come to help," Sam admitted. No words had ever pained him more. "But this show is over. I can't put your lives or the safety of your horses at risk. A damned bunch of cows isn't worth it."

Dick Hummel, off to Sam's left, said, "That's pussy talk, Conacher. We came for a roundup, and we'll by God have a roundup." He took off his hat and slapped it against his leg to dust off the snow. His blue eyes cut through the drifting white like knives. "We're mighty sorry about Annie, Sam. All of us are."

"Damn straight," someone else said. "She was a wonderful lady, and it wasn't fair that you lost your wife while we got to keep ours."

Sam knew they had said these words to him long ago, but he hadn't really heard them then. He did now.

Frank said, "I didn't keep coming around after you kicked me off your place. I regret that now. I should have grabbed leather and hung on for the ride until you were able to talk about losing her. I was pissed at you then. I couldn't understand. But I know all of us failed you in one way or another."

None of these men was responsible for Annie's death. Only Sam held that honor. He had adored his baby girl, but he'd also wanted a son to carry on the empire that he had worked so hard to build. Since meeting Maddie, Sam had tried to shrug off his sense of guilt, but now it sliced through him again like a knife.

"You didn't fail me," Sam said firmly. "I failed myself. I can't accept your apologies, because I don't deserve them. I do deeply appreciate this show of support, though. Problem is, I sold my double-decker, boys. I can only fit five more cows in my stock trailer."

"Hell, Sam," Donahue hollered, "do you think we're dumb asses? Each of us brought a stock trailer. Left them with the ramps down and ready for incoming traffic." He nodded to Cam and Miguel. "Three men aren't enough to do this job. Sam never learned his lesson that he can't drive a spike with a tack hammer."

Sam lost control of the whole operation then. His old friend Frank took over, dividing his men into groups of four and sending them out in different directions. That left Sam to work with Cam and Miguel. "You boys up to several more hours of this shit?"

"Let's do it," Cam said. "My share of the ranch is on the line." He grinned at Miguel. "I'll give you a quarter of what I get."

Sam grinned in spite of himself, and then he fell in with them as they went up the slope. Five hours later, it was colder than a well digger's ass, everyone was exhausted, and a head count of the bawling cows in the trailers was still forty short. It was no small loss for Sam, but it was far better than losing all of them.

Sam walked the circuit to slap backs and shake hands with his onetime friends, thanking each man personally. Then, with the rescued bovines bawling and creating a din with their hooves on trailer floors, Sam gazed through the darkness at the mountain. He made a quick sign of the cross.

"Please, God, don't let the poor things suffer. Take them quick and put 'em on sunny pastures."

"Amen," a chorus of male voices said behind him.

Then Frank stepped up to clamp a heavy gloved hand over Sam's shoulder. "You did the best you could, Sam. Next time you get in a pinch, call me. I'll round up the guys, and we'll help."

Sam got tears in his eyes. He hated like hell for Frank to see them, but his own gloves were frozen, and he couldn't wipe his cheeks. He turned around. "Back at you, pal. I'm sorry I've been such a jackass for the last six years."

MADDIE HEARD ALL THE TRAILERS COMING IN BEFORE SHE COULD even see headlights. Gabriella and Caleb joined her at the window. Kirstin soon flanked her on the other side. They heard what sounded like hundreds of cows bawling inside the containers as they rolled through the ranch proper. Kirstin clapped her hands. Caleb punched the air with his fist. Gabriella smiled and nodded. Rickie, who came running from the living room, shouted with glee and air-boxed with Caleb.

"I'd better get the food on the table!" Maddie exclaimed. "And then I'll pray we made enough."

"No hurry," Kirstin said. "I counted twelve trailers. They'll be a while unloading."

"How do they do that?"

Kirstin grinned. "They back the trailers in through a pasture gate and lower the ramps. Most of the time, cattle can't wait to get out, so all you do is get out of their way. Sometimes, though, you'll have a few that bunch up at the back. That can be difficult if you don't know what you're doing. Fortunately, Dad's friends have been cowpokes all their lives."

Kirstin put Rickie and Caleb to work setting out stacks of plates and flatware on the table while she opened several bottles of wine and climbed on a stool to get extra goblets from a top cupboard. Maddie had decided to serve the meal buffet-style, which would allow diners to feel comfortable about sitting wherever they wished to eat. Sam's table could seat twelve in a pinch, but Maddie hoped they'd have more people.

Maddie decided to call Emma while she was waiting for the front door to open. Her friend had helped her out in a big way at the bar this morning and deserved to get an update. While Maddie chatted with Emma, who was worried about Herm because he wasn't home yet, Kirstin and Gabriella began taking food from the warmers and oven.

Verna had shared with Maddie that Emma often grew anxious when Herm didn't come home. The best thing to do, according to her, was to pretend that Herm was still alive and just away somewhere for an overnighter. Most of the time, Emma woke up the next morning aware that Herm had passed away.

"Emma, you needn't worry about Herm. He helped Sam round up cows today, and he's so exhausted that Sam insisted he stay for dinner and sleep here for the night."

"Oh," Emma said. "But we're right across the road. It's not that far for Herm to drive."

"No, it isn't, but dear heavens, Emma, the roads are so slick! You wouldn't want him to go off in a ditch, would you?"

Emma finally agreed that her beloved Herman would be safer if he stayed all night with Sam. Just as Maddie ended the call, men began filing into the house. She'd never seen so many wet jackets that had frozen stiff. She spread towels on the living room floor. Sam's guests tossed their coats down any old which way, but the Stetsons were treated with the utmost respect.

Kirstin had filled a tub with ice and beer, but few of the men went for it. Realizing her mistake, because all of them were chilled to the bone, she filled mugs with hot coffee and set out cream and sugar. That went so fast that she had to make more coffee.

Chapter Sixteen

MADDIE MET SO MANY MEN THAT SHE PROMPTLY FORGOT most of their names. One exception was Frankie Johnson. She'd never forget him and could only hope he'd retained some of the spelling rules Emma had drilled into him.

Fascinated by all the male humans that had invaded the house, Maddie leaned against a kitchen counter with a glass of white wine and just watched them interact. They were a jovial lot, and once they warmed up, they descended upon Kirstin's tub of cold beer. They elbowed and patted one another on the back with unnecessary force. Even Sam was laughing and occasionally horsing around. It did Maddie's heart good to see him renewing old friendships. She couldn't take her eyes off him.

A wave of guilt washed over her, but she pushed it away. She would always love Graham, but now she had equally strong feelings for Sam. It was confusing, but she couldn't sort it out right now. Later, when she was alone, she couldn't avoid doing that any longer.

The men sat around the table or commandeered spare chairs while they ate. Maddie heard a lot of "remember when" and rowdy guffaws. She decided it was a healing time for all of them. Women would just hug one another, apologize, and cry. Men had to jostle one another, crack jokes, and pretend their feelings didn't run deep. Maddie felt so glad for Sam. He needed friends back in his life. She felt absurdly proud that she had played a part in bringing about this reunion.

One of the men was half the age of the others, probably around thirty-five, like Cam. He shoveled some mashed potatoes into his mouth, swallowed, and glanced at Sam. "I sure would like to work on this ranch again, Sam. Not as your manager or anything. I know that Miguel and Kirstin share that position now. But I'm still a good man with horses and cattle."

Sam smiled. "Well, Jake, I can always find work for you to do around here. Come see me tomorrow, and I'll hire you on."

Jake nodded. "Can I spread the word that you're taking applications again?"

Sam lifted his coffee cup to the younger man. "Absolutely. I have a few positions to fill. Come spring, though, I'll be hiring with a vengeance."

After the last guest left, Sam returned to the kitchen and gathered Maddie into his arms for a long hug. "Thank you for rounding them up this morning. I don't know what you said, but you gave me back my friends."

Maddie leaned against the strong circle of his arms to smile up at him. "Emma was there. She went back into schoolteacher mode and had all of them hanging their heads when she finished with them."

Sam kissed Maddie on the forehead and stepped away, drawing his cell phone from his pocket. He called someone and said, "Hello, Mrs. Pedigrew? This is Sam Conacher."

Maddie's heart leaped. She hurried over to Sam and said in a stage whisper, "Herm is spending the night!"

. . .

SAM STILL LAY AWAKE AT MIDNIGHT, RECALLING THE SHARP STAB of pain that had lanced through him that day over the part he had played in Annie's death. No matter what Maddie said, Annie's doctor had wanted to do a complete hysterectomy, and Sam had begged Annie to wait. *Only six months*, he had pleaded. *Can't you hang in there for only that long?* So Annie had done so, and for no apparent reason, she'd stopped developing the painful cysts. She'd lived for years after that without any hint of a problem. Then she'd been diagnosed with cancer, *ovarian* cancer, and to this day Sam still believed those lethal cells had been hiding in her ovaries all those years.

Kirstin had begged Sam to get counseling, but he'd always resisted, convinced that it was a bunch of nonsense. But the reality was, he still hadn't gotten his head on straight. *Maybe I should call some shrink and make an appointment,* he thought, staring at his dark ceiling. He couldn't go on feeling this way. It was like Annie's cancer, eating him alive.

Sam rolled over and punched his pillow so hard it made his knuckles ache. *Damn. I'm getting so old I can't do jack anymore without it hurting.* He sighed and resigned himself to the fact that it certainly couldn't hurt if he got counseling—and maybe, by some miracle, it would help him to finally put Annie to rest.

MADDIE COULDN'T SLEEP. SHE LAY AWAKE IN HER DOWNSTAIRS bedroom, trying to come to terms with her feelings for Sam. She couldn't understand herself. How could she still be grieving for Graham and also feel such deep affection for someone else? She only knew that she'd come to care for Sam more deeply than she'd ever expected. He was a complicated man, but she felt she understood him in ways that not even his daughter did. She, too, had been left behind. She had experienced the same pain that Sam had, along with the burning anger, the bitterness, and the guilt. She'd even felt frantic as well, terrified that she might lose Cameron or Caleb, as if the Grim Reaper lurked in the shadows, hoping to obliterate her whole life again. The thought of losing her boys and being left alone had filled her with helpless dread.

She couldn't say that she approved of the way Sam had punished everyone around him for his loss. But she did understand it. And because she did, she could forgive him. When he'd realized how wrong he'd been about her son, he'd tried his best to undo the damage he had instigated. He wasn't by nature a vicious person. He'd reacted to the world around him like a wounded animal. Then he'd retreated to a dark place where he could be alone and die. Only a person couldn't wish himself dead. Your heart kept beating, and your lungs kept drawing in oxygen. And no matter how much you hoped you wouldn't, you woke up again in the morning to face yet another day of pain that seemed unbearable.

Sam needed her. Maddie understood that, too. They'd started out as only friends, but she'd have been lying to herself if she pretended that was the case now. When he walked into a room, her heart quickened and her skin tingled. She knew that feeling. It was love, the kind she'd felt for Graham, a heart-to-heart bond, laced with physical desire. She hadn't invited it. She would always love her husband and would never forget him. But even if she was a foolish old woman who was experiencing the emotions of a teenage girl again, she had to open herself to the possibilities and trust Sam enough to explore them with him.

· · ·

THE NEXT MORNING, SAM CALLED A SHRINK'S OFFICE AND MADE an appointment for counseling. He did it in the barn after feeding the cattle. He wanted no one to overhear him. He guessed business wasn't booming for shrinks, because he got a block of time for the very next day at ten in the morning. Toward the end of the conversation, he panicked.

"One other thing. Do I have to lie on a couch? If that's part of the deal, I'm out."

The receptionist had already hung up.

"Damn it to hell."

Sam stared at his phone. *No way am I lying on a shrink's sofa,* he thought. *If I see one in the room, I'll be out of there so fast their heads will swim.*

THAT NIGHT SAM COULD TELL THAT MADDIE HAD SOMETHING ON her mind. She was quiet all evening and barely acknowledged Cam's farewell when he left to visit Kirstin at her house. She'd hardly noticed when Caleb escaped upstairs to talk and text on his phone, either. That was out of character for Maddie. She was nothing if not attentive to her son and grandson.

Sam sat beside her on the sofa. "You're a million miles away." He grasped her hand, gave it a squeeze, and smiled at her. "Penny for them if you'll sell out cheap."

"Oh, Sam." She plopped her head on his arm and twisted at the hips to place her right hand on his chest. She'd never done that. She was affectionate in her own way, but aside from resting her head against him or returning a friendly hug, she'd never touched him in a way that might have been construed as a physical advance. "I've fallen in love with you. I mean really, *really* in love. I'm not sure what to do next."

Sam wasn't certain what to say. There was a romantic glow inside the house from the huge, beautifully decorated spruce in one corner of the living area and the lights that had been strung at the windows. Plus, he wanted her, just as any man with blood still moving in his veins wanted a woman he loved. The next move seemed pretty obvious to him. Only if Maddie was struggling with her feelings for him, she might not be quite ready for a roll in the hay. "Letting it steep like a tea bag isn't working for you?"

Her head jerked back and forth on his arm, signaling that she was shaking it to tell him no.

"Well, Maddie, aren't we a fine pair? I have all my moves down. At this age, God help me if I don't. But it doesn't feel quite right yet as far as the timing goes."

She sighed. "No, it doesn't. It should be impulsive, shouldn't it? No thinking about it required."

Sam had done plenty of thinking about it. "Right. And I think being spontaneous takes some innocent foreplay. We're never alone long enough to make out." He chuckled. "Remember those days? Did you and Graham ever steam up the car windows?"

She giggled. "Oh, dear, don't remind me. One night a cop found us parked on Lover's Peak, and we were putting our location to its intended use. Graham had to wipe the fog away from the glass when the officer rapped on the driver's window with his nightstick. I was so embarrassed when he told us it was past curfew and that teenagers who played with fire usually got burned."

"High school?"

"Yes. We were madly in love."

Sam leaned his head back against the sofa. "Annie was a shy little thing. And, oh, my God, she was beautiful."

"I often stop to admire pictures of her hanging on the wall. She was definitely beautiful. You were a lucky man."

"Does that bother you? The pictures of her, I mean. I guess now that I have another woman in my life, I should take most of them down. For Kirstin's sake, not all of them, of course."

"Don't be silly, Sam. I don't expect you to erase Annie from your life. You can't. And how absurd would it be for me to be jealous of her? You keep the pictures up. They're family history. I have oodles of Graham. They're all in storage for now, but eventually they'll be hanging on my walls. Do you have a problem with that?"

"No. I admire the man. He raised a wonderful son. With your help, of course." He pressed a kiss on her hair. "He also played a part in making you the woman you are. I'm grateful to him for that. And, like you said, he's part of your family history. Neither of us should feel uncomfortable about reminders, I think."

"Agreed." She cricked her neck to gaze up at him. "So when will we start making out?"

Sam bent his head and gave her a lingering kiss, and by the time he broke it off, he felt as if he'd grown a third leg. "That's it for now. Your grandson will come charging down the stairs anytime for his nightly half gallon of milk."

She gazed dreamily up at him. "You're right. We're never really alone, are we?"

"The kids will be married on Christmas morning. After that, they'll be gone for four days for a quick honeymoon, and we'll have Caleb. When they come back and we're relieved of teenager duty, maybe we can sneak off somewhere. I've already got two of my former hired hands back on the payroll. Kirstin and Miguel can handle the ranch. Winter is my slow time. I putter around, fixing equipment. Rub down all the tack. Work with the horses. Feed cattle. Saddle up to ride through the herds to check on all of them. It's a time when I can take off and let someone else do it."

"If we go away together, can we move forward in baby steps?"

Sam almost groaned, but he knew she needed reassurance. "Absolutely. I'm sixty-eight, Maddie. It may take me three hours just to get warmed up." He winked at her and loved the way her cheek dimpled back at him. "Have I mentioned that my night vision went south on me?"

"Yes. When did that happen?"

"I'm not sure, but the night I burned all your books, I realized it was gone. All my life, I could walk into a dark workshop and still see what I was grabbing. That night I grabbed the gas instead of the diesel and nearly blew myself to kingdom come."

"It's hard for me to kneel anymore. At mass, it was a killer."

"I'll get you a special pillow so it doesn't hurt anymore."

Sam was content with the nonsexual turn of their conversation. Women were more sensitive than men when the years tallied up and gravity won the war. By telling her about his diminished night vision, he'd just set the stage for her to feel less self-conscious when he finally made love to her—in the dark.

SAM HAD THE NERVOUS JITTERS AS HE DROVE INTO MISSOULA FOR his shrink appointment. He hadn't dreaded seeing a doctor this much since he'd gone in for his last prostate exam. As he drove, he wondered how these things worked. Did the doctor ask the patient questions, or was the patient just expected to talk? Sam didn't know what to say. *Will it work if I just say my wife died and*

I blame myself for her death? Damn, but he hated the thought of telling a stranger that.

He swung out into the passing lane on Highway 93 to get around some cars bunched up behind a gray Audi SUV. For a moment he thought the vehicle might be Maddie's, but as he cut back over to the right lane, he decided it couldn't be. She wouldn't drive fifty-five in a seventy-mile-per-hour zone. She was from California, for God's sake.

He went back to worrying about his imminent interview with the shrink. He didn't know if it was a man or a woman, or how old the person was. If he walked in and found a young twenty-something blonde waiting for him to spill his guts, he'd be gone in a split second. A woman that age worried about her ovaries only when she might be ovulating. She'd have no idea what it was like to watch a woman you loved with all your heart waste away to skin and bones from cancer, or how it felt when you could touch her nowhere on her body without her screaming in pain.

The memories made Sam feel half sick. *Annie, sweet Annie, you were so damned brave,* he thought. *I would have given my right arm to take your place. What has my life been worth since I lost you?* He pulled over onto the shoulder of the road to think. How could he talk about his feelings with some stranger?

The gray SUV that he'd thought for a moment was Maddie's crawled past him, with a new group of cars braking behind it. Sam couldn't see the driver. The headrest blocked his view. Besides, so what if it was Maddie? She came into Missoula every couple of weeks for physical therapy. She hadn't mentioned that she had an appointment, but they'd been more focused on their relationship last night, with her worrying about taking baby steps before they had sex.

Sam's stomach clenched, and he felt as if he might puke. He loved two women, one of them now only a voice in his head. No question about it, he needed to get help. His feelings had become as tangled as an old set of Christmas tree lights.

WHEN SAM FINALLY PULLED INTO THE HUGE PARKING LOT THAT serviced two medical buildings, he saw the same SUV that had been puttering along the highway in a high-speed zone. It was parked over to the right in an area reserved for only oncology patients. He was glad it wasn't where he'd taken Annie for her treatments. That was all he needed right now, to remember that. He had just pulled his truck into a space and was about to look away when he caught a glimpse of reddish brown as the driver of the Audi climbed out. He could have picked the top of Maddie's head out of a lineup. He'd rested his cheek against her hair so many times that he could almost smell the sweet scent of it.

He remained focused until he saw all of her. Yep, it was definitely Maddie. She wore that gray wool coat that matched her car. People from cities had strange ideas. Who'd know once she entered a building if she clashed with her automobile? He wasn't sure what colors went well together, but women were.

Smiling slightly because he loved her so much, Sam tracked her with his gaze, expecting her to veer left toward the building that housed a multitude of different medical experts, including his future shrink. Only Maddie stepped carefully forward over the ice, aiming for the sidewalk that curved up to the entrance of the Oncology Center. As Sam watched her turn right on the walkway and make her dainty way toward the entrance for cancer patients, an ice-cold knot formed in his stomach. She entered the building through the revolving doors and disappeared. The cold knot splintered and exploded into white-hot rage.

MADDIE WAS EXHAUSTED WHEN SHE GOT BACK TO THE RANCH. SHE felt a surge of gratitude that Sam had Gabriella on the payroll as a full-time employee who kept the house spotless and always had wonderful evening meals cooked. Maddie tried to help her during the day, but mostly she worked on her writing. That was a full-time job. It was going to be so nice to just go inside, slip out of her coat, and sit down to a wonderful dinner. After the kids all went their own ways, she and Sam could snuggle on the sofa, and maybe, if she was lucky, he'd kiss her again. Last night had been fabulous with the soft shimmer of Christmas lights bathing the room.

She sat for a moment, gazing at the huge house. Colored lights outlined the windows and the steep pitches of the roof. It looked like a Christmas wonderland, a place many people would have loved to spend this most special time of the year. She thought of camp and how difficult it would be trying to live there in this weather. Sam had gifted her family with something so precious by inviting them here, a beautiful place to celebrate the holiday. She loved how nice the wreath she'd chosen looked on the door. It had been a perfect choice.

Just then someone she hadn't noticed rose from the porch swing. The next second, a tall silhouette blocked her view of the wreath. She would have recognized Sam's outline anywhere. Broad shoulders topped by a Stetson and underpinned with long, lean legs sheathed by denim. She grinned and opened the car door.

"Sam! You should be inside. Why on earth did you wait for me out here in the cold?"

His voice hit her like a well-aimed Frisbee. "I need to speak to you in the barn."

She could tell by the edge in his deep voice that he was furious about something. She wondered if he'd had a run-in with Cam, or if Caleb, who was sometimes a little outrageous at sixteen, had done or said something that Sam couldn't countenance. If so, he had proven himself to be a reasonable man with kids, and she'd take her grandson to task. This was Sam's house, after all, even though she had been forgetting that lately.

Trying to keep it light, she said, "Oh, in the barn? Be still my heart. Are we going to crawl into the hayloft and hide from everyone?"

He pivoted on his heel without responding and strode toward the huge building. Maddie thought that was rude. Yes, there were yard lights, but a man with good manners would have guided her over the illuminated but shadowy ground to make sure she didn't stumble. Slightly upset by his behavior, she trailed behind him. Sam was Sam, though. She loved the whole package, including his rough spots. Maybe he just wanted the barrier of walls around him before he started ranting about whatever had upset him.

Maddie had been in the barn on a daily basis, with the exception of when she'd been so sick from chemo that she couldn't come. Her cats lived in here now, and she fed them every day, along with Sam's. They slept in the hayloft, cozy and warm. They wouldn't emerge from their hiding places until morning.

As she stepped inside, her eyes had to adjust to the darkness, and she strained to see Sam. She finally picked him out, as his tan jacket seemed to glow in the dim light that slanted in behind her, and when she stepped closer, his eyes shimmered even in the shadow cast by the charred brim of his hat.

She needed to fix that hat for him. Maddie had found a Western milliner in Missoula and spoken with him on the phone. She'd sent him a picture of the Stetson from her cell, and he'd had some fabulous ideas—her favorite: a matching soft overlay of leather at the front to hide the burned edge of the brim, with another overlay at the back to match. To bring it all together, the milliner had suggested a hatband fashioned from the same leather. She just couldn't think how to sneak away the hat without Sam tearing the house apart looking for it.

This time, his voice rammed into her like the dull edge of a machete, almost knocking the breath out of her. "Goddamn you, Maddie. I asked you, again and again, if you were sick, and you looked me straight in the eye and lied to me."

She flinched. Her first thought was *How did you find out?* And then she felt so ashamed. She *had* lied to him, only she *wasn't* sick. She'd gotten her last treatment today. There was no sign of returning cancer, and during her consultation with the oncologist this afternoon, he'd stressed that her surgery was considered to be a complete success. Surrounding tissue had been biopsied. No traces of cancerous cells had been found in any of the samples. Either the different approach to chemo had killed anything dangerous left around her colon, or she'd been in no danger in the first place. Maddie would never know, and neither would the oncologist unless her cancer returned someday. And it didn't appear that was likely to occur.

"Sam, please don't freak out on me."

His tone remained as flat and lethal as it had been when he first spoke. "Freak out. That's interesting. Is that what you call it when you realize someone allowed you to fall in love with her when she was possibly dying?"

Maddie clenched her fists. "I'm not dying, Sam. I'm not even sick."

He walked toward her, and for a moment she thought he meant

to gather her up in his arms. Only he kept on going and strode right past her toward the doors. "Tell it to someone who hasn't experienced the cancer routine. If you make it through the next five years, you'll have a good chance of beating it, but as it stands right now, the odds aren't good."

She whirled around. "Sam!" she cried. "For once, just once, will you listen to someone before you react?"

He spun to face her. Now he was silhouetted against the glow of the yard lights and the shimmer of Christmas cheer. Maddie had come to love every inch of his rangy body. She couldn't see his face, but she had memorized every plane, every imperfection, and every expression that crossed it.

"Spit it out fast," he told her. "I don't tolerate liars."

Maddie bunched her fists at her sides. "I went in for a routine colonoscopy last January. They found a tumor and took a biopsy. It was cancer. I couldn't bring myself to tell Cam and Caleb. It hadn't been that long since we'd lost Graham to the same disease, and I knew they'd be terrified. I chose to keep it a secret and go through it alone. I flew back to Missouri to stay with my sister while I had the surgery. I found a fabulous oncologist. He got all of the cancer, but to be safe, he recommended chemo. Even though the oncologist here in Missoula feels that my cancer is completely gone, I still haven't told the boys. They have endured enough. Can you understand that?"

"Yes. So have I. Endured enough, I mean."

Maddie flinched again. He spoke the unvarnished truth. He was a man who'd been to hell and back because of cancer. He had every right to be terrified, because now he loved *her*, another victim of the disease. Maddie didn't question the depth of his feelings for her. What she questioned now was her own wisdom. When she'd realized that he was falling in love with her, why hadn't she trusted him with her secret? Sam wasn't a blabbermouth. He was a man who analyzed practically every word he said. When he waged verbal war, he took shots that lacerated his enemies. When he wasn't, he spoke judiciously, never, so far as she knew, saying anything that he didn't mean or believe was the truth. "Sam, please, just hear me out. My son and grandson went through hell during Graham's illness, and his death nearly destroyed them." She held up her hands in supplication. "I never lied to them. I just didn't tell them. It was a nightmare I decided that I had to live through by myself. When I first met you, I couldn't trust you with my secret. And later, I knew I had a ninety-five percent chance of surviving. You were a mess over Annie. At first we were only friends. Remember? *Just* friends. And when it became something more, I had almost finished my course of chemo. I was in perfect health. I saw no reason, absolutely *none*, to upset you and possibly ruin the holidays for everyone I love by revealing my secret when it no longer mattered."

"The truth." His tone remained lifeless. "It always matters, Maddie. I looked you straight in the eye and asked if anything bad was going on with you. You met my gaze, never so much as blinked, and flat-out lied to me. I don't like liars. I'm sure as hell not going to love one, especially when she didn't give a shit if she died on me and broke my heart." She could see him working his big hands. He straightened his fingers, and then he bunched them into fists. She could also see his body shaking. "I rolled the dice. I fell in love with you, and you let me. Of all the people I know, you understand me the best. You know how close I came to putting a bullet in my brain after I lost Annie. How could you let me fall in love with you when you knew your cancer could come back? How could you set me up to go through that again?"

Maddie had no answer. She'd been wrong, and now she knew it.

"Sam, I do love you, and I'm so sorry. All of this hasn't been easy." Her throat tightened, and she gulped. "When I met you, I was just trying to make it through one of the most difficult times of my life. I was all alone with my secret in a strange place, and I'd watched Graham die. I was scared to death for myself and even more terrified for Cam and Caleb. In the beginning you and I hated each other. Remember? By the time we became friends and then started to care for each other, I had already . . ." She heard her voice drift away, echoing softly against the hay and plank walls.

"Lied to me?" he inserted. "Just say it, Maddie. You'd already lied to me."

"Please forgive me. I should have trusted you not to let it slip out. I should have trusted you enough to share all my fears with you. But what's between us now was new to me then, Sam. I told you then that I didn't know what to do with my feelings. Remember? I felt as if I was betraying Graham at first. How could I still love him *and* love another man, too? I was confused and struggling to make sense of my feelings. Besides, what I said that morning when you asked if something bad was going on with me is absolutely true. None of us has any guarantees. You could have cancer right now and not know it. Tomorrow you could fall off a horse and break your neck. You can't live a full and satisfying life without taking chances, Sam. You can't love someone without risking your heart."

"I deserved to have an opportunity to decide for myself if I wanted to take that risk. By lying, you took the choice away from me."

"In all fairness, Sam, I didn't really lie except to say I was receiving physical therapy treatments instead of chemo. The other falsehoods were lies by omission. I truly was in perfect health. I did see a doctor. I'd had complete physicals and blood panels done. My heart is fine. And there is absolutely no sign that my cancer has returned or any indication that it might. I had my last treatment today. I wanted to come home tonight and celebrate."

"With who? *Me*? How could I celebrate something I didn't even know about?"

Maddie winced. "I wish now that I had told you."

"I wish you had, too. But you didn't, and we can't turn back the clock. I kept looking for a huge flaw in you, and now I've found it. I'm not perfect, Maddie, but when I say something, I give it to you straight. You'll never pin lying on me, straight out or by omission." He fell silent, kicking at the dirt with one boot and looking down as if he might unearth the mysteries of the universe. Finally, he spoke again. "We're finished. You and your family are welcome to stay until your houses are done. It won't be that long now. We're civilized adults. Right? I'll go in to eat, and then I'll come out to my shop and do my winter thing. When it's bedtime, I'll come back in. It shouldn't be that uncomfortable."

Maddie's throat was washed in scalding heat and tears, and she couldn't speak. She wanted to throw herself into his arms. If she'd only been honest with him.

He spun on his heel and left the barn. Then he came back, giving her reason to hope. He stood there in the yawning illumination of the open doorway, looking like a silhouetted stock photo of a cowboy that would melt the hearts of many women. She could barely hold herself upright. Either her infusion was kicking in, or Sam had just obliterated every bone in her body.

"I just need to say one more thing. We should go out of our way to act friendly to each other. There's no point in upsetting the kids right before Christmas, especially not this year, with the wedding and all."

When he walked away, Maddie's knees gave out. She crumpled to the ground.

• • •

CALEB STOOD IN THE PASTURE WITH HIS HORSE, LATIGO. HE'D taken him for a long ride around their property, and after getting back, he'd spent nearly an hour rubbing the gelding down and grooming him. Now it was pitch-dark. The trees and bushes in the riparian area seemed to press in around Caleb, and if he allowed his imagination to run wild, the bushes could take on the shapes of dangerous animals like bears, cougars, and moose. Caleb figured most kids would hurry back to Sam's ranch, where everything was all bright and pretty for the holidays, but he wasn't afraid to be alone. He had texted his dad to let him know where he was, and he still liked it here a lot even if their camp did feel like a ghost town now.

Trojan, his dad's favorite gelding, nosed his way in and bumped Latigo aside. Caleb grinned. His dad had a philosophy about horses that he'd told Caleb a dozen times. *Even when we don't have time to exercise each of them every day, giving them some attention goes a long way.* Trojan was trying to say that he wanted to be brushed, too.

"Come here, boy," he said to Trojan. "I'll curry you down."

Caleb couldn't stay long enough to give each horse an hour of attention, but he did manage to brush the other three. As he worked, he listened to the night sounds and smiled when he heard the great horned owl call to its mate. He'd seen the female earlier and couldn't wait to tell Gram. She'd get all excited and talk about watching for baby owls this coming spring. This place, a vast expanse of land in Montana along a river or stream, had been his father's dream for as long as Caleb could remember, and now it had come true.

Caleb carried his saddle and tack over to the storage shed. He prided himself on the fact that he didn't need a flashlight. Sam griped about losing his night vision, but so far as Caleb could tell, he still saw pretty good after the sun went down. So did Caleb's dad.

After putting away all his riding gear, he set off for his truck, which was parked by the river near Gram's funny little trailer. After turning the key in the ignition, he listened to the engine sputter and wished for about the thousandth time that he could get a job and save to buy a new rig. His father wouldn't hear of it, though. He was weird about high schoolers working, probably because he'd had to bring in an income when he was only a year older than Caleb was right now.

Looking on the bright side, Caleb reminded himself that he at least had a good stereo, a Christmas present from his dad last year. He could listen to music as he drove back to the ranch. He knew the road well now, but he still drove slowly, watching for wildlife in the yellow glare of the headlights. Elk or deer could get spooked and dash out in front of a vehicle with no warning.

As he pulled in at the ranch, he saw Gram climbing the front steps. In the glow of the Christmas lights, she looked old and tired. His heart caught.

"Hi, Gram!" he yelled as he climbed out of the Ford. "Have you been in Missoula for your physical therapy?"

She paused on the porch and turned to look at him. "Yes," she said in a lifeless voice.

Caleb saw that the front of her coat was covered with dirt, and there was a smudge on her cheek, too. "What happened, Gram? Did you fall down?"

"Something like that. I'm not hurt, though."

Caleb didn't get it. Either she'd fallen down or she hadn't. He hurried up the stairs and took hold of her arm. The wool sleeve of her coat felt icy beneath his fingertips, telling him that she'd been outside for a while. Her face looked almost as white as Sam's hair. "Gram, are you sick?"

"I had a rough day," she told him. "I think I'll go in and lie down for a while."

"Where's your purse?"

At his question, she got an odd look on her face. "I must have left it in the car."

"I'll run and get it and put it outside your bedroom door."

She nodded and turned to go inside. Caleb ran back down the steps, thinking as he did that he needed to get rid of the wheelchair ramp now that his dad no longer needed it. When he reached the Audi, he noticed that the interior was cold. So was Gram's purse. He had no idea where she'd gone outside, but she hadn't just gotten home.

He saw nobody inside the house. As he took the handbag down the hall to his grandmother's room, he noticed that the den door was closed. Maybe Sam was in there doing paperwork. He guessed his dad might be at Kirstin's. He only knew it felt weird with the house so quiet. Just like back at camp, it felt suddenly like a ghost town.

SAM HAD TAKEN REFUGE IN THE DEN UNTIL HE FINALLY HEARD Maddie go to her room. Shortly after that, Caleb, with his distinctive stride, entered the house and left again just as quickly. When all was quiet, Sam couldn't stand to remain inside. The damned place even smelled like Christmas, with evergreen boughs draped in so many rooms. He decided he'd be happier in the barn, where the scents of hay, horses, and cows would surround him. He could shut the doors to block out the sight of twinkling lights and feel as miserable as he wanted without anybody watching him.

The barn was dark, and he hadn't thought to bring a light, so he didn't shut the doors after all. He sat on what he'd come to think of as his hay bale, and as the silence settled in around him, an onslaught of emotions swept through him. He couldn't stamp out his feelings for Maddie, and that terrified him. *Losing her.* He didn't think he could live through it.

Unreleased sobs built pressure in his chest. His eyes burned with unshed tears. He imagined sitting by her bed and spooning broth into her mouth, seeing her wasted body, listening to the death rattle in her chest at the very end, and then pressing a kiss to a cheek gone cold and waxen. He'd done all that once, and no one should have to do it twice.

MADDIE LAY AWAKE, IMAGES FLASHING THROUGH HER MIND LIKE pictures on a television screen, all of them reruns of her times with Sam. He'd come to mean so much to her, and she had blown any chance she had to be with him. She thought back to that moment when she'd first been diagnosed and wondered if she had made good decisions. Had keeping her cancer a secret been the right thing for her to do? It had seemed smart to her at the time, but now she wasn't so sure. Cam would have been supportive and dealt with the stress. He was a strong and responsible man, not a child who needed protection.

She sighed and rolled over to press her face against the pillow. It didn't matter anymore whether she'd been right or wrong. What was done was done. She couldn't change a single thing now, and she had to live with the consequences. She didn't blame Sam for his anger or his sense of betrayal. She *had* looked him straight in the eye and lied to him, whether she'd done it with words or by omission. Even worse, he had deserved a chance to decide for himself whether loving her was worth the risk. It was all well and fine for her to spout platitudes about there being no guarantees in life, but that didn't excuse her for failing to tell Sam that she was a poorer bet than most women.

Sobs welled in her chest and pushed against her throat. When she released them, she muffled the sounds with the pillow, hoping no one came down the hallway and overheard her.

THE FOLLOWING DAY CALEB WENT INTO THE KITCHEN FOR BREAK-fast and found Sam sitting at the table with a mug of coffee cupped in his hands. He smelled like fresh air and hay, which told Caleb that he'd already done morning chores. That normally put him in a good mood. Sam was one of the few people Caleb knew who truly loved working outdoors and caring for animals. But this morning he looked grim. Gram sat in the living room, staring at the Christmas tree. She held a coffee cup in her lap, but he could tell by the scent that she was drinking ginger tea again. That meant she was having another bad day.

Caleb darted a glance at Sam and then at his grandmother. Something was up. Now that they were friends, typically they liked to sit beside each other. He wondered if they were mad at each other for some reason.

Gabriella had pancake batter ready for the skillet, and Caleb could smell warm maple syrup. His mouth started to water. Just as he poured himself a glass of milk, Rickie burst into the house. Gabriella beckoned him to the kitchen, and the younger boy joined Caleb at the table to eat. They both filled up on crisp bacon, scrambled eggs, and hotcakes drizzled generously with heated syrup.

"Can Rickie ride with me this morning?" Caleb asked. "His school is right on my way."

"*Sí,*" Gabriella replied. Then, wagging a finger at Caleb, she said, "No driving speed."

It took Caleb a moment to understand what she meant. Then he grinned. "Ah, you mean no driving fast. I won't, Gabriella. I promise."

Minutes later Caleb stopped on Fox Hollow Road to gaze at their building. "The outside is totally finished now," he observed, smiling at Rickie. "We could live in the workshop area, no worries. Want to go see if they've installed the big propane heater?"

"Do we have time?" Rickie asked. "I've never been inside. It'd be fun to see it."

Caleb pulled off the road, left the engine running so the old truck would stay warm, and piled out of the cab to meet Rickie on the other side. "Last one there's a monkey's uncle!"

For Caleb it was a magical moment when he stepped inside. The overhead heater purred as it pushed warmth into the huge room. He wondered why it was running when no one else was in the building. He guessed that heat might have been necessary to dry out some of the construction material. "At this end we were going to set up a pretend house," he told Rickie. "A living room, a kitchen, and bedrooms. Gram said Dad and I could build some room dividers to make the sleeping areas private."

"Like camping indoors, only a lot nicer!" Rickie exclaimed.

Caleb suddenly remembered. "The plumber promised to make the downstairs guest bathroom kind of functional. Only a tub-shower combo with a flushing toilet, but it sounded fancy to us. Let's go see if he did it!"

Moments later, Caleb flushed the toilet until the tank ran out of water. Rickie ran the tub faucet, flipping his fingers through the stream as if indoor plumbing were a new invention. "Could we maybe sleep over here some night?"

"Wouldn't that be awesome?" Caleb could almost picture it. "You could invite a friend, and I could, too. My dad would probably come over and stay so none of the parents would freak out."

"My dad, too," Rickie cried. "Let's ask if we can do it!"

Caleb tugged his phone from his coat pocket to check the time. "Shit, Rickie. We gotta go, or we'll be late to school!"

Chapter Seventeen

THAT AFTERNOON CALEB WISHED HE COULD DRIVE RICKIE back to the ranch, but the younger boy got out of school earlier than he did and was probably already home. Nevertheless, Caleb stopped to explore the building again and found Murphy, the organizer, on-site to supervise the mud-and-tape process of the downstairs living unit. Now Caleb knew why the workshop heater was running. The walls wouldn't dry properly without warmth.

"Hi, Caleb," the big redhead said. "You guys ready to move in?"

Caleb explained that Sam Conacher had invited them to remain at his house until their own were finished. "I would like to have friends for a sleepover, though, if my dad will chaperone."

Murphy led the way out to the utilitarian end of the structure. He flipped on the overhead lights, and Caleb gasped in surprise. "Oh, wow."

"You have electrical outlets, too," Murphy said, pointing at the white covers along both walls. "And heat. No reason I can see that you couldn't spend the night."

Caleb couldn't wait to reach the ranch and tell his father. "Dad's been waiting for this stage. Now we can build stuff. We do welding and woodworking projects together. Gram needs a new dining room table. She had to leave her big one at the house in

California, because it's too huge for this place. So we're going to make her a new one that looks like a really awesome one we saw in a store."

As he drove the rest of the way to the ranch, Caleb felt bubbles of excitement in his throat. He liked staying with Sam, but he was glad their own place was so close to being finished. They'd dreamed aloud about it so much—how it would all look and how nice it would be—that he was eager to actually live there. He parked out in front of the big house beside his dad's pickup. Glad to see that his father wasn't away working, he bounded up the front steps. At the end of each school day, Gabriella had started making snacks for him and Rickie, and Caleb also wanted to tell Gram hello if she wasn't busy writing.

When he walked in, Gabriella called a greeting to him from the kitchen and then said, "Rickie do homework. Then he come. I make brown cakes."

Caleb cut through the dining room to see what brown cakes were. "Oh, yum, brownies!" he exclaimed when he saw the blue glass baking dish. The chocolaty smell made his stomach growl. "I'll wait for Rickie, though. Thank you, Gabriella. Those will be awesome with cold milk."

Caleb figured Gram must have been writing, but he walked down the hall anyway, hoping to find her bedroom door open. He wanted to tell her about all the progress at their building site. Disappointment flooded through him when he saw that the door was closed. He'd learned long ago what that meant. *Do not disturb.* Gram claimed that interruptions jerked her out of the *zone.*

Caleb started to make a U-turn, but an odd sound from Gram's bedroom made him freeze. What was that? It sounded like someone was crying and trying not to be heard. A cold feeling prickled his skin. He remembered the tension he'd felt between his grandmother and Sam that morning. Now he felt pretty sure he'd guessed right. They were angry with each other about something, and Gram was very upset about it.

Caleb hated it when Gram felt sad. Right after Gramps died, she'd been sad a lot. Now it was time for her to be happy again. Whatever they were pissed at each other about, it couldn't be important enough to let Gram cry and feel unhappy for a whole day.

SAM HAD RETREATED TO THE SHOP TO CONDITION TACK. HE SAT on a three-legged stool with his saddle draped over a post propped atop two sawhorses. Over the summer Sam never had time to care for his gear. Hands slick with saddle soap, he worked a sponge over the leather, taking his time to make sure he got every indentation and crevice. Normally this mindless task soothed him. He could push away his worries and try not to think. Only that wasn't working for him today. Maddie occupied his thoughts. Anger burned low in his belly, and he couldn't shake it off. He had trusted her, and he shouldn't have. She had her own agenda, protecting her kids, and he hadn't factored into her life. Not really. Maybe if she'd told him about the cancer, he would have fallen in love with her anyway. But at least then he would have moved into the relationship with his eyes wide-open. And he would have been aware of the risk he was taking.

The personnel door squeaked open. Sam stiffened, hoping it wasn't Maddie. If he talked to her right now, he might say things he'd later regret.

"Hi."

Relaxing his shoulders, Sam glanced back at Caleb. He'd gotten the boy a handmade saddle for Christmas, a special order to fit his gelding, Latigo. Sam recalled how happy he'd been the day he'd met with the saddler over on the McLendon property to get the horse measured. He'd felt as if he were ordering a gift for his grandson. Now he knew that would never be the case, but he still hoped Caleb would enjoy the new gear.

"Hi," he replied. "Have you ever been taught how to clean and condition a saddle?"

Caleb leaned against a workbench, crossed his ankles, and folded his arms. "My dad showed me. We do it together in the winter, but we don't have the facilities this year."

Sam gestured at the room around them. "Feel free to use mine."

"Thanks."

The boy bent his tawny head. Sam could tell he had something on his mind.

"I, um, just came from the big house," he finally said. "I heard Gram crying through her bedroom door. I know something went wrong. I noticed how you guys were treating each other this morning. She's either mad at you, or you're mad at her, or maybe you're both mad."

Sam's heart caught. He *was* angry with Maddie, but that didn't mean he wanted her to cry. And he couldn't discuss with Caleb what had gone wrong. Maddie had done everything possible to hide her disease from Cam and her grandson. If he said a wrong word, he'd spill the beans.

"Adult relationships can be difficult sometimes, Caleb. And they can also be very private. I'm not at liberty to tell you what went wrong between me and your grandmother."

Caleb nodded. "I understand that. But Gram is really sad. Whatever happened, if you care about her as a friend, can't you at least try to fix it?"

Sam saw no way to undo any of it. Maddie had made her

choices and lied to him. He hadn't been in the wrong, and he couldn't fix the situation. Even worse, neither could she.

All he could say was "Let me think on it."

Caleb sighed and pushed away from the bench. "You came out here to get away from all of us. Didn't you?"

"I just needed some time alone," Sam settled for saying.

"That isn't right. It's your house, not ours. We can go home now and live there until our houses are finished. We'll even have heat. If you'd like us to leave, I can talk to my dad."

Sam took a steadying breath. "Caleb, the situation is complicated. It's almost Christmas. Kirstin and your dad are getting married that morning. Your grandmother and I have agreed that we don't want to upset everyone, so we'll just bide our time until your houses are finished. Then you can go home. That was the original plan."

"How will that work now?" Caleb asked. "Kirstin and Dad will want to live with each other. But you need her here to help with the work." The boy frowned. "It's like nobody except me is thinking about stuff."

A jolt of dread coursed through Sam. Caleb was right. A husband and wife should live together, and Sam hadn't considered what that would eventually mean. The tension in him eased as suddenly as it had struck. "It'll all work out great, Caleb. Your place is almost within throwing distance. Kirstin can live over there and still be here every day. It's a perfect arrangement." Sam truly meant that and realized just how much he'd changed. He no longer needed an iron hold on his daughter. Maddie had helped him get over his irrational possessiveness. "Just think how difficult it would be if your dad lived miles away. She'd be on the road morning and night to work here."

"Our upstairs apartment isn't that big. Kirstin's used to the ranch manager's house, which is huge."

Sam nodded. "The three of you can make it work. Your dad mentioned building a bigger house later. Living in the smaller place will be temporary."

"Just so you understand that we can't live here and leave Gram on the land all alone. From the start Dad said we needed to live close to her. She's getting old, and it may not be that long before we need to watch after her."

Sam, aware of Maddie's battle with cancer, hoped that time wouldn't come sooner than Caleb expected. "Your father is right about that. Your grandmother enjoys her peace and quiet, but she should have loved ones nearby who can check on her and care for her if need be."

"What about you? You're getting old, too."

Sam didn't enjoy being reminded of his age. Caleb apparently thought he was ready for assisted living. He shook his head. "I won't be alone. When Kirstin leaves the ranch, Miguel and Gabriella will probably live in the manager's house. Even if they stay where they are now, they won't be far away."

The boy's shoulders relaxed, and he smiled slightly. "I guess I'm not the only one who's been thinking about it. And with Kirstin working on the ranch, she can check on you while she's here."

Being checked on wasn't something Sam wanted. But he refrained from saying so. "Right. Like I said, it's the perfect arrangement."

WHEN CALEB WALKED INTO KIRSTIN'S HOUSE A FEW MINUTES later, he heard a feminine shriek coming from one of the bedrooms. He ran from the foyer and crossed the living room, almost colliding with his dad as he entered the hallway.

"Kirstin?" his dad yelled. "Where are you? Are you hurt?"

Just then Caleb's future mom came tearing out of a spare

bedroom, wearing a long white dress. Sobs shook her shoulders. She made a fist on the belly part of the gown and held it out from her body. "It's too big! I can't wear this! What on earth am I going to do? Those idiots screwed it up!"

Caleb thought, *Oh, shit.*

His dad said, "It'll be okay, honey. We'll—well, we'll just get it fixed somehow."

A burning glare entered her tear-filled gaze. "Fixed. *Fixed?* There isn't time! My wedding is *ruined*!"

His dad hugged Kirstin. "We can take it to a seamstress. Be thankful it's too big. Taking a dress in should be simple. Adding to it would be a lot harder."

Kirstin buried her face against his shoulder. Between muffled sobs, she cried, "What if it can't be altered, Cam? It's my dream dress. I can't get married in something else."

Caleb had come to know Kirstin really well, and he'd never seen her act this way. She fixed fences. She stood her ground against her dad and Miguel when she thought something was being done wrong. When horses blew up on her, she handled them with calm authority. Now, because a stupid dress didn't fit her right, she was acting like the world had just ended.

He decided he should make himself scarce and let his dad settle her down. If he said something stupid like *It's only a dress,* he had a feeling she might get really mad at him.

ANOTHER WHOLE DAY PASSED, AND CALEB FOUND HIS GRAND-mother standing at the dining room window with tears slipping down her cheeks. Her eyelids were red and puffy. She sniffed, and he wondered how long she had been crying. She was plugged up tighter than the toilet he'd once clogged with bathroom tissue as a little boy.

When he put his arm around her, she felt bony, and it scared him. How come he was the only one who noticed? He guessed his dad had other things on his mind, first and foremost getting Kirstin's wedding gown fixed. Yesterday he'd driven her back and forth between the ranch and the seamstress's place twice and probably had again today. Kirstin was in a total panic, because they were running out of time.

"Gram, don't be sad," he said. "It's almost Christmas. Dad's getting married, too. We're supposed to be happy."

She shook her head. "I'm sorry, sweetheart." She wiped her cheeks with trembling fingers. "I'll cheer up. You're right. It is Christmas, and it should be a happy time."

Caleb turned her toward the tree. "Look how beautiful that is."

With a nod, she said, "It truly is. I wish I'd gone to the storage units and gotten some of our decorations, though. Remember the little angel you made for me? And that picture of you glued onto a sparkly star made with plaster of Paris. I miss seeing that. It doesn't seem quite like Christmas without our own special things on the tree."

Caleb thought of the working heat and electricity back on their property. If Gram wanted to see all her own decorations, he could make it happen for her. He *would* make it happen. Something had gone wrong between her and Sam, and now she was unhappy during the most wonderful time of the year. Caleb knew he couldn't take her home for Christmas because of the wedding plans, but maybe he could do the next best thing and give her a present that she'd never forget.

ON THE FIRST DAY OF CHRISTMAS BREAK, CALEB GOT UP EARLY, threw on his clothes, and hurried downstairs. He found his dad standing in front of the coffeemaker as if he could make the appliance work faster if he stared at it. He looked really tired.

"Morning, Dad. Is Kirstin's dress fixed yet?"

"I wish. By taking it in so much, the trim doesn't meet up. It's a catastrophe."

"Trim? What's that?"

His father grabbed the coffeepot and quickly sloshed coffee into a mug before the machine could leak all over the place. "There are lines in the skirt that are supposed to meet. When they took in the waist, the lines no longer meet, so the skirt has to be adjusted."

Caleb yawned and covered his mouth. "Well, at least it can be fixed. Right?"

"I hope. She has her heart set on that one dress."

Caleb nodded like he understood how important the alterations were, but to him, it was only a stupid dress. As long as it was white, what difference did the lines make? Maybe he'd never get married. His dad didn't seem to be having very much fun.

After grabbing some breakfast, Caleb told his father that he was working on a surprise for Gram and asked if he could be over on their land all day.

"Are you making her something?" his dad asked.

"Sort of. I'll have to run to town a couple of times."

"Do you need money?"

"I've got some of my allowance saved up. I think it's enough."

MADDIE HAD SUFFERED THROUGH THE AFTERMATH OF HER FINAL chemo treatment, and she felt better physically. Her tangled emotions were another story, but she was trying to conquer those, too. Outside Sam's dining room window, fluffy snowflakes drifted through the air, creating a winter scene that was almost postcard perfect. The barn sat off to one side, its doors yawning open to reveal the hay stored along the back wall. Next door to it, the shop, also sided with wood and stained the same reddish brown, emitted golden light from its windows to generate a warm glow. Behind both buildings, towering pines rose above the rooflines, resembling frosted Christmas trees.

Maddie wished that the beautiful surroundings would lift her spirits, but she still felt hollow and sad. Regardless, she had decided that her self-pity party was over. It was high time for her to at least pretend she was filled with Christmas cheer. When she turned from the window, she nearly tripped over Bingo. The other five dogs lay in the kitchen, snoring softly.

She went to put on a CD to fill the rooms with holiday music and began tackling the chore of wrapping all the gifts that she'd been hiding in her room. It was perfect timing—only Gabriella was in the house, and she was upstairs cleaning. Cam had driven into town with Kirstin because there had been another wedding gown disaster. Caleb was over at their property doing something, and Sam was outside puttering. If Maddie hurried, she could get everything under the tree before anyone got back.

As she piled presents at one end of the table and organized the other with rolls of paper, ribbon, scissors, and tape, she hummed along with "The First Noel," wishing she could feel the joy that normally filled her heart when she heard the song. She had every reason to be happy, she reminded herself. She had recovered from her last treatment and wouldn't need another one. Even though she wouldn't officially be a cancer survivor for five years, the odds were strongly in her favor. She could begin looking forward again and believe she had a future. Only, as grateful as she was for that, she couldn't rejoice. Sam had wormed his way into her heart, and now contemplating a life without him made her feel lost.

As she boxed up a set of sound-canceling earbuds for Caleb, she attempted to push all thoughts of Sam from her mind, but while living in his home, she faced reminders of him everywhere she looked. At the center of the table, Kirstin had put out the Conacher family Christmas shakers, sugar bowl, and tiny cream pitcher, which Sam had given to Annie as a gift years ago. It reminded Maddie of all the pain and suffering Sam had endured over the loss of his wife. Guilt weighed heavily on Maddie's shoulders, because she truly had deprived Sam of the right to decide if he wished to gamble with his heart again. Even though she now felt almost certain that she'd beaten the cancer, she hadn't been so sure of that earlier in her friendship with Sam. When their feelings for each other had changed and deepened into love, how could she have continued to tell him she was fine? It hadn't merely been wrong, but also unforgivably selfish of her. Already set on her course, she'd put Cam and Caleb's happiness above Sam's. Who could blame him for questioning her honesty? Or for feeling bitterly angry?

"Jingle Bells" pealed through the house next, but the jolly refrains didn't lift Maddie's spirits. Out of habit, she selected a Santa-patterned gift wrap for her grandson. Always before, she'd used a glue gun to fancy up the gifts she wrapped, but this year, simple would have to do. Her glue gun was in storage, and she lacked the enthusiasm to go to all that bother, anyway.

Oh, Sam, she thought. He was a man who stood behind what he said, and he'd told her in no uncertain terms that their relationship was over. She had to stop hoping he'd change his mind; she needed to accept the consequences of her own actions. As dismal as the future seemed to her at the moment, she had survived losing her husband. Now she would live through losing Sam as well. She had no choice.

Sam was doing everything he could to make things tolerable. When he came in for dinner at night, he was friendly enough, but he avoided meeting her gaze and no longer sat in his recliner, waiting for her to finish writing for the day. She missed their evening chats and feeling his arm around her shoulders. She yearned to hear his deep laugh. She even mourned the loss of his sarcastic comments.

Her book was finally finished and had been sent to her editor. Normally she would have celebrated and felt proud of herself for finishing it up prior to Christmas. Days off loomed before her, allowing time for shopping and baking for the holiday. But her usual enthusiasm evaded her. In short, it didn't feel like Christmas in this huge house where she no longer felt welcome.

She yearned to go back to her trailer, but she couldn't bring herself to ask Cam to make that possible. His mind was on his wedding, the alterations of Kirstin's gown, and planning their brief honeymoon. In order to move back, she would have to tell Cam that she and Sam were at loggerheads. It didn't seem right to spoil this special time in his life with her personal problems. She decided to wait until after Cam returned from Hawaii to drop the bomb. It wouldn't take long to get her trailer inside the building and hooked up to utilities. Caleb could remain on the ranch with his father until the residences were complete.

"Silent Night" came over the stereo next. Maddie closed her eyes for a moment and focused on what the upcoming holiday truly meant. It wasn't about jolly songs and piles of gifts around a beautifully decorated tree. It was about hope and believing in something greater than one's self. Over the coming days, when the situation seemed unbearable, she would remember that.

SAM SAT ON THE THREE-LEGGED STOOL IN THE SHOP AGAIN, RUB-bing the leather of a saddle. With a start, he realized that he'd been circling the sponge in the same spot for several minutes. He was physically present, but his mind was consumed with thoughts of Maddie. Had he done the right thing by ending their relationship? He enjoyed being with her so much. He loved teasing her and laughing with her. He felt as if he had lost his best friend. And no matter how many times he told himself that he had done the right thing, doubts slipped into his mind.

When he'd seen Maddie going into the oncology building, he had reacted without thinking beyond his initial emotions, a confusing mixture of anger and fear. Yes, he'd been justified in his anger. But what he hadn't stopped to consider was that he would lose her for certain if he ended the relationship.

How did that make sense? He'd been terrified of losing her and then he'd done the one thing that would ensure that he did.

Fear. It was an evil enemy that could confuse a man and shift his focus as easily as a sleight-of-hand performer. He'd known two men who had left their wives, not because they no longer loved them, but because the women had been about to divorce them. Their husbands had filed for divorce in order to beat them to the punch. Sam had never understood their reasoning—until now. By filing for divorce first, they had avoided being the ones who got left behind.

Had he essentially done the same thing? Had he tried to avoid losing Maddie by ducking out before she could get sick? By growing angry and accusing her, had he been running from the one thing he couldn't bear to endure again?

Sam had never considered himself to be a coward, but for the first time in his life he understood that cowardice came in many different forms and wore just as many faces. He rested his arms on his knees. The sponge slipped from his now-limp fingers and plopped on the concrete floor. He could almost hear Maddie saying, *There are no guarantees.* She had also warned him that he could never live a happy and contented life if he refused to put his heart at risk. Only he hadn't listened. Hadn't been able to, because every word she'd said had terrified him.

But this isn't about only me and my fears. Maddie has borne the burden of having cancer all alone. Do you think she hasn't felt afraid? Sam wondered how many times she had yearned for just one person she could trust, someone with whom she could share her worries and fears. Sam knew she'd come to trust him at some point, but by then her course had already been set and she had probably felt that it was not only too late but also pointless to confide in him.

Cancer. Merely by thinking the word, he was filled with terror. Maddie believed she was out of the woods, but there truly weren't any guarantees. Sam wanted to deal with absolutes, no ifs, ands, or maybes. *Why have I been given this second great sorrow in my life?*

Sam found himself standing in front of his house on a shoveled path to the porch. Drifts had formed the previous night, creating whimsical snow sculptures. Pine trees shrouded in white clustered around the back of the structure like ladies-in-waiting. Even in daylight the home looked cheery and bright, every roofline and post delineated by tiny lights. The wreath Maddie had on the door was the perfect size, not too small, not too large, but just right.

He pictured her off in a corner crying. And suddenly it hit him with the force of a full-size bus that Maddie had to be every bit as terrified as he was. She was a smart lady. Some individuals truly did win the war. But would Maddie be one of them? She had no way of knowing for sure, and neither did Sam. The only thing he knew with absolute certainty was that he had behaved like a fair-weather friend, turning his back on her the instant he learned the truth.

Filled with regret, Sam walked toward the porch, his thoughts in such a tangle that he barely felt the frigid air cutting through his shirt. Caleb had gone somewhere. Cam and Kirstin were still in town, scrambling to get her wedding gown properly altered before the nuptials. The door squeaked as Sam pushed it open. When he stepped into the entryway, chunks of snow fell from his riding boots onto the dark slate. He moved forward to scan the living room.

Maddie stood in front of the Christmas tree. Shoulders slumped, she hugged her waist as if to ward off a chill. She looked so forlorn. Sam wondered how he could have done this to her. He crossed the room, stepped around her, and crouched to retrieve a professionally wrapped gift box that he'd stowed under the boughs a few days ago. The scent of pine needles filled his senses, reminding him of Christmases past and present.

Maddie said nothing as he tore off the gold foil paper. Holding a fold of soft wool in his hands, Sam pushed erect and moved to stand behind her. "I got this for you to wear while you're writing, but you look as if you need it now."

She lifted her head and grasped the ends of the shawl in her fists to hold it snugly around her shoulders. "Thank you. That was thoughtful of you."

"Maddie, I'm anything *but* thoughtful." Sam enfolded her in his arms and drew her back against his chest. "I'm so sorry for the way I acted when I learned about your cancer. I should have been supportive and understanding, not angry with you."

BEWILDERMENT WASHED THROUGH MADDIE. SHE TURNED HER head to study his face and saw tears in his eyes. This was a sudden about-face, and she was bewildered.

"Don't say anything," he told her. It was more a request than a command. "I need to do the talking. When I found out about your cancer, I felt cursed, as if my life were repeating itself. I'd fallen in love with a woman, and God was going to steal her from me again. Why would God do that to me? But even scarier, Maddie, how would I survive it?"

Maddie could see the raw emotion in his expression. "Whatever comes, we somehow live through it, Sam."

"I know. Only I'm not worried about that now. I've had a lot of time to think about it, and I realize that I haven't been cursed. Instead I've been given a gift, a priceless, precious gift—being able to love again."

Maddie felt tears gathering in her own eyes.

"You won't have to go through this alone any longer if you can find it in your heart to give me another chance," Sam continued. "I understand why you kept it from your kids. Even now they would be devastated if you told them. And you made the decision to keep your cancer a secret long before you met me. I was wrong to feel that you deliberately duped me. You were already up to your eyebrows in the deception. The die had been cast."

"Oh, Sam. I was wrong not to tell you. So very wrong. I love you, and I've felt so lost without you."

He turned her in his arms and held her close, his face pressed against her hair. "God, I love the way you smell. You'll never be without me again, Maddie, unless I go first, and I'll fight dying with my last breath. I want to enjoy this second chance with you. We'll be in this together from here on out. I know how terribly afraid you must be. It took incredible courage for you to come this far alone."

Maddie hugged his neck and began to weep. "I am afraid," she confessed. "I keep remembering Graham's death. Right after his surgery, they said they got it all, only they didn't. How can I be absolutely sure the same thing won't happen to me? I don't want to die that way, Sam. It was so *awful.*"

Sam led her to the sofa. As they sat nestled together on the cushions, he said, "Tell me everything."

Maddie dried her cheeks. "Well, as you know, I didn't want my kids to find out, so when I was diagnosed, I flew to Missouri to have surgery and recuperate at my sister's home. I was incredibly lucky, because I found an oncologist with a new treatment strategy that he wished to try. All he needed was a patient willing to roll the dice."

"What's the strategy?" Sam asked.

Maddie told him about the new chemo drug. "The doctor's plan was to administer infusions in lighter doses and for a longer period of time. As he put it, all it takes is for one tiny cancer cell to survive and then his patient doesn't. He reasons that giving lighter doses of chemo will enable a person to withstand a longer course of treatments and expose any possible cancer cells that remain to the drug. He believes that may increase the odds that those cells will be killed."

Sam nodded. His hair caught the variegated light from the

Christmas tree, making it look like snow dappled with color by a rainbow. "That makes sense to me. I've known so many people who underwent chemo treatments after a cancer surgery only to have the cancer return when the treatments ended."

Maddie nodded. "Graham was one of them."

"And Annie, too."

He tightened his hand around hers. The strength of his grip seemed to lend her strength in equal measure. "It's so good to just talk with you about it. I never even got an infusion port for fear one of the kids might feel it under my clothing or see it. They would have known right away what it was."

Sam drew her closer until she was nestled snugly against him. "Thank you, Maddie."

"For what?"

"For forgiving me. For understanding me. I realized today what a coward I am."

"You, a coward?"

"Oh, yeah. When I first found out I might lose you, I ran."

CAM SAT ON A PLASTIC LAWN CHAIR OUTSIDE THE DRESSING ROOM, waiting for Kirstin to emerge in a pinned-together gown that couldn't be fixed. He was tense, which was evidenced by his clenched hands and the ache of knotted muscles in his shoulders. The dress meant so much to her. Cam couldn't fully understand why, but that wasn't necessary. It mattered to *her*. He was sick-to-death tired of fittings, pins, trim, and tearful outbursts, but he'd never grow tired of Kirstin.

She emerged from the cubicle. Her steel blue gaze clung to his. Her expression glowed with delight. In his estimation, she'd never looked so beautiful, and it sure as hell wasn't due to the dress. "It's fixed, Cam. The piping lines up perfectly and it fits me like a glove."

He pushed to his feet, wishing he could shout *Hallelujah!* Day after tomorrow, it would be Christmas Eve. Even the seamstress would close up shop that afternoon. They'd gotten the dress repaired just in the nick of time. He let his gaze move slowly over her. "You're the most beautiful bride I've ever seen."

She touched her hair. "I'm actually a mess, but the dress is finally perfect." A troubled frown creased her brow. "They say it's bad luck for a groom to see his bride in her dress before the wedding. Do you think there's any truth in that?"

"No," Cam replied. "I've never been superstitious, and I won't start now. And I meant it when I said you're the most beautiful bride I've ever seen. It's not the dress but the woman wearing it. It's gorgeous, of course. I don't mean that it isn't, but it would never look as beautiful on anyone else."

She closed the distance between them and stepped into his arms. "I'm sorry if I've been a little crazy. It's just . . ." Her voice trailed away. "When I was a little girl, I saw a picture of a dress almost exactly like this, and I remembered it all these years."

"I know." Cam heard a thickness in his voice.

"I was starting to believe I'd never get married. You know? And now that I'll have a wedding day, I want every detail to be absolutely perfect. I know that's unrealistic, but I flipped out when the dress arrived and didn't fit. I became a bridezilla, didn't I?"

Cam tightened his embrace. "A sweet and wonderful bridezilla."

The seamstress stepped from the cubicle. She beamed a smile at Cam. "We did it. No one will ever know we tore that dress completely apart and put it back together."

Cam gave her a grin. "It's perfect. Thank you so much for saving the day for us."

• • •

CALEB FROZE WHEN HE ENTERED THE HOUSE AND SAW MADDIE and Sam snuggling on the couch. Exhausted from all the work he had just done, he couldn't help but start to feel angry. *This is just great*, he thought. *You fight for three days and then make up for no good reason.* He went straight to his bedroom and flopped down on the mattress. After a moment, he felt guilty. Gram was happy again. That was all he should have cared about.

Caleb got off the bed and retraced his steps to the living room. "I'm glad the two of you made up," he said. "Now we can have a really wonderful Christmas."

Sam nodded. "Yes, and we'll celebrate as a family."

Just then Kirstin rushed into the house, carrying a large white box. "Mrs. Tamarack pulled it off!" she cried. "My gown is fixed!"

Gram clapped her hands. "Oh, how wonderful. Can we see it, or are you keeping it under wraps until the wedding?"

Kirstin laid the box on the sofa beside her dad. After lifting the lid, she swept the gown from folds of tissue paper and held it against her body. Maddie exclaimed that it was the most beautiful thing she had ever seen. Sam nodded and smiled.

To Caleb it was still only a stupid dress, but it sure was pretty. His dad came up behind him and settled a hand on his shoulder. "I'm so glad it's fixed that I'm tempted to light some candles at church."

Caleb chuckled. "I'll bet you're glad that part is over."

"You have no idea," his dad replied. "I was starting to have nightmares about it."

SAM INVITED MADDIE OUT TO DINNER. HE KNEW OF A SNAZZY joint on Main Street that served good food. He hadn't been there in ages, but he suspected it was pretty much the same. In Rustlers' Gulch time passed but not much changed.

"But Gabriella has fixed a wonderful dinner for us," Maddie reminded him.

"The kids can eat it," he replied. "We planned to go out, remember? And we never have. I'd like to celebrate with you tonight."

Her cheek dimpled in a glowing smile. "What are we celebrating?"

"Mending our fences, for one thing. Knowing that we can't be happy without each other. I can't tell you the other reason out loud."

Maddie went to her room to dress. Sam took the stairs two at a time, hoping he could find a Western sport coat. He hadn't slicked up since Annie's funeral, and the suit he'd bought for the wedding wouldn't be ready until tomorrow. Once in his bedroom, he went to the dresser and opened Annie's old jewelry box. Except for dusting, it hadn't been touched in years, but just as he remembered, a pink net bag lay inside. The funeral home had taken off Annie's rings after the memorial service and given them to Sam. He'd kept them here. Tears stung his eyes as he tugged his wedding band off his finger.

As he opened the small pouch to stow it with Annie's rings, he whispered, "I'll always love you, Annie, but it's time for me to move forward, and I can't do it with one foot planted in the past."

No, of course you can't. Love her well, Sam. Be happy.

Sam stiffened at the familiar sound of his dead wife's voice. Had he imagined it? Was he losing his mind? He stood still and listened. She said nothing more. Finally, Sam smiled. Whether it had been all in his head or not, he liked to believe that Annie had just given him her blessing.

Maddie whistled when she saw Sam coming down the stairs. At the bottom, he held out his arms and did a slow turn for her. "Do I pass muster?"

"You look fabulous, so tall and handsome. But where's your burned hat?"

"Retired. It's time for me to pick a new favorite." He tipped the brim of a black Stetson to her. Then he walked a slow circle around her, admiring how she looked in a Christmas green dress. It was too large for her, but the loose, flowing style allowed for that, and she wore a red belt to cinch in the waist. "Wow. You're beautiful."

She blushed and fiddled with her hair. "Beautiful is for younger women."

"I'll decide what's beautiful and what isn't."

He helped her into her coat. Caleb dashed downstairs just then. "If you're going to a movie, I want to come."

Sam patted his shoulder. "Sorry, partner, but it's a fancy dinner for two. We'll invite you when we're going to see a film."

Maddie wore dainty red shoes with short heels. If Sam recalled correctly, they were called pumps, which had never made any sense to him. His name for them was *impractical*, at least on the ranch. He touched her shoulder with a staying hand and hurried down the steps to open the passenger door of his truck.

When he returned to the porch and swept Maddie up in his arms, she shrieked, which made him laugh. "Easy. I won't drop you. The snow has been shoveled, but it's still slick. I don't want you to slip and hurt yourself."

Once Maddie was safely deposited on the seat, Sam claimed her rosy lips with his own. A zap of desire shot through him, and judging by her dazed expression when he drew away, she'd felt it, too.

"Oh, dear."

Sam chuckled and fastened her seat belt. "Oh, yeah."

Chapter Eighteen

A S SAM DROVE PAST THE McLENDON PROPERTY, HE CAUGHT A flash of red light coming through one of the workshop windows and stepped on the brake. Maddie followed his gaze.

"What is it?" she asked.

There came another flash. Sam had no idea what was causing it and he really didn't want to interrupt their evening by investigating, but he couldn't just ignore it. "I'm not sure. It won't take but a second for me to check it out."

Sam pulled over next to the huge building, put the pickup into park, and swung out of the vehicle. Because it was cold, he closed the door behind him, not wanting Maddie to get chilled. He walked inside and what he saw stopped him dead in his tracks.

MADDIE HAD NO IDEA WHAT SAM HAD SEEN, BUT HE LOOKED stunned when he opened the passenger door. "Brace yourself to be carried again. This snow hasn't been shoveled, and there's something inside that you have to see."

Maddie clung to his neck as he took her to the shop. Once inside, she could only stare at the huge room through tears. The nativity scene that had been in her mother's family for three generations was set up on a hay-strewn tabletop. A towering blue spruce, strung with lights and beautifully appointed with decorations she had treasured for years, stood along the opposite wall. The red flashes came from the star at the tip-top of the tree. Two rectangular folding tables were covered with disposable green tablecloths and adorned with Christmas place mats that sported place settings of her favorite tea rose china. Golden reindeer sat on her coffee table. Candles inside globes stood ready to be lighted. There were even area rugs on the concrete floor.

"It's like entering a Christmas fantasy," she whispered.

Sam carefully set her on her feet. "Pretty amazing, huh?"

Maddie nodded. "Caleb did it. I'm fairly certain, anyway. He caught me by your tree when I was in tears, and I wished aloud for some of my own Christmas treasures." She met Sam's gaze. "I felt out of place at your house after we quarreled."

Sam flicked his gaze over the room, taking in details. "So he created you a new home. Look at it, Maddie."

Her throat had gone so tight that it was difficult to talk. "He must have worked for *hours*, Sam. He created a Christmas room. It's one of the most beautiful things I've ever seen."

Sam nodded. "Hard work and Christmas, spun together with memories and love."

Maddie brushed a tear from her cheek. "What are we going to do? I no longer feel uncomfortable at the ranch. Caleb realizes that. He must think he did all of this for nothing." She pointed at the tables. "We all talked about serving Christmas dinner to those we know who might spend the holiday alone. He even prepared for that. I don't know how he planned to pull that off. Maybe he hoped that his father would help him get it all set up. We have a barbecue smoker and a propane stove. We could cook, if need be."

Sam curled an arm around her. Maddie leaned into him, comforted by his warmth. "Well, we clearly need to bring everything over here tomorrow for Christmas Eve. He put a lot of his heart into this, and it's too precious to waste."

"Dinner and everything?" Maddie couldn't believe he meant it.

"Absolutely. Gabriella and Miguel will help bring the food. While we eat out tonight, we can make a list of people who may be alone tomorrow and invite them by phone to join us for a holiday meal. I can taxi them in."

Maddie could almost envision this huge area filled with people. What a beautiful and meaningful way it would be to celebrate Christmas.

LATER THAT EVENING, CALEB STOPPED DEAD AS HE ENTERED THE living room. Earlier there had been piles of gifts under the Christmas tree and now they were gone. Gram sat beside Sam on the sofa. When Caleb looked at her, she smiled and pushed to her feet.

"We found the Christmas room, Caleb. That's one of the sweetest things anyone has ever done for me. It's a gift I'll always remember."

Caleb felt foolish. He shrugged. "You don't need it now. I did it to make you feel happy on Christmas."

"And I *do*." She slipped her arms around his neck and hugged him. "Sam and I were utterly amazed when we found it, and we've decided we can't allow all your hard work to go to waste. I have several elderly lady friends in my book club who will be celebrating Christmas alone, so we've invited them to your Christmas room for dinner. Sam has some friends who have no family arriving for the holiday, so he invited them to come as well. We'll start cooking early in the morning. Then we'll cart over the food. Ga-

402 · CATHERINE ANDERSON

briella and Miguel are happy to help. Your dad has gone to the storage units to get more chairs so we'll have plenty of seating. He's also going to pile up all the building scraps to have a bonfire. It will be a Christmas we'll never forget."

"A bonfire? On Christmas?" Caleb imagined how bright and welcoming a fire would be. The ghost town would become a home again. "That'll be so awesome. I need to cut some logs into stumps so we'll have more seats around the fire. Plus, I can gather more wood to keep it going. And I should shovel around the pit so none of the old ladies slip and fall."

Gram laughed. "I told them all to bring snow boots. They'll probably love it."

CHRISTMAS EVE MORNING, THE RANCH HOUSE WAS FULL OF AC-tivity. Gabriella had so many helpers in the kitchen that she could barely work. Miguel and Rickie took the Alvarez family's gifts over to the Christmas room, and then they took over treats that Gabriella had made in advance. While all of that went on, Caleb shoveled snow, creating pathways for their guests and a circular seating area at what would be a huge fire pit later.

Sam took charge of the music, the one thing Caleb had forgotten. A boom box was commandeered from Caleb's room, and CDs from Sam's collection of Christmas carols were also collected. The slight echo inside the shop area made the music resound, lending it a magical quality it might have otherwise lacked.

When the food had been prepared for the meal, it was left to stay warm in Sam's kitchen while everyone went over to the Christmas room to open gifts prior to the arrival of guests. When the three families had gathered around the beautiful blue spruce, Caleb and Rickie were put in charge of distributing gifts. Maddie wore the shawl Sam had already given her. Tears came to her eyes when Caleb presented her with a handmade bookrack to stand beside her writing chair. She smiled with delight when presented with a professional photograph of Cam and Kirstin in a gorgeous wood frame, which they referred to as their first family portrait. Cam gave Kirstin a gorgeous gold necklace. Rickie got his first cell phone and smaller gifts from both his parents and new friends. Gabriella squealed in delight when her gift from her husband was an e-reader, which she could use for practicing her English or to read books in Spanish for pleasure. Sam got a new tan Stetson from Maddie, an exact replica of the one Annie had given him for his birthday years ago. Miguel got a new pocketknife and an ax.

Except for the earbuds Maddie had wrapped for him, only Caleb received no gifts.

Cam watched his son with forced solemnity. Sam got up and went into Maddie's as-yet-unfinished apartment. He emerged carrying the most beautiful hand-tooled saddle that Caleb had ever seen. Sam set it in front of Caleb where he knelt by the tree. "Made to measure for Latigo," he told the boy. "In years to come, it'll probably fit another horse just fine, though. It should last you a lifetime."

Caleb couldn't believe it. "You shouldn't have gotten me something so fine, Sam. All I got you was gloves!"

"Which I'll use constantly. Go saddle him up and then bring him over so we can see how he looks in his new gear."

Caleb was so excited that he was shaking. The saddle gleamed in the winter sunlight and slid onto Latigo's back as if it had been made for him, which it had. When Caleb returned to the shop, cell phones flashed as pictures were taken of the horse wearing its new saddle.

On the way back to the pasture, Caleb walked so Rickie could have a turn riding. "Wow, this is a super-great saddle!" The younger boy's dark eyes sparkled with excitement. "Someday my dad is getting me a horse," he told Caleb. "A really nice horse, too! He just can't afford to yet."

Caleb smiled. "You've got a good seat. Someday you'll be a talented rider."

"Sam said he'd give me lessons. My dad says Sam's the best horseman he's ever met, so I'll be in good hands."

As they reentered the shop, Caleb stopped to admire his handiwork. He was glad he'd created the Christmas room. His special gift to Gram would be shared, and that made him feel good.

Gram, sitting on the tan sectional that would eventually go in her downstairs apartment, smiled up at Caleb as he and Rickie came to stand beside the tree. Caleb's dad, who sat beside Kirstin on a love seat, was also smiling. "Except for the saddle from Sam and earbuds from Gram you haven't gotten any presents, Caleb."

Caleb had noticed that. He knew better than to believe his dad or Gram had forgotten to get him something fabulous. He figured they had gotten him something special and were waiting to surprise him with it after everyone else had opened their gifts. *Not a violin*, Caleb prayed. *Please don't let it be a violin.* Now that he'd made friends, he no longer liked playing one.

His dad inclined his head at the tree. "There's something hanging on the tree for you. Gram and I went in together on it."

Caleb turned to look, relieved because something small enough to hang from an evergreen bough couldn't be a string instrument. With that thought, he wondered what they had gotten him. Something really small, for sure, and that was disappointing. On Christmas he usually got big things that he'd been wishing for.

"I don't see anything," he said over his shoulder.

"Keep looking," Gram told him.

Rickie began helping Caleb search. "Keys, Caleb! They got you keys!"

Caleb saw them then. With a shaking hand, he collected them from a drooping branch. He stared down at the black remote lying on his palm. The white outline of a ram's head shone up at him. "A *truck*? You got me a truck! Where is it?"

EVERYONE EXITED THE BUILDING TO WATCH CALEB SEARCH FOR his Christmas present. Sam kept one arm firmly around Maddie so she wouldn't slip on the snow. Feeling her warmth beside him gave him a sense of peace. Whether she survived the battle against cancer or not, he would treasure every moment he had with her. She had been such a special presence in his life, truly a light in the darkness for him. Nothing under the tree could please him more than this sweet, courageous woman. If not for her, he might have lost his daughter. All of his cattle might have died in the high country. She'd also brought his friends back into his life.

Dashing first one direction and then another, Caleb led them on a merry chase to find his new truck. Sam absorbed the sound of voices and laughter. When Caleb finally found the Christmas-red truck Cam had hidden behind Maddie's trailer, he froze in his tracks and just stared.

"Brand-new?" The youth's voice rang with wonder. "Not a used one?"

Cam, who stood with his arm around Kirstin, said, "It needs to last you through high school and college."

Caleb drew open the driver's door. "Oh, man! This is so awesome."

"Look on the backseat," Kirstin called.

Rickie ran to open the rear passenger door. "My present for you is back here. We all got you truck stuff!"

"You knew?" Caleb sent Rickie an accusing look. "And you didn't tell me?"

Everyone laughed when Rickie replied, "It was a secret!"

Sam felt Maddie shiver and drew her closer against him. Together they watched her grandson tear the wrapping off gifts from Kirstin and the Alvarez family. Caleb received a solar cell phone charger for his dash, a wool lap robe, a steering wheel cover, and two thermal travel mugs.

Everyone trailed back inside while the two boys took the truck out for its first spin.

PREPARATIONS FOR DINNER BEGAN NEXT. KIRSTIN AND MADDIE made sure there were enough place settings at the tables. Gabriella went with Sam and Miguel to collect the food. Cam lighted the bonfire, burned the mountain of wrapping paper, and arranged seating. The two boys drove to pick up the elderly ladies who would be their guests.

"Make sure they bring boots!" Cam called after his son. "And don't let anyone slip on the ice!"

Kirstin emerged from the building just then. She came to stand with Cam by the fire. He looped his arms around her and drew her against him.

"This is the best Christmas ever," she said. "Tomorrow we'll be married, Cam. Can you believe it?"

Cam watched the flames lick up through the wood. "It's pretty incredible. Not so long ago, I could only hope to meet my own special someone, and now here you are, in my arms. I'm a man who has everything—a fabulous mom, a wonderful son, and now the woman of my dreams."

She turned to press her lips against his. Then she looked up at him. "And I have the man of *my* dreams. It's amazing."

They turned to gaze at the fire, absorbing the warmth of each other and the flames.

SAM PRESIDED OVER THE HOLIDAY DINNER SEATED AT THE HEAD of the table. Maddie sat at the foot. He led with the meal blessing. Then everyone unfolded their linen napkins and laid them over their laps. He quickly served himself some turkey and held the platter for Mrs. Pedigrew while she forked a piece of roasted bird onto her plate. Bowls and platters followed, and soon everyone had full plates. Sam began to eat, and everyone else joined him.

For the first time in far too long, Sam felt happy at Christmas. He settled his gaze on Maddie at the opposite end of the table. She glowed with contentment and joy as she smiled at him. Laughter rang out. Conversation hummed. Emma Pedigrew thanked Sam at least five times for inviting her over. Her son and his family lived in Seattle, and they hadn't been able to come see her for Christmas this year. Emma could have flown out to be with them, but she didn't like to fly alone. She got lost in big airports.

"It's so nice to be included. Otherwise I would be eating a microwave dinner all alone."

"It's great to have you. And I hope you'll join us again tomorrow for the wedding reception at my home."

"Oh, I'd love that. I put up a small tree and set out decorations, but my house feels so lonely without my kids there."

Sam made a mental note to invite Emma again next year. Not

that Maddie would let him forget. She was a caring woman with a huge heart, and Christmas was a time when people shouldn't be alone.

After desserts were set out, Sam kept an eye on Rickie. When the boy had eaten two pieces of Maddie's pumpkin pie, Sam excused himself from the table and beckoned Rickie over to the Christmas tree. "I have a gift for you, Rickie, but I waited until now to give it to you."

Sam plucked his cell phone from his pocket and pulled up his picture gallery. Thumbing through several images, he found the one he needed. He handed the device to Rickie. "His name is Lightning," he told the child. "I trained him myself. He's a really great horse."

Rickie looked bewildered as he stared at the palomino. "He's pretty. I've petted him through the fence lots of times."

Sam realized Rickie didn't understand and chuckled. "He's yours now. I'm giving him to you as a Christmas present."

Rickie's eyes widened. "He's mine? Oh, *wow!*" Then his expression clouded. "That's very nice, Sam, but I'll have to ask my parents if it's all right."

Sam laughed again. "I'm a step ahead of you. I already asked."

Miguel walked over and put a hand on his son's shoulder. "He's a beautiful animal, son. It's very generous of Sam to let you have him."

Rickie shouted, "Caleb!" Then he ran to find the older boy. The next instant, both kids raced from the building.

Sam met Miguel's startled gaze. "I think we'd better follow them over. You'll want to supervise during Rickie's first ride. That's why I waited until after dinner to give Rickie his present. I knew he'd bolt."

Both men circled the room to say good-bye to the guests, who would be taxied home by Sam's friends, and then they drove over to the ranch in Sam's truck. Rickie was beside himself with excitement. Caleb was showing him how to saddle the gelding. Sam swung up to sit on the fence rail. Miguel joined him.

"This is a dream come true for my son," Miguel said. "Thank you, Sam. I will make sure he takes good care of the horse."

Sam nodded. "I know you will, Miguel. Not a doubt in my mind. Lightning is perfect for a boy his age. He's intuitive, and he won't go any faster than Rickie can handle."

MADDIE HATED TO LEAVE THE CHRISTMAS ROOM, BUT IT WAS growing dark, all the guests had left, and mountains of dishes awaited her at Sam's place. Even so, she lingered to gaze at the nativity scene and admire the beautiful tree. Caleb had strung lights around the windows and along the walls. The room glowed with Christmas cheer.

Sam startled her when he stepped up behind her and enfolded her in his arms. "Penny for them."

Maddie sighed. "I feel as if this is the end of a chapter, Sam. I know it's silly, but Caleb has only two more years of high school, Cam is getting married in the morning, and changes I haven't considered are coming."

"Yes." His deep voice curled around her like tendrils of warm smoke. "But the next chapters will be just as wonderful."

Maddie smiled. "Maybe we'll share a grandchild soon. That will be lovely."

Sam joined her in admiring the room. "Caleb sure worked hard to transform this place. It's a gift of love to you. I know it'll be hard to turn out the lights and walk away."

Maddie nodded. "I took pictures. Not that I need them to

remember this. It'll remain in my mind, just as it is, for the rest of my life." She leaned back against him. "My little boy is growing up, Sam."

"He's a fine young man, Maddie, and he loves you very much. No matter how old he gets, that'll never change."

They walked arm in arm to take a last tour of the room. Then they slipped on their coats, walked to the door, and turned off the lights.

WHEN THE KITCHEN AT THE MAIN HOUSE WAS CLEANED UP, KIRSTIN and Cam slipped away to her house. Assailed with a sudden case of bridal jitters, Kirstin went over her checklist to be sure she had forgotten nothing.

"Calm down, Kirstie." Cam grasped her elbow and twirled her into his arms. "You've checked that silly list dozens of times. The flowers have been delivered to the church. The altar society ladies will put them out right after the public mass is over."

"Poor Father! He'll be exhausted by the time he finishes our nuptial mass."

Cam chuckled and nibbled her neck. "*Really*? You're going to worry now about Father's energy levels?"

"Don't laugh. Tomorrow is the most important day of our lives, Cam. I want it to be perfect."

He ran a hand over her hair, which felt like silk against his fingers. "And it will be. Our parents have become best friends. Nobody made any mistakes at the rehearsal. Your dress is fixed. What can go wrong?"

"Do you like the dress? I got so focused on re-creating the one I saw as a little girl that I never asked if you like it."

He trailed soft kisses along her cheek. "It's a fabulous gown, but quite frankly, I think you're beautiful wearing anything or nothing at all."

Kirstin grabbed his hand, led him to the bedroom, and said, "Prove it."

"That's an invitation I can't turn down."

AFTERWARD THEY LAY IN EACH OTHER'S ARMS, CONTENTED AND relaxed. The soft illumination of Christmas tree lights came in from the living room, touching the shadows with shimmering color. Cam felt as if everything was right in his world.

"I'm so glad I stopped at the Cowboy Tree that afternoon," Cam told her. "I know we would have met eventually, but I'm not sure we would have connected so fast emotionally under other circumstances."

Kirstin giggled. "I may have thought of you as the hillbilly next door." She sobered and snuggled closer. "I'll always feel that God led you to me that afternoon."

"Me, too," Cam whispered. "You were the answer to my prayer."

IN THE MORNING, THE MONTANA SKY WAS A STEEL BLUE AND HOV-ered low over the valley, a forewarning of snow that began to fall as they drove to the church. Kirstin rode with Sam, her gown and accoutrements protected by plastic. Maddie would help her dress in a back room. Sam would cool his heels in the vestibule, waiting for the bride so he could walk her down the aisle. It sounded simple, and Sam hadn't screwed anything up at the rehearsal. But he was still nervous.

As wedding guests wandered in, he greeted them and then let the ushers take over. St. Anne's had always reminded Sam of an elegant old lady. From his vantage point, he could see inside, and today the church sparkled. Christmas trees draped with tiny white lights and gold-trimmed angels flanked the altar. Snow blew against the stained-glass windows, damping what sunshine there was outside so that the nave beckoned to visitors like a beacon. When altar boys ignited the candlewicks, the sanctuary glowed like a small earthly corner of heaven.

As the church began to fill with people, Sam grew jittery again. Kirstin still hadn't joined him. The organist blasted the pipes with a trill of music, and he nearly parted company with his skin. He took a deep breath to calm down. Then he focused on details around him to remain that way. The right front pew had been reserved for the family, he recalled, and there would be no bride or groom's side. Sam and Maddie wanted to sit together as their children were joined together in holy matrimony. Sam noted that the ushers were seating guests on both sides. Everything was proceeding as planned.

Cam and Caleb appeared at the front of the church, both of them looking sharp in black tuxedos. Gabriella, Kirstin's matron of honor, looked splendid in a simple pink dress. She stood opposite Miguel, who was Cam's only groomsman.

Just then Kirstin entered the vestibule by a side door. She looked so beautiful that Sam got tears in his eyes. "Ah, sweetheart, I wish your mother were here to see this."

"She is, Daddy. She is." She lifted her veiled face to smile at him. "I like your new suit. Nice Western cut. It's perfect for you."

Sam laughed. "I couldn't walk you down the aisle wearing shitkickers and jeans."

"Not if you plan to live to see your first grandchild." She placed a hand at her waist. "Oh, Dad, I'm so nervous."

"Don't be. You look beautiful."

"I don't have a flower girl."

"You said you didn't need one, remember? You wanted a simple wedding."

"And Rickie is a little old to be our ring bearer." Her mouth curved in another smile. "Oh, but look how handsome he is!"

Sam took in the boy's suit and hoped Miguel hadn't broken the bank to buy it for him. "At least Rickie won't drop the rings. That's a plus. Gabriella looks beautiful. She was a smart choice as your matron of honor. Imagine what a pain in the ass bridesmaid dresses would have been."

Kirstin giggled. "Don't be irreverent."

Sam heard the organist play a warning refrain. He offered his daughter his arm. "Are you ready, baby girl?"

"Yes, Daddy. I am so very ready. When I leave this church, I'll be Mrs. Cameron McLendon."

KIRSTIN HAD EYES ONLY FOR CAM AS SHE WALKED DOWN THE AISLE. His blue gaze remained fixed on her. His hair glistened like warm honey and fell in slight waves over his forehead. As he stepped forward to take her hand, she realized she was shaking with nerves.

The ceremony began, a blend of the liturgical rituals of a mass and the nuptials. Kirstin lost track of the words and fell back on habits ingrained in her since childhood. She was acutely aware of Cam beside her. Everything else was a blur. It seemed to her that the ceremony lasted for a small eternity and might never end.

But then she and Cam made their vows, promising to love and honor each other for the rest of their lives. Seeing the tenderness in his eyes and hearing the strength in his voice made this the most beautiful moment of her life. She trailed her gaze over his chiseled features, every line of which had been indelibly etched in her memory. *Cam.* His name whispered through her mind, and she knew that joining hearts and hands with him this morning was the best Christmas gift she'd ever received. Even better, she knew that he felt the same way.

SNOW HAD CONTINUED TO FALL WHILE THEY WERE INSIDE THE church, and Sam held on to Maddie's arm as they made their way down the front steps and across the parking lot. She wore heels with slick soles. He didn't want her to fall.

"That was one of the most beautiful weddings I've ever seen," he remarked.

Maddie sighed. "How could it fail to be? Did you see the love they feel for each other in their expressions?"

"I did. It'll be a good, solid marriage, Maddie." Sam saw Caleb climbing into his snazzy new Dodge and yelled, "Don't speed on the way home. The roads will be dangerous!"

Caleb shouted back, "I'll be careful."

Sam helped Maddie into his truck. When he slid in under the steering wheel, he said, "I'll follow close behind him just in case he goes off into a ditch. Did you hear all the sighs and sniffles when Caleb insisted on hugging his new mother before he'd let Cam take her up the aisle?"

"I did. I think every heart in the church melted." Maddie sent him a smile. "He's a dear boy."

"He is that," Sam agreed, "and I don't want him getting in a wreck going home."

"He should be fine. Northern California gets plenty of bad weather. He learned to drive on snow and ice." She glanced over at him. "Is my makeup smeared? I couldn't help it and cried my eyes out as they exchanged their vows. It was so beautiful."

Sam smiled. "Your makeup is perfect. How's mine? I cried, too."

She laughed and settled back against her seat. "I'm so glad we have two hours before people start showing up at the house. I'm exhausted. I'm going to enjoy a leisurely glass of white wine and rest for a while with my feet up."

"I'll second that. I'm sure glad Kirstin wanted a small wedding and kept the guest list short. I don't know how to cook for crowds."

"That's the problem with holiday weddings. It's impossible to find a caterer on such short notice."

"I didn't want a caterer, anyway. People might start thinking I'm fancy. Besides, no professional can outshine Gabriella."

Sam kept Caleb's red truck in sight as he drove through Rustlers' Gulch on snow-covered streets lined with old buildings.

"I love this town," Maddie said. "I've seen communities that try to look old, but they can't compete with the real thing."

"Some of these buildings were built way back in the eighteen hundreds."

"Yes. I've read the history. It's fascinating. And the feeling here is one of the things that convinced me to buy our land."

"Tonight after the kids leave for the airport, we should come back here for the caroling. On Christmas night, groups from St. Anne's go out to sing."

Maddie nodded. "Once I can take off these heels and put on walking shoes, I'd love to do that."

When they reached the ranch, Sam helped Maddie out of the truck. Caleb, already parked near the porch, ran over to grasp her other arm.

"Gram, after I help you get inside, can I go see a couple of friends and show off my new truck?"

Snowflakes drifted around them, a reminder to Maddie that the roads were slick. "The driving conditions are bad, darling."

"I know, Gram, but my friends live on Fox Hollow Road, so I won't be going very far."

Maddie reached the porch, where no snow had collected. Sam relaxed his hold on her arm, and she turned to regard her grandson. "Do you promise to drive slowly?"

"I promise!" Caleb bounced back down the steps. "I'll only be gone about an hour. Then I'll come back to help with the reception."

Maddie curled an arm around Sam's waist as she watched Caleb drive away. "Oh, to be that young again," she said with a sigh.

"There's nothing more exciting to teenage boys than a brand-new set of wheels."

Sam led her into the house, where they removed their coats and hung them up. Then Maddie kicked off her heels. Still dashing in a dress shirt and slacks, Sam turned on the tree lights, put on some Christmas carols, and returned to the living room with two glasses of wine, offering one to Maddie. They retired to the sectional and sat side by side.

"This is lovely," she told him. Then she glanced at her watch. "Quiet before the storm. Thank goodness we did all the prep work last night."

"Just don't get in a dither. The guests will be old friends. If necessary, they'll roll up their sleeves and help."

"Like one big happy family?"

He nodded and smiled down at her. "Merry Christmas, Maddie."

She tipped her head to study his face, which had become so dear to her. "Merry Christmas, Sam. There was a time when I couldn't have imagined this. Our kids are married! What does that make us, parents-in-law?"

His expression remained serious. "I'd like to change that up and make us husband and wife. I'm not much good at being romantic, so I'll just ask you straight out. Will you marry me, Maddie?"

Maddie wasn't taken off guard by the question. She had come to love Sam with all her heart and knew that he loved her. So instead of saying yes, she asked, "When?"

He grinned. "I thought about waiting a while, maybe even a year. The kids' Christmas wedding was really beautiful. I don't want to waste that much time, though. No guarantees, remember? I want to enjoy every day I can with you."

She nodded, because she felt the same way. Every moment they had together was precious.

"Cam and Kirstin will be back for New Year's Eve. We'll have Caleb until then. So I've been thinking about getting married New Year's Day. A small wedding followed by a reception in the back room of the Cowboy Tree. Then we'll make our escape to somewhere in the tropics."

"That sounds fabulous, Sam. Just the two of us."

"Yep. We can practice making out until we spontaneously combust."

She laughed. Then she sobered and gave him a questioning look. "Are you certain you're okay with no guarantees?"

"I don't come with any, either. I'll take my chances, you'll take yours, and if the worst happens, I'll be grateful for whatever time God gives us to be together."

"Will Father Merrick allow us to get married that quickly? What about posting the banns and all that?"

Sam grinned. "He allowed Cam and Kirstin to tie the knot fast. Why would he hesitate to let two old warhorses like us get married?"

Maddie swirled the wine in her glass and took a sip. "I'm still not sure about physical intimacy, Sam. You're in fabulous shape. Without any clothing, I *look* like an old warhorse."

Sam gazed at the tree. The play of light on his face cast his rugged features into sharp relief. "Don't get pissed, but I've already seen you without your clothes on."

"What?"

"It was an accident. I swear. Back in the beginning, when we were feuding, I developed a bad habit of riding upstream across the river and using my binoculars to see what crazy thing Cam had done next. He did some pretty amazing stuff, you know. I wanted to laugh at him, but instead, as much as it rankled, I couldn't help but feel impressed sometimes. Early one morning, you stepped in front of the trailer window wearing nothing. I had just brought the glasses up and was trying to focus in. Bam. There you were. I was a gentleman. I looked away real quick and only got a glimpse. But with only that glimpse—well, I thought you looked pretty damned good. So did the four fishermen who were floating downriver."

Maddie gasped, and her eyes went wide. "Fishermen? I remember that morning. My towel slipped! It was the most mortifying moment of my life. I never saw you, though."

"I'm glad. I was the only one using binoculars, and you would've thought I was deliberately spying. It would have been another reason on a long list for you to hate my guts."

Maddie covered her face with one hand. Sam chuckled. "It was a while back. No point in getting embarrassed all over again. Besides, you're a handsome woman. If those guys didn't catch any fish, they still had something to smile about."

Maddie sighed. "I have another problem that eclipses how embarrassed I felt that morning. I need to tell the kids about my cancer. My daughter called yesterday, and I almost blurted it out, but I just couldn't do it to her on Christmas. And I absolutely can't tell Cam until after they go on their honeymoon. The timing is awful."

"You'll know when the moment is right. Don't worry about it now." He took her glass of wine and set it aside on the refreshment console beside his own. Then he stood and held out his hand to her. "Dance with me."

Maddie laid her fingers across his hard palm and let him pull her to her feet. "Silent Night" played on the sound system. In her mind, this was the most wonderful Christmas day of her life. Sam drew her gently into his arms and smiled when he realized she was too short to hug his neck.

"Step up on my boots," he urged.

Maddie did as he suggested and nearly moaned with delight when her body made full contact with his. "I love being in your arms," she whispered.

"And I love having you in them. I want you to be within hugging distance for the rest of my life."

Maddie closed her eyes and swayed with him. There had been a time not so very long ago when she couldn't have imagined loving another man after Graham. Oh, how wrong she had been. Life was full of beautiful surprises, and for her, Sam Conacher was one of them.

Russian Tea Cookies

Every year before Christmas my mother made these delightful cookies. I am not sure where the name came from, but it is a family recipe, so I think it came from my grandmother, who probably got it from her mother, and so on. If you look the name up online, these are nothing like the Russian tea cookies or cakes that people make today.

However, to me, they have always been Russian tea cookies! They were my favorites, and when I make them now, they still are. Mama paid a farmer to deliver raw milk to us in gallon jars. She let the milk sit until the cream rose to the top so it could be skimmed off. She made whipped cream with it. Each week, she put the two gallon jars out on our front porch so the farmer could reuse them, but she must have forgotten to do that a couple of times, because she put our Christmas cookies in those big milk jars and set them under our Christmas tree. I can remember sitting by our tree to rob the cookie jar, and I invariably went for these cookies first. Sometimes my older brother would join me. Mama would wonder aloud where all the Russian tea cookies had gone. Then she would smile and make some more.

I hope you enjoy them as much as we did!

—CATHERINE ANDERSON

¾ cup granulated sugar
¾ cup vegetable oil
2 eggs
2 teaspoons vanilla extract
1 teaspoon lemon extract
1 teaspoon grated lemon rind

2 cups all-purpose flour
2 teaspoons baking powder
½ teaspoon salt
jam or jelly to your taste
powdered sugar

1. In a big bowl, blend sugar and oil. Stir in eggs, flavorings, and lemon rind. In a separate bowl, blend together flour, baking powder, and salt. Make sure they are thoroughly mixed; then slowly add to the mixture of sugar, oil, eggs, flavorings, and lemon rind. Make sure the two mixtures are completely integrated.

2. Use an ungreased cookie sheet. Take a rounded tablespoon of dough and roll it into a ball with the palms of your hands. Press each ball down on the cookie sheet with an oiled glass that has a smooth bottom (nowadays you can use nonstick cooking spray to oil the glass) and has been dipped in granulated sugar. Continue to oil and dip the glass in sugar each time you flatten a cookie. Then slightly depress the center of each cookie with your thumb or a teaspoon to create a round well. Be sure not to push too hard so you don't go clear through the dough.

3. Fill the cookie wells with ¼ to ½ teaspoon of jam or jelly. Sprinkle lightly with powdered sugar. My mother used different flavors of jam or jelly, which created a variety of tastes.

4. Bake at 400 degrees Fahrenheit for eight minutes or until the jelly sets. Cool on wire racks. Store in an airtight container until served.